# FIT TO BE TIED

He was mocking her, and guessing by the combative spark that appeared in her eyes, Lucy Thomas knew it.

"Mr. Mulroney, I do not know where you get your outlandish ideas. But since you are able to publish them, you are morally obligated to give those who would oppose you an opportunity to rebut your arguments."

"I am, am I?" He leaned back in his chair and put his boots up on the scarred desk his predecessor had left behind. Locking his fingers behind his head, he assumed a position of studied indifference. The truth was, he wanted nothing more than to leap up from his seat and do his best to get his hands on the woman who stood ramrod straight and glaring at him.

His smile wasn't meant to charm. It worked, because she backed up a step as if instinctively putting some distance between herself and the danger he posed.

"And what do I get if I publish your letter, Mrs. Thomas?"

She gasped and marched back toward his desk, quivering with outrage. "How dare you! I had no idea that you were so despicable!"

# BOOK YOUR PLACE ON OUR WEBSITE AND MAKE THE READING CONNECTION!

We've created a customized website just for our very special readers, where you can get the inside scoop on everything that's going on with Zebra, Pinnacle and Kensington books.

When you come online, you'll have the exciting opportunity to:

- View covers of upcoming books
- Read sample chapters
- Learn about our future publishing schedule (listed by publication month *and author*)
- Find out when your favorite authors will be visiting a city near you
- Search for and order backlist books from our online catalog
- Check out author bios and background information
- Send e-mail to your favorite authors
- Meet the Kensington staff online
- Join us in weekly chats with authors, readers and other guests
- Get writing guidelines
- AND MUCH MORE!

**Visit our website at
http://www.kensingtonbooks.com**

# THE BOOK OF LOVE

## PAT PRITCHARD

ZEBRA BOOKS
KENSINGTON PUBLISHING CORP.
http://www.kensingtonbooks.com

*The people and events in this book, including both the town of Lee's Mill and the Luminary Society itself, are strictly products of my imagination. However, I would like to express my gratitude to all those nameless real women who dared to take the first scary steps toward the future for the benefit of us all.*

*Thanks, Ladies.*

# Chapter One

Enough was enough. Lucy leaned back in her chair and allowed herself the small pleasure of resting her eyes from the drudgery of poring over the neat columns of figures. Too many long hours spent balancing the ledgers had taken their toll, leaving both her head and her back aching. However, for the first time since sitting down, she felt like smiling. A profit, no matter how small, was an accomplishment to be savored.

A familiar noise interrupted her brief respite. Wearily she rose to her feet, prepared to answer the call of the brass bell that announced the arrival of a customer. One glance at the clock over the counter gave her some forewarning as to who her guest might be.

Just as she suspected, she found nineteen-year-old Cora Lawford looking agitated as she paced back and forth through the clutter in the store. With each step, the younger woman muttered under her breath and glared at the newspaper in her hand as if it had been written by the devil himself. And probably, to Cora's way of thinking, it had been.

So much for Lucy's good mood. She resigned herself to at least thirty minutes of listening to Cora rant and rave about whatever Cade Mulroney had spewed forth in his latest editorial. Without yet having read a single word, she silently wished the man straight to perdition because the way he enjoyed stirring up trouble was enough to turn a saint to sinning.

As soon as Cora spotted Lucy, she started waving the paper in her hand.

"That . . . that man!" Cora made the last words sound like the most vile epithet she could imagine.

Knowing she was only postponing the inevitable, Lucy held up her hand to stave off Cora's plan to read the offending editorial aloud.

"You might as well wait for the others to arrive. I have no desire to hear his vile scribblings over and over again." Without waiting for Cora to agree, she crossed the room to the stove and put the kettle on to heat.

"Tea won't help anything."

She offered her young friend a placating smile. "No, but it won't hurt, either."

Just about the time the water reached a full boil, she heard the sound of several pairs of feet marching across the wooden porch leading right to her door. Bowing to the inevitable, she reached for several more teacups and set them down on the counter. No doubt, this was going to be another futile discussion about what to do about one Mr. Cade Mulroney.

Her headache worsened at the very thought of it. She decided that the best thing for her to do was work around the store, taking care of the endless little details that a storekeeper had to see to every day. The others could argue all they wanted, but the truth was, there wasn't much they could do about the content of the *Clarion*, the town's only newspaper.

Except ignore it.

She winced when the door slammed open, rattling the glass panes until she feared they would break. After the last woman was inside the store, Lucy decided that it would behoove her to turn the window sign to read *Closed*. It might not make for good business, but it definitely made good sense. All she needed was for certain menfolk in town to find almost the entire membership of the Luminary Society holding an impromptu meeting in the middle of the afternoon.

It was considered scandalous enough that the group had agreed to start meeting two evenings a month. If their critics thought that they were gathering more often than that, well, who knew what kind of trouble would be stirred up? She knew who'd be the one doing the stirring, however. Which brought her thoughts full circle back to Cade Mulroney.

Her mood wasn't improved by the self-appointed leader of the latest arrivals. Mrs. Overland led the charge, her face alight with moral outrage. "Lucinda, have you seen this? I warned you that these radical ideas of yours would cause nothing but problems! I shudder to think what Mr. Overland will have to say about this."

*Only what you allow him to,* Lucy thought to herself. Mrs. Overland was one of the few reasons that Lucy secretly wished that they hadn't opened up membership of the Society to any and all of the ladies in town. The woman and her followers resembled nothing so much as a gaggle of geese with their feathers all ruffled. Uncharitable as the thought might be, this particular woman always talked as if her husband were an absolute despot. The truth was, the poor man was henpecked beyond belief. The very idea of him daring to criticize his formidable wife was almost laughable.

Lucy, on the other hand, knew all too well what it was like to live in fear of a man. Both her father and her late husband had taught her that lesson firsthand. Ruthlessly she pushed those ugly memories back into the recesses of her mind. Both men were long dead and buried, along with any desire she'd ever had to tie her life and fortune to that of another of the male sex.

Willing herself to maintain a facade of calm, she set about distributing cups of hot tea. That done, she stepped behind the counter and began straightening several bolts of fabric while the other women whispered among themselves. Finally, Cora's patience ran out. She picked up the newspaper again and held it up for the others to see.

"Not all of you have read today's *Clarion,*" she announced while singling Lucy out for a long look. "Once again, the men in this town have availed themselves of a convenient forum from which to attack us."

Several of the others nodded in agreement. Before they could start chattering among themselves again, Cora spread the newspaper out on the counter and began reading aloud. She did so with such fervor and expression that Lucy fought the urge to smile. Her friend certainly had a flair for the dramatic.

> *"Once again the ladies of our town seem determined to venture into areas that are far beyond the normal purview of the fairer sex. It is the opinion of this editor that a woman should seek enlighten-*

*ment by concentrating on the comfort and care of the men in her life. After all, man has the right to expect that his needs will come first when he has given both his name and protection to a woman."*

Lucy slammed a bolt of fabric down on the counter. The fabric muffled the noise, so no one took particular note of her strong reaction. She glanced around the room and was relieved to find that everyone's attention was riveted on Cora's recitation.

Normally, Lucy was able to ignore Mulroney's barbed comments. This time, however, he'd gone too far. Maybe in an ideal world a woman could feel safe with her husband or father, but not in this one. As a man, Mulroney had no idea what it was like to be trapped in a marriage with a man who neither sheltered nor protected his wife. Her own experience had been bad enough, but there were women in this very town who had good reason to fear for their very lives.

With a great deal of effort, she maintained her air of calm as Cora finished the last of the editorial.

*". . . not to be ignored is the direct threat to our very way of life if these women persist in their present course of action. With the elections fast approaching, we shall watch carefully to see what the candidates for mayor of our town plan to do about it."*

For several seconds, those last words hung in the air as the women looked at each other in confusion. Lucy didn't blame them. It was hard to comprehend the jump in logic that turned the Luminary Society from a forum for women to improve their minds into a direct attack on the men of Lee's Mill.

Things were definitely getting out of hand. Clearly, someone needed to take charge. Unfortunately, when Lucy looked around the room again, all eyes were trained right on her. She did the only thing she could do.

"I will meet with Melinda Smythe to discuss this matter. Now, however, I need to reopen the store. We don't want to give Mr. Mulroney any more ammunition for his column than is necessary."

Cora, of course, wasn't about to be pacified that easily. "I think we should march right next door and tell that man exactly what we think of him."

Her words had the opposite effect from the one she'd hoped for. If nothing else, Mrs. Overland and her cronies hurried out of the store even faster. For many of them, just joining the Society had been a daring step. Open confrontation with a man, especially one not of their family, was simply out of the question.

Playing the good hostess, Lucy left her work behind the counter and walked her guests to the door. When all but Cora had gone, she changed the sign in the window again. With a sigh, she took up where she'd left off in straightening the fabric and notions.

"This blue is especially nice."

Lucy had little hope that her attempt to distract Cora would work. Despite her youth, Cora wasn't one to be deterred from any path she had chosen. She'd already resumed her pacing.

"How can they hear that and then just walk away discussing the weather? Have they no pride? That man has no right to be stirring up harsh feelings about our group."

Lucy put the last of the fabric in its place and then looked around to see what else needed to be done.

"He probably sees it as his job. It's a sad but true fact that controversy sells more newspapers."

Cora threw up her hands in complete disgust. "Then let him find some other place to look for trouble. We were doing fine without a newspaper before he came to town."

The tinkling of the bell saved Lucy from having to respond. A young couple hesitated before crossing the threshold. She sized them up with one quick look. While he was thin to the point of looking sickly, his wife was hugely pregnant. One glance at their worried faces, and Lucy knew they had no money to spend, which didn't necessarily mean a lot. A good portion of her business was done on a barter system.

"I'm Lucy Thomas, and I don't believe we've met." She came out from behind the counter and greeted them with a bright smile. "I'm always pleased to welcome new customers to my store."

At a nudge from his wife, the man whipped off his hat and nodded at Lucy. "I, uh, I mean we are new here, ma'am. I'm John Horn, and this here's my wife Emma. We was wondering if you could see fit to extend us credit until I get our first crop in."

His wife nudged him again and nodded at the basket she held clutched in her hands. "We do have some eggs to trade, fresh from this morning."

"Well, that's a good start. Bring them over here to the counter and set them down." She accepted the basket from Emma. "While I figure out your credit, you go on and have a look around. I'll fill your order in a minute."

The young couple lost themselves in the wonder of the variety of goods Lucy kept stocked. She'd always prided herself on being able to meet the needs of most folks who came in. While John and Emma dreamed about what they couldn't afford, she peeked into the basket. Seven lonely eggs lay cushioned in a faded scrap of shirt material.

So much for the small profit she'd made over the past week. She closed her mind to the echoes of her late husband's cutting remarks about her being too soft to run the business. Her store existed to serve the town, and the town was made up of people, not dollars. She met Cora's amused gaze across the room as the young couple whispered by the canned goods.

While she waited for them to make up their minds, she emptied the basket of its meager contents. Before they could see what she was doing, she filled the basket with flour, coffee, a small piece of sugar, and a sack of dried beans. It wasn't much, but far more than the value of their trade goods.

Finally, John led Emma back to where Lucy waited. "We'll take what you can give us in flour and beans."

"Already done. You came at a good time when I was fresh out of eggs. I pay top dollar whenever that happens." She smiled and pushed the basket across the counter. "Keep me in mind for any butter or eggs you can spare. If I can't use them myself, the hotel and boarding house in town will take any extra off my hands."

John gave her a surprised look when he hefted the basket, but he didn't say anything. He clearly wasn't fooled by her words, but for his wife's sake he'd accept the small charity.

"Thank you, ma'am. I owe you."

Cora spoke up for the first time. "Mr. Horn, I heard tell the mill owner is needing some extra help right now. If you know of anyone looking for a job, you might pass that news along."

"I'll do that." He offered his arm to his wife.

"We'll be going now. Again, thank you for every-thing."

After they'd gone, Cora picked up the newspaper from where she'd laid it on the counter.

"I know you don't want to confront Mr. Mulroney, but someone is going to have to sooner or later. It's not right for him to go on attacking us when he hasn't even attended one of our meetings. He has no idea what we're doing."

Arguing only made her weary, so Lucy concentrated on picking some lint off a bolt of navy blue fabric. "I still say that as long as we don't respond in kind, eventually he'll find a new target for his venom."

When Cora didn't immediately respond, she looked up from the counter in time to catch her friend dabbing her eyes with a handkerchief. Lucy immediately hurried to her side.

"What aren't you telling me?"

"My aunt is threatening to make me stay home from the meetings." She sniffed a bit and then tipped her nose up toward the ceiling and did a wicked imitation of the older woman who was her guardian. "According to Aunt Henrietta, a lady doesn't embroil herself in controversy. Far better to never be seen at all than to be seen keeping company with scandal."

Lucy knew she shouldn't laugh, but she couldn't help herself. Henrietta Dawson was certainly the most rigid, self-righteous woman she'd ever met. Although she'd taken Cora in when she was or-phaned, she'd done so only out of a sense of duty, not because she cared a whit about the girl herself. Henrietta would never let it be said that she didn't know what her duty had been, but she and Cora had been at odds from the first day.

Lucy could only sympathize with her friend. The

aunt controlled her niece's money, and therefore her life, for at least another year and a half, until Cora reached the age of twenty-one.

"I'm sorry. I didn't know." Lucy gave Cora's hand a squeeze. "I'll talk to Melinda Smythe when I see her. Maybe she'll have some ideas."

"I'd better be going. I told Aunt Henrietta that I'd only be gone for an hour. I don't want to give her the excuse she's looking for to make me a prisoner in the house."

"Now, Cora, she's not that bad."

"You don't know what she's like. Sometimes I think if I have to spend another evening locked in that house with her, I'll lose my mind."

There wasn't much Lucy could do but offer her sympathy. She walked Cora to the door and waited until she was out of sight before coming back inside. Not for the first time, she realized how lucky she was to be on her own. It might get lonely, but at least she had no one to answer to.

Looking around the store, she decided there was just enough time to write up her order for supplies before the late-afternoon rush of customers would start. Humming an off-key tune, she began counting the canned goods.

The amber liquid hit the bottom of the shallow glass, splashing and swirling back up to the rim. Cade tipped the bottle back a bit, not wanting to waste a single drop. When the glass was two-thirds full—the most he allowed himself this early in the day—he set the decanter down and carefully put the stopper back in.

Gently swirling the glass, he carried his brandy to the window and looked out at the town he now called home. He liked what he saw, even though he'd chosen to settle in Lee's Mill for no other reason than that the town had a printing press and no one else qualified to use it. Now that he was here, he intended to put down roots as deep as the rocky Ozark soil would let him.

With a final flurry of reds and oranges, the sun was quickly disappearing behind the Ozark Mountains to the west. He smiled, knowing that the entire demeanor of the town changed every night with the setting of the sun. As darkness settled over the town, all the so-called decent folks scurried home for their evening meals. As quickly as they went to ground, the others—the wilder half of the population—came out from their daylight lairs.

Not long after shadows shrouded the streets, the two saloons would fill up with men intent on having themselves a damn good time.

And all Cade would do was watch, being a man who neither belonged entirely to the light nor to the darkness that swallowed men whole. These days, he restricted himself to merely observing, taking notes, and then using paper and ink to hold a mirror up so the town could see itself. Sometimes his neighbors liked what they saw of themselves in his paper. More often, though, he stepped on someone's toes, especially if he'd done his job right.

He finished off his small allotment of brandy and set the glass down. Deciding he deserved a little extra in light of the day's accomplishments, he repeated the ritual. It had been a long time since he'd had any sort of victory in his life. After all, when a man had fought for the South in the late war, he learned the taste of defeat only too well. But for once, a small victory was his, at least according to the letter he'd received in the morning mail.

It had taken him several hours even to work up

the courage to open the heavy envelope. He'd been so sure of defeat that he'd almost burned the damn thing without reading it. But to his surprise, a judge in far-off Chicago had decided that he at least deserved a hearing in his efforts to regain custody of his daughter.

He picked up the small photograph that represented his sole knowledge of his only flesh and blood. His bitch of a wife had seen to it that he'd had next to no contact with his daughter. If Louisa hadn't managed to get herself killed, he would have been sorely tempted to take care of the job himself.

But Louisa was dead and buried, about the only thing she'd done that he approved of. He supposed he shouldn't be quite so bitter, but what the hell. He figured she hadn't been all that fond of him, either, or else she wouldn't have spent most of her time in other men's beds while he was off fighting the war.

Even that wouldn't have bothered him so much if her choice of lovers hadn't all been wearing blue uniforms. Of course, knowing his wife, they weren't wearing those uniforms for long once she set eyes on them.

He tossed back the last of his drink, wishing like hell that something could wash away the memories of his past. Picking up the small picture of his daughter again, he did his best to concentrate on the future. Tomorrow he'd make the necessary arrangements to journey to Chicago to meet with his attorney and the judge. His hope of bringing Mary back into his life had almost died away completely, but now it flickered back to life. He would not admit to any possibility of defeat.

To that end, he had other plans to make. He reached for pen and paper to prepare a list of things to buy, at least the bare necessities to make Mary comfortable in his home. There'd be time to get the rest once she was in Lee's Mill and settled in.

With that in mind, he thanked whatever gods had inspired him to buy the small house behind the newspaper office. Living with her maternal grandparents, Mary wouldn't have lacked for anything. The small living quarters at the back of the newspaper office, although fine for him, wouldn't have been at all acceptable for her.

After making a few notes, it occurred to him that he knew next to nothing about the needs of a six-year-old girl. Perhaps that starched-up woman next door who owned the dry goods store would have some suggestions. Of course, she might not be willing to speak to him after reading today's editorial. His lips twitched in amusement. He hadn't missed the parade of indignant women heading directly for her store within an hour of the paper's coming off the press.

No doubt he'd insulted their delicate sensibilities with his editorial. But if the women of Lee's Mill would stay home and take care of their families like God intended, they'd be too busy to worry about what he had to say. Besides, his comments were meant for the voting public—the men of the town. If those men were blind to what their women were doing, then by damn, his job was to point it out to them.

He could tell them from firsthand experience what happened when a woman was allowed to run free. Once again, he found himself wishing he could banish all memories of his life before the war, when he'd been naive enough to think he was enough of a man to keep Louisa happy. Over time, she'd made it abundantly clear that he'd been lacking in every way, from his choice of uniforms to his ability to please her in bed.

He slammed his fist down in a sudden surge of re-membered anger and hurt, spilling the bottle of ink all over the list he'd started. Cursing with all the in-ventiveness he could muster, he blotted the ink up with his handkerchief before it could soak through to the desktop. After wadding up his pitiful attempt to list what his daughter would want or need, he tossed it into the fireplace.

Deciding that he needed to get out of the house before he managed to spoil his good mood com-pletely, he picked up his hat and let himself out of the house. Once he was outside, he paused to de-cide which of the two saloons in Lee's Mill would better fit his needs for the night. While they both served the same cheap liquor to anyone with the money to pay for it, the similarities ended there.

While Joe Tanner's place boasted a few tables dedicated to the fine art of poker, it offered very little else in the way of diversion. If a man wanted to play a few quiet hands of cards or spend a few hours sipping whiskey with a friend, it was the place to go. The River Lady, located only a few blocks away, was a world apart. The piano player's music wasn't the only entertainment offered in the brightly lit saloon.

Deciding he'd rather look at the women who worked in The Lady, he walked around to the front of the newspaper office. He peered in the window and checked to make sure his assistant had locked up before leaving for the night. Deciding every-thing was in order, he started to go on his way, only belatedly hearing someone walk up behind him.

Even after all the time that had passed since the war, he still had to fight the instinct to attack. With some effort, he reminded himself that the fighting was over. Even so, his hand found its way to the handle of his revolver before he turned to see who it was.

Damn, it was the woman from the store. At first he wondered if she was coming to read him the riot act for attacking her precious Luminary Society. He hung back in the shadow of his doorway and waited for her to pass by. She was so intent on the package in her hand that he doubted that she even realized that she was no longer alone.

"Evening, Mrs. Thomas."

She let out a satisfying squeal as she jumped about a foot straight up in the air. Instinctively using the manners his late mother had all but beaten into him, he reached out to take her arm, intending merely to keep her from falling.

"Don't touch me!"

There was no mistaking the flash of some strong emotion in her eyes as she jerked her arm free of his grasp. He moved back, not wanting to crowd the woman. Touching the brim of his hat, he apologized. "I'm sorry to have frightened you, Mrs. Thomas. I assumed that you had seen me standing here."

She swallowed, as if forcing her emotions back under control. "Well, you assumed wrong, Mr. Mulroney. Now, if you'll excuse me . . ." Then she lifted her skirts only far enough to keep them from catching on the rough wood of the sidewalk and tried to brush past him.

Her abrupt dismissal of him rankled, testing his already uncertain mood. He stared after her, wishing like hell he'd let her land in the dirt rather than sully her with the touch of his hand. And this was the woman he'd hoped to approach for advice on his daughter. There was no way in hell that he'd let a man-hater like her within ten feet of Mary.

Needing a drink more than ever, he marched across the street to the Lady. The bright lights and feminine laughter beckoned to him, hurrying his steps. It was only as he pushed open the bat-wing doors that he finally realized what he'd seen reflected in the depths of Lucinda Thomas's dark eyes—fear. Pure, intense fear.

"Damn it all to hell."

He stopped midstep, and shading his eyes from the bright lights pouring through the door, he searched the street for Mrs. Thomas. He spotted her hurrying around the corner, probably going to visit one of her friends. It wouldn't hurt to make sure that she reached her destination with no further mishaps. Not wanting to question his motives too closely, he told himself that it was only more of his mother's teachings that had him following yet another woman who couldn't bear his touch.

Lucy flexed first one hand and then the other, trying to stop them from trembling before she reached Melinda's door. Her friend was all too observant, and Lucy had no intentions of explaining what had happened a few minutes ago that had her in such a dither.

She cursed herself for a fool. After all, it was hardly Cade Mulroney's fault that her reaction to his sudden appearance had been all out of proportion to what the situation had warranted. The man was despicable for many reasons, but he shouldn't take the blame for another man's misdeeds.

She would have apologized, but he was all too clever at ferreting out secrets. Let him think what he would. Pausing to take a deep breath before crossing the last distance to Melinda's gate, she heard something. Turning her head to the side, she listened for it again.

Footsteps. They came from somewhere behind her. It suddenly occurred to her that the sun had set. Despite the new sheriff's best efforts, the streets of Lee's Mill were no place for a woman to be all alone after dark. With that thought spurring her on, she practically ran the last few steps to Melinda's gate. Pushing it open, she risked a backward glance before scurrying up onto the porch.

She didn't see anyone along the street but still couldn't shake the feeling that she was being watched. Praying that Melinda had gotten her note and was expecting her, she rapped sharply on the door frame. She felt no little relief when the curtain next to the door was pulled to the side, revealing her friend's face. As soon as Melinda saw it was Lucy, she unlocked the door and opened it wide to welcome her inside.

Just as she feared, her friend took one look at her flushed face and knew something bad had happened.

"Lucy, whatever is wrong? Are you all right?"

Now that she was safely inside, Lucy felt a little foolish for letting shadows frighten her.

"No, I'm fine, really."

As if to convince herself as much as Melinda, she peeked out the nearest window. "I left the store later than I meant to and didn't realize how dark it had gotten. In my hurry, I literally ran right into that awful Cade Mulroney. Poor man, I think I scared him pretty badly when I screamed."

"Oh, Lucy, you didn't!" Melinda's eyes danced with laughter.

"Yes, I did."

"Well, he deserves that and more for that latest editorial. The nerve of that man, preaching at us

24 *Pat Pritchard*

like that." Melinda shook her head in disgust. "But let's not let him ruin our evening. I'll pour you a nice cup of tea to sip while I put the finishing touches on dinner."

Lucy followed Melinda into her small kitchen and set her package down on the table. Despite her assurances to her friend, her legs still felt a bit shaky. It was with some relief that she sat down and cradled a cup of tea in her hands. The warmth soothed her jangled nerves.

Melinda tasted the stew she was stirring and added a pinch more salt. That done, she cut off several thick slices of bread and put them on a plate. In quick order, she had the table set for the two of them. As she arranged the dishes to her satisfaction, she eyed the bundle Lucy had brought with her.

"Is that package what I think it is?"

"Yes, it came with today's shipment."

"Does anyone else know?" Melinda slid around the edge of the table until the package was right in front of her.

"Just Cora, and she won't tell anyone."

"I suppose it would be best if we waited until after dinner to open it."

"Yes, it would." Lucy managed to keep a straight face, but then she relented. "Go ahead and cut the string. We can at least see what they look like before we eat."

Melinda snatched up a handy paring knife and sliced through the twine. Then she began unwrapping the heavy brown paper that protected the treasures inside. With growing excitement, both of them reached inside at the same time.

Lucy traced the first title with her fingers. "Until I held the package in my own hands, I didn't really believe they'd come." She started to pick up one of the books but then withdrew. Melinda did the same.

"Let's eat and then we can start."

Over steaming bowls of stew, the two of them kept up a steady conversation about mutual friends and local gossip.

"Henrietta is giving Cora problems again." Lucy reached for another slice of bread. She wished she had Melinda's talent for baking, and told her so.

"I know it isn't very kind of me to say so, but that old woman has a rock where other people have hearts. I sometimes think Cora would have been better off with no family to take her in."

"I don't know that I'd go that far. Besides, Cora knows she has her trust fund to look forward to. Henrietta may have her shortcomings, but dishonesty isn't one of them. When the time comes, Cora's money will be there for her. Once she comes into her inheritance, she'll be free to do as she pleases. We both know there are worse fates for a woman."

Melinda was one of the few people who knew the truth of Lucy's marriage. "You're right, of course, but that isn't going to make the next year or so any easier for Cora to bear."

"Well, enough of that," Lucy said as she carried her empty bowl to the sink. "After we get these dishes washed up, we can look at our books."

"No, wait. I'll clean up the kitchen after you're gone." She hurriedly cleared the table and wiped it down with a clean rag. "We need to get started if we're going to be ready."

Since Lucy was just as anxious, she didn't argue. Instead, she gently picked up the top book and handed an identical one to Melinda. After looking through it for several minutes, she set it down and reached for another.

"Do you think we should start with *Romeo and Juliet* or *Hamlet*?"

"I've been giving that some thought. Don't you

think the others would prefer *Romeo and Juliet*? It has a simpler plot. Besides, all women like a good romance."

Lucy didn't, but she wasn't going to argue. "You decide. After all, you're the teacher."

Melinda looked at her with knowing eyes. "Lucy, I know you don't want to believe it, but not all men are like your husband or your father."

"Name one." It was a familiar argument between the two of them, one they would never resolve.

"Sheriff Hughes."

"He's paid to be nice."

"Reverend Hayes."

"It's his job, too."

Melinda held her hands up in surrender. "Sometimes I think that I could name every saint in the Bible and you'd find fault with them."

Lucy smiled, just as her friend intended. "I will concede that Romeo, apparently, sincerely loved Juliet. Does that make you happy?"

"It will do for now."

"I can't wait until the meeting to show everyone the books. I only wish we could have afforded enough copies for everyone. But considering how hard we worked to scrape together enough money for even these few books, I shouldn't complain.

"Don't worry. We'll take turns reading. Or we could assign parts for people to read."

"That sounds good to me. Will you be starting your classes right away?"

Although it had been Cora's idea that they form the Society, it had been Melinda who'd pointed out that they couldn't discuss literature if their members couldn't read. To solve that problem, she'd volunteered to tutor anyone who needed help in that direction.

"I only have one student so far, and she isn't sure how often she'll be able to come."

The clock began tolling the hour. When Lucy realized that it had chimed ten times, she rose to her feet. "I'd better be going now. We'll work out the details at the meeting."

"Will you be all right getting back to the store by yourself? I'll walk with you if you're at all nervous about it."

"And then who'd walk back with you? We could end up going back and forth all night long." She smiled at the picture that made.

Melinda unlocked her front door. "Well, be careful. I know it's not far, but there have been some unsavory types riding through lately."

"At least Sheriff Hughes makes sure they keep right on going."

Lucy stepped out onto the porch and gave her eyes several seconds to adjust to the darkness before starting home. She instinctively hurried her steps, wishing that Melinda's small house weren't so far off the main street through town.

At least there were several other folks out and about. Although she didn't recognize any of them, she found their presence reassuring. No one was likely to bother her as long as there were people within hollering distance. Even so, she was relieved when a familiar voice called out to her.

"Mrs. Thomas, would you like me to see you to your door?"

"It is kind of you to offer, Sheriff, but I should be fine. I have only a short distance left to go."

"It's not out of my way." He caught up with her easily and then shortened his long stride to match her shorter one. "Been out visiting?"

"Yes, I had dinner with Melinda Smythe."

"She's the new schoolteacher, isn't she?"

"That's right. She'll be starting classes as soon as the school is built."

"Folks will be right pleased to have their children in school again."

The last teacher had left with no notice, leaving the town scrambling to find another qualified teacher. Melinda had only been in town just a few months.

The two of them continued on in companionable silence. When Lucy reached the front of the store, she pulled out her key. To her surprise, Sheriff Hughes took it and unlocked the door for her.

"That was right smart of you to leave a light burning for yourself, Mrs. Thomas."

She wondered if he'd noticed that she often left a light burning all night long. Probably. He wouldn't be as good at his job as he was reported to be if he didn't notice details like that.

"Thank you again, Sheriff. I would have been fine on my own, but that doesn't mean I don't appreciate knowing you're close by."

Just then, gunshots exploded down the street as a couple of men came staggering out of The River Lady, hollering and whooping it up. Mitchell Hughes muttered something under his breath. Lucy was just as relieved not to have understood a single word he'd said.

She also noticed that the soft-spoken gentleman who had escorted her to her door was gone. In his place was a cold-eyed lawman, ready to face whatever trouble was brewing in The River Lady.

When he walked away without a word, she scurried inside and locked her door, glad to be alone again. She picked up her lamp and headed up the narrow staircase that led to her living quarters upstairs.

For certain, the lamp would burn all night long.

# Chapter Two

Cade hesitated outside Thomas Mercantile. Although he'd been inside the store before, he no longer felt sure of his welcome. Shaking his head at his own cowardice, he deliberately approached the building directly from the front to make sure that the usual group of women was not inside.

He could face down one woman, perhaps even two or three, should it become necessary. But no man in his right mind would take on an entire roomful of irate females. Feeling more than a little bit foolish, he reached for the doorknob and walked inside. As usual, he wished the bell chiming directly over his head would shut the hell up. He understood why a woman alone would want to know when someone came in, but it sure made it hard to be inconspicuous.

Once inside, however, he had no choice but to act like a potential customer, not that he had more than a hazy concept of what he was there to buy. He breathed a sigh of relief to see that Lucy Thomas was already occupied with another customer, leaving him free to scout out the territory.

He ducked behind a tall shelf full of canned goods and studied his surroundings.

He'd purchased a few things at the store during the short time he'd been in Lee's Mill, but he'd never taken the time to really look around. His needs were few since he took most of his meals at the hotel down the street. Once Mary joined him, though, that might have to change. As he studied the dry goods on the shelf, he made a mental note to start asking around for a decent woman who'd be interested in being his housekeeper.

For now, he was more interested in the store itself. After only a moment or two, he realized that while he might not approve of some of the owner's beliefs, there was no denying that she kept her place of business immaculate. There wasn't a speck of dust to be seen even on the highest shelves that he could reach. With grudging approval, he inspected the display of ready-made clothing in the front window, designed to draw the eye of even a casual passerby.

Hell, even the lowly spittoon tucked away in the corner shone brightly from a recent polishing. He wondered if any man had ever had the audacity to actually use it. The thought amused him.

Having satisfied himself with the quality of the establishment, he quietly maneuvered himself into a position where he could study the owner herself. She was still helping a young woman select some fabric. The two women stood with their heads bent over several bolts of material, no doubt discussing the mysterious attributes of the brown versus the green.

After a brief glance, he dismissed the other woman. If he wasn't mistaken, she and her husband owned a small farm not far from town. Although he suspected that she'd yet to see her twenty-fifth birthday, she had the look of someone who'd already spent years toiling under a hot Ozark sun. Her beauty was a bit faded around the edges, but to his eye, she seemed happy enough. At least she laughed easily over something Mrs. Thomas had said.

Lucy Thomas was a different matter. Someone— he didn't remember who—had told him that she was somewhere in her mid-twenties. Running a store big enough to serve the needs of a town the size of Lee's Mill was a big responsibility, one meant for shoulders far broader than her slender ones.

One sure couldn't accuse Lucy Thomas of being flashy. Her clothing was dark, almost somber-looking. Her hair, a rich dark brown, was pulled back into a neat knot at the back. She carried herself with quiet dignity. And while not exactly beautiful, there was something in her face that caught a man's eye.

He fought down a surprisingly strong surge of admiration for her. He knew next to nothing about the woman, but anyone who'd managed to make a success of a business on the heels of the late war had to have either a talent for it or the devil's own luck.

"Mr. Mulroney, were you wanting something?"

Damn, he'd been so caught up in his thoughts that he hadn't realized that the other woman was about to walk out the door, leaving him alone with Mrs. Thomas. He stepped forward as he reached for the list he had tucked in his pocket.

"I need to purchase a few, uh, gifts for a certain young lady. I was wondering if you could make some suggestions?"

Lucy pursed her lips and narrowed her eyes. "I'm certain that I do not carry anything that would be at all suitable. Good day, Mr. Mulroney."

Without waiting for him to respond, she turned her back and walked away. What the hell had he said to ruffle her feathers? He followed her to the counter.

"Considering you haven't even looked at my list, how would you know that?" He made a show of looking around the store. "I can see at least half a dozen things that any six-year-old might like just fine."

"Any six-year-old? I thought . . ." Two bright spots of pink stained her cheeks. "Well, never mind what I thought." She held her hand out for his list without meeting his gaze. After studying it for several seconds, she left him standing at the counter while she gathered up several of the items.

"I'm afraid that I don't have much in the way of dolls right now, but I can order whatever you want. Does she prefer china dolls or rag dolls?"

"What's the difference?"

Lucy gave the matter some thought before answering. "Well, I would say that the china dolls are prettier—fancier, if you will. But the rag dolls are easier to hug."

He wasn't about to confess how little he actually knew about his own daughter. "Maybe it would be better if she were to pick out her own."

For the first time, Lucy gave him a genuine smile. "That might be best. Will there be anything else, or shall I total up your purchases?"

He looked down at the pitifully few items he'd managed to think of and felt a stab of pain somewhere in the vicinity of his heart. Damn his wife and her family for ensuring that he didn't know enough even to pick out a damned doll for Mary. Well, with luck and a friendly judge, all that would change. And it would be a cold day in hell before his in-laws would get their hands on his daughter again.

Realizing that Lucy was still waiting for his answer, he pulled out his wallet. "I'll pay now."

He watched as she neatly wrapped the items in brown paper. With a sense of accomplishment, he picked up the small package and tucked it under his arm.

"Thank you for your help and your advice, Mrs. Thomas."

"You're welcome, Mr. Mulroney."

Touching the brim of his hat as a final salute, he escaped to the fresh air outside the store. He fought the urge to get a drink at The River Lady across the street. Instead, he headed directly for the stage office to book his fare on the next eastbound coach, figuring he'd be gone at least three weeks and perhaps as long as a month.

As he walked, he studied the town in an effort to see it through the eyes of a child. Most of the buildings on the north side of town were only a few years old because a good part of the city had been burned to the ground during the war. Folks still argued about whether the Redlegs or the Bushwhackers had been responsible for the fire, but there were few scars left from the damage. In recent months, a new church had been built on the ashes of the old one, and construction was well under way on the new school, on a location a short distance from town.

He liked what he saw. Lee's Mill may not be Chicago, but he'd found some degree of peace since moving here. He was certain that with time he and Mary could build a good life for themselves, if only the judge would see things his way.

Cade wasn't a religious man, but that didn't

keep him from muttering a quick prayer over the
outcome of the scheduled hearing. He walked inside the stage office and laid his money down on
the counter. Trying to convince himself that he
had no doubts about the final outcome of the trial,
he bought one ticket to Columbia, where he'd
catch the train to Chicago, and two tickets for the
trip back.

An hour later, Lucy was still wondering how one
man could fill up a place. She wasn't sure, but
looking back, it seemed as if her store had shrunk
down to one very small room by the time Cade
Mulroney had finished his business with her. Even
though she'd kept her attention on Martha Neal,
she'd been almost painfully aware of him from the
minute he'd walked through her door. She'd
watched him out of the corner of her eye, trying
not to be obvious about it.

He sure enough was a puzzle. His editorials
were loud, full of bold words and anger. In person,
he seemed . . . She couldn't quite put a word to his
behavior. Not quite flustered but definitely uncomfortable, especially when confronted with an
array of dolls to choose from.

Like most men, he'd probably never taken the
time to acquaint himself with the necessities in a
young girl's life. It finally occurred to her to wonder who the child was that he was buying for. So far
as she knew, he lived alone in the small house behind the newspaper office. Perhaps he had rela-
tives in another town who were coming for a visit.

She picked up her feather duster and took a few
swipes at the closest shelves. Melinda and Cora
were due to come by in a few minutes to finish
planning the Thursday night meeting of the Lu-

minary Society. She paused in midmotion to savor the thought. Who would have ever thought that she would be part of planning something so wonderful?

Melinda, the only one of them with a formal education, was going to lead the reading of the play and the discussion afterwards. Cora, who had belonged to a similar group back in St. Louis, had planned out the format that the meeting would follow.

And she, Lucy Thomas, was going to call the meeting to order. The very idea delighted her soul. Without telling the others, she'd sent off to St. Louis for a gavel. Presumptuous, she knew, but she personally thought it would lend dignity to the whole endeavor.

In years past, she'd belonged to various circle groups through the church. Although she enjoyed herself and had made several lasting friendships, she'd found herself wanting something more. Piecing quilts and memorizing Bible verses were important to her, but she needed to stretch her mind.

She liked to think that she'd found kindred spirits with Cora and Melinda, despite the differences in their ages and backgrounds. The three of them were determined to make a success of the Society. So far, they'd only held one brief meeting, more of an open house, really. Besides posting notices, they had used word of mouth to invite all the women in town who were interested in joining. They'd asked for a small donation from those who could afford it, to help purchase books and the few supplies they'd need.

Everything had gone smoothly until Cade Mulroney caught wind of their plans. She still wondered what was really behind his attack on the

Society. It could be just a ploy to sell more papers, fanning the flames of a controversy that didn't really exist. Somehow, though, she feared there was more to it than that.

Which brought her back full circle—the man was definitely a puzzle.

The sound of the door opening snapped her out of her reverie. She set down her duster and turned to greet her friends.

"Sorry we're late, Lucy, but Melinda had a guest when I stopped by to get her." Cora had a wicked smile on her face. "A gentleman caller, in fact."

"Really? And do I know this gentleman?" Lucy watched in amazement as the normally unflappable Melinda turned bright red.

"He was not a gentleman!" she declared. When she realized how that sounded, she covered her mouth with her hand and glared at her young friend.

Cora started giggling. "Don't you think the townspeople would be shocked to find out that Reverend Hayes wasn't a gentleman?"

"That is not what I meant, and you know it." Melinda pushed past Cora and headed for the small staircase in the back that led to Lucy's room upstairs.

There was no mistaking the hurt in her voice. The other two women looked at each other.

"I didn't mean to upset her." Cora watched as Melinda disappeared up the steps.

"I'm sure she knows that. We'll give her a minute or two to compose herself while I close up for the day."

Cora helped her by locking the door and blowing out the lamps that cast golden pools of light around the store. Although Lucy frequently stayed open later than this, her customers were used to her somewhat erratic hours. Running the store by herself necessitated that some days she close just to have time to take care of her own personal business. Folks knew that if they needed something badly enough, they could pound on her door, and she would open up the store long enough to serve them.

Satisfied that all was secure, she picked up the last lamp and followed Cora upstairs. Melinda had set herself the task of boiling water for tea to go with the cookies that Lucy had baked earlier. The three of them gathered around the table in the small kitchen and spread out their materials.

Lucy started the discussion. "Cora, I've been thinking about what you said last week, and I think you are right."

Melinda nodded. "I agree. We need to set down some rules and then follow them. We want to give everyone an opportunity to participate. By limiting each member's time during the discussion, no one person can take over."

The kettle picked that moment to start boiling. Lucy got up to finish making the tea. While she poured, she expressed her one concern.

"I have to admit that I am concerned about offending people if we ask them to sit down before they are finished speaking. Did your mother's group ever have that problem?"

"At first," Cora admitted. "However, we found it was the best way to maintain control of the proceedings. Most of our members came to appreciate knowing that the rule ensured they'd get their chance to speak. Just imagine what my aunt would be like, not that she'd be caught dead at such a scandalous affair."

"Is she giving you much trouble about going?"

Cora shrugged. "No more than usual. I swear, if

she had her way, I wouldn't set foot out of the house except to go to church. I can't imagine what she'd do if a man ever came calling."

"I know it isn't much comfort, but you'll be twenty-one before you know it. Then you can make your own plans."

Cora reached across the table and patted Lucy on the hand. "Keep reminding me of that, will you? Sometimes I . . . Well, never mind. We have more important things to discuss than Aunt Henrietta."

"Let's make notes about how we will conduct the meeting. After we've written down our ideas, we can copy them over in some kind of order."

Lucy set out a clean piece of paper and opened her bottle of ink. She waited expectantly for the other two to tell her what to write. Melinda started them off.

"We will call the meeting to order promptly at seven o'clock, without exception. We don't want people coming in and thinking that it is all right to stand around gossiping and wasting all our time."

Lucy wrote the rule down in her best penmanship. She decided now was the perfect time to share her purchase with her friends. If they objected, she would put it away. Somehow, she thought they'd approve.

"I'll be back in a minute. I have something to show you."

Upon her return, she resumed her seat and set the small box down in the middle of the table. "I thought we might need to be rather forceful the first few times to get everyone quiet and ready to start. You know how we are at circle meetings. All it takes is a birth announcement, and we spend the rest of the evening gossiping."

With a sense of drama, she gently lifted the lid

of the box to reveal the wooden gavel nestled inside. Her friends' reactions were all that she could have hoped for. Lucy whooped and made a grab for the gavel and the small wooden pedestal that went with it.

"Can I?" she asked as she tested the feel of the gavel in her hand.

"Sure. I already have."

Cora gave the pedestal a satisfying whack before passing it on to Melinda. She fingered the wood with a look of approval on her face. "This is perfect, Lucy. I would never have thought of it, but this makes it all feel so . . . so—I don't know—official, maybe."

She tried it out and then handed it on to Lucy. "I bet you can hardly wait to call the meeting to order."

"That's true," she agreed as she tucked the gavel back in its box, "but we won't have much of a meeting if we don't get the rest of the rules figured out."

Once they got started, the rules began taking on a life of their own. In only a few minutes, they had a list that filled the front of the paper and spilled over onto the back.

"When the meeting has been called to order, we will handle the business of the group first. I think it would be best if we posted the list of things that we need to accomplish at each meeting. That way, everyone will know what is expected of them."

"Do you think a five-minute limit for each person is too long during the discussion period?"

"Should we trade jobs around right away or every few months?"

"Melinda should be in charge of assigning people to read the book or play we're studying and to report back."

"But that will limit who gets to participate. Not everyone who wants to come can read."

"Yet. I hope to fix that as time goes on. I'll be bringing slates and primers for those who want to stay after the meeting to learn."

"I hope Josie Turner can come. She seemed so excited about the chance to learn how to read and write."

Lucy's excitement dimmed. "I wouldn't count on it, though. Her husband doesn't seem the type to let his wife do anything to better herself."

"We can only hope that she can work something out." Melinda hesitated and then asked, "Do you think I should ask Pastor Hayes to talk to Oliver Turner? Maybe a word from him would help."

"NO!" Lucy almost shouted. She fought to regain her composure, but she knew only too well how even such a well-intentioned action would be received by a man like Oliver Turner.

"I'm sorry; I didn't mean to overreact, but I am certain that it would only make it harder for Josie." She offered her friends a shaky smile. "Let's see how things go for a while and how often she can come before we interfere."

"Why does she put up with Oliver treating her as he does?" Cora sounded purely disgusted.

Lucy knew all about the shame, the need to believe that no one suspected, but it wasn't her place to disillusion Cora. "Perhaps she loves him, or maybe we're wrong about Oliver. But until she asks for our help, there isn't much we can do."

"Except teach her to read and write. That alone will go a long way toward helping her." Melinda's mouth was set in a determined line.

For several seconds the three of them sipped their tea, each lost in her own thoughts. Finally, Melinda spoke up.

"Well, that's what the Luminary Society is all about. Helping all women to improve their minds. To learn how to think for themselves." She set her cup down. "I think we've done enough for tonight. We'll convene at seven, go over the rules, and then post them. Cora, I think you should be the one to do that since you have the most experience in conducting a meeting."

"I'll do my best, Melinda, but remember that it was my mother who helped run the meetings. Daughters were treated more like guests or junior members."

"Well, that's more experience than either of us have. You'll do fine." Lucy glanced over her notes. "I'll copy these over twice. Once to post on the wall in our meeting room and one for the official Society records."

Melinda scooted her chair closer to look over the list. "I'm still worried that five minutes is too long. But I guess as long as we make it clear that the rules are subject to change, we can try it. Anyway, after Cora goes over the rules, we'll start the reading. I figure we'll be lucky to get through Act One during the first evening."

"That sounds about right to me. I don't know about the others, but I want to savor the experience, not rush through it." Cora rubbed her hands together in anticipation, but then she frowned.

"There is one other thing I'm worried about. Do you think that horrid Mr. Mulroney will try to come to our meeting? He seems to show up at the most inopportune times."

"He didn't mention it." Lucy regretted her words the instant they were past her lips.

Melinda frowned. "When did you talk to him? Was he bothering you about our meetings?"

"The subject never came up at all."

"Then what did you talk about?" Cora demanded.

Lucy shot her a wry look. "Do you want me to discuss your every purchase here at the store with other customers?"

"Well, no."

"I didn't think so. He came in and purchased a few items, just like a dozen other people today. I do run the only store in town, after all."

"How did he act?" Melinda asked. "Pastor Hayes insists that Mr. Mulroney is a gentleman, but I have a hard time believing that when he writes such outrageous things."

"I found nothing objectionable in his behavior toward me. Truly, he handed me his list, I gathered his purchases, and he paid for them. After I wrapped everything up for him, he left."

Lucy thought about turning the tables on Melinda by asking her about Pastor Hayes, but she didn't want to upset her again.

Cora checked the time. "Oh, dear, I had better be running along."

Melinda stood up. "I'll go with you. That way, your aunt can't complain that you were wandering the streets alone."

Lucy followed them downstairs. She gave each of them a quick hug. "I'll make sure our meeting room is ready for tomorrow night. What time do you think you'll be coming?"

"I was planning on stopping by Cora's house about six-thirty and then coming straight here, but I can make it earlier if you need my help."

"No, that's fine. There really isn't much to do other than set out the refreshments."

She followed them out onto the porch. The evening air felt good as she watched them disappear around the corner. If she closed her eyes and listened hard enough, she could just make out the soothing murmur of the river that curved around the town below the bluff. She leaned against the railing and took pleasure in a few minutes of quiet.

The sound of footsteps brought her back to her surroundings as she stepped back toward her door. Just then, all hell broke loose as a group of mounted riders came tearing down the street. There was little doubt that they'd already had too much to drink as they came bellowing past. To her horror, she realized that they had their guns out, preparing to shoot.

Before she'd gone two steps toward the safety of the store, someone slammed into her, knocking her to the ground. She couldn't breathe and fought to get free of her attacker.

"Damn it, Lucy, it's me—Cade Mulroney. Hold still unless you want to risk both of us getting shot! Those idiots are coming back this way."

All the fight went out of her when she realized that it was Cade Mulroney holding her down in an effort to protect her. Even though he didn't sound any happier about their current position than she did, she took note of the fact that he'd situated himself between her and the potential danger.

He rose up long enough to take another look around. "Son of a bitch, where is Sheriff Hughes?"

From her current position, Lucy couldn't see past Cade to what had him cursing. Meanwhile, she was becoming uncomfortably aware of Cade's body pressed along the length of hers. Her reputation could very well suffer if anyone were to see the two of them lying on the porch, legs and arms entangled, no matter what the reason. She felt his weight shift as he looked around again. The mob sounded farther away this time.

"Is the door to the store unlocked?"

She'd been trying to see past Cade, but then she looked up to answer his whispered question. For a long heartbeat, the rest of the world disappeared as her eyes met his. Never before had she realized how long his eyelashes were, or that he had smile lines radiating out of the corners of his eyes.

Somewhat impatiently, he repeated his question, this time spacing the words out as if she were slow-witted.

Feeling foolish, she nodded.

"On my signal, let's try for it. If those boys are in the mood for some ugly fun, we don't want to stay out here much longer."

The shots were getting closer again. In a sudden move, Cade pushed himself up and offered his hand to Lucy to help her. He practically jerked her off her feet in his hurry to get them both inside. She slammed the door shut and led the way to the counter, putting as much distance as possible between them and the rowdies outside.

When she looked to see if Cade was following her, she noticed that he was limping.

"You're hurt! Where did you get shot?"

"In Columbia," he answered, looking grim as he favored his right leg. He leaned against the counter, taking the weight off his foot.

She was too busy looking for blood to realize at first that his answer didn't make sense. Then it dawned on her that he was referring to a battle injury. "You were wounded in the war."

"Yeah."

"Does it hurt?"

"Only when I abuse it some."

It was clear he didn't want to say any more on the subject. He stood with his head tilted, as if listening for something. When she followed suit, she realized it had gotten quiet outside.

"Right about now those boys are going to be right sorry they shot up Mitch's town. He frowns on that sort of thing." Cade smiled, changing his whole demeanor. "He won't rest until he has them rounded up and brought before the judge. I'm betting they'll be on their way to jail by the end of the week."

"Serves them right. Lee's Mill is a civilized town, not one of those wild cow towns in Kansas."

She cast about for something to offer her unwanted guest. "I don't suppose you'd like a cup of tea."

He gave her a studied look. "I'm betting you don't have anything stronger."

She shook her head. "I don't keep spirits of any kind."

"Then no thanks. I don't think there'll be any more trouble tonight, so I'll be going." He pushed himself away from the counter and almost, but not quite, disguised the need to favor his leg.

She refrained from commenting on it, since it was obvious that he'd learned to live with the pain. And she knew all about a man and his pride. Even so, she followed him to the door.

"I want to thank you for what you did, Mr. Mulroney. You very likely saved my life."

"You're welcome, Mrs. Thomas. Lock up after I'm out, and I would suggest you stay inside tonight. Just in case."

*Like I couldn't figure that out for myself,* she thought with disgust. But considering everything, she bit back the urge to tell him so.

"Good night, Mr. Mulroney. And thank you again."

She watched him walk away from her door, curious about where he was headed. The River Lady seemed a likely destination for him, but from what she could see, he headed straight for the newspaper office. As she sought her own room upstairs, she refused to wonder why that pleased her so much.

Melinda and Cora came flying up the stairs to find Lucy. She could hear their excited voices from the second they entered the store below. Not that she blamed them. Tonight was the night that they'd find out if all their hard work would pay off. Despite all the interest in their group, there was no guarantee that people would actually attend the meeting.

A quick peek at the clock told her that they were right on time. She let them reach the top of the stairs before going out to greet her friends. She couldn't wait for them to see what she'd done with the large storeroom that she'd converted to a meeting place for the Society.

"In here, ladies," she called.

Their reactions were all she could have hoped for.

"Lucy Thomas! When did you find the time to do all of this?" Melinda hurried to Lucy's side and gave her a quick hug.

Cora, on the other hand, stood in the center of the room and spun around slowly, taking in every detail. Finally, she gave Lucy a slow smile, full of approval.

"It is perfect. Absolutely perfect."

Lucy beamed with pride. She had worked hard to get the room ready in time. The curtains on the window were new. Makeshift benches were arranged in straight rows with an aisle down the middle. At the front, she'd placed a long table where the officers of the Society would sit.

Perhaps as time went on, they would be able to

obtain more comfortable chairs and even a podium for speakers to use. But it was a worthy beginning.

"Did you leave anything for us to do, or did you want to hog all the glory for yourself?" Melinda wagged her finger at Lucy.

"Cora, I thought you could arrange the refreshments while Melinda and I set out the books for tonight."

All too quickly the clock began to chime out the hour. The three of them stopped fussing with last-minute adjustments, ready to greet their guests. Lucy paused at the top of the stairs to take a deep breath before walking down the steps with all the dignity she could muster. The others followed her example.

Once they reached the front door, Lucy opened it wide to let a satisfying number of women inside.

Feeling like they were taking a huge step forward in the civilizing of Lee's Mill, she announced to all those present, "Welcome to the momentous occasion of the first official meeting of our Luminary Society. May knowledge and friendship light our way."

Their spontaneous applause both surprised and pleased her.

# Chapter Three

Two sharp raps of the gavel were all it took to render the women speechless. Several of them looked stunned by Lucy's action, but once they were quiet, they stayed that way.

"Ladies, I am now calling our meeting to order. I now yield the floor to Miss Cora Lawford. She will explain the rules of our organization. Please give her your full attention. Thank you."

After Cora stood up, she cleared her throat before speaking. "First, let me begin by saying that these rules have been proposed by Lucy Thomas, Melinda Smythe, and myself based on my experience with a women's society that I attended with my mother. I ask your patience and willingness to try them out for a few meetings before you offer any suggestions for improvement. Until such time as we all agree on any amendments, these will be posted for all of us to read and follow."

Lucy noticed that Mrs. Overland was already frowning, although far more of the women present were nodding in agreement. She thought it boded well for the success of their group if they could start off without any major arguments.

As soon as Cora finished reading off the rules, she stepped away from the table to tack the paper on the wall so everyone could see it. Although they wouldn't be able to read it from their seats, it would serve as a reminder to one and all that the rules existed. Satisfied, she returned to her seat.

"I now yield to Melinda Smythe."

Melinda, far more used to speaking to a group than either Lucy or Cora, launched right into her introduction of the play they would be reading. She asked for a show of hands for volunteers to read the various parts, making sure that she picked women of differing ages and backgrounds. One of the rules was that all members had to participate in some fashion.

Mrs. Overland looked surprised to be among the first ones picked. Lucy suspected Melinda had done so to appease the older woman's sense of importance. If it kept her happy, that was fine with Lucy. She might not be her favorite person, but the woman had a definite following among the potential members. If she threw her weight behind their efforts, it would go a long way toward ensuring their success.

Although Melinda continued to direct the reading of Act I, Cora and Lucy were satisfied to be little more than spectators. Cora had read the play before, and Lucy wanted just to savor the success of the evening.

And as with all good things, the evening passed too quickly. When the last of the ladies had filed back out of the store, she found herself fighting back the urge to cry. Melinda noticed despite her efforts to hide her reaction. She immediately gave Lucy a hug.

"I hope those are tears of pride I see sparkling in your eyes. We did a good job with this first meeting."

"Now if only they come back for the next one and the one after that."

"Judging by the satisfied looks on their faces as they left," Cora said as she finished sweeping the floor, "they'll be back and bring more of their friends." She leaned on the broom and considered her next words. "Keep in mind that not everyone can come to all the meetings. More likely, we'll end up with a core of regulars, some that come often, and a few others that show up when they don't have anything better to do. But that's all right."

Lucy carried her good plates back to the kitchen to wash up later. Melinda followed behind her with a tray full of teacups and saucers.

"I'll finish cleaning up the rest of this. You two better head home before Henrietta gets worried."

Cora muttered something under her breath but didn't argue. She and Melinda gathered their things and let themselves out. Lucy decided the rest of the dishes could wait until morning. She made one last check to see that all the lamps had been extinguished and the fire in the stove was banked for the night. Satisfied with the day's accomplishments, she picked up the last lamp and headed for her bedroom.

As she went through her nightly preparations for bed, she replayed the night's events in her head. It was definitely worth at least two pages in her journal, maybe even three. She'd record all the details first thing in the morning, before she opened the store.

With that happy thought, she climbed into her bed, satisfied with her life and the world in general. This would be one night when she wouldn't need the lamp on to help her sleep.

Cade Mulroney had done it again.

Lucy smoothed the newspaper back out on her counter and read the hateful words for the second time. Halfway through her first attempt, she had wadded the editorial page up and thrown it into the kindling box by the stove. Only the knowledge that she'd have to read it some time kept her from tossing Cade Mulroney's offensive words straight into the stove.

If only the man himself were as easy to dispose of. The wretched beast had outdone his previous efforts at attacking the Luminary Society. She gritted her teeth and forced herself to finish the rest of his article.

> *While the men of Lee's Mill should be flattered that their womenfolk are trying to imitate them, it is imperative that these same men take a firm stand against the so-called Luminary Society. The only things this group is shedding light on are the families being neglected while these wives and daughters attempt to use their minds in ways that are both foreign and unsuitable to the feminine gender.*

This time she did toss the offending paper in the fire and watched it turn to ash, with a great deal of satisfaction. That odious man could say whatever he wanted to without affecting her, but that wasn't true for all of their members. At the very least, Cora would likely have more problems with her aunt. And although Melinda was not married and had no man to answer to, her very job was vulnerable to his attacks. As the new schoolteacher, she had her reputation to consider. If the townspeople decided that there was even a hint of scandal attached to her name, she could be dismissed with no references.

This time, Lucy wasn't going to sit back and let that man's viciousness go unanswered. Since she owned the only store in town, she was the least vulnerable to any retribution he might try to extract. Mustering up all her resolve, she locked up the store and marched next door, intent on giving Cade Mulroney the sharp side of her tongue. No doubt, he'd report the incident in his paper, but she didn't care. Someone had to take up the standard for their cause.

To her surprise there were already a handful of people gathered outside the newspaper office. A couple had their faces pressed up against the windows, trying to see in, but the others were reading a notice that had been tacked on the door.

With her anger still propelling her forward, Lucy forced her way through to the front of the group. A man she didn't recognized grumbled something about pushy women, but she ignored him as she read the paper that had captured all their attention.

The statement was short and simple. Cade Mulroney had been called away on personal business, and the office of the *Clarion* would remain closed until such time as he was able to return.

The dirty scoundrel! How dare he stir up such trouble and then run away before the battle could be joined! He deserved to be horsewhipped. She shoved her way back out of the crowd and returned to her store.

The news about Mulroney's unexpected departure would spread like wildfire through the town. She wondered what could have dragged him away. Certainly, his advertisers wouldn't be pleased, not to mention the town council. After all, they'd looked long and hard for someone qualified to run the newspaper for the town.

The reason had to have been something extraordinary. She could only hope that it kept him gone long enough for the furor to die down about the Society. If only he had given them a chance to show that the women only wanted to improve their minds, not destroy their families.

For the moment, the store was quiet. She decided that it was time that she unpack the shipment that the freight office had delivered the previous afternoon. Several people in town had placed special orders, which may have come in. Picking up the bills of lading, she compared each item as she uncrated it. The freight company down the street had proved to be reliable but not infallible. If she'd learned anything from her husband, it was not to trust anyone completely.

After a few minutes, she'd sorted through everything. Just as she'd hoped, the medical supplies the new doctor had asked for had arrived. No doubt, Henrietta Dawson would be pleased to know that the bolt of black wool she'd asked for had come. Rather unkindly, Lucy wondered why the old woman ever bothered making a new dress when all she did was wear black. Her niece, however, would definitely be interested in the new Butterick pattern book. Lucy glanced through it briefly before setting it aside but decided that she'd save back some of that nice peacock blue fabric for herself. If she worked hard, she could have a new dress ready for the next meeting.

She came out of the back storeroom with the

fabric just as her front door opened. She wiped her hands on her apron, preparing to greet her customer. Melinda came through the door followed by the new pastor, the Reverend Daniel Hayes.

"Melinda, Reverend, welcome." She came out from behind the counter to hug Melinda. Turning to her other guest, she held out her hand. "Reverend Hayes, it's always good to see you. I'm sorry, but those hymnals still haven't come in."

Pastor Hayes accepted her hand and covered it with his other one. "I wish that was why I was here, Mrs. Thomas. I regret to say that I've come to talk to you about the Luminary Society."

Lucy looked to Melinda for an explanation, but her friend only frowned.

"Perhaps you would like a cup of tea, Reverend, unless you prefer coffee. We can adjourn to my quarters upstairs, where we can discuss things in private. I'll close up for a short time so that we won't be interrupted."

"Splendid idea, Mrs. Thomas. Tea would be fine."

Within a few minutes, the three of them were seated around Lucy's kitchen table, sipping tea and enjoying the last of the cookies from the night before. Although the good reverend seemed to be enjoying himself, Lucy noticed that Melinda seemed distracted.

It was the pastor who decided that they'd socialized enough. "I hate to be the bearer of bad news; however, I never like it when the person being talked about is the last one to know.

Lucy's stomach lurched. She might be the only storekeeper in town, but that didn't mean that she was totally impervious to criticism. If enough people were offended by her behavior, then they might just drive the extra ten miles to the next town to do their business.

"I assume this has to do with the Luminary Society."

Melinda spoke for the first time. "I cannot believe how small-minded some people are! The whole thing is utterly ridiculous."

"Now, Mrs. Thomas, I happen to agree with Miss Smythe, but that doesn't mean that the situation can be ignored."

"Well, it's not fair. We've done nothing wrong."

Melinda's eyes sparkled a bit too brightly. When she blinked rapidly several times, Lucy knew her friend was close to tears. Since the schoolteacher was normally one of the most serene people she'd ever known, things must have gotten very bad very quickly.

"I don't suppose that Mr. Mulroney's editorial has helped matters, either. Perhaps you'd better tell me what is being said."

Pastor Hayes's eyes were sympathetic behind his spectacles. He gave her a reassuring smile. "Certain people in town are questioning the real purpose behind an organization such as the Luminary Society."

"Those certain people being . . . ?" Lucy prompted, although she bet she already knew a few of them. "No, let me guess. Mr. Mulroney is one of them, of course. Henrietta Dawson, another. I would even go so far as to guess that Mrs. Overland may be having second thoughts."

"I am impressed, Mrs. Thomas. All three of those people have been in touch with me in the last few days. However, after Mrs. Overland and I had a long discussion, I wouldn't be at all surprised to find that she will continue attending the meetings. The other two, however, were much harder to dissuade from their current opinions."

Lucy clutched her hands in her lap as she struggled for control of her emotions. Hurt warred with anger for control. The tears almost won out over them both. Melinda took up the standard.

"Henrietta Dawson is a bitter old woman. God himself would have a hard time living up to her standards."

Pastor Hayes suddenly had a coughing fit that sounded suspiciously like smothered laughter. When he was again breathing normally, he gave Melinda a reproachful look.

"Now, that's not a very Christian attitude, Miss Smythe. However, I will admit that there is a certain rigidity to her thinking. As for Mr. Mulroney, I do not know the man well enough to understand why he has chosen to take such a vocal stand against the group. I personally see nothing wrong with people trying to improve their minds."

"I'm glad to hear that, Pastor," Lucy told him as she poured him another cup of tea.

"As you probably know, Mr. Mulroney has been called away for an unknown length of time. Once he returns, I will make a point of calling on him. Perhaps he has some concerns that I can speak to."

"Until then, what would you advise?"

The young minister gave the matter some thought. "I would go ahead with your plans. I will continue to encourage folks to give your group a chance to prove itself beneficial to the women in this town. And, should it become necessary, I will preach a sermon on the matter."

Unfortunately, like Melinda, he was relatively new in town and had yet to gather a large following among the citizens. It was hard to guess how much influence he would have if things really turned ugly. She wasn't going to say so, because at least he wasn't going to preach against them.

"I can't believe how people always resist change of any kind." Melinda shook her head. "I declare that if life was left up to some folks, we'd never make any progress."

Pastor Hayes rose to his feet. "I think that's probably been true since Adam and Eve left the Garden of Eden, Miss Smythe. People went through a lot during the war. They're just now getting used to peace again. Anything unsettling makes them nervous."

Turning to Lucy, he smiled. "Thank you for the tea and cookies, Mrs. Thomas. Please feel free to come see me if there is any thing I can do to help. I think if we tread carefully, we'll all weather this storm in good fashion. Please don't get up. I can see myself out."

Lucy happened to glance at Melinda as they waited for the pastor to leave. Her friend had a strange expression on her face, but then it was gone as quickly as it had appeared. Before Lucy could puzzle out what she'd seen, Melinda was on her feet and reaching for the empty cups. Ordinarily, Lucy would have insisted on cleaning up her own kitchen, but Melinda seemed so agitated that she let her work out her frustrations.

"I am so angry about Cora's aunt and that odious newspaperman. How dare they sit in judgement on us? Mrs. Overland is another matter altogether. After all, this is something new for her. If she has concerns, she's right to consult Pastor Hayes on the subject. But for those other two, I would be hard put to find anything nice to say about either of them."

Memories of the other night flashed through her mind. Her conscience made her speak up even though she was not happy with Mr. Mulroney herself.

"Cade Mulroney may have saved my life the other night."

Melinda's tirade was in full swing. "That man thinks . . . He what?" She rounded on Lucy, her eyes wide with shock. "When? What? And why don't I know about this?"

Lucy took pity on her friend. "It was the night before our meeting. I guess in the excitement of holding our first meeting, I forgot to mention it."

"You forgot? Your life was endangered and you forgot?" Melinda dropped back down in her chair, as if her legs would no longer support her.

"It wasn't that important, Melinda. Really."

Her friend crossed her arms across her chest and waited for Lucy to explain herself.

"It happened after you and Cora left. I had finished up for the day and stepped out on the porch for a breath of fresh air when a bunch of rowdies came racing straight through town, hollering and making all kinds of noise. I didn't realize at first that they were shooting their guns, too. Mr. Mulroney, uh . . ." She paused, trying to find a delicate way to say that he'd knocked her to the ground and then covered her body with his. The memory still had the power to make her blush.

"Well, he pulled me to the ground and kept me out of their line of fire. I'm telling you that he deliberately put himself between me and danger. Once those men rode past us, he helped me to safety in the store."

"What was he like?"

"He wasn't here long enough for me to form much of an opinion." That wasn't much of a lie.

She wasn't about to put into words the way his body had felt, pressed against the length of hers, their legs and arms tangled together. No, Melinda didn't need to hear about that at all.

"I will say, however, that he was polite and made sure that I was all right before continuing on his way."

She thought about mentioning the wound Mr. Mulroney had suffered in the war, but decided that he wouldn't appreciate her saying anything. He wouldn't want Melinda's sympathy any more than he'd wanted hers. And then there was the strange vulnerability she'd detected the other day when he'd gravely considered which doll to buy for some unknown little girl.

Melinda wasn't impressed. "Well, I'm pleased that he came to your aid, Lucy, but that hardly excuses his attack on the Society. We have done nothing to warrant his behavior."

Hoping to change the subject, Lucy asked, "How did you happen to be with Pastor Hayes right when he was coming to see me?"

This time there was no mistaking Melinda's strong reaction to the mere mention of the man's name. She blushed right to the roots of her hair.

"I had the urge to bake this morning. Since he likes apple pie so much, I took one over to the parsonage. Mrs. Overland had just left, and he was on his way here."

And how would Melinda know that he liked apple pie? Melinda had never mentioned spending that much time in the man's company. Perhaps Cora had been right the other night. She raised her eyebrows when she met Melinda's gaze.

"It's not like that, Lucy."

"Not like what?"

"Your thoughts are right there on your face. I

was just being neighborly. Other women can traipse in and out of the parsonage all day long, and no one takes notice. I took the man an apple pie. Is that so wrong?"

"Of course not, Melinda. I know it isn't fun to bake just for yourself. It's only natural that you would share with someone you like and respect." There, that should put them back on safer ground.

Some of the tension eased in Melinda's face. "I do respect him. From what I've heard, the last pastor in this town did more to drive people away from church than to welcome them into the fold. Pastor Hayes is having to work far harder than he should have to, just to overcome that man's legacy."

Lucy had sat through far too many of the old minister's sermons herself to argue that point. According to that old coot, there wasn't one person in a hundred miles who wasn't on a slippery slope straight to hell. While he did preach against the wickedness of the men, far more often he lectured women on the ungodly weakness of their gender.

Church should be uplifting, not a burden to be dreaded every week. After a while, she'd quit attending services—one of her few overt acts of rebellion against her husband's wishes. Of course, he and her father had both thought the man a saint.

Shoving yet another sour memory from the past back down, she patted her friend on the hand. "Well, I won't argue that point with you. I have enjoyed going to church since Pastor Hayes came to town." She finished the last of her tea. "Unfortunately, I really must get back to work."

Melinda followed her downstairs. "I surely do look forward to school starting. Some days I'm at a loss as to what to do with myself."

"Enjoy yourself while you can. Once the new building is completed, you'll be busy enough. Since we're sharing a school with White's Ferry downriver, you'll have your hands full with so many students. You'll see."

Her friend was looking decidedly happier. "I can't wait. I have so many plans for the children."

Lucy followed Melinda back down the stairs, doing her best to look interested. The most painful regret about her marriage was that she and her husband had been unable to conceive a child. Since she had no intentions of ever marrying again, she was struggling to come to terms with the knowledge that she would never be a mother.

It was with a great deal of relief that she said good-bye to Melinda. With luck she could lose herself in the soothing monotony of unpacking her supplies and serving the various customers as they came into the store. If she kept herself busy enough, there would be little time for regrets.


Melinda had known the pie was a mistake, one she wouldn't make again. Pastor Hayes had accepted the gift without questioning her motives, but Lucy had recognized the gesture for what it was. A single woman didn't bake pies for a single man unless she was . . . well, interested.

Well, at least Lucy wasn't one to gossip. Not even Cora would hear about it from her, which was a good thing. Cora was a delightful girl and extremely intelligent, but she would think nothing of teasing Melinda unmercifully if she suspected that Melinda had strong feelings about the new pastor.

What a cliché! The old-maid schoolteacher developing a crush on the new minister. If word of it ever leaked out, not only would it embarrass

Pastor Hayes, but it could very well ruin her reputation. And a teacher with a bad reputation was soon unemployed.

She wandered to the front window and looked out. Lucy was right—as soon as the school building was built, she would have plenty to keep her busy in getting ready for the school term. She'd already been working hard on lessons and getting the necessary supplies with the limited amount of money the two towns had given her to spend. Although it wasn't much, with hard work and some creative thinking, it would be enough.

Her eyes wandered toward the steeple down the street. The parsonage sat back from the street, right by the church. If she stood on her toes and tilted her head just right, she could just see the corner of its roof. She wondered if Daniel was there, perhaps working on Sunday's sermon. More likely, he was visiting some of his parishioners. Unlike his predecessor, he felt that it was his duty to reach out to people. He spent most of the daylight hours in his buggy, going from one farm to the next, spending time with each family and getting to know them.

She smiled. He'd told her more than once about being invited to share a meal with someone he'd decided to visit. From the slight shudder he'd given, it appeared that not everyone was a good cook. Melinda prided herself on her cooking, but Daniel might well never find out for himself. A pie was one thing; inviting him to dinner was definitely out of the question.

Firmly she made herself turn away from the window. She was too old to spend her time mooning after a man who'd never been more than polite to her. To give him credit, he was friendly enough to her, but she'd seen him around other people. He treated everyone else the same way.

She looked around for something to occupy her time, not to mention her wayward mind. When she spied the pile of books she'd brought home from the meeting, she decided to reread the play, to prepare for their next gathering. Since she was alone, she made herself comfortable. After slipping off her shoes, she curled up on the sofa with her feet tucked up underneath her skirt. It wasn't exactly ladylike, but she'd always enjoyed reading that way.

She closed her eyes and thought back to her childhood. She'd spent many a pleasant hour snuggled up next to her mother on the sofa. Often as not, they took turns reading to each other, with her father joining in whenever he could. Although her parents had lived long enough to see her finish her education, they both died of diphtheria soon afterward. It still hurt to recall that by the time she received word of their illness, they were already gone.

More alone than she'd ever thought possible, she'd changed jobs every year or two, looking for someplace she could call home for good. She had great hopes that Lee's Mill might just be the place. For one thing, it was the first time that she'd found friends that she would be loath to leave behind. Maybe it was as simple as that: on some level she was ready to let people close again. But she didn't think that was the reason, or at least not the only one.

Lucy Thomas and Cora Lawford had both sustained painful loses in their lives, just as she had. Perhaps one wounded soul recognized another. But whatever the reason, the two women were as close to sisters as she was likely ever to find.

Deciding she'd done enough introspection for one day, she opened the play and started reading it out loud. It made her smile to realize that Juliet, too, had been drawn to the one man she had no business thinking about at all, especially as a lover. Obviously, women throughout history had similar problems. Smiling over that idea, she'd have to find some way to bring it into the discussion the next time the Society met.

After that, she lost herself in the flowing prose.

Cade was all too happy to climb out of the stagecoach. As a means of transportation, it was one step up from being dragged behind a horse on his backside. At least his train wasn't leaving until tomorrow afternoon. There would be time for a long, hot bath, a good meal, and a night's sleep before departing for Chicago.

He waited impatiently for the stage driver to hand down the last of the luggage so he could be about his business. He would need his valise right away, but his trunk would follow along later, once he was settled in at the hotel. He had few fond memories of the time he'd spent in the fair town of Columbia, and no desire to go sightseeing. He had nothing against the place, but just being there made his old wound ache like a son of a bitch. More likely, it was from being bounced around for hours in the stage, but maybe not.

When a man damned near died somewhere, he had little call for remembering the place with any fondness.

He paused at the edge of the stage station. If he asked, someone would fetch a buggy to take him to the hotel, but he decided against the idea. His valise wasn't all that heavy, and the exercise would help work the kinks out of his leg. He'd sleep better if he could ease the stiffness that set in anytime he sat too long.

Not that he was complaining. Far too many of his friends hadn't come through the war at all. Others would give anything to still have a leg, stiff or not.

With that grim thought, he set off through town. After a few minutes, the pain had ebbed to a dull ache. Still noticeable, but endurable. Finally, he caught sight of the hotel the station manager had recommended. According to him, the place was clean and reasonable. Not a bad combination.

He hurried his steps, anxious to be in, out of the hot Missouri sun. Once inside the doorway, he paused several seconds for his eyes to adjust to the dimly lit interior. When he could see more clearly, he crossed the small lobby to the desk.

The clerk looked up from his paperwork. "May I help you, sir?"

"I'll need a room for the night."

"Are you traveling alone?"

"Yes. And I'll also be wanting a bath and a hot meal."

The clerk pushed the ledger across the counter to Cade. As he scrawled his signature, the man selected a key and laid it down on the open book.

"Your room is upstairs on the right. I'll send my boy up to let you know when your bath is ready. Clean towels are included in the cost. Dining room opens at five." For the first time, the man's smile seemed genuine. "My wife makes the best chicken and dumplings west of St. Louis, and there's gooseberry pie for dessert tonight."

For the first time in days, Cade's mood improved. "All of that sounds wonderful. I'll make sure I get down to dinner early. I wouldn't want to miss out on that pie." He picked up his valise. "My trunk should be along presently. I would appreciate it if you'd see to it that it gets to my room."

He started for the staircase but stopped and looked back. "That reminds me, I'll be taking the afternoon train tomorrow, so I'll need transportation to the station around noon. Can you make suitable arrangements for me?"

The man nodded as he made note of Cade's request before turning his attention back to his own business.

Cade made it to the top of the stairs with a minimum of discomfort, but he was really looking forward to soaking in a hot tub in the very near future. His stomach rumbled, reminding him that he'd missed lunch. No doubt, the owner's boy would be able to scare up something to tide him over until dinner.

Not that he wanted anything to spoil his appetite—he dearly loved chicken and dumplings, not to mention gooseberry pie.

The next morning, Cade was awake early. Despite his hunger, he decided to walk off some of his restless energy before breakfast. The bed had been comfortable enough, but he awoke feeling unsettled and out of sorts. No doubt, it had more to do with the upcoming hearing than the quality of the hotel. All because, one way or the other, his life was about to change.

He'd feel a hell of a lot better about things if he knew more about the judge, or even what weapons Louise's parents had in their arsenal. His own attorney wasn't worried, but then, he wasn't the one who stood to lose the one thing that made Cade's life worth living—Mary.

Despite the early hour, the day was already warming up. At this rate, it would be a scorcher by the time his train pulled out. He was glad that he'd left his suit jacket back in his room. As it was, his shirt was already damp and sticking to his skin. Rather than endure the discomfort much longer, he turned back toward the hotel.

Once inside, he headed straight for the dining room. If breakfast came anywhere close to the quality of his dinner last night, he'd be a happy man.

The train was crowded and noisy as it pulled into Chicago. Cade handed a nearby porter some cash to transport his trunk to the cab taking him on to the hotel. His stomach hurt, as tension built steadily as his journey drew to a close. If only he had more confidence in his ability to convince the judge that he could provide a better home for his daughter than her grandparents could.

Hell, he wasn't sure he believed it himself. Questions spun through his mind, stripping away his courage. What did he know about raising a young girl, even if she was his daughter? Would she ever forgive him for tearing her away from the only real home she'd ever known? Was he being selfish rather than a concerned parent?

If he couldn't find answers to his own questions, how could he expect to respond to whatever the judge or his in-laws threw at him? For a few seconds, he almost gave in to the temptation to get back on the train rather than face what lay ahead in the next few days. But that was a coward's way out, and his daughter deserved better than that. With renewed resolve, he picked up his valise and marched forward.

# Chapter Four

Lord of mercy, what had he done?

With the sound of the judge's gavel still ringing in his ears, Cade turned slowly to face his daughter. She stood only a few feet away, cowering behind her grandmother, but it might as well have been the entire continent that stood between them. Even if she didn't understand exactly what had just happened in the courtroom, her grandparents did.

And fury hung around them like a murky fog. He wondered if their anger came more from having to give up their granddaughter, or because they'd lost to him. From the very beginning, their hatred of him had known no bounds. Neither of them had ever forgiven him for daring to touch their precious daughter; now they'd lost yet another innocent to his filthy hands.

Well, to hell with them and good riddance. As soon as he could make the arrangements, he and Mary would shake the dust of Chicago from their feet and never look back. He'd make a success of being a father, not only for Mary's sake, but also to spite the Websters.

He let his lawyer speak to their attorney about the final arrangements needed to transfer custody of Mary to him. Knowing the unbelievable conceit of the people, they probably had not even considered packing any of Mary's things. Well, he'd give them a day to do so before sending a freight company to pick the stuff up.

Mary, however, was going to leave the courtroom with him. He wouldn't put it past her grandparents to spirit her away if he were to allow her one last trip to their house. No, better to make a clean break of things now, before they had a chance to further poison her mind against him.

When the two lawyers were finished haggling over some unimportant detail, Cade stepped forward slowly. When he was as close as he dared, he knelt down to meet his daughter's gaze at her level.

"Mary, honey, why don't you go stand over there with Mr. Greenleaf? I know he has some peppermints in his pocket. He tells me that you like them." Shyly she nodded and sidled away from the protection of her grandmother.

When she was safely out of hearing, Cade braced himself to deal with his in-laws, hopefully for the last time.

"Mary and I will be leaving on tomorrow's train back to St. Louis. I'll send a wagon for her things."

Mr. Webster's face, always florid, looked as if he were about to have a stroke. "Like hell, you will. We aren't done with this matter, not by a long shot."

"I have a court order to the contrary."

The wife spoke up, her fists clutched at her side.

"I can't imagine what that judge could have been thinking. Mary is used to having the best of everything. What kind of life can you offer her in that . . . that village you're dragging her to?"

"I'm her father. She should be with me."

"So you can kill her like you did her mother?"

A ripple of shock rolled through the room. Cade glanced around, taking note of several reporters. It wouldn't bother him in the least to have his name plastered all over the evening papers, but the Websters would hate it. He smiled.

"You seemed to have your facts confused, Mrs. Webster. As I recall, it was one of Louisa's many lovers who killed her. Seems he took exception to finding another man in her bed on an evening he expected to be there himself. As I lay wounded in a Yankee prisoner-of-war camp at the time, you'll have to understand why I was unable to leap to her defense."

The flash of pain in his mother-in-law's eyes shamed him. They might not have approved of him, but there had never been any doubt that they cared deeply for Louisa and, by extension, Mary. With some effort, he reined in his temper.

"Mr. Webster, Mrs. Webster, I am Mary's father, and I do want what's best for her. I should say, what *I* think is best." He held up his hand to stave off their protest. "I know we don't agree on what that means, but I don't want to cut you out of her life. Not completely."

*Like you tried to do to me,* he added to himself. He held out a business card. "If you wish to write to her, I won't interfere. And once Mary has come to terms with her new life, perhaps we can arrange for you to visit her in Lee's Mill."

"You haven't heard the last of this."

Mr. Webster took his wife by the arm and stalked

away, leaving Cade staring after them and shaking his head. He pocketed his card, knowing he felt better for having made the offer. There was little or no chance that the Websters would ever travel to a small town in the Ozarks. He figured it was unlikely that either of them had bothered to learn the fine details of the court order. Knowing the two of them, they would have been too sure of their victory over an ex-Confederate to bother. The judge, however, had made damn sure that their attorney understood very clearly what would happen if they attempted to block Cade from taking his daughter home with him.

Or tried to take her back, by legal means or otherwise.

A meeting with the sheriff was one of the first things Cade planned on doing as soon as they returned to Lee's Mill. Mitch Hughes was a good man. He'd know what Cade could do to make sure that his daughter was kept safe. Any strangers to the town would have a hard time escaping his watchful eye.

Feeling better, Cade joined his daughter and attorney. Reluctantly Mary accepted her father's holding her hand as they walked out of the courtroom. The small gesture went a long way toward melting the knot of loneliness in his heart that had been his constant companion since before the war.

Lucy surveyed the mess in the meeting room, wishing that she could have accepted Cora's offer of help in cleaning up last night after the meeting. On the other hand, Henrietta continued to threaten to forbid her niece's involvement with the Society. One late night could be enough to give the older woman the excuse she was looking for.

Picking up the last tray and carrying it to the kitchen, Lucy started washing the dishes. She shouldn't complain about a few dirty cups and saucers if being a little messy was the worst problem the group had. With the lack of an irate newspaper editor to spearhead any organized opposition, the last two meetings had come and gone with little or no comment from anyone. Maybe the husbands and fathers who Cade Mulroney had been trying to whip into an angry frenzy had realized that it was all a tempest in a teapot.

Just as she dried the last few saucers and returned them to the sideboard, she heard someone knocking at the front door of the store below. Wiping her hands on her apron, she patted her hair to make sure she was presentable and hurried down to answer the summons. She checked the clock to see if she was late in opening the store. Seeing that a few minutes still remained before her normal time, she decided that someone must need something in a hurry.

That optimistic thought died as soon as she opened the shade on the front windows. Although one person could have a need that necessitated her opening early, it was unlikely that the pastor, mayor, and sheriff all had run out of something essential on the same day. Her stomach did a slow roll as she turned the key and stepped back to let her unexpected guests into the store.

Pastor Hayes looked apologetic, while his two companions looked decidedly grim. Deciding she'd feel better with a stout barrier between her and whatever bad news they were bearing, she took up her normal position behind the counter before speaking.

"Gentlemen, what can I do for you?"

"Mrs. Thomas, I am sorry for bothering you . . ."

Mayor Kelly immediately interrupted him. "I said I would handle this, Reverend, if you don't mind."

"But . . ."

"You had your chance to put a stop to this non-sense weeks ago. Now it has fallen to me."

Lucy had never had much use for the mayor. Rather than being the strong leader he thought he was, his position on issues depended on what he thought folks wanted to hear at any given moment. She wondered who'd put him up to calling on her.

"Now, Mrs. Thomas, we are here because of the threat posed by your so-called Luminary Society." The mayor drew himself up to his full height, an unimpressive few inches over five feet. Even all puffed up as he was, she still could meet his gaze head-on.

"You feel threatened by a group of women who gather to read Shakespeare, Mr. Mayor? I'm sorry, I didn't realize how frightening we must be."

Pastor Hayes suddenly found a display of bridles to be riveting, while the sheriff gave her what appeared to be a smile of approval over his employer's balding head.

"I did not say I was frightened, Mrs. Thomas. I am talking about the obvious neglect of hearth and home when women are not in their proper place."

She would have none of that. "And exactly whom would you say that I am neglecting? I live alone, after all. Then there are the other members of our group who are currently single, widowed, or whose children are grown." Her fury, barely controlled, brought her back around the counter. "We are also teaching several of the town's women how to read. Since it is the mother's responsibility to see to the education of their children, I would think that this would indeed be a noble effort on our part."

Although the sheriff stood his ground, the mayor took several rapid steps back toward the door.

"Well, I thought it only fair to advise you that I, uh, we will be keeping a very close eye on the activities of the Luminary Society."

"Fine, Mr. Mayor. I will make sure you have the agenda of our upcoming meetings, so that you can see for yourself what we are doing. I'm sure that Miss Smythe will lend you a copy of the appropriate Shakespeare play to read ahead of time, so that you can contribute to the discussion. I'm sure that whatever you would have to say would be valued by all of our members."

By the time he reached the door, Mayor Kelly was so utterly flustered that he left his two companions behind. As soon as he was safely outside and out of sight, Pastor Hayes gave in to the need to chuckle.

"I apologize, Mrs. Thomas. I insisted on coming with the mayor to offer you my support, but I see that you didn't need a champion. You vanquished him with ease."

Considering how badly her hands were shaking, Lucy wasn't so sure that she'd actually won that battle. "I appreciated your being here, Reverend Hayes." She glanced toward the still-silent sheriff.

"And you, sir. Are you here to warn us against meeting?"

Mitch gave the matter some thought before answering. "Well, ma'am, I would have to say no to that. I see no problem with any group getting together, whatever the reason, as long as they don't break any laws."

"But . . ." she prodded, sensing he was holding something back.

"But I think you should take some of what the mayor said to heart. Some folks, and I don't know why, are stirring up trouble about your little group. It's an election year for the mayor. He can't afford to have everyone mad at him."

Lucy clenched her hands into fists. "*Everyone* being those who can vote. In other words, the men." She didn't bother to hide the disgust she felt. "Well, thank you for warning me. I'll see to it that the others get the message."

Having discharged his duty, Sheriff Hughes started for the door. "Again, I'm sorry we had to bother you, Mrs. Thomas. Pastor Hayes." He touched the brim of his hat in a salute as he walked out.

Since the pastor had made no move to leave, she stepped back behind the counter and took on her role of storekeeper.

"Is there something else you were needing, Reverend? If not, I have a few things I need to see to before the store gets busy."

"No, there's nothing." His shoulders drooped slightly as he bade her farewell.

Lucy felt a twinge of guilt. After all, he could have let the mayor descend on her alone. Instead, once again he'd offered his support to their cause. She had no reason to take her bad mood out on him, one of the few allies their fledgling group could claim.

She hurried around the counter, catching up with the young minister at the door. "No, wait, Reverend Hayes. I didn't mean to be short with you. After all, it isn't your fault that this whole situation makes me so angry. What was it you wanted?"

"All is forgiven." He gave her a tentative smile. "After all, I know only too well how hard it is to be charitable when someone opposes your efforts to accomplish a worthy goal, just because you don't do things the way someone else did."

Lucy found herself smiling back. "I suppose you have run into a few folks who wish you were more like your predecessor." She shuddered. "Let me reassure you that there are far more of us who appreciate the fact that you are so different from him."

As if realizing that he shouldn't be questioning the work of another pastor, Reverend Hayes gave the man his due. "I'm sure his efforts were well intentioned. I know for a fact that he worked hard at his calling."

Figuring he had to say something nice about the old minister, Lucy didn't bother to argue the point. She gave the current pastor an inquiring look, raising an eyebrow in an effort to get him to come to the point.

He took the hint. "Ah, well, what I was going to suggest was that perhaps I could let Miss Smythe know about this morning's events on your behalf." He shifted from one foot to the other as he waited for her response.

"I wouldn't want you to go out of your way. Besides, Melinda normally stops by the morning after our meetings to plan out our next endeavor."

"Actually, she has other plans for this morning. She very graciously consented to let me transport her out to the new school to check on its progress. I have business in that area, too, you see."

Interesting, especially the blush that he couldn't quite hide. Maybe Melinda's interest in the man wasn't unrequited. "That was generous of you to offer to take her. I'm sure she appreciates going. I know she's anxious to get started teaching."

He glanced at his pocket watch. "I had better move on along, then."

"Please tell Melinda not to hurry on my account. We can plan for the next meeting later today or even tomorrow."

She opened the door and followed her visitor outside. He tipped his hat and hurried down the sidewalk toward the parsonage. Lucy was about to step back inside when she heard a small commotion down the street. Just as she suspected, the twice-weekly stagecoach was just pulling into town.

With a cloud of dust and a lot of yelling at the horses, the driver brought his team to a stop right in front of the stage office. The horses shied a bit but then settled down. No doubt they were as anxious as the passengers to be shed of the coach.

The show over, Lucy had started back into the store when she stopped and took a second look at the disembarking passengers. She blinked several times, hoping against hope that she was mistaken. Unfortunately, her eyesight was all too clear.

Cade Mulroney was back in Lee's Mill.

As far as she knew, no one had known for sure where he'd disappeared to. Wherever it was, she wished he had stayed there. If there was smoldering resentment against the Luminary Society, he would be sure to start fanning the flames as soon as he had a pen in his hand. Why couldn't he have stayed away?

That was when she noticed his companion. There was no doubt that this was the person who liked dolls. Her curiosity completely aroused, Lucy lingered on the porch, hoping to catch sight of the child's mother. When the driver slapped the reins, turning the corner for the stables behind the stage office, it became clear that Cade was alone with the small girl.

Interesting.

Realizing that she'd been staring, Lucy looked

around to see if anyone had taken note of her inexplicable interest in the newspaperman and his diminutive companion. Considering how she felt about the man and the trouble he'd caused for her and her friends, she had no interest in him or his personal business.

Deciding that she needed to spruce up the display in her front window, she hurried back inside the store and picked up her feather duster. Taking a position by the window, she turned her attention to straightening the merchandise arrayed there. It was amazing how much dirt accumulated in just one day.

Her diligence paid off with a front-row view of Mr. Mulroney as he walked by her store with the little girl in tow. She noticed that his limp was more pronounced than usual, probably due to the strain of traveling. She herself had no fondness for journeying by coach. Going any distance with a child to entertain and care for had to be even more of a strain.

And what a pretty child she was. Something in the window caught the little girl's eye as they passed by, giving Lucy a clear view of the child's face. With such dark hair and light-colored eyes, there was little doubt that she was closely related to Cade Mulroney. Niece, perhaps?

That seemed unlikely. No, something about the possessive way he held the little girl's hand spoke of a closer relationship. Cade Mulroney had brought home a daughter but no wife. It took her a few minutes more to sort out the complex emotions that swirled through her mind with the new knowledge.

First and foremost was the same jealousy she often felt when she saw someone with the child she herself would never have. But something darker, more primitive, was there, too. After a minute, she gave up trying to analyze how she felt. There was far too much to do to spend her morning lollygagging in the front window, trying to catch sight of a man she had no interest in.

As she walked back to the counter to start filling the boardinghouse's weekly order, it came to her. She knew just how she felt about Cade's lack of a wife.

She felt . . . relieved.

With that disturbing thought, she picked up a sack and started weighing out beans and hoping she was wrong.


Melinda wiped her hands on her skirt, trying to hide her nervousness. She'd almost fallen over in shock when the Reverend Hayes had offered to escort her out to the new school building. Although she knew the building was not quite finished, it was far enough along for the crew to take measurements for constructing all the shelves she needed for storage. The foreman on the project had asked her to stop by this week to discuss the matter with him.

Evidently, the pastor had overheard Melinda talking about it with Cora after church, because he'd approached her with the proposed outing. She was doing her best not to read too much into the gesture, but evidently her heart wasn't as resigned to being a spinster as she'd thought.

And if she'd taken extra care with her hair— well, she had an image to uphold as the town's only teacher. Of course, that didn't account for her sudden urge to wear her best dress. With some effort, she resisted that particular mistake. Looking presentable was one thing; looking like a woman out for a drive with her beau was another.

She could just imagine how that would set all the tongues wagging in the church circles. Henrietta Dawson would lead the attack. Only the other day Cora had mentioned how often the old woman had insisted that the poor minister come to dinner. She'd even gone so far as to hint that she wouldn't find it amiss if he wished to court her niece. Of course, Cora was humiliated by the situation and complained about not ever having anyone her own age to talk to. The foolish girl acted as if Daniel Hayes were a member of her aunt's generation when, in fact, he was at most only a year or so older than Melinda herself was.

The clock behind her chimed the half hour, startling her out of her reverie. She didn't want to appear anxious, but neither did she want to keep her escort waiting. No doubt, he saw this as yet another of his pastoral duties, but what did it hurt to pretend, if only to herself, that it was something more?

Before she could pursue that particular argument any further, a buggy stopped outside her gate. With her heart fluttering in her chest, she waited for the driver to dismount and walk the short distance to her door. She made sure to stay back out of sight long enough to count to ten. Even if the purpose of the trip was business, that didn't mean that the normal rules didn't apply. Since she had no female relative to answer the door for her, she would do so herself, but only after a suitable delay.

Finally, with as much serenity as she could muster, she glided to the door and opened it.

"Pastor Hayes, I hope I haven't kept you waiting," she lied.

"Oh, no, not at all, Miss Smythe. You were very prompt." He snatched his hat off his head and smiled. "We have a lovely day for a ride."

At least the weather was a safe topic of conversation. "Yes, it has cooled off somewhat from the weekend."

Much to her secret delight, he offered her his arm as they stepped off her small porch. For the next few minutes, conversation lagged while he handed her up into the buggy and then walked around to the other side to climb in beside her. With a quick flick of the reins, her companion guided the horse back out onto Lee's Road. They headed west out of town on the River Road.

The new school was a joint effort between Lee's Mill and the neighboring town of White's Ferry. Money was tight as the area struggled to rebuild from the effects of the late war. By combining their resources, the towns could afford both a new building and a real teacher for the children in the area. By last count, Melinda fully expected to have as many as thirty students, ranging in age from five to about fifteen or sixteen.

She mentioned the fact to Pastor Hayes.

"I surely hope that most of the farmers will see fit to send their older children to school. Even if they are going to continue to work the family's land, they still need to know how to read, write, and do figures."

The pastor smiled at her fervor. "I take it you've had some heated discussions with a couple of the folks who live back in the hills."

She looked to see if he was taking her seriously. His encouraging smile was all that she could have hoped for. "Yes, I have. That Mr. Jolly had the audacity to tell me that it was mistake to go filling women's heads with anything other than how to count their egg money. And he has five daughters! Can you imagine?"

"Some things are slow to change, but I think you're doing a fine job. I've talked with enough folks in the area to know that they are really excited about their children attending school." His expression turned serious. "You won't win every battle, but you must not let that discourage you or turn you from your path."

His words pleased her. Now that they'd left the last few houses of Lee's Mill behind them, she felt the tension start to drain away.

"Thank you, Pastor Hayes, for both the kind words and the ride out here. I don't often get out of the town proper."

Behind his spectacles, the pastor's eyes crinkled at the corner. "I would like to think that we have become friends. Please call me Daniel."

"All right, but then, you must call me by my given name, at least when we are alone." Her pulse raced as she waited to hear her name on his lips for the very first time. She hoped he understood the limit she put on the familiarity. Both of them had their reputations to consider.

"Melinda and Daniel it is, then." He flicked the reins, urging his horse into a brisk trot. "We should reach the school in another few minutes."

They needn't be in any hurry, but she didn't give voice to that idea. She didn't want to jeopardize their newfound friendship by seeming too forward, or worse yet, to have him think she'd set her cap for him. Casting about for a safe topic of conversation, she brought up the Society's meeting from the night before.

"Speaking of promising students, I think that

Josie Turner has come a long way in her studies. She is so eager to learn that I regret that our meetings are only twice a month. It is every teacher's dream to have a student who actually hungers to learn."

She frowned, not wanting to be thought gossiping. While she didn't feel she could bring her concerns to the attention of the sheriff, perhaps it wouldn't hurt to hint that all was not as it should be between Josie Turner and her husband. "I can only hope that Mr. Turner will come to appreciate her efforts to improve herself."

Daniel mulled over her words for several seconds. He was all too aware of the uncertain temper of Oliver Turner, but he hadn't quite decided what, if anything, he could do about it. "I will include Mrs. Turner in my prayers."

Melinda seemed satisfied with his response, which pleased him. But then, everything about Melinda Smythe pleased him. While he admired her mind and her vocation, neither accounted for the increasingly strong need to see her, to be with her. He wondered how she would react if she were to realize how hard he was fighting the urge to stop the buggy and kiss her.

Keeping his hands firmly on the reins, he clucked to his faithful mare and urged her on. The sooner they reached the school and the safety of other people, the better.

He still needed to talk to her about the mayor's visit to Lucy Thomas, but the last thing he wanted to do was cast a pall over their brief outing. After they returned to town would be soon enough to spoil the mood. For the moment, she seemed content in his company as they continued in companionable silence.

Just over the next rise, the roof of the new school came into view. Immediately, Melinda sat forward, straining to better see the small building that would soon house both her and her students. She turned a brilliant smile on him.

"They've painted it!"

With some effort, he tore his eyes away from her face to admire dutifully the pristine white structure that sat in a small clearing. Several workmen were putting the finishing touches on the outbuildings. One was a privy, but the other was a small stable, built to shelter the horse Melinda would need to traverse the short distance from her home to the school.

He had to admit to some concern about the isolated location of the school. While he understood why that particular spot had been chosen, he didn't particularly like the idea of her driving or riding back and forth alone each day. When winter came and the days grew short, she would be making the trip in the dark.

He'd take it upon himself to escort her, but that would cause talk that neither of them could afford. As they crossed the last distance to where the foreman stood waiting for them, Melinda began to point out all the features of the school that she wished him to admire.

"The stable will also provide cover to keep the wood dry year-round. I have also asked that both towns furnish a supply of food to keep on hand in case of a sudden storm. This will be my first winter in Lee's Mill, but I understand that heavy snow and even ice storms are not uncommon."

She gestured toward the back of the building.

"Even though no one will be living here, I am pleased that they saw fit to build a root cellar under the building. Tornadoes are not unknown in the area, and the children need a place of safety should the weather become threatening."

"The children will be in good hands, Melinda."

There, he allowed himself the small liberty of using her name since the foreman was still out of hearing. He set the brake and climbed down off of the buggy. Before he could round the buggy, Bud Keller was already helping Melinda down from her seat. Drat the man, anyway.

"Miss Smythe, Pastor Hayes. Nice of you to make the trip out here. I could have cobbled together shelves for you, but I figured they'd suit your needs better if I had a clearer picture of what you have in mind."

Daniel hung back slightly, the better to give the impression that his role had simply been that of transportation. Even from a short distance away, though, he could eavesdrop as Bud and Melinda discussed the intricacies of desks, blackboards, and bookshelves. He tried not to resent Bud's offer to escort Melinda up the steps to the schoolhouse. He followed them inside. The sunshine poured in through the windows, rendering the interior only slightly dimmer than outside.

The room smelled of sawdust and varnish. Although both towns shared the same economic struggles, they had managed to fund a good, solid building that would serve the communities for years to come. He suspected that Bud and his sons were working for less than their usual wages, but then, they had a vested interest in the building. Bud's grandchildren had been among the first students to officially enroll in the school.

"Mr. Keller, you have done an amazing job." Melinda twirled around, her face reflecting her genuine delight in the old man's work. "I was here only two weeks ago. I cannot believe how much you've accomplished."

"The weather's been good. Now, about those shelves . . ."

Daniel watched as the two conferred in the corner. Although he didn't want to risk being caught staring, he let his eyes linger on Melinda as long as he dared. A lone sunbeam struck her hair, setting off sparks of gold and red fire. Several curls had escaped from their pins and danced around the delicate line of her neck.

He wondered what her skin would taste like.

The shock of that thought had him stumbling back in an attempt to put some distance between himself and the temptation of Melinda Smythe. How could he be thinking such things about a lady of her quality? And him a man of the cloth! If she even suspected he harbored such ideas, she would shun his company for good, and rightly so.

And he couldn't bear the thought of never having her smile in his direction again, even if it was just between friends. He closed his eyes and prayed hard for the strength to make his wayward mind behave. Otherwise, he would no longer be able to risk spending time alone with Melinda. Even chaperoned outings might not be a good idea if he couldn't learn restraint.

"Reverend Hayes, are you all right?"

Something in Bud's voice told him that it wasn't the first time he'd asked that question. Daniel cast about for an explanation that the man would accept without exactly lying.

"I'm sorry, Mr. Keller. My mind was wandering. Did you need something?" He took off his spectacles and began polishing them with his handkerchief to avoid meeting Bud's gaze.

"Not me. Miss Smythe, though. She asked me to tell you that she'd meet you at the buggy in a few minutes. The freight company delivered a couple of crates for her that we put out in the stable for safekeeping."

"Thank you. I'll go wait for her."

Daniel hurried outside, thoroughly disgusted with himself. He'd been so caught up in his own thoughts that he hadn't even noticed Melinda leaving the room. What an idiot he must appear to both her and Mr. Keller. Once he'd reached the bottom of the steps, he turned toward the small stable on the chance that Melinda wanted to peek inside the crates and needed his assistance.

He met her coming back from the stable. From the expression on her face, she'd found whatever had been delivered to her satisfaction.

"I'm sorry, Daniel. I didn't mean to keep you waiting. I'm sorry this all took longer than expected."

He offered her his arm as they veered back toward where he'd left the buggy. "No apologies necessary, Melinda. I know this is an exciting time for you. Besides, I have no set time that I'm due anywhere."

She looked puzzled. "But you said that you had business out this direction."

That was true enough, even if it was business he'd arranged after he'd offered to bring her out to the school.

"I do, but I told the Davidsons not to expect me at any particular time." He shook his head and laughed. "It seems Mr. Davidson wants me to pray over his pregnant mare. I must admit that I have never done such a thing before, but I didn't see how I could refuse. The family depends on this particular horse a great deal. Evidently, they al-most lost her the last time she foaled."

Melinda smiled. "I think it is sweet of you to even consider it. From what I've heard about your predecessor, he wouldn't have. I'm sure the Davidsons will appreciate whatever you come up with."

He handed her up into the buggy. They both waved good-bye to Bud and his sons before head-ing down the road. The family he needed to pay a call on lived only another mile or so down the road. His business shouldn't take long.

Already he was looking forward to having Me-linda's undivided attention for the ride back to town. And he planned to savor every moment.

# Chapter Five

Cade looked at his daughter and then back at the note in his hand. He crumpled the piece of paper and prayed for guidance. He'd known that juggling his business and his duties as a parent would likely be more difficult than he expected, but so far it had been sheer hell.

He'd already missed out on one story and could ill afford to miss out on another one. With the town election fast approaching, the local politics were heating up. Evidently, the mayor had decided to call an emergency town council meeting for that night. Cade checked the time.

He couldn't very well take a six-year-old to The River Lady, no matter what the reason. Where was he supposed to find someone of good character to watch over Mary while he was gone? He'd started asking around since they'd returned to Lee's Mill, but respectable widows were a rare commodity. Pastor Hayes had offered to make some inquiries on his behalf, but it was too soon to expect much in the way of results.

Of course, he could send Will, his typesetter, in

his stead, but he'd already tried that once. What little sense he could make of Will's notes had resulted in an article all of two lines long—not nearly enough to fill the front page of the paper. No, he had to be the one to go, but how?

The only woman he knew by name who didn't work at The Lady was Lucy Thomas. Her image filled his mind in surprising detail, considering how little contact he'd actually had with her—if he didn't count the night he'd ended up stretched out on top of her in front of her store.

His mind might have almost forgotten that little incident, but his body evidently hadn't. It had been some time since he'd felt any sort of attraction toward a woman, but he still remembered what it felt like. And now was no time to be thinking along those lines. Not if he wanted to ask the woman for a favor.

"Mary, would you mind coming with me for a few minutes? I need to step next door to the store."

Without a word, she closed the book she'd been reading and stood up. Just as silently, she crossed the room to take the hand he held out, and let him lead her out the front door. He tried hard not to let her continued silence bother him, telling himself that she would talk when she was ready.

But it hurt to think that he'd done this to her, stealing the light from her eyes by making her leave behind all that was familiar to her. He'd already spoken to the doctor down the street, who had advised patience and gentleness. Any show of temper could very well drive the girl further into her melancholy.

Cade drew what comfort he could from the fact that she showed no fear of him. Perhaps she'd always been on the quiet side, but he had no way of knowing that. And of course, he sure as hell couldn't ask her grandparents for advice. No, he was on his own and feeling blind.

The two of them stepped out into the bright sunshine. Mary blinked a couple of times and then turned her face up to the warmth of the sun. For a brief second, she smiled. The sight warmed Cade's heart.

"Do you like being outside?" He kept his voice soft, not wanting to frighten her.

Mary tilted her head to the side, as if to give the matter serious thought. After a bit, she looked around until she spotted a buggy coming down the street in their direction. With more excitement than she'd shown to date, she pointed at the horse and driver and looked up at Cade with a world of questions in her huge eyes.

Wanting to keep the mood light, Cade took his hat off and knelt in front of his daughter. "Why, Miss Mulroney, would you do me the honor of going on a buggy ride with me tomorrow? I could arrange a picnic lunch for the two of us."

To his amazed delight, Mary giggled and nodded vigorously. He would have to rent a rig, but no matter what the cost, it was well worth seeing the return of joy to his daughter's eyes. He offered her his arm.

"Well, then we both have something to look forward to." He took her hand again. "For now, I need to speak with Mrs. Thomas."

For once, he didn't mind the bell announcing his arrival. He was too busy watching his daughter do just as any other child would do when confronted with the wonders of penny candy. She dropped his hand and scampered off to stand right in front of the rows of glass jars, her eyes wide with wonder. He reached in his pocket for some change, figuring she'd enjoy the candy more if she picked it out and paid for it herself.

"Mr. Mulroney."

There was a definite chill in Mrs. Thomas's voice, which did not bode well for his purpose in calling on her. Still, he had an ace in his pocket, or rather, one standing by the candy display.

"Mrs. Thomas, may I present my daughter, Mary?" He stepped back from Mary's side, revealing her to the storekeeper. Just as he'd hoped, he diverted Mrs. Thomas's attention away from himself. He wondered if she was still angry over the last editorial he wrote before leaving for Chicago. Leave it to a woman to know how to nurse a grudge.

"Hello, Mary. My name is Lucy Thomas."

To give the woman credit, she didn't seem to take it amiss when Mary offered up a shy smile by way of a greeting but didn't say a word. When his daughter abruptly turned her attention back to the candy, Lucy shook her head and smiled at Cade.

"I should know better than to compete with peppermints and taffy."

"Thank you for understanding. I don't know that she's ever had the chance to pick out her own sweets before." He hated to admit to that, but for some reason, it seemed important that this woman not think ill of his daughter.

"Well, then we shouldn't rush her, not when there are important decisions to be made. Take your time, Mary. Just come get me when you're ready."

Cade realized that Lucy was showing surprising sensitivity to his daughter's needs. Perhaps she was that way with all children, but all he knew was that he appreciated it on Mary's behalf.

He dropped his voice. "May I speak with you alone for a moment, Mrs. Thomas?"

When she didn't immediately agree, he pointedly looked in Mary's direction and then back to Lucy. "Please."

Lucy didn't like the feeling that she was being manipulated by Cade Mulroney. But short of making a scene, she had no choice but to lead him to a quiet nook on the far side of the store. Although the shelves full of sewing notions would afford them some degree of privacy, they would still be able to keep an eye on his daughter.

She waited not too patiently for Mulroney to spit out whatever had him fumbling for words. As mean-spirited as it was, she took some pleasure in watching him struggle to find a way to ask whatever question he had stuck in his craw. Even so, she resisted the urge to tap her foot.

"As you've probably surmised, Mary has only recently come to live with me." His eyes looked past Lucy to where his daughter stood counting the change in her hand.

"She's lovely," Lucy said, taking note of the fact that he offered no explanation as to where Mary had lived prior to her arrival in Lee's Mill. Curious as she was, Lucy knew she wouldn't ask. Not yet.

"Thank you for saying so."

And for what she didn't say, if she'd correctly interpreted the look he gave her. "It's nothing less than the truth." She decided to take pity on him and help him along. "I assume your question has to do with your daughter."

He gave her a wry smile. "You'd think that a man who makes his living with words would have an easier time stringing some together, wouldn't you?" Cade took a deep breath and plunged in.

"You see, we only returned three days ago. My work requires somewhat erratic hours, and I'm frequently called away at the last minute to cover a story. Although I have been looking, as yet I have been unable to located a suitable housekeeper."

What did this have to do with her?

"A housekeeper would seem sensible. Have you talked to Pastor Hayes? If anyone could help you find someone, it would be him."

Cade nodded impatiently. "I've already spoken to the pastor, and he promised to give the matter some thought. But my problem is this: I need to attend the town council meeting tonight. I have no one who can stay with Mary, and I can't take her with me."

Knowing the mayor always insisted on holding the meetings at The River Lady, Lucy applauded his decision. Although she herself had never set foot in the place, she knew it was no place for a young girl, even if the bar did close down for the duration of the meeting.

"If you're asking if I'd be available to stay with Mary, the answer is no. As a businessman, you must understand that I cannot close my store . . ."

Before she could finish her sentence, she noticed they were no longer alone. Mary was beside her, holding out her coins and tugging on Lucy's sleeve. Lucy laid her hand on Mary's thin shoulder.

"But if Mary wouldn't mind helping me with the evening chores around here, I would be glad for her company."

Mary's eyes, so like her father's, widened in surprise. She looked from one adult to the other, asking her questions without words.

Cade knelt down to her level. "Mary, remember when I showed you my office and the printing press? And how I'm responsible for the newspaper here in Lee's Mill?"

Lucy found herself wanting to answer for the little girl, who nodded in response to her father's questions.

"Well, tonight I have newspaper business to see to. I have to go to a place that isn't suitable for someone your age."

Another nod, although a little slower this time, as if saying she understood but wasn't sure she liked it.

"Well, Mrs. Thomas says you can stay with her for the time I'm gone. Seems she would like your help with some of her chores, just like you've been helping me with mine."

Two pairs of silver-gray eyes looked to Lucy for confirmation. Even if she could have refused the father, there was no way she could refuse the daughter.

"That's right, Mary. I'd love some company while I dust the shelves and such. Now that I think about it, tonight's my regular night for refilling the candy jars. I know I could use some help with that."

Mary's smile was all that Lucy could have hoped for. "Well, young lady, we'll have a fine time while your father is off doing men's business. And we all know how important that is." She wrinkled her nose and shuddered, exaggerating for the little girl's benefit.

"Now, we'd better get to picking out that candy."

Lucy skipped away, all her attention focused on the treats to come. On the other hand, Cade was back to looking as if he might have made a tactical error. "I'm grateful, Mrs. Thomas. I think."

"I have to admit that I'm surprised that you

would think me suitable company for an impressionable young girl. After all, I might try to teach her to think for herself or some other dreadful thing."

Cade winced at the tartness in her voice. So much for his hope that she wasn't fostering a grudge. If his daughter hadn't been standing just across the room, there was little doubt that she would have told him exactly what she thought of his opinions and his paper. Well, there was always tomorrow.

Three hours, four cups of coffee, and two cigars later, Cade Mulroney walked out of The River Lady with Mitch Hughes.

"Well, that was a total waste of time."

Cade flicked his cigar ashes over the railing. "I'd have to agree with you there, Sheriff. I've never seen it take so damn long to accomplish not a blessed thing. If the mayor had some purpose in mind other than working his jaws or boring half the town to death, I sure as hell don't know what it was."

"Election years have a way of bringing out the worst in politicians. From what I've heard, he was bad enough last time, when he was running unopposed. Now that the banker has come out against him, we can expect more of the same."

Cade grinned. "Can I quote you on that, Sheriff?"

Mitch stopped short. "Aw, hell. I forgot who I was talking to. You quote me, and I'll be looking for a new job five minutes after the paper comes off the press."

Slapping Mitch on the back, Cade hastened to reassure his companion. "I can't deny that I like to print the truth as much as I can, but I'm not stupid. The council might not mind me stirring up a hornet's nest over some things, but they wouldn't appreciate me making them look like fools."

When they came up even with the newspaper office, Mitch slowed down. "In case you didn't notice, you live here."

"I left Mary with Mrs. Thomas next door. I was lucky she took a liking to my daughter, because she made it pretty clear how she feels about me."

"Well, it is her hornet's nest you've been poking with a stick. I can think of several ladies in town who aren't real fond of you right now."

That was just fine with Cade, but he suspected that the sheriff might have a slightly different take on things. Mitch, although friendly enough, wasn't given to talking much about his past. If he had a woman in his life, no one knew about it.

"They're entitled to their opinion, I guess." He savored the last of his cigar for a moment while he chose his next words. "The role of a newspaper editor is to educate the public, to let them know what's important and what needs to be watched. If I was looking to be popular, I would have chosen a different line of work."

Mitch looked up and down the street, his lawman's eyes never still. "Personally, I would . . ."

The distant sound of glass shattering and running feet brought both men to full alert. Mitch's head swiveled from side to side as he tried to trace the sound. It seemed to come from behind them. Mitch drew his gun and signaled for Cade to go on into the store. Cade was more worried about his daughter than catching some unknown vandal. Not wanting to scare Mary, he kept his hand on his own gun but didn't draw it. He slipped inside the door as Mitch moved off down the narrow alley between the store and the newspaper office. He

waited there until he heard Mitch call back that all
was clear outside.

"Lucy!" he called, pitching his voice to carry no
farther than the counter. When there was no immediate answer, he worked his way toward the
back of the store and the stairs that led, presum-
ably, to her private quarters.

There was no sign of any trouble on the main
floor, so he started up the steps, calling Lucy's
name softly every few seconds. His pulse raced at
breakneck speed, but he kept his movements slow
and careful. There was no reason to think that his
daughter was in any danger, he kept telling himself. But why the hell wasn't Lucy answering when
he called her name?

Finally, he reached the top of the stairs. Since
he'd never been in that part of the building before, he slowly raised his head high enough to
look around. No use walking into trouble.

He'd scanned about half the room when he saw
them. His first instinct was to scoop his daughter
up in his arms and rush her back to the safety of
their own house. With some effort, he resisted the
impulse, taking the time to observe his daughter
and Lucy as the two of them sat studying a chessboard at the table. When Mary reached out to
move her pawn, she looked to Lucy for approval.

Once the little girl had set the piece down, she
sat chewing her lip while Lucy reached for her
knight and explained her own move. Something
told Cade that Lucy had more than a casual interest in the game. He tried to imagine his late wife
playing a game any harder than checkers and
couldn't bring the picture into focus.

Slowly, not wanting to disturb them, Cade came
the rest of the way up the stairs and walked toward
the kitchen table. Lucy immediately looked up,

but Mary was too intent on her next move to take notice.

"How was your meeting?"

"My what? Oh, the meeting." He decided to be tactful. "The mayor had a lot to say."

Lucy's eyes sparkled with amusement. "Any of it worth listening to?" But before he could respond, she had already turned her attention back to Mary. "Now remember, bishops move at an angle. If you leave your pawn there, I can take it." She accompanied her explanation with a demonstration.

Mary immediately snatched her piece back to safety. Back to biting her lip, she looked for a move that wouldn't cost her one of her men. Finally, she moved her knight into position to threaten two of Lucy's pawns. There was no doubt that she knew exactly what she'd done, because she sat back, arms crossed over her chest, and waited to see what her opponent would do.

"Good girl!" Cade beamed with approval of his daughter's newly acquired skill.

Mary looked at him and pointed at the situation she'd created. He placed his hand on her shoulder as he leaned down to study the board.

"You've got her on the run. It will take some quick thinking to save those pawns."

He suspected that Lucy would let his daughter go on to capture her soldiers, but he understood what she was doing. His own father had taught him the game the same way. Whenever his moves showed some forethought, his father would play along, letting Cade learn what strategies were worth pursuing. If he made only random moves, his father would move in for the kill.

It was one of the memories he'd cherished during the hours he'd spent in hell as a prisoner of the Union army. Sometimes the life he'd lived in his mind had been more real than the squalor and misery that had surrounded him. But that was all in the past—and in the occasional nightmare— and he wanted nothing to color the present.

Mary definitely had Lucy on the run. After a couple of quick moves, she knocked over a knight with fiendish glee. The two adults laughed along with her.

"Well, Miss Mary, you'll have to give me a re-match soon." Lucy reached across the board and tapped her small opponent on the nose. "If I'd known how much you'd enjoy beating me, I might have thought twice about teaching you how to play."

Her complaint did little to dampen the victor's spirits. Only reluctantly did Mary take her father's hand when he held it out.

"Come on, we'd better go before we wear out our welcome." Without thinking, he prompted her, "Did you thank Mrs. Thomas for letting you be her guest for the evening?"

For one second and then another, silence filled the room as they waited for Mary to respond. He felt terrible for having put them all in an awkward position.

Then the world righted itself when Mary whis-pered, "Thank you, Miss Lucy."

Cade thought his heart would stop at the sound of his daughter's voice. He didn't know whether to dance and celebrate the end of her long silence or be furious that a relative stranger had coaxed Mary into uttering the first words he'd ever heard from her. In the end, he said nothing.

"You're welcome, Miss Mary. I've enjoyed your company this evening." She met Cade's gaze over his daughter's head. "I mean that. Until you can make other arrangements, she's welcome to visit me."

"I appreciate it. All of it."

"I'll see the two of you out." She picked up a lamp to light their way down the stairs. "Don't forget your candy, Mary. I think you left it on the counter."

His daughter skipped down the steps ahead of him with single-minded purpose. He followed closely on her heels. Lucy had the door opened for them before he remembered that there had been a prowler in the area right before he'd come inside.

"Make sure you lock up as soon as we're outside." He didn't want to scare his daughter but felt that he should warn Lucy. "Mitch thought he heard someone out back awhile ago. I'm sure if there was a real problem, he would have stopped back by to tell us. Still, it doesn't hurt to be careful."

"I always am." She stood rubbing her arms as if she'd received a sudden chill.

"Well, we'll be on our way, then. Thank you again."

He stopped long enough to hear Lucy turn the lock before hurrying home with Mary. He tried not to get his hopes up too much that her long silence was finally over. If not, he at least knew that she could talk and perhaps would do so more often as she grew comfortable in her new surroundings.

And while he might not approve of everything Lucy Thomas did, he definitely owed her a debt of gratitude he might have a hard time repaying. He wasn't sure how he felt about that, but there was nothing he could do about it tonight.

* * *

"If their parents disapproved of them seeing each other, they were wrong for sneaking around like that. After all, the Bible says to honor thy father and thy mother."

"But this isn't a Bible story. It's a play."

Mrs. Overland was under a full head of steam. "But this Shakespeare fellow should have known better than to let a couple of teenagers run wild like he did. No wonder they came to a bad end."

"It was a tragedy, that's for certain."

Josie quietly raised her hand. When Cora called on her, she drew a deep breath. "Well, I don't think their families had any business dictating who they should marry."

It was the first time Josie had offered up an opinion on her own. Lucy wanted to applaud for that reason alone.

"I mean, if they'd left the two of them alone, maybe they'd have found out they were all wrong for each other. Seems to me, the parents gave them no choice but to sneak around."

Before anyone else could respond, Lucy saw that it was time to bring their meeting to a close. She raised the gavel and brought it down smartly on its pedestal.

"Ladies, I'm sorry to say that we're out of time. Josie, you and Mrs. Overland will have to pick up this discussion right where you left off in two weeks."

Her announcement resulted in a satisfying mix of groans and applause. So far, the attendance had remained pretty constant, increasing slightly with each successive meeting. No one ever seemed to be in a hurry to leave even when the meeting was officially over.

Melinda's voice rang out over the others. "I put out a paper so that you all could sign up to bring refreshments for the next few meetings. I know we all appreciate Lucy Thomas's generosity in providing cookies up until tonight, but we need to share the duty."

A few women immediately lined up to sign the paper. Although Lucy didn't mind baking, she didn't always have the time to do so. Especially since she'd had Mary staying with her an hour or two almost every day. Not that she was complaining. So far, Cade had not been able to find a suitable housekeeper, and she wasn't sure she wanted him to.

Mary was a sweet child, even if she didn't talk much—or sometimes at all. If Lucy assigned her a task to do, the little girl worked hard to finish it. And Lucy was having fun sharing some of her favorite books with her. Perhaps she wasn't being wise in allowing herself to become so attached to Cade's daughter, but she couldn't seem to help herself.

The members of the Society began filing out. Melinda and Cora straightened the meeting room and gathered up the books and papers that were scattered over the front table. After a bit, Cora hurried down the stairs to make sure that everyone was gone.

Melinda picked up the top copy of the play and began flipping through the pages. "I'm almost sorry that we've almost finished with this play. Everyone is just now starting to open up and talk." She set the book down. "Did you hear Josie? I was so proud of her!"

Lucy handed her a couple of books that had been left on the seats. "She stood right up to Mrs. Overland, didn't she? Actually, I thought the two of them handled their discussion very well. Neither of them was willing to give an inch, but they respected the other's right to disagree."

"I made notes on the points they each made to refresh their memories for the next discussion."

Cora rejoined them. "I'll take the dishes to the kitchen."

Lucy followed behind her with the last of the tea. "Melinda, how is Josie coming with her lessons?"

"Terrific. I've never known anyone so eager to learn. Why, only yesterday she recited all the sums I had assigned her to memorize."

"Think she'd like a job? I've been thinking about taking on someone a few hours a week while I do paperwork and write out orders. These last couple of months, business has been almost too good for me to get everything done by myself."

Melinda frowned. "I have no doubt that she'd be a willing worker."

"But . . ."

"Well, I just don't know if that husband of hers would see fit to let her." She sounded as if she wanted to say more but was reluctant to.

"It shouldn't be up to him!" Cora rolled up her sleeves and began washing the cups and saucers.

"A husband has a lot to say about what his wife is allowed to do."

"Well, I wouldn't put up with someone like Oliver Turner. I don't know what she ever saw in him to begin with."

With some effort, Lucy refrained from responding. Cora was too inexperienced to know that not all marriages were made in heaven. A man could be charming right up until he had his ring on a woman's hand, but after that, she was at his mercy twenty-four hours a day.

"It's getting late. You two had better be going." She dried the last cup and set it back on the shelf. "I think tonight's meeting was the best one so far."

Melinda gathered up her things. "Yes, let's savor

the moment. Because come morning, when Mr. Mulroney's paper comes off the presses, we might have more complaints to deal with."

"He makes me so mad." Cora's footsteps echoed angrily down the steps. "This time, if he even so much as mentions the Society, he's going to hear from me."

Melinda shooed the younger woman out the door ahead of her. "I'll be by tomorrow afternoon. If he's complaining again, we'll figure out a plan of attack together."

Lucy bit back the impulse to defend Cade Mulroney to her friends. She waited until they were gone and she was back upstairs before giving in to the urge to picture him in her mind. Granted, her contacts with him were usually brief, but she knew him to be both a gentleman and a good father. Although he had yet to explain the sudden appearance of a daughter in his life, she had no doubt that he was doing his best to take good care of Mary. It wasn't easy for a man alone to raise a child, but he never complained.

Cade's contradictions puzzled her, taking up far too much of her energy in trying to figure him out.

It would be nice if she could talk to someone about him. Cora was too young to understand Lucy's past experience with men. Melinda would listen, but she'd have a hard time setting aside her anger over Cade's editorials. Besides, she didn't know exactly what she needed to think through in the first place.

Taking care of his daughter only served to remind her how much she was missing in her own life. She cherished each moment with Mary, knowing that it was likely the closest she'd ever get to mothering a child. Eventually, Cade would make other arrangements, although as far as she knew, his name had never been linked with a woman's in town. He seemed to be in no hurry to find a wife; certainly her feelings on that subject didn't bear close inspection.

Her long-held belief that she had no desire for another husband evidently didn't extend to feeling no desire for a man at all. It was true that toward the end of her marriage she'd come to dread the rare nights when her Harold had exercised his husbandly rights. But earlier, before things had gone horribly wrong between them, there'd been times when she'd found pleasure in sharing his bed.

Something about Cade made her remember those times—the touching, the holding, the heat. She wasn't sure she'd forgive him for making her feel achy and needy. The memory of his body against hers, unbidden and unwanted, made her blush as she sat alone at her kitchen table.

No, neither Melinda nor Cora would understand. She'd keep her own counsel and hope that she'd get over this . . . this . . . infatuation. Soon. *Please, God, soon.*

"Here's the test copy, Mr. Mulroney."

Cade gingerly accepted the still-damp newsprint from Will, his typesetter. He held it at arm's length to study how it looked.

"You did a fine job once again, Will. The headlines you came up with really catch the eye."

Will cleared his throat and sent a wad of wet tobacco flying in the general direction of the spittoon that Cade had bought for his use. More often than not, Will managed to hit it. When he missed, Cade tried not to complain. Some dried spit and tobacco splatters on the floor were a small price to pay for the services of a first-rate typesetter. Until the day Will had staggered into Cade's office drunkenly demanding a job, Cade had spent far too many hours trying to get the newspaper out on time. Now that Mary was living with him, he planned to hold on to Will and his services if it meant tying the man to the press.

"I'll read over everything and let you know if there are any corrections before we start the final run."

"Yes, sir." Will dragged the back of his hand over his mouth and sort of sidled toward the door. "While you do that, I think I'll wander on over to The River Lady for a bit."

Cade glanced up from the paper long enough to give his employee a dark look. Nothing would stop Will from his daily visit to the saloon, but Cade could hope that some feigned disapproval might limit the number of beers the man consumed to a manageable amount.

"Be back in half an hour."

That pronouncement had Will scurrying out the door. The quicker he reached The Lady, the more time he'd have to drink. Cade barely flinched when the door slammed. In the quiet of his office, he studied the paper.

He gave most of his articles only a cursory glance. He trusted Will to get things right, at least when he was sober. His own editorial, though, was giving him some second thoughts. Once again he'd gone after the Luminary Society with both barrels. He read it over slowly, trying to decide why his conscience was pricking at him when he firmly believed that he was right on target about the group.

If his opinions were that firmly entrenched, why the sudden urge to shy away from the harsh words he'd put to paper? He frowned, knowing that it didn't take a genius to figure that one out. The reason lived right next door.

He closed his eyes and pinched the bridge of his nose between two fingers, trying to ease the threat of a headache that had been following him around all morning. A deep breath and then another helped some. What the hell was he going to do?

If he succeeded in offending Lucy Thomas to the point that she would have nothing to do with him, what would he do with Mary? Worse yet, how could he explain to his daughter that it was her own mother who had sent him on this crusade to keep women at home where they belonged? Hell, if Louisa had been faithful or at least discreet, maybe he wouldn't be so riled up over a few women with pretensions of being intellectuals.

That was the real problem. The memory of Lucy explaining chess to his daughter bothered him more than he cared to admit. There'd been little doubt that the woman understood the finer nuances of the game. To his knowledge, she was the only woman he'd ever met who might just offer him a real challenge across the board.

Truth was, he'd never given much thought to the idea that not all women would be satisfied with studying the latest fashion trends or trading recipes for cakes and pies. He couldn't imagine spending hours over fancy needlework and housework himself, but his mother had seemed content with her lot. Why would other women need more than that?

No, he would stand by his words of condemnation. He'd even managed to piece together a couple of good quotes from the mayor's farce of a speech the other night. That would leave the other candidate no choice but to take a stand on the issue as well. Maybe with a little prodding from Cade, the two men would make the Luminary Society and all the problems that came with it one of the central issues of their campaigns.

Ignoring the last-ditch effort of his conscience to change his mind, he scrawled his approval across the top of the paper and left it for Will. By five o'clock, people would be reading his words, his ideas. He liked the power it gave him.

And if Lucy Thomas didn't approve, that was just too damn bad.

# Chapter Six

"I'll go with you to deliver it."

Melinda slowly looked up from the letter she was writing as she considered the offer. She was determined to tell Cade Mulroney what she thought about his continuing attacks against the Society, but that didn't mean that she relished the thought of facing him alone in his newspaper office.

Pastor Hayes stood waiting patiently for her to answer. When she met his gaze, he gave her an encouraging smile.

"I'll wait outside, if you'd like. I'm sure that Mr. Mulroney will act the gentleman, but I'd still feel better knowing that you weren't completely alone."

She thought it was important to attack the problem from a show of strength—which meant a woman standing up to the editor. Even so, having Daniel close by would be a comfort. What harm could it do if a gentleman escorted her the short distance from the meeting room above the store to the newspaper office next door?

"I would like that, Pastor Hayes."

"I thought we'd agreed you'd call me Daniel

when we were alone." He softened the small criticism with a smile.

Trying not to blush, she tried again. "I would like that, Daniel."

"Fine. Take your time finishing your letter. I'm in no hurry to get anywhere."

He pulled out the chair next to her and sat down. He stretched out his long legs and leaned back, giving credence to his statement that he had all day to wait for her. Just that quickly, all the sentences she'd so carefully crafted in her head before putting them to paper became all muddled. She closed her eyes, trying to pull her scattered thoughts back into some semblance of order.

But instead of constructing powerful rebuttals to Cade's latest attack, she sat wondering if Daniel would have chosen to sit so closely if he knew the effect his proximity was having on her. She wanted to touch him, to test the strength she saw in his lean build. And those eyes—his spectacles did little to tone down their beautiful blue. Then there was the matter of his smile that melted her heart and made her tingle all over.

"Need help with the wording?"

Oh, Lordy, she'd been sitting there staring at the paper like some kind of ninny! "Ah, no. I was trying to decide how to get my point across without resorting to the nastiness Mr. Mulroney uses himself."

Drawing on all her willpower, she managed to finish the essay. Laying the pen aside, she blew on the paper gently to dry the ink. She read it over again one last time to make sure that her meaning was clear and that it was letter perfect. That man already thought women were intellectually inferior; she wouldn't prove it to be true by misspelling a word or using an ill-constructed sentence.

She had no desire to give their opponent any more ammunition in his campaign against them.

Satisfied that she'd managed to finish the letter, she turned to hand it to Daniel, only to find him already reaching for it. His hand touched hers as she held it out. A powerful surge of awareness shot up her arm to center somewhere near her heart. Even in her confusion, she was aware that the effect wasn't one-sided, because Daniel jerked his hand back just as quickly.

The letter fluttered to the floor and lay there waiting for one of them to be brave enough to reach for it again. Daniel gave her a crooked smile as he bent down to retrieve her letter.

"I'm sorry, Melinda. I didn't mean to startle you."

"That's all right. I guess all this hubbub is making me jumpy," she lied. The editorial had not a thing to do with what—or rather who—was jangling her nerves.

Daniel immediately turned his attention to her writing, giving her a much needed respite from the warmth of his gaze. On the other hand, she had the perfect excuse to sit and watch him as his eyes traced her words down the page. He might not have the classic good looks of Cade Mulroney or the powerful build of the sheriff, but she didn't care. He had the strength of his beliefs, which drew her to him in ways no other man ever had.

She had to admit that in all likelihood he would have also offered to escort Cora or Lucy if they were on their way to Cade Mulroney's office. But he'd never invited them to use his first name; she held that little bit of knowledge close to her, savoring the sweetness of it.

About the time he was reading the last paragraph, she made herself look away, not wanting to be caught staring at him. She busied her hands with putting the stopper back in the ink bottle and gathering up the rest of the stationery she'd borrowed from Lucy.

Daniel set the letter down on the table. For several long seconds he studied it before looking up to Melinda. Her stomach fluttered, and she feared that somehow she had offended him with her strong words. Slowly he got to his feet and reached down to put his hand on her shoulder.

Looking so very serious, he said, "Melinda Smythe, something tells me that I should have had you writing my sermons for me."

Then he grinned. "Seriously, you've done a wonderful job of countering each of his points with strong ones of your own. His pride will make him print the letter, but I'm sure he will not like doing so."

The combined feeling of relief and pleasure that he approved of her efforts robbed Melinda of all caution. She jumped to her feet and threw her arms around him, intending to give him the kind of hug that a friend gave a friend. While the embrace started out that way, something changed.

Suddenly, she wasn't the only one doing the hugging, and her lips were in direct contact with his. Her heart tripped over itself, beating wildly as the sweetness of the moment settled around them. Her imagination had not done the strength of Daniel's arms justice. Inside his embrace, she gloried in the unfamiliar feel of a man's body so close to hers.

His hands gathered her closer; she went willingly. Never again would she have to sit and daydream, wondering what a man's touch—specifically *this* man's touch—would feel like. She now knew: it felt like heaven.

Slowly Daniel ended the kiss, brushing his lips across hers one last time before pulling back, but not far enough to leave her feeling abandoned. He rested his forehead against hers and sighed.

"Do you have any idea how long I've wanted to do this?"

Her eyes flew open and looked up into his. Was he telling her that she wasn't the only one with daydreams?

He smiled down at her. "I think it was the first time I saw you working in your garden. Something about the way you attacked those weeds, determined to protect your flowers from them. You came to the gate to introduce yourself." He closed his eyes, lost in the memory. "There was a smudge of dirt on your nose, but I remember thinking how very beautiful you were. Do you think badly of me, a pastor, wanting to kiss a member of the congregation the first time we met?"

The heat in his gaze gave her the courage to be daring. "No, I don't. In fact, I wish you'd do so again."

"It would be my pleasure."

This time she knew better how to tilt her head so that their lips met at the perfect angle. But that's where the similarity between the two kisses ended. It was the difference between a spring rain shower and a summer thunderstorm. The first was pleasant, but the other was all power and heat raging out of control. Needs she'd never known and didn't understand burst loose inside her as Daniel deepened the kiss. His tongue slid over hers, teasing and tempting.

Savagely he broke off the kiss and lurched backward, leaving her feeling raw and hurt. Daniel stood panting, as if he'd been running a long distance as he stared across the short but impassable space between them. Melinda felt the sting of tears and blinked, trying to ward them off.

"Miss Smythe, I apologize for my behavior."

Following his example, she fell back on formality as a lifeline. "Apology accepted, Reverend Hayes, if you will forgive my own forward behavior. I don't know what came over me."

That was a lie. It was lust, pure and simple. After years of maintaining her excellent reputation, she'd thrown it over without hesitation for the chance to be in this man's arms. She pulled her tattered pride around her like a cloak.

"Miss Smythe . . . Melinda . . ." Daniel clasped his hands behind his back as if to keep from reaching out to her.

Another voice startled them both. Cora breezed in through the doorway, blissfully unaware of the terrible tension that shimmered between the two of them.

"I was wondering if you'd finished your letter yet. Do you think we should deliver them all at once or . . ." Her words trailed off as she got a good look at Melinda and Daniel. Without hesitation, she spun around and headed right back to the door. "Excuse me. I, uh, forgot something downstairs."

Before she could disappear, Daniel caught up with her. "No, please stay, Miss Lawford. I was just leaving."

Melinda wanted to follow after him, but her feet seemed to be nailed to the spot. The tears she'd been fighting won the battle and poured down her cheeks. She swiped them away with her fingers, but more followed. Cora's arms enfolded her. They didn't feel the same as Daniel's, but they kept her from shattering into little pieces.

"Cora, I've made such a fool of myself. Now he'll hate me."

Her friend leaned away from her, holding Melinda at arm's length. "Don't be silly, Melinda. I don't claim to understand men, but that wasn't hate I saw on Pastor Hayes's face just now. He had the look of a man who'd been knocked senseless." She tilted her head to the side. "So is he a good kisser?"

"Cora Lawford!"

"Well?" Her friend's smile was impish. "Was he? I promise I won't tell anyone."

"Well, yes, he surely was." She wasn't going to lie, not about something this important.

"Details, I need details." Cora pulled a handkerchief out of her pocket and wiped away the remains of Melinda's tears. "Did he hold you close? Who started it?"

Enough was enough. She knew that Cora would carry no tales, but that didn't mean she wanted her to know everything. Perhaps when she herself managed to come to terms with the whole episode, she'd need to discuss it with someone, but not now. Melinda threw back her shoulders and stood tall.

"Never you mind. Nothing will come of it, so it's best that we all forget what just happened." As if she ever would.

"That didn't look like 'nothing' to me. In fact, I'd like a little of that kind of nothing in my life." Then Cora relented and changed the subject. "Lucy sent me up to find out how you wanted to handle the letters. Should we go together or deliver them separately?"

Half an hour before, Melinda might have been able to face down the newspaper editor on her own. Now, however, with her nerves feeling raw, Cora's company would be appreciated. She picked up her letter from where Daniel had laid it on the table. The memory of his approval gave her a new surge of courage.

"Let's go together. Perhaps a united front will convince him that we are a force to be reckoned with."

"I like the sound of that. Think we can rout him? Maybe chase him down the street, waving our letters like avenging swords?" Cora linked her arm through Melinda's, tugging her toward the door.

Cade heard footsteps approaching his office. Knowing from the way they sounded that it wasn't Will, he looked up to see which member of the Luminary Society had decided to pay him a call this time. So far, half a dozen had invaded his office, determined to put him in his place.

This time, his uninvited guest was at least a familiar one. Lucy Thomas peeked around the door frame, looking unsure of her welcome. He knew without asking that she was here on behalf of the Society. If there had been some problem with his daughter, she wouldn't have hesitated about walking through the door.

He immediately rose from his chair. "Mrs. Thomas, please come in. What can I do for you? Would you care to sit down?"

"No, thank you, Mr. Mulroney. I won't be here long."

Cautiously she crossed the small room. Just before reaching him, she pulled a white envelope from her purse and tossed it on his desk. "I would appreciate it if you would see fit to publish this in the next issue of your newspaper."

He left her missive where it landed, and picked up a stack of others. "I must say, I've never had such an influx of letters to the editor in all my years in this business. If I were to print them all, there would be little room left for news."

Her chin took on a stubborn tilt. "Are you implying that the citizens of Lee's Mill wouldn't be interested in our reaction to your libelous editorials, Mr. Mulroney?"

"I wouldn't say that exactly, Mrs. Thomas. There might be some who would find them interesting." He was mocking her, and guessing by the combative spark that appeared in her eyes, she knew it.

"Mr. Mulroney, I do not know where you get your outlandish ideas. But since you are able to give them free rein in such a public arena, you are morally obligated to give those who would oppose you an opportunity to rebut your arguments."

"I am, am I?" He leaned back in his chair and put his boots up on the scarred desk his predecessor had left behind. Locking his fingers behind his head, he assumed a position of studied indifference. The truth was, he wanted nothing more than to leap up from his seat and do his best to get his hands on the woman who stood ramrod straight and glaring at him.

His smile wasn't meant to charm. It worked, because she backed up a step as if instinctively putting some distance between herself and the danger he posed.

"And what do I get if I publish your letter, Mrs. Thomas?"

She gasped and marched back toward his desk, quivering with outrage. "How dare you! I had no idea that you were so despicable!"

"How dare I what?" His boots hit the floor with a loud thud. "I am a businessman, Mrs. Thomas. I expect to be paid for my services."

"What services? You are the editor. Those are

letters addressed to you. Print them. How difficult is that for you to understand?"

She was being so damned cute, more like a kitten than the angry lioness she thought she was. He leaned back again to consider her question. He had already made up his mind to publish at least a couple of the letters. As always, his driving motive was to sell his product, and controversy sold newspapers. By allowing the ladies their say, he gave the appearance of being fair.

Then he would calmly rip their efforts to shreds. If they actually attacked him with their words, he could point out how unladylike that behavior was. Not to mention that no genteel female would want her name to appear in the paper except in the social news.

But something in him didn't want to twist Lucy Thomas's words to his advantage. She'd never said a disparaging word to him about her late husband, but he recognized her as a kindred spirit. Her marriage had left scars that only another wounded in the same way would recognize. A pretty widow like her would have had suitors. If she was still unmarried, it had to be by choice.

Hell, he even respected her and how she lived her life. Instead of the bitterness that he sometimes wallowed in, she offered everyone she met a smile and kindness. Even before he'd come to know her personally, he'd heard stories about her generosity. Hardly a person in town hadn't benefited from the way Lucy Thomas conducted business.

Deciding he'd had enough fun at her expense, Cade stood up. He picked up her letter and tossed it back across the desk.

"I understand far more than you do. If the illustrious members of the Luminary Society want to speak their piece, fine. I'll print what I can of the others, but I won't print yours. That's the deal. Take it or leave it."

This time she reacted with puzzlement. Frowning, she picked up her unopened envelope. "Why not mine?"

He repeated himself, making it clear that no further explanations would be forthcoming. "That's the deal."

She wisely accept the small victory. "Good day, Mr. Mulroney."

"Good day, Mrs. Thomas."

And when she walked out, the brightness of the afternoon dimmed.

"What are you going to do about these women getting out of hand, Mr. Mayor? After all, if you can't control them, how are you going to run this town?"

The question shouldn't have come as a surprise to anyone. But from the way the mayor flushed and shuffled papers, it wasn't one he was prepared to answer. Cade glanced around the room to see how the rest of the men in the room responded to both the inquiry and the mayor's hesitation. While no one seemed to be all het up about the issue, the longer the politician fumbled for an answer, the more attention he drew.

"Well, I don't know rightly how to answer that, George. The ladies have always had meetings and such."

A voice in the back of the room shouted out, "But that was always church business, Mr. Mayor. Who knows what these women are up to? Hell, I've heard tell that some towns are having problems with women trying to shut down saloons!"

That got everybody sitting up straight and taking notice. A few meetings were one thing. Messing with a man's right to drink was another. The mayor, known to frequent The River Lady fairly often himself, rose up on his toes, trying to see who had thrown out that last remark.

"There's been no indication that the ladies are doing anything but reading a play and talking about it. You've seen their letters in the paper."

"Are you defending them?"

This from Cletus Bradford, the banker. He had yet to corner Mayor Kelly into an open debate of the issues, so he had to make do with heckling his opponent at town council meetings. Cade made note of the question and waited for the mayor's answer.

The mayor rose to the occasion with his usual blustering. "No, Cletus, I'm not defending anybody. All I said was that as far as anyone knows, the ladies are reading Shakespeare. No one has said a word about your God-given right to drink."

The banker jumped to his feet. "Are you calling me a drunk?"

Others in the audience were starting to get in the spirit of things by yelling at both the mayor and the banker. Cletus, recognizing opportunity when he saw it, marched with great dignity up to the front of the room and, by sheer size alone, overshadowed his opponent.

He held out his hands, calling for order in the room. "Gentlemen, gentlemen. Please."

After several seconds, he had regained everyone's attention. "Now, don't be hard on our fine mayor."

He bowed his head in Mayor Kelly's direction as a gesture of respect. Cade didn't buy it for a minute. A man didn't become a successful banker by being a fool. No, he was up to something for certain. A story was brewing right under Cade's nose, one that would make tomorrow's edition fly out the door. He made note to remind Will to run extra copies.

"Mr. Kelly can't be expected to know everything." *Or anything at all* went unspoken but was still implied and understood. "I am here to suggest that someone should attend the next meeting by the Luminary Society and report back to us—ahem, I mean the mayor. Then we'll all better understand what should be done about the problem."

Mayor Kelly somewhat belatedly realized that control of the meeting he had called had somehow been wrested away from him. With some effort, he planted himself back in front of the banker. Since the banker stood head and shoulders over the mayor, Mayor Kelly's effort was only marginally successful. Even so, he did his best to reassert his authority.

"I move that since Cade Mulroney has been following this whole Society situation closely, that he be the one to attend their next meeting." The mayor's eyes roamed over the room until they lit on the back row, where Cade was doing his best to hide behind a couple of ranchers.

"I see you, Mulroney. Don't you be trying to duck out on us."

Cursing his own bad luck, Cade tried to salvage his pride. If he was going down, he was going to take everyone responsible with him.

"Yes, sir, Mr. Mayor. I will look forward to accompanying you and Mr. Bradford to the next meeting of the Luminary Society. If I remember correctly, that would be tomorrow night at Thomas Mercantile."

Cade stood to leave only to find the sheriff blocking his way. He hadn't even noticed that Mitch had slipped into the seat beside him.

Glaring down at his friend, he snarled, "Go ahead and laugh. You know you want to."

Mitch shifted a toothpick from one side of his mouth to the other as he considered the matter. "Well, I've got to say that even if I find it amusing," he drawled, holding up his hand to forestall Cade's explosion, "I seriously doubt the ladies will."

"Well, that's too damn bad. At least they *want* to be at their meeting. I don't. On top of that, I have to sit between those two idiots."

The two of them watched as the other men in the saloon either filed out through the door to go home or lined up at the bar to start drinking. Cade pulled out his watch to check the time. He'd promised to pick up Mary by seven-thirty. Judging by the length of the line inside the saloon, he figured he'd better join those going out.

Mitch fell into step beside him. "Remember that prowler we heard the other night?"

Cade had almost forgotten the incident. "Yeah. I figured nothing came of it, since you hadn't said anything."

"Well, I'm not sure anything has come of it, but I've found footprints twice in the last week right between your place and the store."

That brought Cade up short. He didn't like the idea of anyone sneaking around Lucy Thomas's place, much less his. "Any idea who it is or what they're looking for?"

"No. I'll be keeping an eye on things, but I thought you ought to know."

"Have you told Lucy—I mean Mrs. Thomas—yet?"

"I didn't want to scare her for no reason, but I figured on telling her tonight. You headed that way?"

Cade hurried his steps. "Yes. Mrs. Thomas has been watching over Mary for me whenever I have to be away."

The River Lady was only a short distance from the store. After they crossed the street, both men paused long enough to listen for any suspicious noises. Unfortunately, enough men were still leaving the saloon behind them that it was impossible to hear anything clearly.

"I'll go in with you to speak to Mrs. Thomas and then circle around from the back. Maybe I can catch the son of a bitch that way." Mitch fiddled with his toothpick some more. "Out of curiosity, when are you going to tell Mrs. Thomas that you've invited the mayor and Cletus Bradford to her next meeting?"

"Does it make a difference?" The very idea of sitting while a bunch of old hens butchered the Bard was enough make him curse a blue streak.

"Not particularly. I figure I'm paid to keep the peace around here. If she and the others light into you with rolling pins, I want to be close by in case you need rescuing." His laughter sounded rusty, but it was clear that he was enjoying himself at Cade's expense.

"Go to hell, Sheriff."

His companion turned serious. "I've already been there" was his cryptic reply.

Cade had too many secrets of his own to want to go prying into someone else's. Besides, there wasn't time for soul-searching discussions. They'd already reached the store front.

"I told her to lock up and that I'd knock. The

first time, she left it open for me, but I didn't think
that was safe."

"Good advice, considering."

Cade pounded on the door with the side of his
fist. Although he couldn't see the staircase from
where he stood, he could see the shadows in the
store shift as soon as Lucy started downstairs with a
lamp. He moved back from the door so that she'd
see both him and the sheriff clearly before she
turned the lock.

"Sheriff Hughes, Mr. Mulroney, please come
in." If the sheriff's presence concerned her, she hid
it well. "You timed your arrival perfectly. We just
finished a rousing game of cribbage with Melinda
Smythe."

Mary came dancing down the stairs, holding on
to the schoolteacher's hand. Cade braced himself.
The last encounter he'd had with the other woman,
she'd told him in no uncertain terms what she
thought of him, which wasn't much.

Mitch tipped his hat to both of the women and
then knelt down to smile at Mary. "Evening, ladies.
And Miss Mulroney, it's nice to see you again."

Cade's daughter gave the sheriff a shy smile before reaching out to her father. He picked her up
and settled her in his arms. She yawned loudly and
laid her head on his shoulder.

"Come on, sleepyhead. We'd better get you home
and tucked in bed." Over her head, he smiled at Lucy.
"Thank you again, Mrs. Thomas. I don't know
what I'd do without you."

He nodded in Melinda's direction. "Miss
Smythe, I assume you'll excuse us."

"Certainly," she agreed, giving him a cool look.
But then she stepped forward and patted Mary on
the back. "You'll have to give me a rematch soon,

missy. I'm still not sure that I believe that was your first time playing the game, not when you helped to trounce me so thoroughly."

As Cade stepped out into the night, he hugged his daughter up close. No matter what he thought of the Society as a whole, he certainly appreciated the kindness some of its members had shown to him and his daughter. While he still felt he had the right of it when it came to what the group was doing, he had to admit that once again his conscience was bothering him about the effect his words might have.

He'd managed to slip away without telling them about the threesome who planned on inflicting themselves on their next gathering. Promising himself he would do so first thing the next morning, he let himself into the house and carried his daughter upstairs to bed. In a matter of minutes, he had her in her nightgown and stood overseeing her prayers.

Although he wasn't a religious man himself, each night when she knelt whispering by her bedside, he found himself hoping that she included him among her prayers.


Lucy was dead tired and ready to retire for the night, but the lawman seemed to be in no hurry to follow Cade and his daughter out the door. In fact, he looked rather puzzled by their abrupt departure.

"Was there something you needed, Sheriff?" she asked, forcing a welcoming smile.

He seemed to consider his words carefully before answering. "I'm not given to going around scaring folks unnecessarily, Mrs. Thomas. But Mr. Mulroney and I both thought you should know that someone has been snooping around in between your store and his newspaper office."

She shrank back from the doorway. "Who? Why?"

"I don't rightly know, ma'am. The other night I heard someone back there when I was on my rounds, but he was gone before I could catch him. Knowing you live alone, I've been checking every night. Although I haven't actually heard or seen anyone again, there have been footprints."

"People cut through between the buildings all the time, Sheriff. I've done it myself," Melinda interjected. "Surely it's only someone taking a shorter way home."

"Maybe, but I'd feel better if I knew that for sure." Mitch moved closer to the windows and stared out into the night. "Things are quieter in Lee's Mill than they used to be, but there are still some rough characters around. I hated to even mention it. But now that you know, you'll need to be real careful about locking up."

Lucy appreciated his concern, even if his news was unsettling. Certainly, she'd start leaving a lamp lit every night, not to mention locking the door even if she was only going upstairs for a few minutes. She told him her plans, leaving out the part about the lamp. No one needed to know that sometimes she needed one to keep the night shadows at bay.

"Well, I'd better finish my rounds. Miss Smythe, if you're ready to leave, I'd be right glad to see you get home safely."

"I would appreciate your company." Melinda gave Lucy a worried look. "Lucy, are you sure you'll be all right? I could stay the night if it would help."

As much as she didn't want to be alone, one

night of company wouldn't change things in the long run.

"No, you go on along while you have a safe escort. I'll lock up and go upstairs."

"If you're sure. I'll get my things and be right back, Sheriff." She hurried upstairs and out of sight.

Lucy waited with the silent lawman. "We do appreciate all you've done since you've been in Lee's Mill. I think I speak for most of the town when I say that we sleep better at night knowing you're around."

He acknowledged her comment with a nod. "I'll make sure my deputy knows the situation, Mrs. Thomas. And Mr. Mulroney will be on alert as well."

"Thank you again, Sheriff."

Melinda was already coming back down the steps. She wrapped her shawl around her shoulders and then gave Lucy a quick hug. "I'll be over in the morning to see how you are."

Lucy gave them both a brave smile as she let them out and locked the door. She waited until they were past her windows before retreating to her bedroom upstairs. Once there, she cautiously approached the window that looked down on the newspaper office. Nothing was moving in the narrow space between the buildings. She angled her head to better see the small house that Cade shared with Mary. All the windows were dark except one on the lower floor. Even as she watched, she could see the outline of a man walking around inside.

Cade was still awake, too. She wondered if he was feeling restless or if he still had work to do. From a few comments he'd made, she knew he wrote much of the newspaper at night after Mary was asleep. He managed to confuse her as no other man ever had. How could he be so nice to her in person and such a beast in print? It still rankled that he'd refused even to consider her letter for his paper. Why had he accepted the others and not hers?

Did he think she couldn't write a coherent sentence?

Not that any of her friends had anticipated his reaction to their strong words of criticism. While he had printed the letters as written, he'd gone on to use them as yet another weapon in his arsenal. It had taken a lot of talking on her part to keep Cora from acting rashly in retaliation. Melinda probably wasn't any happier about it, but she'd seemed more distracted than angry the past day or two.

As she was turning away from the window, a movement on the ground below caught her attention. Before she could decide what to do, she recognized the tall form of the sheriff. Her pulse immediately slowed down, but the brief episode had left her shaken. Turning away from the window, she considered what to do next.

Sleep would be a long time coming, so it would be a good night to bathe and wash her hair. Besides, brushing her hair dry would help soothe her nerves. That decided, she laid out a clean nightgown and started heating the water.


Later, as she lay still wide awake and tense, she realized that for the first time since her husband's death, she wished she weren't alone in her bed. Closing her eyes, she tried to imagine having a man next to her, his strong arms open to offer her sanctuary.

As appealing as the image was, the make-believe companion she'd created in her mind looked far too much like Cade Mulroney for comfort. He was hardly the stuff that dreams were made of, but in her limited circle of acquaintances, there was no one else who came to mind. Why was that? she wondered. Frankly, she'd always preferred men with light coloring, but the streak of silver in Cade's dark hair was undeniably attractive. Something in his gray eyes spoke of secrets and remembered pain.

Not for the first time, she considered what kind of woman had taught him to think the way he did. Most likely, she'd been his wife, probably Mary's mother. And as adamant as he was that the proper role for females was to be at home, she figured that the mysterious lady in Cade's life had sought her satisfaction elsewhere.

If so, no wonder he hurt. But Cade's past was none of her business, except for the impact his attitudes were having on the Society. She had better things to do than worry about one bitter newspaper editor.

Reaching out, Lucy dimmed the lamp on the table next to the bed until it offered only a small cocoon of light. That small glowing circle was enough to hold her night fears at bay. In the lonely solitude of her bed, she curled up on her side, firmly shut her eyes, and waited for sleep to overtake her.

# Chapter Seven

"You will not be welcome."

"I never thought I would be." Cade reached in his jacket pocket for a cigar. Before he could bite the tip off and light it, Lucy grabbed it out of his hand and threw it on the floor.

"Hey, I paid good money for that," he protested. Before he could retrieve it, she stepped on the innocent roll of tobacco and ground it to pieces with the heel of her shoe.

"We do not allow smoking." She glared up at him, her hands on her hips. "Although if I have to chose between a cigar and you, I'll take the cigar."

Damn, she was cute. Cade knew better than to laugh at her show of temper, but it was a hard-fought battle to maintain a serious expression. "Now, Mrs. Thomas, I must remind you that my being here was not my idea. The mayor and Mr. Bradford practically ordered me to attend your meeting."

"They had no right to do so. Besides, it's not just my meeting, Mr. Mulroney. The Luminary Society belongs equally to all the women in Lee's Mill who

choose to attend. Our membership will have to
bring the matter up for discussion and then a vote.
I cannot condone uninvited guests without everyone's approval. It would be a serious breach of our
rules."

He would be only too glad to retire from the
field, but he hadn't told her the worst of it yet.
"The mayor and Mr. Bradford are already on their
way as well. You might succeed in running me off,
Mrs. Thomas, but if you turn them away as well,
everyone will think you women have something to
hide."

For a moment, he thought she would fly apart
at the seams, her anger was so great. Instead of
lashing out at him, she drew herself up to her full
height and did her best to stare him down.

"This is my home, Mr. Mulroney. No one—especially no man—has a right to walk up those steps"—
she gestured in the direction of the staircase—
"without a specific invitation from me. I think if
you checked with Sheriff Hughes, you would find
that such an action would be defined as trespassing. Shall we go see him?"

This time he couldn't help himself. He laughed,
knowing it was the wrong thing to do. "I'm sorry,
I'm sorry." He held up his hands to stave off an explosion. "But the very image of Mitch marching
both the mayor and Mr. Bradford off to the pokey
is more than my poor mind can handle."

His explanation did little to defuse the moment.
He tried again. "Mrs. Thomas, as you know, I am
not exactly a fan of the Luminary Society."

"That, sir, is the understatement of the year. If
you'd kept your nose out of our business, we
wouldn't be having this discussion at all."

He ignored the interruption. "Be that as it may,
I can tell you this much. I will leave, if you insist.

You may even be able to repel the mayor and his opponent. But if you do, you will rue this day."

"Are you threatening me, Mr. Mulroney?" Her voice had gone all cold and brittle.

"No, Mrs. Thomas, I'm not, but I am trying to explain the facts to you. If you keep us out, you're going to fan the flames of protest against your group. Tell us we can't come in, and not a single man in town will believe that you aren't all up to something."

"Father, are you and Lucy mad at each other?" Mary pushed herself between the two adults, her eyes darting from one to the other as she looked for reassurance that all was well.

He offered her the comfort of his arms, lifting her high against his shoulder. "Everything is all right, funny-face. Sometimes grown-ups can get loud when they feel strongly about a subject. That doesn't mean they are mad." He looked past Mary, daring Lucy to contradict him. "Isn't that right, Mrs. Thomas?"

Lucy's smile, aimed at his daughter, was a bit ragged around the edges. Still, she managed to convince his daughter that she wasn't mad. "We were only talking, little one." She tugged on Mary's pigtail. "I'm sorry if we worried you."

It wasn't the first time that he had envied Lucy's easy manner with his daughter. He was growing more comfortable in his role as father, but he still felt awkward whenever confronted with a new situation.

"Mary, why don't you take your father into the meeting room and show him what a nice job you did arranging the refreshments." Then, with another smile for his daughter but not one for him, she walked away and disappeared down the steps.

Mary wiggled to get down. "Come on. Lucy let me

put out the cookies and the plates and the napkins
and the cups and the saucers." She frowned. "I wanted to carry the teapots, but she didn't want me to
get scalded. I would have been careful, though. I
know I could have done it."

"Well, Mrs. Thomas knows how much you like
to help, but some things are for grown-ups to do."

Mary gave a heavy sigh as she led the way. "That's
what she said, too."

Once inside the inner sanctum of the Society,
Cade paused to look around. The women had
come up with a far better meeting room than The
River Lady. For one thing, it didn't smell like old
cigars and cheap liquor. He tried to picture the
mayor conducting a meeting while his listeners
nibbled on fancy cookies and sipped tea.

The image made him chuckle. He wondered if
Lucy's baked goods were as appealing as everything else was about her. When he reached out to
sample one of the cookies, his daughter slapped
his hand.

"Those aren't for you. They're for the ladies."

"They won't miss one cookie, will they?"

Mary considered the matter. "I guess not." She
picked one out for him and then quickly re-
arranged the remaining cookies to hide the empty
spot.

"Will you be all right by yourself while I go to
the meeting with Mrs. Thomas?"

She rolled her eyes, looking far more mature
than she was. "Yes, Father. I'm a big girl. Lucy gave
me a book to read, so I'll be fine."

To that end, she walked away and settled herself
in a comfortable chair in the small room that
served as Lucy's parlor. Left alone, Cade felt at
loose ends. Finally, he gave up and took a seat in
the back row of benches, figuring it would give

him the best opportunity to observe the ladies in action. Glancing at his pocket watch, he prayed that the next couple of hours would fly by.

The last thing he wanted to do was waste an entire evening listening to a bunch of women pretending to be men.

Melinda hurried her steps, as if she could outrun her troubles. A headache throbbed behind her eyes, making her wish she could simply stay home for the night. Sheer stubbornness kept her feet moving in the direction of Lucy's store.

One mistake, one moment of passion, was not going to drive her indoors, her head hung in shame. She'd done nothing so very wrong and certainly nothing she was sorry for. If she harbored any regrets at all, it was only that Daniel Hayes seemed to view the whole incident in a different light. Since he hadn't so much as spoken a word to her since he'd kissed her senseless, she had no real way of gauging his mood.

They couldn't go on avoiding each other forever, not in a town the size of Lee's Mill. Nor did she want their first encounter to be a public one. If he wasn't going to seek her out, she would find him. If necessary, she would wait until it was dark one evening and confront him at the parsonage. No lady would do such a thing, of course, but she wasn't feeling particularly ladylike at the moment.

Why, if he thought one embrace was so shocking, she would . . . Before she could complete that thought, she was brought up short by the sight of the mayor and another man—was that Mr. Bradford?—knocking on the door to the store. What could they be wanting? By now, everyone in town ought to know that the store was closed two

Thursdays a month for their meetings. Cade Mulroney had seen to that.

But there the two men stood staring at the locked door. Cautiously, Melinda approached them.

"Can I help you, gentlemen?"

Mayor Kelly looked his most officious, warning her she wasn't going to like his answer.

"Ah, Miss Smythe, now that you are here, perhaps Mrs. Thomas will answer our summons."

"You realize, of course, Mr. Mayor, that the store is closed tonight." She stepped past him to knock on the door herself.

The banker entered into the conversation. "We know, Miss Smythe. In fact, that is why we're here. We intend to get to the bottom of this Luminary Society meeting business."

Had she heard him correctly? What business was he talking about? Before she could ask him to explain himself, Lucy opened the door. She stood in the opening, clearly blocking the entrance to the store.

Lucy nodded in the direction of the two men, but then her eyes met Melinda's, shutting them out of the conversation. "I'm glad you're here, Miss Smythe. I appreciate your coming early to help." Turning to the mayor, she gave him a cold smile. "I apologize for leaving you standing out here until the meeting begins, gentlemen, but you'll understand, I'm sure."

She surprised them all by taking Melinda by the arm and yanking her through the doorway. It all happened so quickly that the mayor and banker could do nothing to prevent her from shutting the door and locking them out. Once inside, she all but dragged Melinda to the back of the store.

"Lucy, what is going on? What are those two doing here?"

"Let me catch my breath and then I'll explain."

While Melinda waited, she kept an eye on the front door, fully expecting the two men to start knocking again.

"Seems that the mayor has got it into his fool head that we're up to something. There was a town council meeting last night. When the subject of the Luminary Society came up, those two idiots out there decided to come to our meeting, uninvited and unwanted. They ordered Mr. Mulroney to attend, as well, so he can report on our activities."

"How dare they!" A surge of anger intensified Melinda's headache. "What gives them the right? The Society is not subject to public scrutiny, or at least it shouldn't be."

Lucy paced the length of the storeroom. "I tried to tell Mr. Mulroney that we'd bring the problem before the Society as a whole and then allow the membership to vote on the matter."

She punctuated each word with a wave of her hand. "I explained that we had rules that had to be followed." Finally, she slowed down. "He told me—and I believe him—that if we block their entry completely, we will only make matters worse. I have no idea what they think we're up to that is so worrisome to the men in this town, but they're bound to think the worst."

"Well, then I don't see that we have a choice but to let them in." Melinda thought for a few seconds. "I do think that we can and should ask them to wait outside the room upstairs until we explain their presence."

"I suppose that will be better than nothing. I'm just worried that when it comes time for discussion, no one will want to talk. Not as long they have to worry about what Mr. Mulroney will print in tomorrow's paper."

"He's been holding that ax over our heads for some time. If we ignore him, he prints what he wants. If we respond to his allegations, he prints what he wants. Either way, he sells newspapers, and we bear the brunt of his success. I don't know how you can stand that man."

The two of them started out of the storeroom. Before they started up the stairs, Melinda glanced out the front window. "When is the great newspaperman supposed to arrive?"

"I'm already here, Miss Smythe."

The softly spoken words brought Melinda up short. Slowly she turned to face the nemesis of the Society.

"Mr. Mulroney, did no one ever tell you that eavesdroppers rarely hear anything good about themselves?"

"That may be true, but then, as a newspaperman, I've developed a pretty thick skin."

"How nice for you," she told him sweetly with sarcasm dripping from every syllable.

She hated that his laughter made her want to join in. To her surprise, Lucy did. Finally, she gave in to the urge to smile. "Mr. Mulroney, one of these days you will go too far."

"No doubt." He didn't look the least bit worried. "Well, now that the pleasantries are out of the way, are you ladies going to keep the mayor and Mr. Bradford standing outside all evening?"

Both women turned to study the two men in question. Bradford was leaning against the porch railing while the mayor cupped his hands around his face and tried to look in the window.

"Well, as tempting as the thought is, we'll probably have to let them in." Lucy looked to Melinda for confirmation.

She nodded. "Maybe you can take them upstairs

for now while I wait down here for Cora and the others. That way I can let everyone know what's going on."

"Good idea. I think it is better if everyone is forewarned, but I don't want the men to think anything is going on or that we're trying to hide something. It's bad enough that we have to let the fools in at all."

Realizing that she'd just insulted Cade, Lucy blushed. "Oh, dear. I didn't mean to include you in that comment."

"If it's of any help, I didn't hear any of it." Cade grinned. "I was too busy watching the fools trying to pick your lock."

"They wouldn't!" Lucy charged across the room and threw the door open. The mayor tumbled across the threshold at her feet. Lucy swept her skirt back out of his way while he clambered to his feet. "Mr. Kelly, would you like to come in? Oh, and you, too, Mr. Bradford."

She led the flustered mayor and the banker upstairs, with Mulroney trailing along behind. Melinda didn't envy Lucy having to keep the three of them entertained while the women of the Society gathered. Since the meeting was due to being in about ten minutes, the ladies should come filing in soon.

While she waited, she stepped outside to catch a breath of the evening air. Already she saw several groups of women headed her way. Then she spied an all too familiar form walking straight for her. Her first urge was to duck back inside to avoid him, but she was no coward. Trying to appear far more casual than she felt, she waited for the pastor to close the distance between them.

"Good evening, Miss Smythe." He took his hat off and nodded.

She winced at his use of her full name. There

were too many people close by for him to risk
using her given name, but still it hurt. She responded in kind.

"Reverend Hayes."

"I'm here to offer my support." His gaze met
hers and then darted away.

"To me? Whatever for?" She kept her own smile
cool and distant.

"To you and the others, of course. I heard that
the mayor and company were descending on your
group  I thought you might like another man
there who is firmly in the Society's corner, so to
speak."

"Well, that would be kind of you, Reverend, but
we wouldn't want to take up too much of your
time."

The first group of members had reached the
porch. They gave Melinda and the pastor a questioning look but didn't say anything. She didn't
give them the chance.

"Good evening, everyone. There's been a slight
change of plans. The mayor and two other men
have decided to observe our meeting tonight. Since
we couldn't figure out a way to avoid it, we thought
you should know what was coming."

While none of the women particularly liked her
announcement, no one walked away. She found
that encouraging. "Go on in as usual. Lucy will
keep them occupied until the meeting actually begins."

By then, there was a steady stream of women
coming. Although Melinda didn't say another
word to the pastor, she remained acutely aware of
his presence. She had half expected him to follow
the first group upstairs, but to her surprise, he remained right where he was. Maybe it was his way of
showing his support, but she wished he would

leave before she did something foolish, like asking why he'd been avoiding her. Or crying.

Cora saved her from her own foolishness. She joined the two of them on the porch. She was breathing hard, as if she'd been running. "Melinda, is this rumor I heard about men taking over the Society true? My aunt is so upset, she almost refused to allow me to come."

"Well, if that's the rumor around town, it's only partly true. There are three men here to observe the meeting."

"Four men." Pastor Hayes planted his feet firmly in front of the door.

Melinda frowned at him. "I guess if you're going to insist, then indeed there will be four men attending tonight: the mayor, the banker, the newspaper editor, and the pastor. Quite a cross-section of the male population, don't you think?"

"I don't understand. Why are they here?" Cora asked as she slipped past Daniel into the store.

"It seems we're making the men in town nervous with our secret meetings and wicked doings."

"Now, Miss Smythe, not all men are worried," Pastor Hayes chided. "Some of us actually admire the Society's efforts."

She knew that, but she was in no mood to approve of anything the man did or said.

"Anyway, I was appointed to let all the members know what they were walking into tonight. I think everyone is here, so we can go on upstairs. Lucy and I thought we'd keep the men out while the meeting is called to order. Then we'll allow them to enter as long as they keep their mouths shut and sit in the back."

"I'm willing to abide by those rules," Daniel promised when they reached the top of the stairs.

He followed too many rules, Melinda decided,

but now wasn't the time or the place to point that out. At least he was talking to her again, even it was only because of the Society.

Still, it was a start.

"The meeting will come to order." Lucy banged the gavel three times before most of the talking subsided. She gazed around the room, meeting each member's eyes. "We have some serious business to discuss and not much time in which to do so."

The final murmurs faded away. Several of the women straightened in their seats, their expressions grimly serious. Cora rose to her feet.

"As you all know, we're about to have four special guests." Her tone left no doubt that the men were anything but special. "We have been given no choice about them being here, but we do have some say in how they are treated. We cannot risk offending them, as tempting as that thought may be. However, other than to announce their presence, we will not acknowledge them in any way. They cannot be allowed to participate in the business or activities of the Society."

She paused again for affect. "All in favor of this being our policy, please respond by raising your hand."

Every right hand in the room shot up. There was no need for a count. Looking pleased, Cora looked to Lucy. "Please write down that the members of the Society unanimously vote to ignore the men."

There was a short ripple of laughter in the room, but as soon as Melinda started to open the door to let in their unwanted guests, the room went completely silent. Lucy found the men's obvious discomfiture amusing. Of the four, only Cade seemed blissfully unaware of the waves of disapproval. Pastor Hayes led the way to the back row, while the mayor and his companion looked decidedly uncomfortable in their surroundings.

Once the four of them were seated in the back, their presence was no longer acknowledged by so much as a glance or a welcoming smile. Cora immediately launched into the business portion of their meeting.

"The treasurer's report has been posted." She gestured toward the wall. "It has been suggested that we sponsor a bake sale in two weeks after church to raise money for another set of books. All in favor, please so indicate."

Once again, the women solemnly voted.

"Melinda Smythe has agreed to head the committee to choose the next book. If you're interested in serving with her, please raise your hand."

A sprinkling of hands went up. Lucy was pleased to see that Josie Turner was among the volunteers. From what Melinda had told her, Josie was making good progress in her reading.

"That concludes tonight's business. I yield the floor to Miss Smythe to lead the discussion of last week's reading."

Cade hated to admit it, but he may have been wrong. He still felt the community would be better served if all of these women stayed home and took care of their families; that hadn't changed. However, it was obvious that a fair number of the ladies were perfectly capable of running a businesslike meeting and discussion. Hell, he'd been tempted to throw out a comment or two himself.

For one thing, Romeo wasn't a tragic hero. Hell,

no. He was a damn fool for letting a woman tie
him all up in knots that way. He'd have been better
off to satisfy his needs with a whore back in old
Verona rather than kill himself over Juliet. Cade
knew all about pretty women and their ways. If the
two lovers and their friends had survived, he had
no doubt Juliet would have been casting looks
Mercutio's way inside of six months.

Bored with the discussion and the ugly memories it was stirring up, Cade let his eyes drift
around the room. With unsettling regularity, they
kept wandering in the direction of Lucy Thomas.
Although she'd said very little over the course of
the meeting, he found himself straining to hear
every word she spoke. She never raised her voice,
but all the women took her comments seriously.
Even that old harridan Mrs. Overland shut up
whenever Lucy had the floor.

Not that he agreed with a word Lucy had said.
He didn't know it for a fact, but he suspected that
her own experience with marriage hadn't been
any better than his. That sure as hell didn't keep
her from spouting a lot of romantic nonsense
about honor and loyalty. And the rest weren't
much better.

The Lawford girl stood up and announced that
when people had no say in how things were done,
they became desperate and acted rashly. He hoped
like hell that she wasn't hinting that women should
have the vote. The very idea was enough to give a
man nightmares.

The only one who occasionally said anything
that made sense to him was a thin woman who sat
in the back corner. He studied her profile, trying
to place her. Finally, it came to him. She was the
one with the misfortune to be married to that son
of a bitch Oliver Turner. If so, no wonder she seemed

down on fathers choosing spouses for their children. Hers had picked a dandy for her, even if she seemed reluctant to speak out about it.

The mayor, seated beside him, stirred restlessly and then leaned over to whisper to Cade. "How long do we have to sit here?"

"I'd guess until it's over." Served the idiot right for letting himself get maneuvered into attending in the first place. Cade would have found it amusing except for the fact he'd been roped into it along with him. He leaned forward slightly to see how Bradford was faring.

The bastard was smiling, but Cade was willing to bet it wasn't because the man was enjoying himself. There was too much hunger and cold in his expression for that. Cade couldn't quite put his finger on what bothered him about the way Bradford's eyes roamed around the room, especially when he kept looking in Lucy's direction. As if he suddenly sensed he was being watched, Bradford's expression abruptly changed as he glanced at Cade, looking as bored and restless as the mayor.

If Cade hadn't been looking directly at the banker when the change came over the man, he would have missed it entirely. Even so, it would have been easy to think he'd imagined the whole thing. He'd only had limited contact with Bradford, so he didn't know the man all that well. As far as he knew, he had a reputation for dealing fairly with the bank's customers.

No one seemed real surprised when he declared himself a candidate for mayor. Everyone within a hundred miles knew that Kelly was a pitiful excuse for a mayor. He'd only been elected because his opinions didn't offend anybody—after all, he really didn't have any. A weather vane didn't have anything on him when it came to shifting each time the wind changed directions. Bradford stood a good chance of being elected.

Cade had thought that the change might be good for the town, but now he had to wonder. It might be worth his while to do some quiet snooping around. The man might be the upstanding citizen most folks thought he was, but then, maybe not. Lots of men came out of the war as heroes but didn't deserve the reputation.

Satisfied with his plan of action, Cade turned his attention to one other man in the room. He wondered if anyone else questioned the motivation behind the good pastor's interest in the Luminary Society. Perhaps he truly felt that the ladies were entitled to meet and talk about whatever they damned well wanted to. It wouldn't be the first time that a man of the cloth became embroiled in a crusade for one fool cause or another.

But if that was the case, why did the man's eyes stay riveted on the new schoolteacher for the entire evening. On occasion, he did look around the room and nod at something that was being said. But having done that, his gaze immediately turned back to Melinda Smythe.

Cade considered the target of the pastor's interest. As schoolmarms went, the woman wasn't badlooking, especially with that fire-colored hair of hers. And she had shown a fair amount of gumption the other day when she'd confronted him in his office. If the minister had a taste for strongwilled women, far be it from Cade to question it. His own taste these days ran to female storekeepers, not that he planned on pursing that avenue.

He allowed himself a gratifyingly long look in Lucy Thomas's direction. There was strength in her as well. A woman had to work twice as hard as a man to run a successful business. And despite her doing a man's work all day, there was something very feminine about her that he ached for during the dark hours of the night.

He wondered what she'd do if she even suspected how much time he spent wondering what it would be like to have her underneath him as he buried his need in her willing body. He shifted restlessly, wishing he dared get up and leave. The bench he sat on wasn't the only thing that was hard and uncomfortable at that moment. If this blasted meeting didn't end soon, he'd go anyway.

The rap of the gavel jarred him out of his inner tirade. Lucy Thomas rose to her feet as the room fell quiet.

"Thank you, ladies. Don't forget to sign up for refreshments for the next meeting. Those of you who are to read with Melinda, pick up your books on the way out."

And just that fast, the women began filing out of the room. At no time had any of them paid the least bit of attention to the four intruders in the back row. Even now, not a single woman even glanced in their direction. He smiled. Cade and the others had descended on the Society with little or no warning, and still the women had managed to close ranks against them.

And that was precisely the reason he disapproved of the whole damn idea of women banding together for any reason. All the passion they were pouring into this farce of a meeting should be redirected in a more appropriate direction—their families and their homes.

It hadn't escaped his notice that the three ringleaders were all currently unmarried and likely to remain so, either by choice or lack of opportunity. He shot a dark look in the direction of Cora Lawford and Melinda Smythe. He had to admit that neither of them was lacking in the areas necessary to attract a husband. Hell, if he was reading the pastor correctly, the man was more than mildly attracted to the teacher. From the way the two kept glancing in each other's direction, the feeling was not one-sided.

He stood up, muttering a curse under his breath. Why weren't a home and family enough for a woman? What the hell did it take for a man to satisfy a woman? Of course, if he'd known that answer, maybe he'd still be married himself.

It was time to get the hell out of this place. Without a word to either the other men or the few women left in the room, he marched out to Lucy's parlor to find his daughter.


He picked up a handful of rocks, looking for the perfect one. He examined each one carefully but decided none of them would do. It had to be the right size, the right shape, the perfect opening salvo in his own personal war. When he bent down to check out a likely-looking specimen, his hat fell to the ground. The breeze picked it up and sent it rolling along the ground toward the river. Cursing a blue streak, he caught up with it at the edge of the river. It wasn't much as hats went, but it served to protect his balding head from the effects of the hot sun.

After jamming it back on his head, he looked around to see if anyone was watching. It was doubtful that anyone would wonder why he was walking along the river. Most folks in town took the occasional stroll along the River Road on a hot summer evening. And tossing rocks into the river was a favorite pastime for young and old alike. If he threw all the rejects into the water, no one would find it strange that he was picking up one rock after another.

Eventually, he found the right one and slipped it into his pants pocket. Just to make sure that no one took note of his actions, he continued along the river for another half an hour, still skipping the occasional rock across the water. Finally, when the road began to wind back up along the side of the bluff, he quickened his pace.

Darkness would be upon them soon, and he had work to do. Fingering the cold limestone in his pocket, he smiled and nodded at his neighbors as he wended his way home. Yes, tonight was the night that the first battle would be waged.

The evening had been a stressful one for her. First, the men had stuck their unwanted noses into the Society's business. Granted, not one of them had dared to speak out during the course of the evening, but every woman in the room had been painfully aware of their presence. It had been impossible to ignore them completely, what with the banker gloating over something, the mayor tapping his foot, and Cade sitting there glowering at everyone in the room.

At first, she thought he'd actually looked interested in the topic being discussed. A couple of times he'd nodded in approval or shaken his head in disgust when one of the women made a point. It had been tempting to ask him if he had something he wanted to contribute to the discussion.

Then, toward the end, all of a sudden he'd looked as angry as the editorials that had stirred up this whole mess in the first place. Were all the women he came in contact with going to have to pay the price for his wife's wrongdoing, whatever it had been?

It hurt more than she cared to admit that she was being punished in some way for a crime she had never committed. Not that she wanted more out of Cade Mulroney than to be a good neighbor.

She chastised herself for that particular lie. Neighborly feelings didn't leave a woman restless and achy during the night. Nor did they make her want to soothe the frown lines from around a man's mouth or brush an errant lock of hair back from his forehead.

She punched her pillow, trying to find a more comfortable position. If she could coax herself to sleep, she wouldn't have to lie here and think about an irascible newspaper editor and his adorable daughter. Finally, out of sheer force of will, her eyes began to drift shut as her body relaxed under the warmth of her blankets.

Seconds later, all thoughts of sleep disappeared with terrifying sounds of shattering glass and running feet.

# Chapter Eight

With her heart in her throat, Lucy jumped out of bed and grabbed a wrapper off the peg by the bedroom door. For what seemed like an eternity, she waited in the shadows, listening for footsteps. Had someone broken into the store below?

Her ears strained to hear the slightest sound that didn't belong, but there was only silence. She looked at the lamp beside her bed and debated whether or not to turn up the wick. Right now, the light illuminated the room enough for her to see but kept the corners shrouded in darkness. She hovered just outside its glow, wishing she weren't such a coward.

She had to do something besides stand in a corner and shake. If she didn't investigate, she would spend the entire night awake and terrified. If something was wrong, she'd need to go for help.

After picking up the lamp, she left the dubious safety of her room and cautiously approached the stairs leading to the store below.

Even the quiet was frightening. What waited for her below? Determined to find the answer to that question, she slipped down the steps one or two at a time. Upon reaching the bottom, she drew a shaky breath and waited, for what, she wasn't sure. Finally, deciding she couldn't stand there all night, she reached to turn up the light.

No sooner had she done that than the pounding began. The loud noise almost startled her into dropping the lamp. It was coming from the door across the room.

"Lucy! Lucy Thomas!"

Her name was accompanied by another round of pounding on the door, which rattled the windows.

"Damn it, woman, open up. It's me—Cade!"

She didn't even hesitate. Taking only the time to set the lamp down, she ran for the door and drew back the lock. Cade was inside before she could back out of his way. He grabbed her shoulders roughly, angry concern written all over his face.

"Are you all right?"

She nodded.

"I was just going up to bed when I heard glass shatter. Which window was it?"

"I don't know. I was just coming down to see when you got here."

"I'll look. You stay here."

She almost cried out in protest when his hands dropped away from her, leaving her cold and alone and frightened. He was back in seconds with a large rock clutched in one hand. In the other was a crumpled-up piece of paper. He shoved it into his pants pocket.

"Let's get you away from the door and back upstairs." He shifted both items to one hand in order to take her arm.

She pulled back. "No, I want to see the paper. And the window."

Before he could stop her, she was already on her way toward the small window in the back. There wasn't much to see except a scattering of glass shards on the floor. The cool evening air was seeping inside the large hole in the center of the window. It was obvious that this was no accident, that someone was trying to frighten her. She took another step forward, to do what, she didn't know.

A sharp pain shot up her leg, causing her to cry out. Cade was beside her in an instant.

"What's wrong?"

The worry in his voice did a lot to soothe her jangled nerves.

"I seemed to have stepped on a piece of glass."

The words were no sooner out of her mouth than he was cursing as he swept her up in his arms. The unexpected sensation of being crushed against the strength of his chest had her struggling to get free. He tightened his grip as he headed upstairs.

"Damn it, Lucy, hold still," he growled. He climbed the flight of steps with little effort. Even the extra burden of her in his arms didn't keep him from berating her. "I can't believe you were stupid enough to walk around barefoot over broken glass. Never did know a woman who showed a lick of sense!"

That did it. She kicked her legs in an effort to get free. "Don't you dare lump me in with every other woman you've known, Cade Mulroney. Now, put me down this minute!"

He only tightened his hold on her. "Hold still before you make both of us fall and break our necks."

With a burst of speed, he hauled her unceremoniously up the remaining distance. Once there, he seemed to be momentarily at a loss where to go in the darkness of her home. She took charge, trying to regain some control over the chaos her life had become in the past few minutes.

"The kitchen," she ordered. "There's a lamp and matches on the table."

Cade shifted her weight in his arms and carefully maneuvered them through the doorway. He quickly set her down and then dealt with the lamp. He poured water from the pitcher into a basin and then reached for a towel.

She wasn't sure which hurt more—the glass digging into her foot or the sudden separation from the heat and strength of Cade Mulroney. A sorrowful sigh escaped from her mouth before she could stop it.

The sound startled Cade into slopping water down the front of his shirt and pants. He looked more worried than angry.

"Is it your foot?"

That struck her as a funny question. "If it's not, I'm going to give it back and ask for one that doesn't hurt."

He muttered something that sounded obscene under his breath as she gave herself over to a fit of the giggles. On some level, she knew that it was fear and something else that didn't bear close examination that had her emotions so out of kilter.

With some effort, she managed to rein in the need to laugh. She bit her lower lip as she concentrated on the wonder of Cade Mulroney kneeling in front of her. The lamplight glinted off the silver threaded through the blackness of his hair. Her wayward hand reached out to touch it. She snapped it back before Cade took notice.

With more of his unexpected gentleness, Cade wiped away the blood that had caked around the wound on the bottom of her foot. He cushioned her heel in the palm of his hand; the sensation sent shivers up her leg to pool somewhere deep inside her.

"I'm going to pull the glass out now. This might hurt." His dark eyes looked apologetic.

She gripped the seat of the chair, determined to show him what she was made of. It took several attempts for him to get a grip on the sliver, which was slick with her blood. Finally, he managed to pull it free from her skin. He then held a clean towel over the wound and applied pressure until it quit bleeding. He continued to cradle her foot through the whole process.

For the second time, she felt bereft when he let go of her and stood up.

"Will you be all right while I send for Mitch? He needs to know about this."

Calling in the law would make the whole nightmare seem too real. "Do we really need to involve the sheriff? I'm sure it was only some kid playing pranks."

He rinsed her blood off his hands and wiped them dry with a towel. "I sure as hell don't go running to the law for every little thing, but in this case, Mitch already thinks someone has been sneaking around. He'll want to know he was right."

"But surely no one meant any real harm."

Cade gave her a thoroughly disgusted look. "What does it take to convince you? Someone actually breaking into the store? Next time he might not be satisfied with only throwing a rock through your window. Besides, kids playing around don't usually take the time to write a note." He pulled a wadded-up piece of paper from his pocket and tossed it in her lap.

She'd forgotten about the paper he'd found downstairs. Reluctantly she picked it up, giving up all pretense of hiding the trembling in her hands as she carefully straightened out the note and held it closer to the lamp to read. At first the words didn't quite sink in, but the second time through she repeated the words aloud. The shock of what she was reading kept her from stumbling over the obscenities.

*"Disband your precious society, bitch, or I'll disband the damned thing for you. Stop corrupting the women of this town or you'll find yourself on the road to hell. Next time I'll break more than a window."*

The paper slipped from her fingers as her whole body went cold and then hot. She had to do something—run, cry, scream, something. Lurching to her feet, she stumbled forward, right into Cade. He caught her, once again offering her a haven in his arms.

Shaming herself for a coward, she burrowed into his embrace. He loaned her his strength as he stood motionless. Then, slowly, the embrace that started out to comfort changed into something far more as the horror of the note gave way to the warmth of a man's body pressed along the length of hers. The thin cotton of her nightgown and wrapper did little to cushion her from Cade.

A feeling hot and sweet slowly slipped loose, making her ache deep inside. Telling herself she needed to step back for the sake of her sanity, instead she tilted her head back to find Cade's mouth only inches from hers. The expression on his face was intense, but she couldn't tell if he was angry or only confused at how they came to be clutched in an embrace that stretched from chest to thigh.

She couldn't have told him and didn't really care. At that moment, the only question on her mind was how that hard mouth would feel if he kissed her.


He knew he was damned, but he'd go to hell with a smile on his face for a kiss from Lucy Thomas. To that end, he slowly closed the small distance between her mouth and his, giving her every chance to protest. To his wonderment, instead of slapping him stupid for even considering such a thing, Lucy let her eyes drift shut as she offered herself up to his kiss.

It had been so damned long since he'd felt the sweet touch of a woman in his arms. Cursing them both for fools, he angled his head to better capture her mouth, coaxing her into deepening the kiss. The shy touch of her tongue to his almost brought him to his knees.

She moaned as she tangled her fingers in his hair. He let his own hands do some wandering of their own, tracing the elegant lines of her back down to her waist and onto the flare of her hips. Cupping her bottom, he fitted her against the length of his desire. There was no way she could miss how much he wanted her—and bless her, she didn't seem to mind, not one damned bit.

Running his hand down her thigh and back up, he dragged her gown with it. When his fingers first felt the smooth skin underneath, it was if he touched silk made of fire. If he got any hotter, he'd explode.

He rained a series of quick kisses along the length of her jaw and back to her ear. It had her panting his name, urging him on.

"Cade . . . please."

She tugged his face back down for another bone-melting kiss as she pulled his shirt loose from his pants. The sharp pleasure of her nails digging into his back was almost enough to send him over the edge. He wasn't sure he'd last as far as the bedroom.

He pushed her back against the support of the table, determined to take her as far as she was willing to go. His fingers turned clumsy as he tried to untie the ribbon at the top of her gown. Finally, it slipped loose, allowing him access to the sweet woman's flesh underneath. She arched her neck back, offering herself up to his questing mouth and hands.

He kissed his way down the small valley between her breasts as he molded them to fit his palm. Nothing had ever tasted so sweet. He reached for the buttons on his pants, needing to bury himself in this woman. But before he had slipped one free, he realized somewhere in the back of his mind that the pounding he heard wasn't his heart or even Lucy's.

Someone was downstairs wanting in. It had to be Mitch Hughes, if anything Cade's befuddled mind told him could be trusted. He froze, trying to regain control of his scattered thoughts and lusting body. Pushing back from Lucy, he did his best to close the neck of her gown and then tugged the skirt back down over her legs. Just that quickly, the light died in her eyes.

Given the choice of embarrassment or fury, she chose anger. "Cade Mulroney, how dare you!"

He wasn't doing much better himself, but he'd

made a promise never to lie to himself. "I dared because you wanted it as much as I did."

She gasped and back away. He hated the disgust reflected in her dark eyes. Only moments before, she'd craved his touch; now she was revolted by it. He'd been right all along. Lucy Thomas might talk nicer and act nicer, but underneath it all, she was no different than Louisa had been.

"If you don't want Mitch Hughes knowing the truth about what we've been doing up here, you'd better keep your voice down. He probably saw the broken glass and wants to make sure you're all right. I'll let him in on my way out." He charged down the steps.

The added realization that he'd left Mary alone and undefended to take care of this cold-hearted bitch filled him with pure disgust, both at himself and the dark-haired temptress upstairs. He reached the door and yanked it open just seconds before Mitch was going to kick it in.

"I saw the window. Is Mrs. Thomas all right?" If the sheriff wondered at Cade's presence, he didn't say.

"She cut her foot on the glass but otherwise seems to be fine. I heard the window break and came running. No sign of who did it, but he left a note, though. Lucy—uh, Mrs. Thomas—has it upstairs." He brushed past the lawman to go out the door. "I left Mary home in bed. If you want to talk to me, that's where I'll be."

Mitch caught him by the arm. "Before you go, how long ago did this happen?"

"About half an hour or so."

The sheriff looked purely disgusted. "Hellfire and damnation. The bastard's long gone by now. I've been down at The River Lady for the last hour trying to sort out which idiot started the fight this time. Finally, I locked up the whole bunch to make sure I got the right one. It made me late starting my rounds. I'll go talk to Mrs. Thomas."

"I don't think she'll be able to tell you much, but you'll find the note interesting. I'd like to get my hands on the son of a bitch who goes around scaring women like that." He didn't want to feel sorry for the woman upstairs, not after she'd looked at him as if he'd just crawled out from under a rock, but he did.

"Go on and check on your daughter. I'll see to Mrs. Thomas."

Cade nodded and walked out before he did something stupid, like offer to bring Mary back here and spend the rest of the night watching over Lucy Thomas. After almost taking her right there on the kitchen table, he was the last person she'd want protecting her virtue. Besides, there was no way she'd believe she would be safe from his unwanted attentions, especially when he didn't believe it himself.

He stepped out into the night and firmly turned his steps toward his own home, wishing it didn't seem like the wrong thing to be doing.

Morning hurt.

Lucy groaned and tried to bury her face back in the pillow, knowing it was futile. She was awake, and there was a day waiting out there to be faced. Slowly she sat up and swung her legs over the edge of the bed to the floor. Having managed that much, she tried to decide whether her legs would support her if she stood up.

Her gown caught in the rumpled covers, pulling it high around her legs. The sensation brought back unwanted memories from the night before, when it was a man's hand that had tugged her gown up to her hips. The image of Cade caressing her bare flesh immediately brought her to her feet. Maybe if she kept herself busy, she wouldn't have to think about what she—no, they—had done during the dark hours of the night.

She poured a basin of water and tried to wash away the memories along with the last vestiges of sleep. It didn't work. One look in the mirror, and she wanted to scream. Instead of her hair being neatly bound in its usual braid, it tumbled down past her shoulders in a tangled mess. Obviously, Cade had undone her braid.

When had he done that?

Her brush snagged in the tangles, but she was merciless. The small pain seemed too little a price to pay for her wanton behavior. She, of all women, should know better. The temptation of one man's kiss had trapped her in a marriage straight from hell once before. There was no room in her life for another mistake like that one—she'd barely survived the first experience.

Not that Cade Mulroney was likely to come courting. He'd made it perfectly clear on more than one occasion that he had little use for women in general. He had no more desire to shackle himself to a marriage than she did. But how to explain the flash of fire, white-hot and all consuming, that had flared up between them?

She didn't want to think about that anymore, much less how much she'd liked the way Cade Mulroney's body felt against hers. After slipping on her plainest dress, a drab brown that she usually reserved for heavy cleaning, she ate a light breakfast and hurried downstairs to open the store.

After unlocking the door, she went into the storeroom to get the broom and dustpan. Her sore

foot served as a reminder that there was broken
glass to be cleaned up before someone else stepped
on it. She didn't need any more blood on the floor.

Once she had the last of the shards swept into a
pile, she scooped them up and deposited them in
the trash. Feeling the need to keep busy, she
looked around for something else to occupy her
hands. A shadow appeared at the broken window,
causing her to drop the broom and scream.

"Damn it, Lucy, I swear you could wake the
dead."

The fact that it was Cade at the window did little
to soothe her jangled nerves.

"What do you think you're doing?"

"I'm getting ready to board up this window, if
that's all right with you. It looks like it's going to
rain."

Without waiting for her approval, he covered
the lower half of the window with a board and
began hammering. Lucy wanted to protest that
she could have taken care of it herself, but the
truth was, she appreciated his thoughtfulness.
She'd even tell him so, once she decided whether
or not she was still speaking to him.

Deciding there wasn't anything for her to do
there, she picked up her broom and headed out to
sweep the front porch. Mary was playing with her
doll outside the newspaper office. As soon as she
caught sight of Lucy, she came scampering over to
the edge of her father's porch.

"Good morning, Lucy." She frowned as she held
up her well-loved rag doll. "Bridget can't talk, but
she says hello, too."

"Good morning to the both of you, then." Lucy
curtsied, making the little girl giggle as she tried to
do the same.

"I'd come over there, but Father said he'd nail my toes down if I left this spot."

"Then you'd better stay over there." Lucy had no trouble smiling at this member of the Mulroney family. "Maybe he'll let you visit later, after I get my morning chores done."

"He promised I could have a couple of pennies to spend on candy if I was good."

"Then I'll see you for certain because I know what a good girl you are."

One who she wished were her own daughter. Shoving that pain aside, Lucy turned her attention to clearing a layer of dust off the wood planks of her porch. She glanced at the sky, deciding that Cade's prediction of rain was likely to come true. If so, it would be a quiet day. Folks were more likely to stay indoors, where it was dry, than to make a trip to town for supplies.

What she didn't want was time on her hands.

Inside, she noticed the hammering had stopped. She'd have to measure the window before ordering the replacement glass. She always had a few pieces in the storeroom, but none of them would fit that particular window.

Heavy footsteps warned her that she was no longer alone in the store. To her relief, it was Mitch Hughes.

"Morning, Mrs. Thomas."

As always, he tipped his hat, reminding her that at least some men acted like gentlemen. Not like some folks she could mention.

"Good morning, Sheriff. Thank you again for checking up on me last night."

"Mulroney is the one you should be thanking. I didn't get here until way after the damage had been done. I'm right sorry about that."

"You can't be everywhere. Besides, no real harm was done except to that one window." She didn't want to think about the threat contained in the note. She'd been relieved that Mitch had taken it with him last night.

"Well, just know that I'll be keeping a closer watch on things around here for a while. I don't hold with cowardly weasels scaring women, not in my town."

His gruff concern reassured her.

"I know you'll get to the bottom of things. But I have to admit that I'm worried about some of the others in the Society. Melinda Smythe and Cora Lawford, for example."

"I already checked with both of them this morning. They were a bit upset to hear about your problems, but neither of them have had any trouble."

"That's good."

"Well, I'll be going. If you have any trouble, anything at all, send someone running for me or my deputy."

Knowing the sheriff had a sweet tooth, Lucy called him back. She hurriedly filled a small sack with penny candy and held it out to him. When he reached into his pocket for some change, she shooed him on out the door.

"That's little enough thanks for all you do."

He popped a candy in his mouth and gave her one of his rare smiles. "It's thanks enough."

She started to close the door behind him, but another man filled the door frame, this one much less welcome.

"Thanks for boarding up the window." She forced the words out but made no effort to be more than barely polite.

"When you get the replacement glass, I'll put it in for you."

Trying not to notice how strong his arms looked with his sleeves rolled up, she kept her gaze averted. Looking at his face didn't help, not with those knowing eyes looking straight into hers. Last night they'd been molten silver, and that harsh mouth had tempted her soul.

"That won't be necessary." She busied her hands straightening a pile of burlap sacks.

"Someone has to do it." He sounded so reasonable that she wanted to smack him.

"I don't want to impose. I'm sure you have enough work of your own to do. You know, all those nasty editorials to write and such."

His laughter rang out, full and deep. "Tell me, Lucy Thomas, what makes you madder? The fact that I disapprove of your precious little society or the fact that I know how much you liked what happened upstairs last night."

Truly outraged and thoroughly embarrassed, she fought the urge to throw something straight at Cade's thick skull.

"Nothing happened last night," she lied. Her pride was all that kept her from slinking away in shame. How could she have let herself fall so low? One word from him in the wrong place, and her reputation would be in tatters. She turned her back on her tormentor, hoping he would simply disappear.

Instead, she felt the warmth of him as he closed the distance between them. Her wayward body wanted to lean back against the strength of him. He didn't touch her, but there couldn't have been more that a breath of air between them. Her very skin ached for his heat.

"Maybe you can convince yourself that nothing happened last night," he whispered from somewhere close to her ear, "but I was there. We both know that if Mitch hadn't gotten there when he did, I could have—would have—taken you right then. I guess we both owe him a debt of gratitude for stopping what would have been a mistake of monumental proportions."

The sheer nastiness of his last words left her reeling in pain as he walked out, slamming the door behind him. She didn't know a single word vile enough to describe how she felt about him.

Or herself.

Cursing herself for a coward, she retreated to the storeroom to collect her scattered emotions. How could she have allowed herself to become embroiled in such a mess? At the very least, she could have been honest with both of them about what happened. Denying the passion they'd experienced didn't make it any less real.

She wasn't going to lie to herself anymore. There was something about Cade Mulroney that drew her. Perhaps it was as simple as recognizing another survivor or as complex as her woman's heart needing more than itself for company.

The reasons didn't matter. He was not the right man for her. No one was, but especially not him. Her friends would feel betrayed, and she needed them in her life far more than she needed Cade with all his complexities and scars. But for one guilty minute, she closed her eyes and relived those first few perfect moments she'd spent in his arms.

The bell over the door chimed once and then again. Knowing it was likely to be Melinda and Cora, Lucy did her best to compose her features before hurrying out to meet them. With luck, they would assume that the lines of strain around her eyes and mouth were due to the broken window and anonymous threat.

She'd guessed correctly. Both her friends were

waiting by the counter for her. Melinda held out her hands as she rushed to Lucy's side with Cora right behind her.

"Lucy! Are you all right? Tell us everything."

She let herself be gathered into their sympathetic arms and soak up their concern, even if they were blissfully unaware of the real reason she was upset. She didn't like keeping secrets, but they'd no doubt feel betrayed if they found out that Cade had done more than make sure that she was not harmed last night.

"I'll make tea." Cora hurriedly filled the kettle and put it on to boil while Melinda led Lucy over to one of the straight-backed chairs that flanked the wood stove.

"There's nothing much to tell. I went to bed about the normal time. I had trouble going to sleep—you know how it is when you can't seem to quit thinking about things." She closed her eyes, trying to forget how it had felt to huddle in the shadows of her room, wondering if she was about to die.

"The sound of the window shattering woke me up. Before I could even reach the bottom of the staircase, Mr. Mulroney was at the door."

That got their attention. Melinda frowned, while Cora's eyes were blazing with fury.

"It's bad enough that he forces his way into our meeting and berates us with his newspaper, but now he's taking to throwing rocks through your window? I hope they throw him in jail and leave him there to rot!"

Lucy was appalled. "Cade would never do that, not to me!" No matter how angry she was with him, she didn't want his reputation tarnished with unfounded rumors. If necessary, she would defend him to all comers, even her friends.

* * *

Melinda was glad that Cora was too busy being outraged on Lucy's behalf to notice that something wasn't quite right about the way their friend was acting. Oh, Lucy's worry about the vandalism was genuine enough, but her defense of Cade Mulroney was a bit too emphatic.

When Lucy had come out of the storeroom, she'd looked pale and shaken, just like someone who'd been badly frightened. Now, though, the color in her face was high, and her eyes sparkled with a powerful emotion. Her use of the editor's first name hadn't escaped Melinda's notice, either. What was going on here?

"Lucy, no one is accusing him of anything."

"But he's the most likely culprit," Cora insisted. "Who else feels so strongly about the Society?"

"It wasn't him, I tell you. Even if you don't trust him, we all know Mitch Hughes is a good judge of character. If there was reason to suspect Mr. Mulroney, the sheriff would have him in jail right this minute. Instead, he thanked him for being here until he could come himself."

"So how long was Mulroney here last night?" Melinda did her best to sound casual.

Lucy actually blushed. For her sake, Melinda was glad that Cora was busy pouring tea and didn't notice.

"About half an hour. No more than that, I'm sure. And he was a perfect gentleman." Her eyes pleaded with Melinda to believe her.

"Well, I'm certainly glad that you weren't alone." There was more to what happened last night with Cade Mulroney; she was certain of it. But now wasn't the time for prying. That would come later, when Lucy wasn't so obviously on her guard.

"The sheriff promised to keep a close eye on

things for the next few nights." Lucy studied her hands, folded in her lap. "I'll feel better knowing he's out there."

The bell chimed again as a local rancher came through the door. Lucy looked a bit too relieved at being called to duty in the store. Something was definitely up, and apparently it was between Lucy and the cold-eyed newspaper editor next door.

Melinda might have dared to express her disapproval, except that she knew firsthand what it was like to be drawn to the wrong man. She had no business offering advice to her best friend when she had the same problem herself.

Sympathy was an entirely different matter.

Daniel paced the length of the church and back again. A raging argument had him muttering to himself and marshaling his best defenses. His opponent was his own conscience and the need to do the right thing. He paused to look up at the pulpit from which he preached each Sunday. His faith had never been in doubt, his calling clear from his earliest memories. No, he was God's man and always would be.

But he lived in the world of men, and that world had rules and expectations of its own. And if he didn't think of something soon, he was going to break one of those rules: he, a single man, was going to spend the night lurking outside Melinda Smythe's house.

In the usual course of events, he would never think of doing such a thing, but ever since he'd heard about the attack on Lucinda Thomas's store, he'd been worried sick that Melinda might be the next target. She lived alone and was vulnerable to attack. How could he sleep peacefully in his own bed while the women in the town were not safe? Especially that woman.

Mitch Hughes had announced very publicly that he would be patrolling the next few nights, but he was only one man. If he was centering his efforts on Mrs. Thomas's store, he certainly couldn't keep a close eye on Melinda's place as well. No, it would take at least two men to do the job.

And if it wouldn't have scandalized the entire town, Daniel would have marched right into the sheriff's office and volunteered his services. Instead, he was going to wait until dark and then slip out of the parsonage and down the street to take up his self-appointed post. He'd already picked out a spot from which to watch Melinda's house. He would have preferred to observe from a distance, but there wasn't any place along the other side of the street that would have offered both cover and a clear view.

He was going to hide behind the tall bush in the corner of her small backyard. He figured no one would be stupid enough to approach the front of her house. Why risk being seen by anyone on the street? Therefore, the only logical choices would be the sides of the house or along the back. From his chosen vantage point, he should be able to see if anything was amiss.

He would feel better knowing Melinda was safe. But if anyone caught sight of him, both of their reputations would suffer. The resulting scandal might very well cost them their jobs.

Unless he married her.

The idea stopped him dead in his tracks. The very real possibility of being forced into a hasty marriage should have him on his knees and praying for guidance. Instead, he felt like smiling for the first time in hours. Melinda might feel differently, but he could think of far worse fates than spending the rest of his life with her by his side.

Like never again knowing the sweetness of her kiss.

He stopped midstep and closed his eyes. Now, even days later, his pulse raced with remembered passion. But if it were only lust that had his hands shaking and his heart pounding, he would have fallen to his knees and prayed himself past the crisis, but his need for Melinda went bone deep. With that realization came a calm he hadn't felt for days.

Tomorrow he would seek her out and lay his heart on the line. But for tonight, he would stand guard and keep her safe.

For the tenth time in as many minutes, Melinda slipped from one window to the next. Someone was out there; she could feel his presence, although so far she'd seen nothing more threatening than the familiar shadows in her backyard. Caution had her standing to the side of the window. She didn't want to be in the way of shattered glass if another idiot decided to start throwing rocks.

She wondered how Lucy was sleeping. Not well at all, if she had to hazard a guess. Even with Sheriff Hughes and that odious Cade Mulroney keeping an eye on things, Lucy had to be worried.

A slight movement to the left of the woodshed caught her attention. She stared long and hard, but nothing seemed out of place. Putting it off to an active imagination, Melinda decided it was time to turn in for the night. No amount of pacing and jumping at shadows was going to make the long night ahead pass any faster.

Her bare feet made no sound on the floor-
boards of her room. The cool smoothness of the
wood was replaced by the knobby feel of the
braided rug she'd made last winter that lay along-
side her bed. She stripped off her wrapper and
laid it across the foot of the bed and then turned
back her covers. She knew she should crawl into
the big brass bed, which had belonged to her parents, and go to sleep.

But with the windows all closed and locked, the
room was stifling. There was no way she'd be able
to sleep without at least a slight breeze. Figuring
she'd been safe enough for the past few weeks with
the window next to the bed open, she reached for
the latch when a man's outline detached itself
from the shadows of her backyard.

She threw her hand over her mouth to hold
back her need to scream. If he knew he'd been
spotted, the intruder might very well feel cornered
enough to go on the attack. She snatched her
wrapper back off the bed and debated whether
she could make it out the front door and to the
neighbor's before whoever was out there knew
what she was about.

Trouble was, her elderly neighbor wouldn't be
any better prepared for handling the situation
than Melinda herself was. She looked around, trying to find something she could use as a weapon.
The only thing she could think of was the large
cast-iron skillet in her kitchen. If she left her position, though, the man might move again, and then
she'd have no idea where he was.

For the moment, indecision had her frozen in
that spot, staring out into the night until her eyes
hurt with the effort.

He changed locations again. This time, he moved

farther back into the yard, but something in the way he moved caught her eye. She'd seen this man before; she was sure of it. What was it that looked so familiar? Then he happened to look up at the sky, and she knew. The dim moonlight reflected off what could only be a pair of spectacles.

What on earth was Daniel doing lurking in her backyard in the dark of night?

There was only one way to find out. She hurried through the house to the front door, pausing to complain when she stubbed her toe cutting a corner too closely. Taking care to keep silent, she threw back the lock on the door and slowly turned the knob. When the door was open wide enough, she limped out into the night air.

Lord, if anyone caught her running around outside barefoot and in nothing more than her night-clothes, her reputation would be shot. She didn't care. Right now, she had to find out what the good pastor was up to. Her good name might be in jeopardy, but folks would think he'd taken leave of his senses.

She made it off the porch and around to the dark side of the house without seeing anyone. So far, so good. Trying to keep to the shadows, she reached the back corner of the house. There was no sign of Daniel where she'd last seen him, but that didn't mean anything.

She decided to risk a whisper. "Daniel! Is that you?"

No response.

She inched forward another couple of feet. "Daniel, I know you're out here. Where did you go?"

A pair of arms snaked out of the darkness and yanked her back into the bushes. A hand, clamped firmly over her mouth, kept her from screaming. She flailed her arms and did her best to kick her assailant.

"Melinda, it's me. Settle down before we wake your neighbors."

As soon as she recognized Daniel's voice, she relaxed into his embrace. The strength of his arms felt like heaven as she twisted around to face him. He seemed to be in no hurry to release her. Snuggling against his chest, she let the strong rhythm of his heartbeat soothe her.

Finally, he stirred.

"Melinda, you've got to go back inside. If anyone sees us out here, we'll both be ruined."

That he continued to hold her close made her feel daring. "I'm not sure I care."

He tipped her chin up to face him. "You know that's not true, Miss Smythe. Neither of us can afford such scandal."

"Then why were you lurking in my yard, Daniel Hayes, if you're so worried about your reputation?"

His hand went back over her mouth. She started to protest when he shook his head and whispered near her ear, "Hush—someone's coming."

Despite her earlier claim not to care, she did. Very much, in fact. Lee's Mill had become home to her; she didn't want to lose it. For the longest time, the two of them huddled in the shadows, waiting for the approaching footsteps to pass by and then fade into the night. Finally, when all that could be heard was the drone of a few cicadas, Daniel loosened his hold on her and stepped back.

"That was too close for comfort."

"You still haven't answered my question. What

are you doing here?" Despite the heat of the summer night, she felt chilled to the bone without Daniel's arms surrounding her.

"Now isn't the time for long discussions. If that was Mitch, he'll be back by." He raked his hand through his hair. "Will you go back inside if I promise to answer all your questions in the morning?"

She considered the offer. There was some powerful emotion underlying his words, one that made her feel all shivery inside.

"Please, Melinda. I'll come back at first light."

It must be important if he was willing to be seen entering her home at that hour. Hope and despair both fluttered in her chest.

"All right, I'll go in."

Before she'd gone two steps, those same arms caught her again, and Daniel's mouth found hers. The sultriness of a summer night in the Ozarks had nothing on the white heat that flashed between the two of them. She moaned as she parted her lips in response to his gentle assault.

And his hands, Lord of mercy, they burned through the thin cotton of her nightgown and wrapper, setting her skin aflame. As abruptly as the kiss began, it ended, leaving both of them shaken and gasping for breath.

"Go in, Melinda." He motioned in the direction of the front porch.

"But . . ."

"Please, while I'm strong enough to let you go." He stood with his hands clenched at his sides, as if he didn't trust himself.

"Good night, Daniel."

She brushed past him on her way to the front door. The man was temptation itself, but she didn't tell him that. Instead, she quietly walked away and began counting the minutes until sunrise would bring him back.

Daniel waited until he heard Melinda's door open and close. Once she was safely inside, he slipped around to the back of her house. In just a few seconds, she appeared in her bedroom window, and unless he was mistaken, she was waving. He melted farther back into the bushes, convinced she was only hoping he was still there. Surely, he couldn't really be seen that clearly.

Before he could take another step, a heavy hand had Daniel by the scruff of the neck, flinging him to the ground. The impact jarred the breath out of him, taking all hope of secrecy with it.

# Take A Trip Into A Timeless World of Passion and Adventure with Kensington Choice Historical Romances! —Absolutely FREE!

Enjoy the passion and adventure of another time with Kensington Choice Historical Romances. They are the finest novels of their kind, written by today's best-selling romance authors. Each Kensington Choice Historical Romance transports you to distant lands in a bygone age. Experience the adventure and share the delight as proud men and spirited women discover the wonder and passion of true love.

4 BOOKS WORTH UP TO $24.96— Absolutely FREE!

# Get 4 FREE Books!

We created our convenient Home Subscription Service so
you'll be sure to have the hottest new romances delivered
each month right to your doorstep—usually before they
are available in book stores. Just to show you how
convenient the Zebra Home Subscription Service is,
we would like to send you 4 FREE Kensington Choice
Historical Romances. The books are worth up to $24.96,
but you only pay $1.99 for shipping and handling.
There's no obligation to buy additional books—ever!

## *Save Up To 30% With Home Delivery!*

Accept your FREE books and each month we'll deliver 4
brand new titles as soon as they are published. They'll be
yours to examine FREE for 10 days. Then if you decide to
keep the books, you'll pay the preferred subscriber's price
(up to 30% off the cover price!), plus shipping and
handling. Remember, you are under no obligation to buy
any of these books at any time! If you are not delighted
with them, simply return them and owe nothing. But if
you enjoy Kensington Choice Historical Romances as
much as we think you will, pay the special preferred
subscriber rate and save over $8.00 off the cover price!

# Chapter Nine

Cade stared out into the night. He should be in bed but knew he wouldn't get much in the way of rest. Was Lucy having any more luck getting to sleep? He doubted it. The events of the night before were too strong to be ignored.

Rage stirred inside him. When Mitch found the sneaky bastard who'd thrown that rock, Cade wanted first shot at him. He might have no use for the Society, but he had even less for a weasel who threatened women.

Especially one particular woman.

He let loose a string of profanities that would have done a bullwhacker proud. Everyone made mistakes in life. With luck, you survived them, learned from them, and didn't repeat them.

Last night, in Lucy's kitchen, he'd come close to forgetting exactly what he'd learned from loving Louisa. Only a fool would take his broken heart, paste it back together as best he could, and then hand it over to the care of another woman.

His conscience pricked at him because his training as a newspaperman demanded that he report only the truth. And yet, here he was lying to himself. He knew full well that Lucinda Thomas was nothing like Louisa Webster. First and foremost, his late wife had never stood on her own. Initially there had been her father; later, for a brief time, she'd let Cade be the one who cared for her. But when the war had called him away, she floundered on her own. It should have come as no surprise that she would have sought out other men to give her life stability. What he'd seen as femininity was, in truth, weakness.

Lucy, on the other hand, had picked up the pieces of her life and made it whole again. She didn't seem to need anyone—especially a man— to lean on. He would have admired that about her, if she hadn't gone and started encouraging other women to seek fulfillment outside their homes. He knew firsthand where that road led.

On some level, he was still that idealistic young fool who had wanted a wife and family of his own. In his mind's eye, he'd pictured coming home from work to a welcoming wife, a hot meal, and children at his feet. Instead, here he was, years down the road and no closer to that goal that he'd been back then.

Almost against his will, he was drawn back to the window, to stand guard over the woman next door. He didn't need to. Hell, he'd lost count of the number of times he'd seen Mitch and his deputy prowling between the two buildings. If given her choice, he had little doubt that Lucy would pick their stalwart sheriff to stand between her and any more trouble.

But Mitch Hughes wasn't the one who had comforted Lucy or fanned the fire of passion in her dark eyes. No, by God, it had taken a soul-weary ex-Confederate, who carried more scars than the one that left him with a bad leg, to make Lucy Thomas burn like a fire in his arms. Nothing more would come of that one encounter, but he knew he wouldn't forget it soon. Neither, he suspected, would she.

That thought made him smile.

A noise overhead reminding him that unlike Lucy, he wasn't completely alone. Mary, the one bright spot in his life, humbled him with the simplicity of her acceptance of his sudden appearance in her life. He cocked his head toward the ceiling, waiting to see if his daughter was merely stirring in her sleep or if she had need of his comforting presence.

After one last glance out the window, he left his self-appointed post, picked up the lamp, and trudged up the stairs to Mary's room. Before opening her door, he turned the wick down as far as it would go. The soft glow would be enough for him to check on her without disturbing her with a sudden brightness.

Inside her room, he set the lamp on the bedside table and breathed in the sweet scent of his daughter. She lay on her side, curled up in the center of her bed. He smiled and tugged the blankets up around her shoulders. There were far too many nights when he'd missed out on the chance to tuck her in, so he often stopped in long after she'd been asleep, to give her one last kiss. She might never knew how often he adjusted her covers or brushed her hair back from her forehead during the dark hours of the night, but each time restored a part of his soul.

She smiled in her slumber and scooted down into the covers. Maybe on some level she did sense his presence, and that was all right, too.

Perhaps now he could rest.

* * *

The stupid bitch thought a board and a few nails would stop him. Well, he'd just see about that. There were other windows and other weapons.

Slipping back into the safety of his room, he had to admit that the note might not have been a good idea, because the sheriff had been furious. Mitch Hughes took pride in his job; he wouldn't rest until he found out who had thrown the rock and written the threat. So far, he had no suspects, but he wouldn't give up easily.

On the other hand, time was running out. Tonight he had chosen another target, but thanks to the combined vigilance of Mitch and his damned deputy, he hadn't gotten close to the teacher's house. This time, the note had been more specific about what he had planned for the women who dared to belong to the Luminary Society.

*Luminary* meant light, and light came from fire. He fingered the note in his pocket. Let them rest tonight. Let them think that Mitch had scared him off.

For now, he'd sleep the sleep of the virtuous. Tomorrow night or the one after would be soon enough to further enlighten the whole damn bunch of them.

*Enlighten. Luminary. Fire.* It all went together perfectly.

The knock at the door, while not unexpected, still caused Melinda to jump. It had to be Daniel; no one else would come calling this early. With fumbling fingers, she unlocked the door and opened it.

He stood, hat in hand, looking uncertain of his welcome.

"Good morning."

"Good morning." She didn't know what else to say. For several awkward seconds, they stood and stared at each other.

He glanced back toward the street. "Well, I would say the next move is for you to either invite me in or to say good-bye. Either way, standing out here would only invite gossip."

"I'm sorry, Daniel. Of course, please come in."

The second he crossed the threshold, he sniffed the air appreciatively. "Something smells good."

"I baked some fresh bread this morning. Would you join me for some breakfast?"

"You don't have to go to all that trouble on my behalf."

"I have to eat, too, you know. It doesn't take much effort to crack a couple of extra eggs." She led the way to the kitchen table. He took a seat across from hers and sat quietly as she prepared a simple meal for the two of them. Once she sat down, he bowed his head and said grace.

Then he dug into the meal with satisfying enthusiasm. She relished every minute of the experience. It seemed so homey for the two of them to be sharing a meal at this hour of the day. If she closed her eyes and pretended, she could almost imagine the two of them doing so for years to come. But that didn't answer the question of why he'd come calling at the break of day.

When every scrap of food was gone, Daniel pushed back from the table, looking well satisfied.

"I hate to say it, but if I ate that way every morning, my poor horse would refuse to carry me on his back. That was delicious."

She basked in his praise, pleased that he'd enjoyed eating at her table. But that also meant the moment was upon them. She didn't know whether to be relieved or worried.

"I suppose you're wondering why I'm here." His normally cheerful countenance settled into grim lines.

"And why you were hiding in my yard last night," she reminded him. "But let's not talk here. Let's go to the front parlor, where we can be more comfortable."

Daniel allowed her the small respite it took to relocate to the other room, before speaking. "As far as last night goes, it was simply that I was worried about you. Until Sheriff Hughes catches the culprit who threatened Mrs. Thomas, I can't feel that any of the Society's leadership—Lucy, Cora, or you—are completely safe. I couldn't sleep, knowing you might be in danger, so I decided to keep an eye on things myself. I know it sounds crazy now, but at the time it seemed like a reasonable thing to do."

She reached out to touch his hand. "That was sweet of you, Daniel. I have to admit that I was worried, but you risked an awful lot. What if you'd been seen?"

His eyes turned bleak. "That's just it. I was."

Daniel watched as the full import of his words sank in. Melinda turned pale as she slumped back in the chair.

"Who? How?"

"Well, if there's anything to be happy about, it was Mitch Hughes who caught me. Right after you went inside, I went back around the house, figuring I had the best cover to get away undetected." He shook his head at the memory. "That man must have the eyes of a cat. Anyway, he grabbed me by the neck and tossed me to ground like a rag doll."

The memory wasn't one of his finest moments,

but he found some comfort in that Melinda's first concern was for him.

"Did he hurt you? Are you all right?"

"Injured in dignity only." Although the ease with which he'd been captured still rankled. She didn't need to know that part.

"What happened then?"

Now that he'd told her the worst, the words came easier. "He dragged my sorry carcass off to the parsonage as soon as he recognized me." Daniel chuckled. "You could tell he wanted to curse a blue streak but didn't want to offend me. He said something like 'What kind of a . . . stupid son of a . . . I mean . . . what an . . .' He still managed to express his displeasure, but it wasn't easy on him."

Melinda wasn't laughing, not that he blamed her. The situation was grave, indeed. "If it's any comfort, we both know that Mitch won't say a word to anyone."

"But if someone saw him with you, or even if his deputy finds out . . ." Her voice trailed off. When she met his gaze, a single tear slid down the smooth curve of her cheek.

This was where he got to be the hero. Drawing a deep breath, he slid to the floor on one knee, directly in front of her. "I created this mess, so I will do the only thing I can think of to fix it." He took her chilly hand in his. "Melinda Smythe, will you do me the honor of marrying me?"

He didn't know what reaction he'd been expecting, but the look of pure horror on his intended's face certainly wasn't it. Melinda jerked her hand free of his as she visibly struggled to speak.

"Fix it? I'm not some piece of broken furniture that needs a few nails and a fresh coat of paint!"

"That's not what I meant," he protested.

"Then what did you mean, Daniel?"

"I, uh . . ." Words failed him completely. He was beginning to feel like a fool, kneeling before a woman who was looking at him as if he'd grown a second head. He tried again. "I'm offering to marry you."

Melinda no longer looked pale and shaken. No, she definitely looked absolutely furious. She glared down at him, her arms crossed over her chest. "And exactly why is that?"

Something in her tone warned him to back away. He pushed himself back up onto his feet to put a little distance between them.

"I explained it. The sheriff saw me in your backyard."

"So, you're proposing marriage to me solely because someone caught you in the bushes outside my house."

He nodded, glad that she was finally understanding the situation. But if so, why didn't she look any happier about it? The protection of his name would save them both if even a hint of last night's events leaked out.

Melinda stood up and walked over to the front door. Throwing it wide open, she pointed outside. "I think you need to leave."

"But . . ."

"Now, Daniel. Thank you for coming."

Perhaps she needed to think things through. "I know this has all come as a shock to you, Melinda. Obviously, you need some time to consider my offer."

She looked to the heavens as if praying for patience. "No, I don't need time, Daniel. My answer is no. Now, leave."

Knowing he had no choice but to do as she ordered, he picked up his hat and started out the door. "I meant what I said."

"I know you did, Daniel, and for that I thank you. But I've seen marriages based on love and marriages based on duty. I want what my parents had, and I'm not willing to settle for less."

Once the door closed behind him, he blinked up at the morning sun. He didn't know whether to feel relieved or angry that she'd thrown his offer back in his face. He'd come to terms with the idea of marrying Melinda, but obviously she had no such illusions about him. He tried to decide where he'd gone wrong. No doubt, he'd gone about it wrong, but what he could have done differently, he didn't know.

She couldn't possibly have expected a long, drawn-out courtship. That would have been ideal, giving them both time to get to know each other. But that simply wasn't possible, not under these circumstances. He had thought they were friends— more than friends really, considering the few kisses they'd shared. Hadn't that been enough to build a marriage on?

He glanced back in hopes that she was watching him. But no, the door was firmly closed, and there was no hint of her through the lace of the window curtains. Feeling more alone than he had in years, he walked the short distance to the church. Perhaps he'd find answers there.

A knock at the door brought Lucy from behind the counter. Most folks knew to walk right into the store, but she couldn't see anyone through the glass that comprised the top half of the door. Events of the past few days had her far more cautious than normal.

With her heart pounding, she slowly turned the knob and peeked out. Relief coursed through her as she recognized a familiar dark head. She opened the door wide and pretended not to see anyone.

"Why, I thought for sure I heard someone knocking." She looked this way and that, deliberately overlooking her small caller.

"I'm down here, Miss Lucy."

Lucy put her hands on her hips. "Well, now I'm hearing voices. What is going on?"

A small hand tugged at her skirt. "You can see me, Miss Lucy. I know you can."

Feigning surprise, Lucy looked down at Mary Mulroney. "Why, I declare, Miss Mary, I didn't see you there. Were you invisible for a minute?"

That had the little one giggling. "No, silly. I'm here to deliver this letter." She dropped her voice to a loud whisper. "It's from me and my father." She held up a note written in her childish scrawl.

"How long have you been working for the postal service?" Lucy accepted the envelope.

"Oh, not long." Mary danced from one foot to the other, waiting impatiently for Lucy to do something besides talk.

"Come along inside. A letter this fine calls for special treatment." With Mary right behind her, she headed for the desk, where she kept her important papers and correspondence. Reaching for her letter opener, she made a big production of slitting open the envelope to retrieve the note inside.

Mary watched each movement with gratifying delight. Finally, she couldn't stand the suspense another second. She blurted out, "It's an invitation to a picnic with us. This very afternoon."

The startling announcement almost caused Lucy to drop the letter in shock. Although she wasn't surprised that Mary might want her along on an outing with her father, she had a hard time picturing Cade allowing the invitation to be delivered. Quickly she scanned the brief note. Right below Mary's carefully drawn signature was a masculine scrawl. If she tilted her head at just the right angle, she could almost believe it said *Cade Mulroney*.

"Mary, are you sure your father wanted to include me on your picnic? I would love to go, you understand, but I'm sure he meant for it to be some special time for the two of you."

Mary shook her head emphatically. "No, he said I could bring along a friend, and I picked you. He swallowed kind of funny when I said that, but he said it was all right with him. Then he said something like, if you could stand it, he could. Can you stand it, Miss Lucy?"

Heavy footsteps warned Lucy that the other member of the Mulroney clan had just joined them.

"I'm interested in hearing the answer to that question myself, Mrs. Thomas."

She wondered if the fox felt the same way when he realized he was trapped, good and proper. There was no way she wanted to disappoint the pair of silvery eyes looking up at her and pleading for her to agree. On the other hand, there was another pair the same color daring her to accept. Well, she could survive an afternoon in Cade's company. If nothing else, she'd spend her time playing dolls with Mary. That should keep the little girl's father at arm's length.

"I would love to go, Miss Mary. Let me see if Miss Smythe or Miss Lawford can keep the store open for me for a few hours."

Cade smirked, knowing that if her friends couldn't cover for her, she would have a convenient excuse for staying home. He probably thought he'd have the best of both worlds then—his daughter knew he was willing to accommodate her wishes, without his really having to go through with it.

Knowing she was punishing herself as well, Lucy decided to thwart him. "But even if they can't, I'll be glad to close up the store for one afternoon. Everyone should take a day off for a picnic now and then." She put her arm around Mary's shoulders. "Now, scoot off so I can get some work done before it's time to go."

"We'll come by for you at about noon, if that's all right with you."

"That will be fine." Something about the gleam in Cade's eye bothered her. If she didn't know better, she would suspect that she'd just played into his hand.

"Do I need to bring anything?"

Cade chided her on his way out of the door. "Now, what kind of manners do you think I have? A gentleman never invites a lady on an outing and then tells her to bring the food. Don't you think I'm capable of putting a luncheon together?"

Despite herself, Lucy blushed. She hadn't meant to insult the man. "I'm sorry."

"Well, I should think so. Any man who doesn't know how to go over to the hotel and sweet-talk the cook out of some fried chicken and apple pie has to be a complete fool." He was laughing when he pulled the door closed behind him, cutting off any chance she had to respond.

For several seconds, she stared after him, wishing she could figure the man out. But despite her misgivings about the entire enterprise, she found herself smiling. A picnic with Cade Mulroney— who would have thought it?

\* \* \*

Melinda leaped at the chance to take Lucy's place working in the store. The last thing she wanted at the moment was free time on her hands. Waiting only long enough to watch Lucy bustle out the door, intent on her afternoon in the sun, Melinda put on a heavy apron and set to work.

Picking up the feather duster, she began at one side of the store and worked her way to the other. No doubt, Lucy had done the same thing in the past day or so, but better too clean than not enough. Afterwards, she'd take the broom and start in the storeroom and sweep her way to the porch out front. With luck, she might be able to keep her mind too busy to let thoughts of Daniel Hayes plague her.

What could the man have been thinking?

A stack of cans went toppling over when she hit them with a little too much enthusiasm. She picked them up, wishing it were this easy to set her life back in order.

Noble fool that he was, Daniel would have shackled himself to a woman for life in the name of honor. Well, he would find his honor to be cold comfort indeed if he married a woman he didn't love, no matter how she felt about him. How dare he offer her the protection of his name when he wasn't willing—or able—to offer her his heart?

If a scandal did arise from their behavior last night, so be it.

She didn't want to leave Lee's Mill, but she would if and when it became necessary. If eyebrows were raised and questions asked, she would shoulder the full blame and declare Daniel innocent of anything but lacking good sense. There had to be a town somewhere that needed a teacher badly enough that its citizens would overlook one minor indiscretion.

She paused, before starting on another shelf, to blink back another bout of tears. After she'd shown Daniel the door, her resolve not to weep had lasted all of thirty seconds. How much could a woman cry without drying up and blowing away with the hot summer breeze?

Fingering the small brooch pinned at her neck, she wished her parents were there to advise her. What woman's wisdom could her mother have handed down just as she had the small piece of jewelry? Melinda closed her eyes and remembered the comfort of her father's strong arms protecting her from harm. Her family had been gone for a long time now, yet the pain of their passing still left her feeling raw and abandoned.

In their absence, she had come seeking Lucy's pragmatic advice, only to find her friend making plans to spend the day at the river with Cade Mulroney and his daughter. Under other circumstances, she would have questioned Lucy's decision to accompany Cade anywhere, much less on a picnic. No matter how much Lucy had insisted that she was going as Mary's guest, not her father's, something didn't ring quite true.

Would Lucy change into her second-best dress and pinch color into her cheeks to spend time with a little girl?

But then, who was she to second-guess what anyone else did? In light of last night's affair, Melinda had good reason to call her own judgment into question. She winced. *Affair* was definitely the wrong word to use. Surely even the most conservative thinkers in town wouldn't consider a few stolen kisses an affair.

Her conscience decided to join in on the discussion by reminding her that a few kisses were one thing, but the fact that she had been clad only in her gown and wrapper was another. She closed her eyes and let herself remember the way Daniel's body had felt against hers when his hands had . . .

The bell above the door yanked her back to reality. Telling herself to be grateful for the interruption, she slipped around the end of the shelf to see who had disturbed her solitude.

There was no mistaking the mayor. He hadn't seen her yet, and something had her hanging back, waiting to see what he was up to.

"Mrs. Thomas?" he whispered.

How odd—if he really wanted Lucy to answer, why didn't he call out her name like everyone else did?

Deciding she'd hesitated long enough, Melinda deliberately bumped into a length of chain hanging at the end of the aisle. If the noise startled her, it was nothing compared to the way Mayor Kelly jumped straight in the air. Melinda would have laughed, but good manners dictated that she act as if nothing had happened.

She took a few seconds longer than necessary to straighten the chain, making sure that it was still hanging securely on a nail. Then she braced herself and turned a bright smile on the mayor. "I'm sorry if I startled you, Mr. Kelly."

Frowning, the mayor looked past her, as if waiting to see if she was alone. "I was looking for Mrs. Thomas."

Melinda set down the duster and stepped behind the counter. "I'm sorry, but Mrs. Thomas asked me to watch the store for her this afternoon while she's, ah, away. Can I help you?"

"No, I really stopped by to make sure that she was all right. The sheriff only just now saw fit to tell me about the problems she's been having." Clearly, the man was upset. "The mayor shouldn't be the last to know when there's trouble in town."

"Well, I assure you that Lucy is fine, Mr. Kelly, but I know she'll appreciate your concern. I also know that the sheriff is being quite diligent in his investigation." For some reason, she felt the need to defend Mitch Hughes's efforts, even if he was being more closemouthed than the mayor liked. She had her own good reasons to appreciate the lawman's discretion.

The mayor's eyes flitted from side to side, as if to avoid meeting Melinda's gaze head on. "Well, then, I'll be going."

How strange. The man was certainly acting oddly, but perhaps he was truly upset that he hadn't known there was trouble in town. She watched him practically run for the door.

"I'll tell Lucy that you were asking about her."

That stopped him cold. He looked back over his shoulder from the doorway. "That's all right, Miss Smythe. Don't bother. It's enough to know that she wasn't harmed."

With that, he quickly slipped outside, closing the door behind him. Melinda crossed to the front window and watched as the mayor disappeared down the street in the direction of The River Lady. Since that was known to be one of his favorite haunts, she decided that she was reading more into his behavior than was warranted. After all, her own emotional state was none too stable at the moment. No doubt she was jumping at shadows.

Sighing, she headed for the storeroom. She'd just picked up the broom when the bell chimed yet again. No wonder Lucy sometimes complained about never getting anything done when she was interrupted every few minutes. Once again, Melinda wiped her hands on her apron and forced herself to smile pleasantly.

One look at who was waiting at the counter had her wanting to jump back into the storeroom and bolt the door behind her. The last person she wanted to face at that moment was the cause of her emotional turmoil in the first place. Sheer stubbornness propelled her forward.

"Reverend Hayes." His formal title felt strange to her tongue. Two people who'd tasted passion in the dark of the night shouldn't need to put such distance between themselves.

"Miss Smythe."

The silence dragged on painfully. She had nothing left to say to him. Since it was his foolishness that put this strain between them, he could be the one to make polite conversation.

"I take it that Mrs. Thomas is not here."

"No, she's not. Why don't you come back when she is?"

"Stop it, Melinda." There was more than a bite of anger in the words.

That little show of emotion pleased her no end. Her own temper kept her prodding his. "Stop what, Pastor Hayes? I'm sure I don't know what you're talking about. You said you were looking for Lucy. I simply told you to come back another time when she was here."

That did it. His eyes, normally the color of a summer sky, darkened to a stormy gray-blue. He threw his hat to the floor.

"Don't patronize me, Melinda. I won't have it."

That did it. She looked around for something to throw as well. She settled for slamming the broom handle against the wall. "You won't have it? Whoever gave you the idea that you have any say at all in what I do? My behavior is none of your concern."

When he was standing across the room, she felt safe in hurling words at him from her side of the counter. Suddenly, without her realizing how he managed it, Daniel was right in front of her, his eyes blazing down into hers. His hands grasped her shoulders, firmly but with the same underlying gentleness he'd always shown her. It made her want to scream.

"Let go of me, Daniel. This is what got us into this trouble in the first place."

Reluctantly he let his hands drop, but he stood his ground. "That's why I'm here, Melinda. We need to talk about this."

"We already did. Your pride made you offer to marry me."

"It was more than my pride that had me down on my knee this morning, and you know it."

She didn't want to hear the hurt underlying his words. Turning her back to him, she insisted, "It *was* your pride talking—that and the need to protect our reputations. Not much to base a marriage on, if you ask me."

"That's it exactly—I did ask you, if you'll remember. I asked you to be my wife."

Pain rolled through her in waves. "Daniel, please go. I cried all morning over this. I don't think I can take any more."

He moved closer to her again. She could feel the warmth of his body seeping through the thin protection of her dress. The need to lean back against him was a powerful temptation. But accepting his comfort now wouldn't change anything and would only make things worse when he did walk away.

"I think you at least owe me an explanation, Melinda. After what happened between us last night, I have to think you harbor some pretty powerful feelings for me."

She did, but unless he felt the same way, it didn't matter. "What if I told you that you weren't the only man I had ever kissed that way?"

"Then I'm afraid I'd have to call you a liar."

Something in his voice had her turning back around. "Why? Because no other man would look at me that way?"

"Now you're fishing for compliments. Shame on you. A man would have to be blind not to see what a desirable woman you are." He inched closer. "But a woman like you has too much pride to let just any man trifle with her."

"And I suppose you think you aren't just any man?"

"Let me tell you what I think." His hand cupped her face gently, forcing her to look at him head-on. "After I left you this morning, I sat alone in the church for hours. It finally came to me that I was worried about all the wrong things—our jobs, what people would think, our reputations."

"Those things seemed pretty important to you this morning." And that was what hurt the most—that he cared more about what everyone else thought about him than how she felt.

"And I was wrong. None of that's important. What matters is this . . ."

His words trailed off as his mouth sought hers. She moaned his name as his arms wrapped around her, pulling her close to his heart, right where she wanted to be. If ever there was a moment in her life when she needed something to hang on to for dear life, this was it. She snaked her arms up around Daniel's neck and kissed him back with every bit of courage she could muster.

There may come a time when she might wish that this moment had never happened, but for now she prayed it would never end.

Finally, Daniel gentled the kiss and then broke it off. "Melinda Smythe, I've always prided myself on my self-control, but one kiss from you turns me weak. You are temptation itself."

She considered his words, trying to decide if that was a good thing or not. But considering what his kiss did to her, she had to agree with him. The touch and taste of Daniel Hayes made her want to forget all sense of propriety.

"I managed to figure out one thing for sure while I was sitting there all alone." He kissed her again, playfully brushing his lips across hers.

"And what was that?" she murmured, wishing he'd get down to business and really kiss her.

"That I didn't want to be sitting there alone, not anymore. I wanted you there beside me. Today, tomorrow, always." He punctuated each word with another kiss. Before she could react, he plunged his tongue into her mouth, sending her world careening off course completely. She wasn't sure where Daniel left off and where she began.

Abruptly, almost violently, he broke off the kiss that threatened to set them both on fire; he gasped out the words she needed to hear. "I love you, Melinda Smythe. Marry me and make me whole."

With her eyes brimming with tears and her heart overflowing with a newfound joy, she could only nod and whisper, "Yes, Daniel. Oh, yes."

# Chapter Ten

The sun danced down through the trees above them, painting the ground with dappled shadows. Cade had picked the perfect spot for their picnic. The trees were thick enough to offer protection from the heat without interfering with the slight breeze. A convenient log offered her a comfortable seat while Cade spread out the blanket he'd brought.

Mary fairly sparkled with pleased excitement. She giggled as she chased after a bright orange-and-black butterfly while the two adults looked on and smiled. Even if the two of them were at odds over some things, Mary was the one point of agreement they shared. It was amazing how easily such a small child could wrap two full-grown people around her little finger.

"Thanks for coming with us. It meant a lot to Mary."

And nothing to her father? Lucy tried not to let that idea hurt.

"She's such a charmer that it is hard to say no to her about anything." That was true, as far as it went.

But Mary wasn't the only reason that Lucy had accepted their invitation.

Cade sat down beside her on the log, far enough away to be proper, but close enough to please her. "I know. It's so hard to refuse her anything that it would be easy enough to spoil her. Considering how her grandparents doted on her, it's amazing that she isn't already."

That was the first time Cade made mention of Mary's life before coming the Lee's Mill. Lucy's curiosity was aroused. She decided to pry a little if he was in the mood to talk.

"Was she living with your parents?"

Cade had been watching his daughter's antics, but he turned to face Lucy before answering.

"No. My in-laws."

Judging by the grim set to his mouth, there was no love lost between Cade and his wife's parents. And where was his wife? It only just occurred to her that if he was still married, she had no business being alone with him like this.

"And your wife?" She held her breath as she waited for him to answer.

"Thank God, she's dead and buried." He picked up a stick and snapped it half.

His bitterness burned through his words like acid. His words should have shocked her—and on some level they did—but since she'd had the same feelings about her late husband, she was in no position to judge.

Cade seemed surprised at her calm acceptance of his comment. "Aren't you going to tell me that is no way to talk about the dearly departed?"

"No, although I would caution you against saying such things within Mary's hearing. No doubt, she loved her mother, whatever the woman's shortcomings might have been."

"Mary has never heard a word of criticism about Louisa from me."

Louisa—now the mysterious woman had a name. Lucy wished it didn't make the woman seem more real, as if she were suddenly sitting there between them.

"If Mary is anything to judge by, I would guess your wife was beautiful."

"I suppose I thought so at one time."

"I'm told that my husband was considered handsome." She offered that tidbit up as payment for trusting her with his confidences.

To her surprise, Cade reached over and took her hand. "It's amazing how hard it is to see beneath a pretty veneer to the real person underneath."

"The worst part is knowing that no one would believe you if you tried to tell them the truth. Everyone who knew my husband, including my own father, thought he was a saint."

"Did he hit you?"

Cade's gentle question surprised her into answering truthfully. "Only once." She closed her eyes and let the memories come. "I defied him one too many times, I guess. He'd ordered me to attend a church service with him, but I wouldn't go listen to that hateful preacher. Harold lost his temper and slapped me across the face."

She felt chilled despite the heat of the afternoon sun. "I think it startled him more than it did me. He begged me to forgive him, but I never really did." Images of the past flowed through her mind. "Mostly he used words as his weapons. I left him once, but my father wouldn't allow me back in his house. He said that a woman's place was with her husband."

"I bet that hurt more than anything your husband ever said to you."

"You know, I've never told anyone else all of this." She looked down at their hands, still entwined. "Thank you for listening. It helps."

Cade shrugged. "No one wants to admit how much of a fool he's been. In my weaker moments, I'd like to think that if the war hadn't happened, things would have been different for Louisa and me. But most of the time, I know that I'm just fooling myself. Sooner or later, she would have found her way into another man's bed anyway." With that, Cade moved away, as if he'd said way more than he'd meant to, and needed to put some distance between them.

"I need to check on Mary," he announced, although his daughter was in plain sight only a few yards away.

Lucy hurt for him, although she new better than to offer her sympathy. Instead, she gave him her anger.

"Cade . . ." She waited to see if he was listening.

"Yes?"

"The woman had to be a complete idiot. She had everything and threw it all away."

He didn't want to believe the truth of her words. "She made it clear that I didn't satisfy her—in bed or out of it."

Lucy had felt his passion, however briefly, and knew the truth of how well Cade could satisfy a woman. "Like I said, she was a fool," she whispered as he walked away.

His steps seemed to falter a bit, leaving her hoping that it was due to his bad leg and not because he heard what she'd said. Because he continued on his way without looking back, and because it would embarrass her otherwise, she let herself believe that she had the right of it.

But just in case, she spent the rest of the afternoon concentrating her attention on the younger member of the Mulroney family.

"One rock, two rocks, three rocks, four," he sang softly, stacking them neatly on the shelf. "A few more warnings and they won't meet anymore."

The simple rhyme brought him a great deal of pleasure. He liked it when things turned out better than expected. Each step he took required careful planning. Tonight was the night when, once again, he'd take to the streets and make his presence known.

He liked that idea.

People respected a man who stood out in a crowd. By the time he was finished, his name would be on everyone's lips. Power was a more valuable commodity than gold.

He studied the rocks again. Each one had its own personality. It was his job to match them to their targets. On impulse he picked up the first one, but immediately returned it to its appointed spot. His hand hovered over the second before finally settling on the third.

He hefted the rock, learning its weight and texture. The feeling was right. This one was for the store owner. The second choice was easier. He'd known all along that the fourth stone had the right feel for the schoolteacher. His knowledge of the Lawford girl, though, was sketchy at best. He tried telling himself that either of the other two rocks would work, but he hated guessing at something so important.

Finally, it came to him. He pointed at one and then the other, each time saying a letter from her name. "C-O-R-A-L-A-W-F-O-R-D." So it was the first one after all. He'd leave the last one up on the shelf as a reminder of all his hard work. He only hoped that the men of Lee's Mill would someday appreciate all that he'd done, all that he was willing to sacrifice, to make the town a good place to live.

Now that he had the rocks laid out in the correct order, it was time to start working on the notes. He reached for pen and ink. Words were often harder to choose rightly than the rocks had been, but he'd been mulling them over for days. Once he started writing, the ideas seem to flow from the pen right along with the ink.

The message would be clear, not that these women would heed his warning. That was half the fun, knowing he'd given them every chance to mend their ways and the stupid bitches wouldn't. No, not at all.

"One rock, two rocks, three rocks, four . . ." he hummed happily to himself.

The first note was done. The clock on the mantel chimed the half hour. If he kept at it, the other two would be done before dinnertime. Not a bad day's work.

Dust hung in the air, stirred up by the horse's hooves and held there by the humidity. Lucy fanned herself with the brim of her hat, but nothing much helped. She normally endured the heat of an Ozark afternoon as best she could, but this one had been pure pleasure. Rare was the day when she got away from her duties at the store for more than an hour or so. To spend several hours strolling along the river in the company of a handsome man, well, that was something special indeed.

She glanced at her two companions. Curled up

against her father's side, Mary was more than half asleep. The child had played herself nearly to the point of exhaustion chasing butterflies, wading in the shallows, and playing games of tag with Cade. Lucy wasn't sure she'd ever heard anyone giggle as much as Mary had. Looking back over the short time she'd known her, the little girl had truly blossomed. Living with her father obviously agreed with her.

Cade himself looked more relaxed than she'd ever seen him. He had discarded his jacket not long after they'd reached the river. Later, as a concession to the day's heat, he'd rolled his sleeves up to his elbows. More than once, Lucy had caught herself staring at his strong forearms, admiring the sheer masculinity of the man.

He'd been so cute when Mary had talked him into shucking off his boots and socks to go wading with her. He, in turn, had teased Lucy into joining them. She knew he'd found it amusing that she'd made him turn his back while she rolled down her stockings and slipped off her shoes. No doubt he'd been remembering the liberties he'd taken the night her window was broken. It was a bit late to worry about her modesty, but a woman had to have certain standards.

"You're being awfully quiet." Cade flicked the reins, encouraging the horse to step lively.

"Sorry, I didn't want to disturb her," Lucy whispered, using Mary's drowsiness as an excuse. Better the small lie than to confess the truth of the matter. Cade didn't know that she'd been daydreaming about him, remembering the taste of his kiss, the feel of his body.

"Once she falls asleep, Sherman and his entire army wouldn't wake her up."

The two adults shared a smile over the sleeping

child. Lucy wondered if Cade appreciated what a gift his daughter was. Seeing the look of protective wonder on his face, she had to believe that he did. Seeing his joy only made her more aware of the gaping hole in her own life.

"What's wrong, Lucy?"

"Nothing at all," she lied. "I'm fine."

"You forget that I'm damned good at knowing when someone's not telling me the truth. One second you were smiling, and the next you looked as if you'd received bad news." The sympathy in his eyes softened his words. "I thought we'd become friends. You can trust me with your secrets."

He made it surprisingly easy to pour out her secret sorrow. "There's not much about my marriage that I miss, but I do regret that my husband and I never were blessed with a child."

"You're a young woman, Lucy. There's still plenty of time left in your life for motherhood." He was looking straight ahead at the road and so missed the wince of pain his words caused.

"I may not be old in years, but in experience I am. I have no intention of ever marrying again." She clenched her hands in her lap, wishing she'd kept her mouth shut about the whole business.

"You can't think that all men are like your husband and father."

She considered the matter. "No, I can't say that I do, any more than you should think all women are like your wife. The problem is in figuring out which ones are. I thought my husband was a kind man, but obviously my judgment is faulty when it comes to the nature of men."

"Oh, I don't know about that. You seem to like me well enough. That alone proves that you are an excellent judge of character." The corners of his mouth tilted up in a grin that invited her to join in.

"My friends would question that, you know. Melinda about fainted dead away when she heard about my plans for the afternoon."

"I'm surprised she didn't rush out to round up the entire Society to save you from my clutches."

"There wasn't time." And then there was the small matter that she rather liked his clutches.

"Well, make sure that they all know that I was a complete gentleman. I wouldn't want them coming after me."

They'd reached the outskirts of town. All too quickly, Cade maneuvered the rented buggy to a stop. He eased Mary down to lie on the seat. Freed of his sleeping burden, he was able to assist Lucy in alighting. Instead of offering her his hand, he slipped his hands around her waist and lifted her down.

She instinctively put her hands on his shoulders to steady herself. When he set her down, she was standing delightfully close to him. Was he going to kiss her right there on the street? He wouldn't dare, would he? Her heart fluttered, with what could have been either fear or hope.

The moment of uncertainty ended abruptly when the door of the store flew open. Melinda came charging out, looking excited—a decided change from the way she'd been earlier when Lucy had last seen her.

"Lucy, I thought you'd never get back!"

"Why? What's wrong? Did something happen?"

Before Melinda could answer, the pastor joined them on the porch. "Nothing bad, I assure you, Mrs. Thomas. Miss Smythe, Melinda, that is . . ." He put his arm firmly around the teacher's waist and pulled her close to his side. "What I'm trying to say is that Melinda has made me a very happy man today by accepting my proposal of marriage."

Lucy stepped back, bumping into Cade. His solid presence was reassuring as she gathered her scattered thoughts. She realized that Melinda and her betrothed were both waiting for her to respond. Despite her own feelings on the subject of marriage, she could only be pleased for her friend. She moved forward to give Melinda a tearful hug while Cade shook the pastor's hand.

"When? How?" she managed to stammer.

Since both members of the happy couple managed to blush, she knew the story would be worth hearing. At the same time, standing out on the street was not the place to press for details.

It was Daniel who managed to come up with an acceptable response. "We've been friends for some time but only recently realized that our feelings had deepened into something far more lasting."

Lucy blinked back some tears, although she knew they were more for herself than for her friends. If anyone could make a marriage work, she was convinced it was these two.

"I'm very pleased for you both," she told them honestly. "Pastor, since Melinda is like a sister to me, I hope that you will become the brother I never had."

"That would be my hope as well, Mrs. Thomas."

"Under the circumstances, perhaps you could begin by calling me Lucy."

"Lucy it is. And please call me Daniel." He pulled out his pocket watch and checked the time. "I'm sorry, but I must go. I have several of the church elders coming to talk to me in only a few minutes."

It was then that Lucy realized that Cade had deserted her some time in past few minutes. She must have been more dazed by Melinda's news than she'd realized, because she hadn't even heard the buggy pull away. The coward had left her alone to face Melinda's radiant joy. She would curse his name, but in truth she would have run for the hills herself if given the opportunity.

Forcing what she hoped was a sincere smile on her face, she looped her arm through Melinda's and led her back into the store and straight upstairs. Once they were settled in her parlor, she shook an admonishing finger at her friend.

"All right, I heard that flimsy excuse for an explanation from your Daniel. Now I want details, details, details." To her great amusement, Melinda blushed again. "Most especially, I want to know what went on between you and the good pastor that has both of you looking so guilty."

Melinda had her eyes fixed on the floor and wouldn't look up. That, more than anything, convinced Lucy that there was more to this sudden engagement. She also sensed that Melinda needed to talk about it.

"Come on, Melinda. There's only the two of us here, and nothing you tell me will leave this room." She gave Melinda a few seconds to consider her words before adding, "You do want to marry the man, don't you? If you're having second thoughts, now is the time to tell him, before the news gets all over town."

Melinda's response was gratifyingly fast in coming. "Oh, I do want to marry Daniel. I really do." But then the joy in her friend's eyes dimmed.

"Then what's wrong?"

"I only hope that it isn't only his sense of honor

that made him propose." A few tears streamed down Melinda's pale cheek. "I would hate to think he felt forced into marriage with me."

Lucy fought to keep her voice calm, but alarms were going off. "Melinda, this is difficult for me to ask, but I want the truth. What, exactly, happened that makes you think he offered to marry you only because he had to?"

Her friend's gaze went right back to the floor. "He kissed me."

"I can't believe that he's the only man to have ever kissed you. That is hardly a matter for scandal."

"It is if you consider the fact that I was in my nightgown at the time."

"What! You allowed Daniel into your bedroom?" Not that she was in any position to judge. She'd allowed Cade to do far more than kiss her when she was wearing her nightgown.

"Heavens, no, Daniel would never compromise my reputation like that!"

"Then how?"

"I saw him hiding in my backyard, and I went out to see what he was doing." She sighed. "Seems he got it into his head that I was in danger from the same man who broke your window. He knew the sheriff was busy watching your place, so he took it upon himself to stand guard over mine."

That sounded exactly like something the earnest young preacher would do. "That was foolish but sweet of him. Was that when he kissed you?"

Melinda nodded. "He made me go back inside, but before he managed to get back to the parsonage, the sheriff caught him."

"Mitch Hughes would never carry tales."

"I know, but Daniel was worried enough that he was at my house at first light."

"Was that when he proposed?"

"The first time. I turned him down that time."

"Because you were convinced he was doing so for the wrong reasons? I take it he didn't take no for an answer."

"He followed me here after you left. He said he realized that he needed me by his side." The tears were back. "He says he loves me."

Lucy joined her friend on the small sofa and put her arm around her shoulders. "Then I'm sure he does. Daniel Hayes is a man of his word. He was honest about what he proposed the first time, wasn't he? And you believed him."

Melinda gave her a tearful nod.

"Then why don't you believe him this time? He didn't look like a man who was facing a life sentence out there on my porch. More like someone who'd just been granted his heart's desire."

Hope replaced the fear in Melinda's expression. "He did, didn't he?"

"Yes, he did. Now let's get your face washed up," Lucy ordered her friend. "We have a wedding to plan."

Son of a bitch, he was purely disgusted with himself. Cade sat back in his office chair and put his feet up on the desk. Cradling a glass of brandy in his hands, he thought back over the day's events and wished he could figure out what was going on in his head.

He'd never thought himself a coward, but faced with the obvious happiness of Daniel Hayes and Melinda Smythe, he'd turned tail and run. He hadn't even taken time to thank Lucy for spending the afternoon with Mary—and him. With luck, they'd all think he'd been in a hurry to get his sleeping daughter home.

Damn it all to hell, he knew full well that he had no business taking a woman like Lucy Thomas on a picnic. Even though she claimed to have no desire to marry again, more than one man had been fooled into thinking he was safe. It wouldn't do at all for folks—and especially Lucy herself—to get the idea that the two of them were keeping company. Hell, she'd be right at the top of his list if he were ever so foolish as to risk marriage again, but it would only be because Mary needed a mother. Right now, he had the best of situations. Lucy was providing the feminine influence that his daughter needed, without his being plunged back into the hell of marriage.

Feeling restless, he dropped his feet back to the floor and crossed the room to look out the window that faced the store next door. The boards he'd slapped up over the broken glass infuriated him all over again. He might not have much use for women, but no one should go terrorizing them.

He'd tried to convince himself that it was a one-time incident, most probably a drunken prank, but his gut instincts told him differently. Trouble was brewing. If he thought it would work, he'd argue long and hard to force Lucy and her friends to give up the Society. Now that Daniel Hayes had more than a pastor's interest in Melinda Smythe, maybe he'd back Cade's play. Mitch would for certain if it meant keeping peace in town.

He tossed back the last of his brandy and set the glass down on the windowsill. There weren't enough words in the world to convince the stubborn woman next door that she was endangering herself and her friends by inciting the women to organize. Even if they were satisfied for now to limit the business of the Society to literature, it was only a matter of time before that changed.

Like most newspaper editors, he kept up on current affairs in the East by telegraph, so he was learning that the Luminary Society was hardly unique. Since the war, similar groups had sprung up all over the damned country. Already they were a force to be reckoned with in some areas, preaching temperance and pushing for women to get the vote. The very idea made him shudder. He closed his eyes and tried to imagine a government with women in positions of power.

Based on the zeal with which the ladies had conducted their meeting the other night, it was just possible that women might run men right out of office. As much as he hated to admit it, Lucy Thomas would likely be a better mayor than Otis Kelly. For one thing, she was always sober, which was more than he could say for the mayor.

Speaking of the mayor, if the damned fool didn't do something soon, he was going to find himself kicked out of office by the banker. Cade didn't much care which of them won. The election made news, and that was good for his business.

He'd left Mary alone long enough. She was good to entertain herself with her dolls and such, but she was too young to see to her own needs for long. His office was only a short distance from the back door of his house, but that didn't mean he felt comfortable leaving her alone after dark. He stepped out the door, pausing to listen to the early-evening sounds. The sound of the river murmured underneath the usual noises of the town. A few crickets were making their usual racket.

It was too early for the lightning bugs to start their flickering dance in the woods back of town, but he knew Mary would be watching for them. Having grown up in the city, she found the Ozark woods that surrounded Lee's Mill a constant source of entertainment. He'd even gone so far as to teach her how to buzz June bugs by tying a string to their leg and flying them around her head. Tenderhearted thing that she was, she'd tried that trick once and then immediately set the emerald green beetle free, apologizing and promising never to do such a thing again.

Mary was waiting for him in the parlor. It still made his heart melt to have her here in his house, in his life. The way she smiled when he entered the room was enough to have him walking on air for hours.

"Well, my lady," he said, bowing deeply, "will you do me the honor of accompanying me to dinner at the hotel?"

Her curtsy did her grandmother's training proud. "Yes, Father, I would be delighted to eat with you." She spoiled the formality of their actions with a happy giggle. "Besides, they cook better than you do."

She danced back out of reach when he charged at her, pretending outrage. "That might be true, little one, but you don't need to be so eager to say so."

Despite his grumbling, she settled her hand trustingly in his. Together they strolled down to the hotel. He noticed that since Mary had come to live with him, more of the townspeople spoke to him as they passed. He hoped it was a sign that those roots he needed so badly to set down were starting to take hold in Lee's Mill. Perhaps his neighbors considered a child a man's stake in the future of the town.

Once they reached the hotel, Mary led the way to their favorite table in the back corner of the dining room. Almost immediately, the owner's wife, Belle, was there to tell them what was on the menu for the night. She always managed to slip his daughter an extra cookie or other sweet whenever she thought Cade wasn't looking.

Shortly after she'd left with their order, Mitch entered the room. He started right for Cade's table as soon as he spotted him. He nodded to Mary. "Miss Mulroney, Cade."

"If you're here to eat, why don't you join us?" Cade offered, since it was obvious that Mitch had something stuck in his craw.

"Don't mind if I do."

Cade always took the seat that put his back to the wall. It amused him to see that Mitch took the other one that offered a full view of the room while preventing anyone from being able to sneak up behind him. The unconscious choice spoke volumes about the lawman's experience in life.

Belle swung by their table again, to get Mitch's order on her way back into the kitchen.

Since it was doubtful that whatever the sheriff wanted to talk about was appropriate to discuss in front of Mary, Cade steered the conversation to a safer topic.

"I assume you've heard that our young minister has decided to take himself a wife."

"Yes, I did hear that. I suspect that Miss Smythe will make a fine pastor's wife."

There was something about the glint in Mitch's eyes that set Cade to wondering. He tested the waters. "I have to say that it came as quite a surprise to some of us."

"I'm sure it did." The closemouthed lawman stubbornly kept his gaze firmly away from meeting Cade's.

Now Cade was sure that Mitch knew something that no one else did. Normally, he'd feel obligated to push for details, but now wasn't the time. Not with Mary sitting there listening to every word.

"Miss Melinda is getting married?"

He turned to his daughter. "I forgot that you were asleep when we heard the news. She and Pastor Hayes announced their engagement just this afternoon."

Mary frowned. "Will she still be my teacher when school starts? She promised I could sit right up front."

"I'm sure Miss Smythe wouldn't break an important promise like that one." But it was a good question. The town council had looked long and hard for someone qualified to teach the children. Folks wouldn't be too happy if they had to start searching for a new teacher all over again before the school was even finished.

"I'll have to ask her tomorrow night before the meeting."

Mary's statement had both men sitting up straight and staring at her.

"Uh, Mary, what meeting is that?"

His daughter looked up from playing with her doll. "The Society meeting. Miss Lucy and the ladies invited me."

"They did, did they?" He'd have something to say about that idea. But what had him more worried was the fact that the Society wasn't due to meet for another week.

"Are you sure you have the right night, Miss Mary? The ladies wouldn't normally meet again this soon." Mitch's gentle tone belied the worried frown on his face.

"It's the right night, all right," Mary assured them. "Lucy and Cora and Melinda want to meet every week now."

"Aw, hell," Mitch muttered, not quite under his breath.

Before either of the men could figure what to

say next, Belle appeared with their dinners. Cade tried without success to do justice to the excellent meal that she set in front of him. Judging by the way Mitch was pushing his peas around in his plate, he wasn't the only one whose appetite had just been ruined. Finally, both of them pushed their plates back, giving up all pretense of eating. Two perfectly good steaks had just gone to waste.

Lucy Thomas and her friends had a lot to answer for.

Trouble was, there was someone out there who was threatening to make them pay.

# Chapter Eleven

"This meeting is now called to order." Lucy banged the gavel on the pedestal with more force than usual, but it got the job done. The whispers of a few women in the back of the room faded away when she stared in that direction.

"We appreciate everyone coming together on such short notice, but we felt that it was necessary that we take a stand on the problem of the men in this town interfering with our organization."

Her remarks were rewarded with a gratifying number of nodding heads and even a ripple of applause.

"We all know that there have been editorials written urging the candidates for mayor take a stand against the Luminary Society. And after last week's meeting, we know for certain that the men in this town have taken to discussing our business in their little town council meetings."

Even though keeping her voice calm, Lucy let her outrage shine through, encouraging the other ladies to feel the same way. She'd argued long and hard with Cora against responding to the men's actions with a show of temper. No, far better that they take a firm stand but act with dignity. She was firmly convinced that if any of them threw a tantrum, it would force the men's hands.

Melinda took over for the moment.

"I have discussed this matter at length with Pastor Hayes." She blushed as she added, "My fiancé."

Cora led the rest of the members in a spontaneous round of applause, making Melinda turn even redder. Finally, she held up her hand, asking for a return to silence.

"He agrees that we should be allowed to continue on as we have been. The fact that a woman wants to improve her mind does not lessen her dedication to the other areas in her life."

Lucy, as well as the others, was riveted by Melinda's words. It was vital that Pastor Hayes continue to support their cause.

"Women played vital roles in the war, often doing the work of men who were away fighting. We've all heard stories about those valiant ladies who nursed the wounded even while the battles raged on around them. In fact, early on, if it hadn't been for women gathering food and blankets, men of both sides would have starved. Even here in Lee's Mill, you all organized to roll bandages and to gather food to send to the men at the front. It doesn't matter which side you supported; you all saw your duty and you did it."

She looked around the room, letting her words sink in. "And now, we have another obligation to meet, but this one is to ourselves. If we let the men interfere with our Society and its goals, then we are failing not just ourselves, but generations of women to come."

A trained preacher couldn't have done a better

job, Lucy decided as the ladies of the Society considered Melinda's words and then rose to their feet in a show of support. Of course, now came the hard part.

If the Society was to expand beyond the strictly educational goals that they started with, what should they do next?

It was Cora's turn to speak. She smiled at Lucy, clearly pleased with the way things were going. The girl was fearless, but then, she wasn't the one who'd been directly threatened. Neither Lucy nor Melinda were the type to cower, either, but perhaps the few years' difference in their ages and Cora's had taught them a greater sense of caution.

"First, ladies, we'd like to propose that we continue to meet weekly rather than every two weeks. Now, I realize that not all of you can come that often, and that's all right. As always, we will post minutes of the discussion from each meeting so that everyone is kept informed."

"All in favor of weekly meetings, please raise your right hands."

The vote was almost unanimous.

"Secondly, we would like to expand the list of subjects that we will consider suitable for discussion."

Mrs. Overland's hand shot up.

Cora acknowledged the woman's need to speak with a nod. "I yield the floor to Mrs. Overland."

"We've all heard rumors that Lucy there received a threat against her life."

Slowly Lucy rose to her feet. "Some coward threw a rock through my side window with a note attached. So far, that's the only tangible threat that we've received." She half expected the room to empty out in response to her confirmation that the threat had been real.

But the women of Lee's Mill were made of stronger stuff than that, surprising Lucy and quite possibly themselves. Mrs. Overland was the first to show her resolve. The formidable woman had remained standing while she awaited Lucy's reply. She positively vibrated with indignation.

"Well, I never!" she huffed. Looking around at her companions, the older woman stood ramrod straight and announced to one and all, "I, for one, will be here at every meeting. No one, least of all one who's too cowardly to show his face, is going to keep me home against my will."

Her words seemed to hang alone in the air, but then thunderous applause and shouts of agreement rattled the windows. Lucy, taken aback by the spontaneous support, looked to her friends only to see the same pleased astonishment reflected in their expressions.

Finally, the uproar died back, leaving in its wake an uneasy silence, waiting for someone to fill the void.

One by one, every person in the room looked to Lucy for guidance. She closed her eyes, praying for a strength she wasn't sure she would find. Once she opened her mouth, though, the words came easily.

"I move that we form a committee to consider additional topics for us to discuss. We shall not abandon our primary purpose of continuing to educate ourselves in the areas of literature and history. Rather, we are looking for other appropriate avenues of enlightenment." Deciding that they'd already crossed a line from which there would be no retreat, she went for broke.

"First among these new areas of discussion should be issues facing our community as a whole."

There were several "Hear, hears" and even one

rather loud "Amen!" in response to her pronouncement. Cora rose to her feet and signaled that she had something to add to the conversation. Lucy was only too glad to yield to the younger woman.

"Even though we do not have the vote, we still should decide which candidate would best serve our interests, and throw our support behind him."

Shock rippled through the room as first one woman and then the next looked to their neighbors to see if they'd heard rightly. Finally, a tentative hand went up in the back of the room. Cora immediately recognized Josie Turner.

"How do we know that either candidate will want our backing? I mean, if we can't vote, why would they care what we think?"

Melinda stepped in to answer before Cora could. Although they both appreciated Cora's enthusiasm, the girl often spoke without thinking things through completely.

"Maybe neither Mayor Kelly nor Mr. Bradford will want our support . . ." She paused for effect. "But by the time the next election rolls around, and the one after that, we will have had time to build a sound foundation for our opinions to count. Right now, we can't even get our words printed in the newspaper without them being twisted and turned every which way. But we will learn how to bring pressure to bear, to make sure that our voices are heard."

Cora moved to stand at Melinda's side. Lucy hurried to join them, showing a united front to all in the room. Melinda let the other members buzz and talk among themselves for several minutes before urging Lucy to bring the meeting back to order. This time, it only took one loud rap of the gavel to have everyone returning to their seats, ready for business.

"Do I have volunteers for the committee to discuss possible topics for future meetings?"

A gratifying number of hands were raised. Rather than accept them all, which would have resulted in an unwieldy number on the committee, Lucy wrote down everyone's name and posted them as a slate of candidates. A quick vote reduced the number by half. She promised the others that they would be on the committee for the next series of discussions.

All too soon, it was time to end the meeting. As the members of the Society vacated the room, the immensity of what they had accomplished over the past couple of hours hit Lucy full strength. She sank down on the closest chair and did her best to assimilate all that had been said and done.

"We're on treacherous ground, ladies."

Melinda looked rather pale herself, but then, her whole life had gone through huge changes in the past couple of days. Only Cora looked blissfully unaware of the gravity of what they were about to undertake.

"Well, well, well." It was all that Lucy could think to say.

Melinda smiled. "Well, indeed." She looked around the room. "I suppose we should get things cleaned up a bit."

"Leave it. I'll do it in the morning. I don't think I have enough energy left to lift a spoon."

Her two friends didn't look too disappointed about escaping their usual housekeeping duties. Cora practically skipped down the stairs, but she stopped to wait for Lucy at the bottom.

"Don't you go doing all that by yourself. My

aunt is visiting friends tomorrow, so I'm free to come help first thing in the morning."

Lucy was only too glad to accept the offer. Friday was the day she normally wrote up her supply orders for the week, which wouldn't leave much time for dishes or cleaning.

"I'll take you up on that, Cora." She gave the girl a quick hug. "I do appreciate all that you do."

Melinda opened the door of the store and peeked out. From the way her face lit up, Lucy knew exactly who her friend was looking for. Her suspicions were confirmed when Pastor Hayes appeared in the doorway.

"Evening, ladies. I made sure my meeting ended in time to walk you home, Melinda." His greeting was for all of them, but his smile was for his intended. "Miss Lawford, I would be glad to act as your escort as well, if that is acceptable."

"I know my aunt would appreciate your thoughtfulness." Cora hurried through the door to join them. "See you in the morning, Lucy."

As soon as they were gone, Lucy locked the door. For once, she knew she wouldn't have any trouble sleeping. The meeting had exhausted her, both physically and emotionally. She still had trouble believing how unified the women were when it came to the Society. On any given topic, there was often heated discussion. But after tonight, it was obvious that when it came to the group as a whole, everyone was ready to stand together.

What would Cade Mulroney have to say about that in his next column? No doubt, his words would ring out in outrage and disapproval. Too bad, she thought, feeling pretty smug. The men in this town were just going to have to get used to the women having a say about things.

But what things? At least Melinda was heading

up the committee to choose which issues the group would study and discuss. She could trust her friend to lead them all in the right direction. It wasn't a bad thing that Melinda had the pastor's ear, not to mention the rest of him. That last thought had Lucy chuckling on her way up the stairs. If she was any judge of such things, she suspected that Melinda and her beau would not want a long engagement.

Why, only a few minutes ago, the two of them were looking at each other with such ardor as to almost set the air aglow around them. No, the wedding would be soon. Despite her own jaundiced view of marriage, once again Lucy knew in her heart that these two people would be happy together.

But to get back to the matter at hand, the women of Lee's Mill would be able to count on Daniel's help in the weeks and months ahead. That thought eased the last knot of tension left over from the evening's events.

Once inside her room, she set down her lamp and dimmed the light. It felt good to pull the pins from her hair and let it fall free down her back. She finger-combed the tangles out of it before loosely braiding it for the night. After changing into her nightgown, she walked to the window and looked down toward Cade's house.

He'd kept Mary home tonight. Perhaps that had been best, considering the nature of their meeting, but she was sure her young friend was probably disappointed. He hadn't expressed his disapproval of their hastily called meeting in so many words; nevertheless, his feelings on the matter were crystal clear. She could only hope that he wouldn't let that interfere with her friendship with his daughter.

She would greatly miss her afternoons with the little girl. It had been a long time since Lucy had seen the world through such innocent eyes. Mary found anything and everything interesting, from June bugs to the Sears, Roebuck catalog. Just the other day, the two of them had spent what seemed like hours watching a spider build its web.

No, she would have to make sure that Cade continued to share his daughter with her.

The last light in Cade's house suddenly winked out, reminding her that it was time to seek out her own bed. After she slid in between the cool sheets, she thought about the other member of the Mulroney family. In the dark of the night, with no one else around to hear her words, she allowed herself to whisper her dreams.

"I would miss Mary, it's true. But I would miss her father just as much, maybe more."

Having made her confession, she slipped into dreams of silver eyes, and kisses that could melt her soul.

Mitch felt an itch right down the middle of his back. Keeping his moves slow and deliberate, he paused at the railing outside the newspaper office and looked around. Try as he might, he couldn't find the bastard.

He was out there, all right, playing his sneaking games, toying with Mitch and his town. As the sheriff, it was Mitch's job to catch the son of a bitch before he did more than throw a rock through Lucy Thomas's window. But there was more to it than that. Mitch had failed to protect those in his charge once. He still had the night shakes over the cost to his friends and to his own soul. This time he wouldn't fail.

Keeping to his usual routine, he continued down the sidewalk, looking in windows and checking to make sure doors were locked and secure as he passed the various stores along the way. But when he reached a particularly dark stretch of shadows, he slipped between the buildings and doubled back. If his quarry was depending on Mitch to follow his usual route, he might just be able to catch the culprit.

He sure as hell hoped so. Three nights in a row of pulling double shifts were taking their toll. He had to let his deputy have a night off or the man would up and quit on him. That left Mitch to cover the other six nights, not to mention the days. Hell, he couldn't remember the last time he'd been able to spend more than a few stolen hours at his ranch, but that was a whole other problem. For now, he'd give up sleeping and eating both before he would let harm come to the women in this town.

There—a block or so down the road, someone disappeared between the bank and the hotel. From this distance, it was impossible to see who it was, only that it was most likely a man. Mitch left the safety of the shadows along the buildings to run in the street. His boots would make far too much noise on the boards of the sidewalk.

He could only hope that this time he'd catch someone other than Pastor Hayes, trying to be a hero. The look on the minister's face when Mitch had hauled him out of the bushes the other night had kept him laughing for hours afterward. If it had been anyone else, Mitch would have shared the incident with Cade Mulroney. But the good pastor's intentions had been good, almost noble, even if he had all the stealth of a drunken miner.

Mitch was one of the few people in town who

hadn't been totally surprised by the sudden announcement of Daniel's engagement to Melinda Smythe. At first, he had worried that they were marrying only because they were concerned about her reputation. One look at the two of them together had dispelled that idea.

In fact, he was a little jealous. He wouldn't mind having a woman look at him that way someday.

Now wasn't the time for thinking along those lines. At the corner, he slowed to a walk, listening hard to the night sounds. He ignored the normal ruckus from The River Lady. He turned his head one way and then back again. There. A footstep from off to his right. The bastard was still sneaking around back in the shadows.

Drawing his revolver, he charged around the corner. What he saw had him cursing a blue streak.

"Damn it to hell, Oliver. How many times have I told you to quit pissing in people's gardens?" He approached the rancher cautiously. The man was a mean drunk, and as far as Mitch could tell, he was drunk a good part of the time. This time he got lucky—Turner was in a pleasant fog.

After fumbling to button up his pants, Oliver touched the brim of his hat. "My apologies, Sheriff."

"Can you make it home, or do you need to sleep it off here in town?" It wouldn't be the first time that Mitch had hauled the sorry bastard into a cell for the night for his own safety.

"I left my horse over there somewhere," he waved vaguely in the direction of The Lady. "Want to get home to my loving wife. Need to do my duty as a husband. My father wants grandchildren, you know, even if they're off the daughter of the town drunk."

The image of Josie Turner flashed through Mitch's mind. More than once he'd seen the fading bruises on her face and arms. If there was one thing he hated more than a mean drunk, it was one who took his temper out on a woman. Josie was a little bit of thing, no match at all for the bastard she was married to.

Maybe he'd do her a favor and keep her husband locked up until he slept it off. Trouble was, Oliver Turner was no better sober. He was still debating the issue when he heard the unmistakable sound of glass shattering.

"Son of a bitch!" He left Oliver to his own devices and took off at a dead run for Lucy Thomas's place.

Cade came charging out of his house, gun in hand. He'd only caught the barest glimpse of someone running between the buildings—not enough to recognize who it was. But no sooner than the shadowy figure had passed by than another of Lucy's windows exploded into a thousand pieces.

Once outside, he was torn with the need to catch the bastard and the urge to find Lucy and offer her what comfort he could. Mitch made the decision for him. The lawman came charging between the buildings with such fury in his eyes that Cade found himself backing up a step and holding his hands up in the air.

Luckily, the lawman recognized him immediately. "Which way?"

Cade pointed behind him. "You want help?"

"Check on Mrs. Thomas first; then come on if you want. I have a sick feeling that he's not done for the night."

With that cryptic remark, Cade ran for Lucy's front door. Just like the first time, he could see the flicker of the lamp that she was carrying down the stairs. He didn't know whether to admire her courage or curse her for a fool for not staying upstairs, where she was safe from broken glass and idiots throwing rocks.

He forced himself to slow down and knock on the door. "Lucy, it's me. Mitch wanted me to check on you."

It took her shaky hands several long seconds of fumbling to get the lock open. Cade slipped inside and slammed the door closed. He didn't question the relief he felt when Lucy flew right into his waiting arms.

She clung to him as if he were all that stood between her and all the evils of the world. He felt the same surge of protectiveness he would have if it had been Mary who had been threatened. For a short time, he allowed himself the secret pleasure of holding this particular woman against him.

Finally, he knew he had to put some distance between them or lose all control over the situation. "Give me the lamp."

She handed it over without an argument. Although it was unlikely that the culprit had done more than break the window, it was only common sense to make sure. The two of them made their way to the back of the store. The dim light from the lamp glittered off the shards of glass that littered the floor.

Cade made sure to keep himself between Lucy and the gaping hole in the window until he asked, "Do you have shoes on?"

"Slippers," she told him as she came up beside him. "Is there a message this time?" she asked, sounding far calmer than he expected her to.

"I don't see one . . ." he started to say when she interrupted him.

"There—in the corner." She pointed to something white lying in the midst of the glass.

He retrieved the object—another rock wrapped in paper. "Let's get back out front."

Lucy hurried to follow him. When they reached the counter, he set down the lamp and turned up the wick. He gently unfolded the paper and spread it out flat. They each read the hate-filled words silently, as if speaking them aloud would give them more power. The burn marks along the edges of the letter made Cade's skin crawl.

"I'll kill him." *Painfully, slowly.*

"I might just let you." Lucy traced the writing with her finger. "I wish I recognized the handwriting."

"That would make it too easy. Whoever he is, he figures he's too smart to get caught that way." Cade picked up the paper and held it up to the light. "Good quality. There can't be that many people in town that would have use for paper like this."

"No, but it is the type I keep in stock. There's no telling how much I've sold over the past five years."

"The ink is probably no more helpful." Cade looked around, trying to decide what to do next. "I've got to get back to Mary."

"Go, then. It wouldn't do for her to wake up all alone. I'll be fine."

Cade stopped short of the door. "Come with me."

"I'm not dressed."

"Damn it, Lucy, be sensible. What's more important—how you're dressed or Mary's safety? Besides, it will only be until Mitch comes back. Once we know that everything is quiet, you can slip back home with no one the wiser."

"But you and Mitch will both know." The protest didn't have much conviction behind it.

"And neither of us will say a word. Now, get your keys so we can lock up and go."

Lucy gave him a considering look, but then she hurried to do as he suggested. He stepped outside first to make sure that no one was watching, and then signaled to Lucy to follow. The two of them hugged the building, keeping out of sight as much as possible. In short order, he had her safely inside his kitchen.

"Have a seat. I want to check on Mary, and then I'll put on a pot of coffee."

He bounded up the stairs to his daughter's room. Mary had kicked off her covers, but otherwise she was sleeping soundly. He tugged the blankets back up around her shoulders. He paused long enough to plant a soft kiss on her forehead before returning to his guest below.

Lucy was sitting just where he'd left her. He'd love to get his hands on the fool who had put the fear in her dark eyes. Normally, she was so strong, so capable, but tonight there was a new vulnerability in the set of her shoulders. No woman deserved to be terrorized this way. He fought the need to pull her into his arms for comfort, remembering what had happened the last time they'd tried that.

"Would you rather have coffee or tea?" It wasn't much, but at least it was something he could do.

"Tea, if it isn't too much trouble."

He stoked up the stove and set the kettle on to heat. Neither of them seem inclined to talk as he went through the motions of being an attentive host.

"It seems sort of strange to be offering you some of your own cookies." He set the plate in front of her. When she took no notice of it, he started to get worried.

"Lucy, are you all right?"

No answer. Damn, it hurt to see her sitting all huddled in on herself.

"Lucy, damn it, answer me!" He knelt in front of her, forcing her to meet his gaze. "Are you all right?"

Her eyes filled with tears that spilled down her pale cheeks. "What did we do that was so wrong? I mean, all we wanted was to talk about books and maybe teach some of our members to read. How is that hurting anyone?"

Knowing that he'd been the one to lead the attack on the Society made him feel small and petty. He stood by his opinion that women belonged at home, but he fought his battles using words, not rocks and threats.

"Now isn't the time to think about that. Mitch is out there looking for whoever is doing this. Once the guilty party is in jail, we'll know more how to handle the situation."

The kettle started to boil, giving him an excuse to look away from the pain in Lucy's eyes. He poured the water over the tea leaves and let it steep for a couple of minutes. When he judged it strong enough to drink, he filled a cup for each of them and then added a dollop of brandy to the hot drink.

"Drink this." He practically shoved the cup into her hands.

She dutifully took a sip but frowned when she tasted it. "What's in this?"

"Brandy. It'll do us both good."

Although she looked rather skeptical, she continued to drink the tea until it was gone. He was relieved to see some color back in her cheeks.

"Thank you for coming to my rescue again."

He hadn't done anything special—no more than any man would do when a woman was threatened—and told her so.

"That's not true, Cade Mulroney." She waved her hand in the direction of the town. "How many other men did you see beating down my door to make sure that I was all right?"

"Mitch Hughes, for one."

She shrugged. "Two men out of the entire town. That isn't saying much."

He felt uncomfortable with her gratitude. Luckily, the sheriff picked that moment to reappear. He rapped on Cade's door.

"Mulroney, I can't get Mrs. Thomas to answer her door. Do you know where she is?"

"She's here, Sheriff. Sorry to worry you, but I didn't want to leave Mary alone, either."

"Good thinking."

The lawman blinked as he stepped into the brightly lit kitchen. When his gaze landed on Lucy, he frowned.

"Are you all right, Mrs. Thomas?"

She gave him a brave smile, although it was a bit shaky around the edges. "I'm fine, thanks to Mr. Mulroney here."

Cade had enough of the niceties. "Did you find him?"

Mitch shook his head. "Not before he broke two other windows and disappeared."

"Who?"

Both men knew Lucy wasn't asking the identity of her assailant. No, she was worried about the other women in town.

"Miss Lawford and Miss Smythe."

"Lord, no! Are they all right?"

Just that quickly, the fear was gone from Lucy's expression. Unless Cade missed his guess, that was fury, pure and simple, that glittered in her eyes. He was relieved to see some of her spirit restored.

Mitch looked worried about the two women, but he nodded. "Yes, they're made of stout stuff, those two. No harm done but for the broken glass."

"Did they get one of these, too?" Cade pulled the note out of his pocket and tossed it on the table in front of the sheriff.

Mitch picked it up and scanned the writing. "Almost word for word. Whoever he is, he sure enough has a grudge against the women in this town."

Lucy corrected him. "Not all the women. Just those of us who belong to the Society."

"And not even all of them. Of course, if he were going to throw warnings at every woman who'd attended one of your meetings, he'd be at it day and night." Mitch shook his head in pure disgust. "Personally, I can't wait to get my hands on him."

"Any ideas who it might be?" Cade handed Mitch a cup of the same kind of tea he'd fixed for himself and Lucy.

"Not yet." The sheriff took one drink of the hot liquid and gave Cade an appreciative smile. "Nice touch with the tea."

"Well, it's that kind of night. Lucy, would you like another cup?" He'd already poured himself one.

"No, one of those is enough for me." She rose to her feet. "Sheriff, would you mind seeing me back to the store?"

"Yes, ma'am. Are you sure you'll be all right by yourself?"

Her spine went ramrod straight. "I certainly will. No one is going to run me out of my home with a few rocks and idle threats."

And maybe the culprit meant every word in the

note, but Cade wasn't about to say so. Lucy had already experienced enough tonight to give her nightmares. No use in adding to it. He followed the two of them to the door.

"If you need anything, come get me, Lucy."

She rewarded his concern with one of her bright smiles. "I don't want to be a bother, Mr. Mulroney, but I do appreciate the offer. Let's hope that things are quiet the rest of the night."

He watched from the window until the light appeared in Lucy's bedroom window. After a bit, the light dimmed but didn't go out altogether. He couldn't blame her for wanting to hold the darkness at bay.

Then she appeared at the window. From this distance, he couldn't tell if she was still in her wrapper, but that didn't matter. Although he knew all too well how the woman felt through the thin layers of her clothing, now wasn't the time for those kinds of thoughts. It was enough to know that she was safe in her room.

And for now, he'd stand watch to make sure she stayed that way.

# Chapter Twelve

He struggled to catch his breath. It wouldn't do at all for someone to notice that he sounded like he was at the tail end of a long foot race when he walked into The River Lady. No, he must keep up appearances if he didn't want that damn sheriff to come sniffing around.

"Howdy, gentlemen." He nodded at a group of habitual card players. He might join them a bit later, after he bought himself a drink to celebrate his victory for the night.

All three messages had been delivered. The last one had been a close call. He'd been about to throw the rock when he'd caught sight of Mitch Hughes running down the street right at him. He'd managed to duck out of sight just in time.

That he'd been able to throw the rock, shattering the window, while the dutiful lawman was still within sight had added to the excitement. He'd taken refuge in the steps leading down into a neighbor's storm cellar and watched Mitch retrace his steps, his frustration clear in the way he cursed under his breath.

The Lawford woman had been a sore disappointment, though. Instead of crying or acting scared, she and that harridan aunt of hers had come boiling out of the house waving rolling pins, ready to do battle. He'd have to try harder to teach them a lesson. No woman should dare stand up to a man. If they didn't know their rightful place in the world, they'd soon learn.

But for now, there was whiskey to drink, cards to play, and more plans to make.

"Do you think we should call another emergency meeting?" Melinda looked to her friends and then to Daniel for their opinions.

"No, I don't think that would be wise." Lucy reached for another cookie, more to keep her hands busy than because she was hungry. "Whoever he is, he's looking to interfere with our group. If we panic every time he acts, then we're just playing into his plans."

"I agree." Daniel patted Melinda's hand. "Word of the attack will spread fast enough when the *Clarion* hits the presses. Mitch thought the story should be told, so that everyone in town knows what's going on."

Cora toyed with her teacup. "My aunt was absolutely furious. I was worried about how she'd react, but I underestimated her. No coward was going to tell her what was right and what was wrong." She smiled. "That's a direct quote, by the way. For now, she insists that I continue attending our little meetings."

Lucy nodded in approval. "Good for her. I knew she was made of sterner stuff than you gave her credit for."

"I appreciated the sheriff coming by last night.

He helped cover our window with a board and checked to make sure no one was lurking around the yard." Cora frowned. "I wish we knew for sure who was doing this." Her eyes flickered toward Lucy and then away.

"I wasn't aware that we had any suspects in mind."

"Well, it seems awfully suspicious to me that Cade Mulroney is so fast to reach your door whenever this happens."

"What do you mean by that?"

"Just what I said. Both times this has happened, he's been the first one on the scene. We all know how he feels about the Society." Cora's chin took on a stubborn tilt, as if she was determined to have her say no matter how hard Lucy objected.

"He was also with the sheriff. Are you suspicious of Mitch Hughes as well?"

"Well, no. But I just think you should be careful around that man."

Lucy wanted to laugh. She needed to be careful around Cade Mulroney, but not for the reasons that Cora had in mind. "I appreciate your concern, Cora. Cade Mulroney may have his faults"— she held up her hand to forestall any further comments—"but I know that he would never lift a hand to harm a woman."

Especially her, but she wasn't going to say that.

Cora clearly wanted a target for her anger. "Well, if it isn't Mulroney, who could it be? Nobody else is as vocal about their disapproval."

"I don't know, but I'm not going to sit by and wait for things to get worse. I think we should attend the next town council meeting and demand some action."

Lucy looked around the table, waiting for her friends to react with something more than stunned silence. Even Cora, the most daring of the bunch, was speechless.

"Well, I do think we should make our concerns known. We may not be able to vote, but that doesn't mean we don't have some rights. I want to know what they are going to do about this threat."

"But, Lucy, the mayor always holds the meetings at The River Lady. My aunt would skin me alive for setting foot in such a place."

Melinda joined in. "Even if they stop selling liquor during the meeting, it's still a saloon, Lucy. Our reputations would be in tatters." She looked to Daniel for his reaction. It wasn't long in coming.

"Mrs. Thomas—Lucy—I understand how you feel, but you must really think about the consequences of such an action. Politics is a dirty business, best meant for men to deal with."

Lucy wasn't about to insult the good minister for thinking like a fool, even if that was how she felt. Every decision the council made affected the women as much as the men. If the men didn't realize that, it was time someone pointed it out to them.

"I will go alone, if necessary. The mayor and Mr. Bradford obviously felt they had the right to invade our meeting. I see no reason why we shouldn't return the favor, especially when all this trouble began when they decided to interfere with the Society."

A heavy silence hung over the table as her friends considered her words. None of them looked happy, but at least they weren't walking out the door. She knew full well that what she was suggesting was outrageous by the standards of most folks, but times were changing. If the town was going to grow up, then all the people who lived here should have a voice in matters of concern.

While she let them mull things over in their minds, she looked out the window toward the newspaper office next door. She could just imagine what Cade would have to say on that editorial page of his. If he thought women had no business meeting together, there was no doubt in her mind how he'd feel about their meddling in local politics.

A smile tugged at her lips. There was a certain pleasure to be had in going toe to toe with him. He wouldn't back down from a good fight, but neither would she. Some powerful energy simmered between the two of them when their emotions ran high.

Maybe she'd announce her plans to him when he came to reclaim his daughter. Or perhaps she should let it be a surprise.

"I'll go with you, Lucy, if you think it is absolutely necessary that we go to the meeting." Melinda clearly wasn't happy about the idea, and neither was her fiancé. It spoke to the depth of their friendship that she would risk the town's censure to support Lucy.

"Thank you, Melinda. We can discuss it some more later. Perhaps we can come up with a better way to handle the situation, but at this point I don't know what it would be."

"I'll pray about it." Daniel picked up his hat and rose to his feet. "Know that whatever you decide, I will be there for the two of you."

"Two? What about me? Don't I get a say in this?" Cora gave Daniel a look that would melt stone.

Lucy played peacemaker. "Cora, of course you have a say, but there is no way that you can go in

The River Lady. I'm a widow, and as such, I have a little more latitude in my actions. Melinda has Daniel's approval and support. You cannot risk your reputation to the same degree that we can."

"But . . ."

"No, Cora," Melinda said firmly. "Lucy is right. Please try to understand that we're trying to improve the lot of women in this town. We can hardly continue to make that claim if we allow you to damage your good name just to make a point."

"I want to go," Cora sighed, signaling her surrender. "But if it would hurt the cause to do so, I will stay home. I don't have to be happy about it, though." She picked up her teacup and set it on the counter. "I'd better be going. We hired someone to make repairs on the window, and Aunt Henrietta wanted me there to supervise."

"We'll see you home," Melinda announced. "I suspect the same man is replacing my window. The sheriff sent John Horn over to see me this morning."

"That's him." Turning to Lucy, Melinda asked, "Is he doing yours as well?"

"No, Mr. Mulroney promised to put in the new glass tomorrow morning after he boarded up the window earlier today."

"He sure seems to be underfoot a lot, Lucy. Anything you want to tell us?" Melinda's eyes danced with a teasing light.

"No, except to say that he feels obligated because I watch Mary for him whenever he has to be away on newspaper business. I figure we both profit from the arrangement."

"Well, I still think we should keep an eye on the man until we know more about who is behind these attacks."

Lucy would be more than happy to take on the

job of watching Cade closely, but not for the reasons that Cora had in mind. She toyed with the idea of telling her friend, but since nothing would ever come of the attraction she felt for him, she held her piece. She wouldn't mind another taste of the passion that they'd shared, but it would only serve to complicate her life. And his.

For now, she would concentrate on the problem at hand. The women of Lee's Mill were in danger, and for no other reason than that they wanted to educate themselves. If the mayor and the council weren't going to take serious action on their own, then she'd do everything within her power to prod them along.

"Are you sure? Absolutely, positively sure?" Melinda lagged behind a step, waiting for Lucy to answer.

"No, I'm not absolutely sure, but I haven't heard any better ideas since we last discussed it."

"Daniel said he would meet us there."

"Good," Lucy said, meaning it. "It will be a relief to have at least one person in our corner."

All too quickly they reached the steps that led into The River Lady. If their course of action weren't so terrifying, she'd be excited about the prospect of finally seeing the inside of a saloon firsthand. The Lady, like all other such establishments, was forbidden territory for any woman of character. She couldn't imagine the allure of such a place for most men except as a means to escape the company of their wives and families.

She didn't begrudge anyone the occasional evening out or a casual game of cards. But some men spent far too much time and money in the place, and their families suffered for it. Josie Turner was one such woman. For Josie and others like her, Lucy would face the demons who waited inside the bat-wing doors of the saloon.

Both women paused at the bottom of the steps to settle their nerves. If they didn't show a united front, the men would no doubt do their best to chase them right back out the door. It was bad enough to know their daring action would be the source of gossip for the entire town by tomorrow. It would be so much worse to be thought cowards.

Lucy went forward with Melinda right beside her. Together they pushed open the doors and stepped into the brightly lit interior of the saloon.

Cade had turned to say something to Mitch when he noticed the ruckus at the door. Since town council meetings rarely stirred much excitement, he stood to better see what the commotion was.

"Aw, hell, I can't believe it!" He sank back down on his chair, trying to decide whether to curse or laugh.

Mitch had been too busy lighting his cigar to take note of the rising excitement, but he looked up to see what had his friend all worked up. Cade waved his hand in the direction of the doorway, still unable to find words to express himself.

"Who?" Mitch started to ask when he realized that The River Lady had two new customers, ones that no one would have ever expected to cross the threshold.

Cade hunkered farther down in his chair. "Tell me that isn't Lucy Thomas and Melinda Smythe standing over there."

"I wouldn't want to lie to you. Besides, they're coming this way."

"Shit. What could that woman be thinking of?"

Resigned to his fate, Cade rose to his feet and pushed his way through the crowd. At least for the moment, the men in the saloon seemed more puzzled than angry by the presence of real ladies in their midst.

As soon as he was within grabbing distance, Cade snagged Lucy by the arm and dragged her to the back of the room, where he and Mitch had been sitting. He felt bad about leaving Melinda to follow as she would, but he was in no mood for worrying about his manners.

He practically shoved Lucy into his vacated chair and then pulled another one over for Melinda. When both women were seated, he stood glaring down at them.

Lucy looked ready to do battle. "Quit hovering over us like that."

He prayed for patience. "What do you think you're doing walking in here like you own the place?"

She had the audacity to sniff the air as she ran her finger over the table . "If I owned it, at least it would be clean. When was the last time these tables were washed?"

Mitch didn't help the situation by laughing loudly. "I'll tell the bartender that you didn't find the place up to your standards."

"Oh, shut up," Cade grumbled. "Seriously, Lucy, what are you doing here?"

She batted her eyes, trying for all the world to look innocent. "It was our understanding that Mayor Kelly has called a town council meeting tonight. Did I hear wrong?"

"So that's what this is all about: payback for us invading your precious little meeting."

She didn't appreciate that comment one bit. "The Luminary Society is an organization for the

women of this town. Men have no place in it. The
town council, on the other hand, makes decisions
for all the citizens of Lee's Mill. That gives us the
right to attend and to address the issues that affect
us all."

Melinda looked a little less convinced that they
should be there, but seemed determined to support Lucy's position. "We've been threatened and
need to know what's being done about it.

"I can't believe what I'm hearing." Cade was
thoroughly disgusted with both women. Turning
to Mitch, he asked, "Can't you throw them out of
here?"

His friend seemed to take the whole incident in
stride. "No, not unless they're disturbing the peace.
You ladies planning on getting rowdy in here?"

Lucy got all huffy with the lawman. "Of course
not. I assure you that we know how to behave in a
meeting."

Mitch raised an eyebrow in response. "Yes,
ma'am, I know that. I just wasn't sure if you knew
what to do in a saloon."

The mayor picked that minute to come strut-
ting into the saloon and right up to the front table.
He shuffled through some papers and then laid
them out in front of him. Glaring at those around
him until they fell silent, he cleared his throat and
called the meeting to order.

"We are meeting tonight to discuss the upcoming
election. Are all the council members here and accounted for?"

A few hands went up. Mayor Kelly looked from
table to table, taking note of each man. His eyes
slid past Mitch and Cade and then back again. The
instant he recognized the two women, his face
flushed white and then red.

"Who in the hell let them in?"

The few men who had missed the uproar when Lucy and Melinda had made their entrance were now staring right at Cade's table. From the looks he was getting, every one of them thought he was responsible for inviting the women to the meeting. He wanted to jump up and deny responsibility but decided it would be both undignified and ungentlemanly. Besides, Lucy had got herself into this mess. She could just get herself out.

Mayor Kelly pushed his way through the crowd to glare at both women. His anger carried over to the two men. "Sheriff Hughes, what is the meaning of this. Why haven't you done something about this?"

Mitch, never a big fan of the mayor, stretched out his long legs and considered the matter. "Well, sir, they've both assured me that they will be on their best behavior. I don't know of any laws that say that women can't attend a town council meeting if they're of a mind to."

Having had his say, the sheriff puffed on his cigar, sending a cloud of smoke floating right into Mayor Kelly's face. The irate politician gave Mitch a disgusted look as he fanned the air to clear it.

"And you," he said, pointing at Cade. "I suppose you're backing their play on this."

Cade hadn't planned on it, but he had as much respect for the mayor as did Mitch. He glanced at Lucy to see how she was handling being the focus of a crowd of scandalized men. He had to give her credit. She met the mayor's gaze head on, refusing to apologize for disturbing the meeting.

"Neither Sheriff Hughes nor Mr. Mulroney are responsible for our presence, Mr. Mayor. Miss Smythe and I are here as concerned citizens of Lee's Mill, here to see what action the council is going to take to stop the attacks on the members of the Luminary Society. These gentlemen were kind enough to allow us to share their table."

That clearly didn't please the mayor one bit. He gave Cade a nasty look, but his comments were aimed directly at Mitch.

"Your job is on the line here, Hughes. I haven't been too impressed with the way things are going around town lately. I'll want a report on what you've done so far about catching the culprit who's been breaking windows and scaring our women."

Cade couldn't resist jumping into the fray. *"Your* women? Why, Mayor, is there something you want to tell us?"

"Shut up, Mulroney, or we'll be looking for another newspaper editor right along with a new sheriff." Figuring he'd had the last word, the irate politician stomped back to the front of the room and began his meeting.

Mitch didn't seem at all concerned by the mayor's threats. He gave Cade a sly look and then grinned at Lucy and Melinda. "Seems Henrietta Dawson took it upon herself to question Mayor Kelly's ability to run this town. The way I heard it, by time she was finished with him, there wasn't much left of him."

"Good for her," Lucy murmured. "I know you're doing all you can, but he has no right to go around talking that way to either one of you."

"He's the one who might very well lose his job come election time." Cade nodded in the direction of the banker sitting off to the left. "Bradford has been talking to a lot of folks around here about how things could be done better. Enough of them are listening to make Mayor Kelly a mite nervous."

Right then the two candidates got into an argument over the need to raise taxes to pay for improvements to the landing on the river.

"I don't see what's wrong with it the way it is."

Bradford jumped to his feet. "Then maybe you need to have Doc check your vision. Any fool can see that half the boards are rotten. If we want to bring commerce to Lee's Mill, we need to make sure we have the kind of facilities to attract river traffic. An improved landing would go a long way toward doing that."

Cade leaned close to Lucy on the pretense of explaining the background of the discussion. The scent of lilacs teased his senses. "The mayor is against the improvements mainly because it wasn't his idea. He says the town can't afford it, but that's not the problem. If he backs it, then he's supporting his opponent's project."

"Well, I'm in favor of the improvements. There are a lot of things I have trouble ordering, because the freight wagons take so long and can carry only so much." She shook her head and sighed. "I have no say in the matter since I'm a mere woman. Of course, I pay all the same taxes as the businessmen in town—who can vote."

After another few minutes, the heated exchange died down, and the mayor moved on to the next item on the agenda. Finally, he said, "If there is nothing else . . ."

Lucy immediately jumped to her feet and waited for the mayor to acknowledge her presence. Instead, he turned his back to her and called for the bartender.

"Mick, the meeting's over. How about a beer?"

Lucy, not to be outdone, announced in a very loud voice, "Well, I see that the men in this town have very different ideas about how to conduct a meeting. Mr. Mayor, I believe I am within my rights to address the town council."

Cade figured that was the quietest it had ever been in The River Lady. Everyone in the place had their eyes trained directly on the mayor's back. Even Mick, the bartender, hung back, unsure whether the meeting was indeed over.

Cletus Bradford seized the opportunity to speak once again. "Well, it is obvious that Mr. Kelly has no attention of addressing the very real concerns of the women in our town. Since they no longer feel safe in their beds at night, I don't blame Mrs. Thomas and Miss Smythe for daring to cross the threshold of this establishment to seek help."

With a dramatic flourish of his hat, he bowed in their direction. "Should I be elected to office, I assure you that it will not become necessary again for you to take such drastic measures to make yourself heard."

Then, before anyone—especially Mayor Kelly—could respond, he marched out of The Lady, with a large contingent of the town council following right on his heels. Whether it was in support of Bradford or to avoid being cornered by Lucy, Cade had no idea.

"Not that he's listening to us now," Lucy complained, looking thoroughly disgusted. "Well, this accomplished nothing, Melinda. I guess you and Cora were right."

"Don't be so sure, Mrs. Thomas. You may well have stirred up quite a hornet's nest tonight by giving Cletus Bradford another club to beat Mayor Kelly over the head with." He ground out the last of his cigar and tossed it into a nearby spittoon.

Melinda looked toward the door. "Pastor Hayes was supposed to meet us here."

"Perhaps his meeting ran later than he expected it to," Lucy suggested.

Mitch rose to his feet. "Since your escort isn't here, if you ladies are ready to go, I'll be glad to see you both home."

"That would be kind of you, Sheriff." Lucy picked up her purse and started for the door.

Cade realized that he was about to be left behind. Having no real desire to hang around with the unhappy mayor, he hurried after Mitch and the two women.

"I'll see Mrs. Thomas home, Mitch." He hustled her along before she could refuse his offer.

Melinda called after them, "Good night, Lucy. You, too, Mr. Mulroney."

Lucy stumbled along beside Cade, calling back over her shoulder, "I'm sure Daniel was just delayed, Melinda. Thank you for your support, Sheriff."

Mitch nodded and offered his arm to Melinda. They turned down the street that led to Melinda's house.

Cade finally slowed down. "I never thought to ask: if we're both here, who is staying with Mary?" Not that he was worried about it. Lucy took her responsibilities for his daughter as seriously as he did.

"Oh, I'm sorry, Cade. I should have told you that Cora was going to stay with her."

"Of course, if you had told me earlier, you would have had to confess what your plans were for this evening."

Instead of feeling guilty, Lucy actually looked rather proud of herself. "How clever of you to figure that out for yourself." Then she turned serious. "I hope I didn't cause more problems for the Society, but I felt like a point needed to be made. Mitch and one deputy can't handle this all by themselves. Two men can't be everywhere at once. They have to sleep some time."

"I'll be sure to point that out in tomorrow's paper."

"Seriously?"

"Hell, yes, but don't misunderstand me, Lucy. I still think the Luminary Society is causing more problems than you will admit. Women can read at home, if that's what they want. But even those who support your efforts are going to have a hard time convincing the men in town that women should invade town council meetings and making demands on the mayor."

That did it. Lucy turned on him with fire in her eyes.

"That goes beyond all reason, Cade Mulroney. You men," she snapped, poking him in the chest with a finger, "can hang around a place like that River Lady all night long, drinking and playing cards and who knows what else. That's all right for you, but let the women decide they want to do something for themselves instead of waiting hand and foot on a bunch of helpless men, and we're destroying society. That makes a lot of sense."

She spun away from him and hurried toward the front door of her store. Once there, she unlocked the door and walked in without waiting for him. He supposed he should be grateful that she didn't slam the door in his face and lock him out.

He caught up with her halfway up the stairs. She ignored him completely until they reached her parlor, where Cora sat reading a book. Cade looked around for his daughter, but she was nowhere in sight.

Cora pointed toward the bedroom. "Mary was tired, so I let her lie down on Lucy's bed. I'd guess she's been asleep for about half an hour or so. I hope that was all right."

"I appreciate your watching her for us, Miss Lawford. Would you allow me to see you home safely? I know Lucy would feel better knowing you weren't out there alone."

Cora looked to Lucy for advice. Considering the fight they'd just had, he was curious what she would have to say on the matter.

"That's sounds like a good idea to me. Since Mary is asleep, there's no reason for you to hurry back if you need to take care of any newspaper business."

"I would like to stop by the office for a little while, if you really don't mind."

Lucy looked suspiciously pleased. "Then it's settled. Cora, thank you again. Stop by in the morning, if you'd like, and we'll talk about the meeting tonight. Josie Turner will be here to handle any customers for me."

That was news to Cade. "I didn't know Mrs. Turner had started to work for you."

"Well, it's only for a few hours a week, but I think she'll be a big help to me."

"I'm sure that any time Josie can get away from that awful husband of hers will seem like heaven to her." Cora suddenly remembered that she and Lucy weren't alone. She blushed furiously and apologized. "I'm sorry, Mr. Mulroney. That was rude of me. Please don't say anything about what I said in the paper. It would only embarrass Josie, and it could put her in danger."

Cade was getting damn tired of Lucy's friends assuming the worst about him. "Believe it or not, Miss Lawford, I do believe that private conversations are exactly that. You don't have to worry that anything you say to me in the normal course of things will end up as tomorrow's headlines." He gave her a reassuring smile. "Besides, if anything, my opinion of Oliver Turner is even lower than yours."

"Well, at least we can agree on one thing." Cora gathered up her things. "I know my aunt will appreciate knowing I didn't have to walk home alone, Mr. Mulroney."

"I'll be back in an hour or so, Lucy. Lock up after I leave."

"I will."

Cade ran down the stairs to catch up with Cora. He offered her his arm but was surprised when she took it. The sun had set some time ago, and the side streets were dark. She shivered with a chill or nervousness—he couldn't tell.

"I wasn't sure you'd trust me to see you home."

Her steps briefly faltered. "Lucy seems to think you're safe enough."

"But you're not so sure." It wasn't a question. She'd made her opinion of him clear enough on other occasions.

"Well, it isn't as if we know each other very well," she hedged.

"True enough." They walked on in silence for a minute or two. He figured that if she had something stuck in her craw, now was the time for her to spit it out. She didn't disappoint him.

"I do have to say that you've been conveniently at hand each time Lucy has been threatened." She glanced at him to see how he'd take her remarks.

"Do I need to point out that both times I was with the sheriff, or do you suspect Mitch of being involved in whatever you think I'm up to?"

"Heavens, no," Cora assured him. "Sheriff Hughes has been a godsend for this town. I usually

don't mind walking alone now. Before he came,
Lee's Mill wasn't safe for anyone after dark."

He made note of the fact that she hadn't yet
said what she thought of him. He supposed that
her letting him see her home meant that she
trusted him on some level. Perhaps she was more
worried about Lucy for other reasons.

"Well, believe it or not, I would never harm Mrs.
Thomas."

They had reached the house Cora shared with
her elderly aunt. Light spilled through the front
window onto the sidewalk where they stood. Before
Cora walked away from him, she looked him straight
in the face, perhaps hoping to find something in
his gaze. She nodded slightly, as if she'd reached a
decision.

"I think I believe that. You might even be good
for her. Good night, Mr. Mulroney."

Stunned by that pronouncement, he managed
to mumble, "Good night, Miss Lawford."

He waited until she disappeared through the
front door before making his way back to his office. After letting himself in through the front
door, he lit a pair of lamps that hung over his desk.
He thought about pouring himself a brandy, but
he had work to do. A short one wouldn't hurt, he
decided. After taking a sip, he pulled out a stack of
fresh paper and reached for his pen.

In his mind, he tried out several different be-
ginnings for his article on the town council meeting. Nothing much had been accomplished; it
wouldn't be the first time he'd said exactly that
about the mayor's frequent meetings. Tonight had
been different, though. Never before had any of
the women in town been in attendance, and he
felt that alone was newsworthy.

How the town reacted—specifically the men—

would in large part be determined by the way he presented the facts. If he made a big deal about Lucy and Melinda daring to cross the threshold of The River Lady, their names would be fodder for the gossips in town for days. Perhaps he could just mention in passing that representatives of the Luminary Society had attended the meeting to express their concern about the recent attacks on their membership.

He wasn't fooling himself that no one would ever find out who the women were, but it was a softer way to handle the matter. That idea brought him up short. He never, ever let the way he did his job be influenced by personal feelings about the people involved. It was a sign of how infatuated he'd become with Lucy Thomas that he'd even consider such a thing.

Cursing himself for a fool, he reached for the brandy and poured himself another half glass. Leaning back in his chair, he reconsidered his position on the issue of women and town politics. On the surface, he would say that he was against it, but the more he thought about it, he wasn't sure why.

After all, the women had every right to be worried about what had been happening. It was equally obvious that the mayor and the council had no immediate plans to organize any help for Mitch. Then there was the fact that none of the three women involved had any men in their lives to step forward and make demands on their behalf. Melinda had the pastor, of course, but he was too new to the town to have much influence.

What a damn mess!

Finally, he picked up his pen and crossed out what he'd already written. After another failed attempt, the words started pouring out across the paper. When he wrote the last sentence, he put the article in his top drawer rather than out by the press, to be typeset. There would be enough time in the morning for another rewrite if he changed his mind yet again.

It was long past time to head over to Lucy's. He knew he should want to get Mary back to their own house and settled in her own bed. But the truth was, he was hoping that Lucy would have a cup of coffee and some of those good cookies of hers waiting for him. A man could get used to coming home to a woman who made him feel so welcome.

He stopped to consider the direction his thoughts were headed. Despite his sworn oath never to leave himself open to the pain a woman could cause, it was obvious that on some level he'd changed. He wasn't sure what it was that he felt for Lucy Thomas, but it felt a hell of a lot better than what he'd felt for Louisa.

The thought made him stop short of the door while he considered the matter. It was obvious that he wanted far more than mere coffee and cookies from Lucy, but exactly what, he didn't know. Having decided that much, it was time to see how much she was willing to give him. He walked out the door with a determined smile on his face.

# Chapter Thirteen

An hour after the meeting, his hands ached with the need to hurt someone. That time would come, but not yet, not tonight. He relished the thought of making those two upstart bitches pay for daring to ruin the meeting. His meeting.

How was he supposed to convince people to vote for him if he couldn't set the stage without interference from outsiders?

Damn, he hated things he couldn't control. Who would have ever thought that two so-called decent women would dare to set foot in The River Lady? Since no one else seemed to be overly upset about the incident, he feared that he was the one who had come off looking bad.

It never occurred to him until too late that he should have handled the situation with patronizing humor rather than anger. If he'd patted that Lucy Thomas on the hand, assuring her that everything would be done to protect her, he would have come out looking like a hero or, at the very least, a concerned leader.

Instead, he'd ended up at the bar, drinking too

much and sulking. What a damn fool! For every step forward, he seemed to slip back two. He couldn't afford to lose the election. Because if he did, he stood to lose a hell of a lot more than a job title.

Maybe he should have hired someone to harass the women instead of doing it himself. If only there had been a way to hire some fool without revealing his own identity, but Lee's Mill was a small town filled with busybodies who made note of every stranger who rode through. No, he'd done right to take action himself.

His eyes itched with exhaustion. Tomorrow would be soon enough to polish the details of his last attack. For now, he needed sleep more than he needed to worry about tomorrow. But, he reminded himself as he crawled into his narrow bed, the time was coming when everyone would show him the respect he deserved.

Lucy stood poised at the top of the stairs, her head tilted, listening for Cade's knock. He'd planned to be gone an hour, but that time had come and gone twice over. Had something else happened?

For lack of anything better to do, she left her post to check on Mary yet again. The little girl hadn't stirred more than an inch in the two hours since Lucy had returned from the town council meeting. Poor little mite, she must have been extra tired to fall asleep so soundly.

The thought made her smile. Mary had come a long way since that day when Cade had first brought her to visit. Back then, only a few weeks before, it had been unusual for the little girl to utter a sound. Now when something interested her, she chattered like a magpie. The two of them had shared long discussions on butterflies, lightning bugs, and whether she should change the name of her rag doll.

Neither Mary nor her father would ever know what it had meant to Lucy for them to share even this much of their lives with her. She and Cade might never agree on what a woman's role should be when it came to family, but she'd never felt so complete in her life.

In part, her newfound satisfaction was due to the Society and the friendships she found there, but through Mary she was experiencing the joys of motherhood. She wasn't fooling herself that a child would have made her marriage a happy one, but at least she wouldn't be so alone now. The only way to change her situation was to remarry. Until recently, she would never have considered that a possibility. That she was willing to entertain that idea, even for a moment, was a major shift in her thinking.

The real question that plagued her was the reason behind her changing attitude. Was it because of Mary? Or was it because of Mary's father?

Rather than follow that line of thought, she resumed her position to listen for Cade. This time, her patience was rewarded with a series of sharp raps at the front door of the store. She drew a calming breath before descending the stairs. A familiar profile filled the window below.

As soon as she opened the door, Cade slipped inside. "I apologize for being so late. I lost all track of time."

"Don't worry about it," she reassured him as she led the way upstairs. Over her shoulder, she asked, "Dare I ask what was so riveting?"

"I needed to finish the article on tonight's town

council meeting." His steps slowed to a stop just short of reaching the top. "I wasn't sure what to say." He sounded more puzzled than frustrated by the situation.

She was tempted to ask what he had decided to report, but tomorrow would be soon enough to face that particular problem. "Why don't you make yourself comfortable in the parlor? I have coffee made if you have time to sit a spell."

"Any chance of having some cookies to go with it?"

She laughed at the hopeful note in his voice. "Yes, Mr. Mulroney, I have a plate of cookies set aside just for you."

He took the last few steps two at a time. "Then in that case, I would love to have some coffee. Would you mind if I check on Mary first?"

"No, of course not. She's slept the whole time you were gone. I don't know what the two of you did today that wore her out, but it must have been quite strenuous. I don't think I've ever seen someone sleep so soundly."

As Cade peeked in on Mary, Lucy carried the coffee and cookies to the parlor. Once there, she faced the dilemma of where to sit. The chair would be more proper, but it would make it awkward to serve the meager refreshments. On the other hand, if she shared the sofa with Cade, he might think she was being forward.

A heavy footstep warned her that her time was up. She quickly set the tray down on the table and perched on the end of the sofa. Let Cade think what he would. She'd made her feelings on the subject of men in general clear to him on more than one occasion. That she was lying to herself as well as to him was beside the point.

When Cade stepped into the room, her heart

stuttered and started racing. She clenched her fists in her lap, willing her wayward body back under control. Several slow breaths did little to ease the ache that stirred inside her.

Knowing full well that her reactions were both foolhardy and inappropriate didn't make a bit of difference. Maybe she was still feeling the effects of the past few days: the attack on her home, attending the meeting at The River Lady, the argument with Cade on the way home. But whatever the cause, even her skin seemed too tight, as if something hot and needy was building up inside her. She could only hope that Cade swigged down his coffee and left quickly before she did something foolish.

Cade sank down on the other end of the sofa, but that didn't leave nearly enough distance between the two of them. If he was aware of her, he gave no indication of it. To give herself something to do other than stare, she leaned forward to pour the coffee.

"Would you like some sugar?" Biting her lip, she hoped that he took that question at face value. Trying to keep her own expression neutral, she glanced at Cade to await his response.

Despite a suspicious gleam in his eyes, he very politely answered, "Yes, thank you."

As soon as she held out his cup, he grabbed a handful of cookies off the plate and then accepted his drink. She fixed her own, all the while wishing she could come up with a topic of conversation that wouldn't stir up trouble of one sort or another.

Cade didn't seem to notice that the silence had stretched on so long, but then, he was happily devouring the cookies one after another. Judging by the satisfied look on his face, they met with his approval.

"It's easy to see where Mary got her sweet tooth," she teased.

He paused between bites long enough to respond. "I like all kinds of sweet things." As he spoke, his voice deepened and his eyes darkened to the color of molten silver, sending a shiver through her when he added, "That includes you, Lucy."

The temperature in the room changed radically in the space of a heartbeat. Whether it was suddenly too cold or too hot was a matter of opinion. Her hands trembled so much that she had to set down her cup rather than risk spilling it.

Cade waited patiently for her response. Words were his business. They didn't come so easily to her. She settled for honesty rather than fancy.

"You frighten me."

He accepted that without comment. Instead, he set down his own cup and put back the last two cookies. Moving slowly, he slid across the short space between them. One hand slipped around Lucy's shoulders; the other cupped her chin gently.

"Don't be afraid of me, Lucy. I'll try to go slowly, but I have to tell you that even this much distance is too much." He leaned in close to brush his lips across hers. "I've wanted to do this since that first night."

She didn't have to ask which night he meant, although he gave her time to think about it. The memory of that experience had been simmering in the back of her mind every time she'd been with him since. As much as she wanted to give in to the temptation of Cade Mulroney, common sense demanded that she protect herself from the pain he might cause.

However, since her husband's death, she'd prided herself on facing whatever problems life threw her way, no matter what. And right now there was one large problem sitting right next to her. She studied Cade's face, taking note of each line etched there by life, the silver glints in his hair, and the stern mouth that felt so right when he kissed her. In truth, the way she felt when Cade kissed her was like nothing she'd ever experienced before. If she let this chance go by, she might very well never find it again.

Feeling as if she were leaping off the bluff to the river below, she gave herself over to the moment and kissed him back. Her eyes drifted shut as sensations flooded her mind. With far more gentleness than she would have given him credit for, Cade teased her lips apart and deepened the kiss. His arms encircled her as he lifted her onto his lap.

She knew she should protest that it was too much, too soon, but she didn't care. He made her ache in places that had been dormant for far too long. Deep inside her, she felt absolutely right about sharing this moment with this man.

Cade halfway expected Lucy to slap him senseless for what he was doing, but instead she had become a willing participant. Considering her enthusiastic response to his kiss, he dared to palm her breast with a gentle squeeze. To his delight, she moaned as she leaned into his hand to increase the pressure of his caress.

He kneaded her soft flesh slowly, letting the tension between them build. Lucy arched her back, offering him better access to nibble his way up her graceful neck. He needed to touch more than the soft cotton of her clothing. One by one, he undid the buttons of her dress. As each one eased free, he expected her to stop him, but when he stopped briefly, she urged his hand to finish its job.

To his delight, she began working on his shirt. When her seeking fingers slid inside the small opening she'd made, he thought he would die of the pleasure. As he tugged her dress down off her shoulders, he took the straps of her chemise with it. The sight of the sweet woman's flesh revealed to him made him burn.

With honest admiration, he whispered, "Lucy Thomas, you are truly lovely." He leaned down, and using lips and tongue, he paid homage to the beauty before him.

Lucy leaned back even farther, pulling him down beside her on the sofa. He fought the tangle of her skirt to get even closer. Finally, with a muttered curse, he reached down and slipped her skirt up to her thighs, giving them both the freedom they needed to discover new sensations as their legs entwined.

"Kiss me again," Lucy demanded, tugging his face to meet hers in a soul-searing taste of heaven itself.

He obliged her. She tugged his shirt loose from his trousers and ran her palms up his back, pausing every so often to dig in her nails, to urge him on. Her legs stirred in restless invitation. Finally, he wrapped one of her legs around his waist, pushing the hard evidence of his need more firmly against the core of her heat.

When he started rocking against her, Lucy whimpered and offered her lush breasts up for more attention. He suckled first one, then the other, drawing in the sweet taste of Lucy's skin. The need to finish what they'd started pounded in his mind, but she deserved the chance to decide for herself.

He pushed himself up on his elbows, but that small distance between them wasn't enough to clear his mind of her scent, her beauty. Drawing a ragged breath, he tried to string together the right words.

"I can stop if you want me to, Lucy. Lord knows that's the last thing I want to do, but I will if you say so. No matter what it does to my sanity."

She stared up at him, her dark eyes sleepy-looking with passion, her lips swollen from his kisses. The feminine power of her answering smile surged through his body, renewing the need to take her right there on the too-small sofa.

He rose up onto his knees and shrugged his shirt the rest of the way off, tossing it to the floor. The need to mount her was riding him too fiercely to allow for such luxuries as dispensing with more than the minimum of clothing. Finally, he yanked her skirt up and his trousers down and took her with one powerful thrust.

She gasped at the sudden invasion, but when he tried to pull back, she protested.

"No, don't stop. I want you."

He kissed her deeply before saying, "I'm afraid I'll hurt you."

"I'm not that fragile, Cade Mulroney." She wrapped her legs tightly around his hips, forcing him closer to the center of her being.

Despite her protests, he started off moving slowly, but his good intentions didn't last all that long. She met him thrust for thrust, panting her approval and driving him on until the whole damn world shattered and spun around them. Lucy's keening satisfaction was almost lost in his own shout of release.

Then, as the world righted itself around them, he savored the sweet satisfaction. The moment of peace was short-lived.

The sound of a sleepy voice came floating down the hall from the bedroom. "Father, Lucy, where are you? Is it time to go home?"

In just that short time, Lucy went from looking well satisfied to horror-struck. Immediately, she began pushing him off her as she struggled to get away from him before Mary came wandering in.

Cade stopped Lucy's struggle by anchoring her hands over her head. "Lie still, damn it."

"Get off me now before she sees us!"

"I will, but take it easy." Then he pitched his voice to carry as far as Lucy's bedroom. "Wait there, Mary, and I'll come get you in just a minute. Lucy and I have something we have to finish."

"All right. I just wondered where you were." Luckily, Mary sounded more asleep than awake.

For several long seconds, both adults strained to listen for the sound of footsteps, but none were forthcoming. Satisfied that they were in no immediate danger of being discovered, Cade eased his hold on Lucy.

Much as he regretted the necessity, he pushed himself back and then scrambled to his feet. Feeling less than gentlemanly at the moment, nevertheless he held out his hand to help Lucy up off the sofa. His temper slipped a notch or two when she refused to meet his gaze and turned her back to him. Taking only enough time to fasten the front of his trousers and to locate his shirt, he waited for Lucy to put herself back together.

It damn well better be embarrassment and not regret that had her acting this way.

"Lucy, she doesn't know what happened between us."

"No, but we do." Her cheeks were stained with patches of red. She pointedly kept her eyes from looking in his direction.

"Yes, we do." He let a little of his own frustration show when he all but yanked her back into his arms. "I'll tell you this much: I don't regret a minute of the time we spent on that sofa or what we did, Lucy Thomas. I hope like hell that you don't, either."

She didn't answer. He took some encouragement from the fact that she didn't struggle to get free of him.

"Lucy, at least look at me."

Slowly she lifted her eyes. He brushed her hair back from her face. "I wish I didn't have to go, but I do."

Lucy nodded and started to step back. He almost let her go, but he needed to reassure her somehow that if it weren't for Mary, wild horses wouldn't have dragged him away from her right then.

A kiss was the best he could do. He could only hope that it was enough. He didn't know what to think when Lucy scrambled back away from him the second he loosened his grasp of her.

"Are you coming, Father?" Mary was starting to sound worried.

He muttered a curse under his breath. "I'm on my way now, Mary." He had no choice but to go.

"Lucy, we'll talk tomorrow."

It hurt like hell that she didn't bother to answer.


Mercifully, for once she'd been able to sleep soundly all night long. That didn't make morning any easier to face, but she was grateful anyway. If only she didn't have both Josie Turner and Cora due to arrive in just a matter of minutes. At least Melinda had plans with Daniel. She simply wasn't up to facing the pastor any more than she wanted to see Cade this morning.

Or ever.

No matter how many times her mirror told her otherwise, she was convinced that one or both of the two women would take one look at her face and know how far she'd fallen. Her memories of the night before hadn't faded one bit, leaving her all too aware of how wantonly she'd behaved. Making love in the parlor of all places! Not to mention that they'd done so on the sofa with all the lamps lit.

Then there was the small matter of Cade's daughter, sleeping only a short distance down the hall. If it weren't for the grace of God, Mary would have come looking for her father instead of calling out their names. How on earth would they have explained to the little girl what they'd been doing?

Lord of mercy, she had herself blushing again. Determined to put the whole experience behind her, she marched downstairs to open the store. Her personal life might be a disaster, but she couldn't afford to let her livelihood suffer right along with it.

No sooner had she unlocked the front door than Josie appeared. Lucy had grown fond of the younger woman. Considering her background, it was a wonder that Josie had managed to hang on to such a cheerful nature. On the other hand, it wasn't at all surprising that around men she was shy and hesitant. Lucy understood why all too well. Anyone married to a vicious weakling such as Oliver Turner had good reason to be cautious.

"Right on time, Josie." She gave her the best smile she could muster. "Do you think you can handle the store on your own for a while this morning? Cora Lawford is coming by in a few minutes, and I need to finish my orders for the week."

Her eyes huge at the thought of all that responsibility, Josie gave her a slow nod. "Yes, ma'am, I'll do my best."

"I know you will." She patted the girl on the shoulder. "Now, you know where I keep the ledgers. If you're not sure what to write down, make notes on another paper, and I'll help you transfer the information later. If someone needs to barter for their purchases, do as you see fit."

From the way Josie worried at her lower lip, that was clearly more than she'd expected to have to deal with. Lucy wanted to help Josie learn new skills, not to scare her off. She put her arm around Josie's shoulder and gave her a quick hug. "Don't let it overwhelm you. Remember, I'll be right there in the storeroom if you need me. If you have questions, come on in and ask them."

Josie's smile brightened right back up again. "I'll get the feather duster and start on the shelves, Mrs. Thomas. Then I'll see to the sweeping."

"Call me Lucy, and that sounds fine." She handed Josie her spare apron. "You'll need this because things get pretty dusty this time of year. I'll go get started on the orders. If Cora comes in, send her on back."

"Yes, ma'am."

Lucy figured it would take a while longer for her new helper to get used to calling her by her first name. As the daughter of the town drunk, Josie had very limited experience dealing with folks she considered her betters.

It had been a real joy to see her blossom under the tutelage of Melinda. Now that Josie was learning to read and cipher, a whole new world was opening up before her. There were still a lot of words she didn't know, but she kept at whatever text Melinda assigned her until she knew it forward and backward. She was a quick learner, and given the chance, she would be able to improve her lot in life.

Lucy frowned. Considering the wealth of Josie's father-in-law, it was an absolute shame that she had to live in that nasty little cabin she shared with Oliver. Unfortunately, Oliver's father considered Josie undeserving of his worthless son. So did most everyone else, but for the opposite reasons.

Well, there wasn't much she could do for Josie except to offer her a job and encourage her to continue with her studies. After all, she had her own plateful of problems to deal with. Leaving Josie to get started on her chores, Lucy picked up her papers and headed into the storeroom.

The familiar routine helped to soothe her, so that when Cora finally arrived, Lucy was in a far better frame of mind.

"Good morning, Lucy."

Lucy had been kneeling down to count the items in a packing crate. She looked up and smiled. "You look particularly chipper this morning."

"Yes, well, Aunt Henrietta left on the stage this morning for Columbia. She sees a doctor there."

"Nothing serious, I hope."

Cora settled down on a handy stack of boxes. "Personally, I don't think she has anything at all wrong with her. Doc, here in town, holds the same opinion, so she thinks he's a fool. The one she sees in Columbia agrees with whatever she tells him. Besides, she likes to brag about needing to see a specialist."

Lucy knew she should disapprove of her friend's flippant attitude about her elderly relative's health, but she figured Cora had the right of it.

"How long will she be gone?"

"A couple of days."

Now, that was cause for worry. "Will you be all right by yourself? Considering everything that has gone on these last couple of weeks, I'm surprised that she left you behind."

"The only reason she would is that I told her that I could stay with you. I hope that was all right, but her decision to go was rather sudden. There wasn't time to ask you first."

"Of course it's fine. To tell you the truth, I'll be glad for the company." *Especially because Cora's presence would prevent any chance of a repeat of last night,* she added to herself. Cora's next statement caused Lucy's stomach to lurch until she realized that her friend was talking about an entirely different subject.

"Well, now that we've settled that, tell me about last night." Cora had a devilish sparkle in her eyes. "What was it like, walking into The River Lady? I want details, details, details. The *Clarion* hasn't come out yet, so I don't even know what Cade had to say about it."

Lucy picked up on Cora's use of his first name. "Cade, is it? Since when are you two on such a friendly basis? Usually, you have much more interesting names for him."

Even in the dim light of the storeroom, Lucy could tell that Cora was blushing. "Well, uh, we had a nice talk last night when he walked me home.

I decided that maybe he wasn't such a bad sort after all."

Lucy put the lid back on the crate before moving on to the one below it. When she tried to lift it, Cora hurried to help her.

"Then you believe me when I tell you that he isn't behind the attacks?"

"I guess. But you know, I almost wish I didn't," Cora admitted as they shifted the heavy boxes around. "It was easier not to be frightened when I thought I knew who was responsible. Now I look at every man I pass and wonder if he's the one."

Lucy shivered despite the heat of the day. "I know. I try to draw comfort from knowing which men are trustworthy." She ticked them off on her fingers. "Sheriff Hughes, Pastor Hayes, Cade Mulroney."

"Three out of the whole town isn't saying much," Cora pointed out. "Surely there are more."

"Oh, I'm sure that's true. But those are the ones I have the most contact with and feel I could depend on in an emergency." She went back to counting the dry goods, hoping Cora had forgotten her original purpose in coming. She should have known better.

"So, quit trying to avoid answering my question. What was it like sitting in a saloon? I've heard there was a painting of a woman over the bar and"—she leaned forward and dropped her voice to a whisper—"she's naked!"

Thoroughly shocked, Lucy lost count. "Where on earth did you hear that? Who have you been talking to?"

Cora giggled. "Never you mind about who. I just want to know if it is true."

"To be honest, I didn't notice." That much was

true. She'd been concentrating too hard on finding a quiet corner in which to hide to really look the place over.

"Didn't notice? How could you miss something like that?" Cora shook her head. "You'd make a poor spy, Lucy, if you missed seeing a naked lady."

"Well, never you mind about such a thing. I, for one, had more to do than to look for tasteless artwork, and I'm sure that Melinda will tell you the same. Besides, a young lady should have no interest in such things."

"Balderdash, Lucy Thomas," Cora said, laughing. "The fact that I'm not supposed to do something only makes it that much more interesting." She tilted her head to consider something. "Since you've turned out to be such a failure in this, I'll just have to ask a certain newspaperman next time I see him."

"Cora Lawford, don't you dare ask Cade . . ."

"Ask me what?"

The unexpected sound of Cade's voice startled Lucy into dropping the crate lid she was moving. Unfortunately, she didn't quite get her foot out of the way in time. Pain shot up her leg, causing her to go stumbling back. She managed to control her fall, landing awkwardly on another crate.

Cade and Cora both rushed to her side, making her feel even more foolish. She waved them back. "I'm fine. Clumsy, maybe, but fine."

"Are you sure?" Cora asked, still hovering over her.

"That I'm clumsy or that I'm fine?" Lucy managed to lighten her tart response with a smile. "My foot hurts but not as much as my pride."

Cade offered her a hand up off the low crate. She hesitated before accepting his help, unsure how she would react to his touch. But to refuse would only make Cora suspicious that something was going on. Gingerly, Lucy put her hand in his. Other than a slight smile, he showed no indication that he'd noticed her reluctance.

Once she was back on her feet, Cade turned his attention to Cora. "Now, what were you going to ask me?"

"Cora, don't you dare!"

"Lucy, you sound exactly like my aunt. If I want to ask Cade a question, I will."

"Well, even Henrietta is right some of the time," Lucy reminded her as she gathered up her papers.

"Oh, come on, Lucy. I just want to know."

Cade leaned against the doorway, looking as if he had all day to wait while the two women bickered back and forth. Finally, he took charge.

"I'll tell you what. Lucy, I assume Cora wants to know something that you consider inappropriate for someone of her tender years." He winked at Cora to let her know that he was teasing. "Lucy, why don't you whisper to me what it is and let me decide?"

Lucy didn't like it, but it was obvious Cora wasn't going to give up until she got her way. "Fine." Of course, it also meant that she was going to have to let Cade get way too close for her peace of mind. She held her breath while he took the few steps to position himself directly in front of her.

"Well?" The corners of his eyes crinkled in good humor, almost daring her to object when he leaned down within kissing distance.

The scoundrel knew full well that his presence was making her jittery, but she managed to maintain a calm demeanor. She pitched her words for his ears only. "She wants to know if there is a painting of a naked lady over the bar at The River Lady."

His laughter rang out loudly in the confines of the storeroom. He grinned at Lucy before turning to shake his finger at Cora. "Miss Lawford, that is no subject for a lady to wonder about, but the answer is no. There's a long mirror over the bar."

Clearly disappointed, Cora announced, "I need a cool drink. Lucy, can I bring you anything?"

The last thing Lucy wanted was for Cora to leave her alone with Cade, but she could hardly say so. "I'd love a glass of water."

When Cora had sailed out of the door, Cade moved closer to Lucy. This time she did back away as her pulse raced. He followed her, finally leaning in close to her, with his hand on the wall over her shoulder. Even though he wasn't touching her, she could still feel the heat of his body as if he were. She desperately tried to think of what to say. Something that had nothing to do with what had happened the night before, even if that was all she could think about, surrounded as she was by his scent and warmth.

"Is that true? About the picture, I mean."

"Why, Mrs. Thomas, did you think I would lie to Cora? Especially when I finally have her convinced that I'm not in league with Lucifer himself."

"Well . . ."

He acted hurt. "No, I told her God's own truth. There *is* a mirror over the bar." His voice dropped low and rough as he whispered, "Besides, the naked lady is on the other wall."

The rogue! His wicked smile invited her to share the joke. She tried her best to look disapproving, but it was impossible to do in the face of such outrageousness. What started off as a giggle grew into outright laughter. She sank back against the wall and held her sides, trying without success to catch her breath.

"Cade Mulroney," she gasped out between bouts of laughter, "you do have a slippery way of using words. Must be from writing all those editorials telling people the truth the way you want them to hear it."

Some of the humor died in his eyes. "Lucy, I don't use my paper to spread lies."

The need to laugh faded when she saw how her comment had affected him. "Cade, I know that. I may not always agree with what you have to say, but I know that you don't use your paper for your own purposes. I never meant to insult you."

She couldn't resist the need to touch him as she offered her apology. Brushing her fingers along his rugged jawline, she followed the caress with a quick kiss on his cheek, breathing in the scent of bay rum.

Cade cocked his head as if listening for something. Lucy looked around him to see what had caught his attention. The sound of approaching footsteps had the two of them moving to put some distance between them. Evidently, Cade was in no more of a hurry than she was to have anyone find out that there was anything going on between the two of them.

When Cora walked back in carrying a tray with empty glasses and a pitcher of water, Lucy was hard at work writing out her order. Cade was in the opposite corner poking around in a pile of new shirts. If Cora suspected anything had happened in her absence, she gave no indication of it.

"I brought one for you, too." She held a glass out to Cade and then gave Lucy the other one.

"Thank you," Cade told her with a smile.

Lucy took note of the slight blush that crept up Cora's cheeks. "This tastes good. This room not only gets hot, but dust collects in here no matter how often I sweep."

Cade drained his own glass and set it back on the tray. "I'd better be going. It's almost time for the *Clarion* to come off the presses."

Lucy had good reason to worry about this particular edition. She couldn't very well demand to know what he'd had to say about last night's meeting, not when she'd already insulted his honor only minutes before.

As if he sensed her concern, he stopped in the doorway. "You'll find today's edition interesting, but I don't think you'll find it upsetting."

With that cryptic remark, he disappeared from sight. Lucy stared at the empty doorway for another heartbeat, maybe two, before Cora cleared her throat.

"Hmmm, now, what was that all about?"

Caught staring like a schoolgirl with a crush. "What? Oh, that. After you left last night, he stayed at his office for quite a while working on his report on the town council meeting." She considered her words carefully. "He wasn't sure what points to emphasize."

Cora was nothing if not persistent. "Which brings us back to why I came over in the first place. What happened?"

"All right, here it is in a nutshell. Melinda and I shook like leaves when we walked in. The whole place immediately got real quiet, and then everyone started crowding around us and staring. Luckily, Cade and Sheriff Hughes saw us come in. Cade invited us to join them at their table." No reason to tell Cora that he'd dragged her along like a dog on a leash.

"Once the mayor started the meeting, he didn't much appreciate seeing the two of us in the audience. He accused Cade of inviting us. Mr. Bradford picked up on the mayor's refusal to discuss our questions and made it into another campaign issue. However, I don't believe either of them is serious about solving the problem."

"I wish I had been there."

"To tell the truth, I wish I hadn't been. Perhaps we'd have been wiser to put our concerns in writing and then have a man represent our views. Pastor Hayes, perhaps, or even Cade."

Josie appeared in the doorway. "I'm sorry to bother you, Lucy, but a customer wants to barter some cut wood for flour, beans, and such. I looked back in the ledgers but didn't see anything similar to judge its value by."

"That's fine, Josie. Tell him I'll be right on out. I was about finished in here, anyway." Turning to Cora, she added, "I've got to get back to work. Can we talk more tonight?"

"That will be fine. I need to gather up a few things to bring with me. Are you sure you don't mind me staying with you?"

"No, I'll enjoy the company."

"Then at least let me cook dinner."

"That sounds heavenly. I do get weary of preparing meals just for myself."

"I'll be back around five."

After Cora left, Lucy looked around the room and decided that she'd done enough to figure out her next orders. Perhaps Josie could stay on a while longer while she wrote them up. For now, she'd go try to figure out how many pounds of flour and beans equaled a load of wood.

# Chapter Fourteen

Cade followed his daughter into the house. Disappointment left a bitter taste in his mouth. He'd been counting on spending the evening with Lucy, but that plan had failed. Although he liked Cora Lawford, he dearly wished she'd gone to Columbia with her nasty old aunt.

He hadn't missed the fact that Lucy was feeling a bit skittish around him. While he knew the reason, he wasn't quite sure what to do about it. She hadn't exactly run when he'd cornered her in the storeroom, but she hadn't exactly thrown herself into his arms, either.

Mary tugged on his sleeve. "Are we going to the hotel soon?"

He looked down into his daughter's sweet face and ruffled her hair. "It's a little bit early to eat. Are you hungry? I could fix something to hold you over until our usual dinnertime."

"No, that's all right. I can wait," she assured him, but she was clearly disappointed.

He knelt down to her height. "All right, Mary,

what's going on? If you're not hungry, why the big rush to eat early?"

"I heard that they have strawberry shortcake tonight."

"And you're afraid they'll run out before we get there." Knowing it was one of her favorites, he didn't phrase it as a question.

She nodded vigorously. "Sheriff Hughes told Lucy that he was going to order his dessert first and then eat his vegetables if he had any room left. He's awfully big. What if he eats it all?"

"Did you tell him that you'd like to have some?" Cade was willing to bet his shy daughter hadn't spoken a word. Although she had become more outgoing when she was around Lucy and her friends, she still seemed to be rather shy around men.

To his surprise, however, she nodded vigorously. "I did. I told the sheriff that you and I would both want some. He said that he might leave a little for me, but you were on your own." She frowned. "I guess I would have to share mine with you. It would be the polite thing to do."

"Well, let's not let it get to that. I don't like the idea of Sheriff Hughes eating all our dessert, either. Let's go see if we can beat him to it."

Mary rewarded him with a hug and a sloppy kiss on his cheek. He held her close, soaking up extra warmth for all the years that he'd missed. If eating strawberry shortcake for dinner and vegetables for dessert made her happy, then so be it. Tomorrow they'd eat extra vegetables to make up for it.

When she wiggled free of his embrace, she immediately skipped out the door and waited impatiently for him to follow. Once he was outside, he cast one last longing look at the store next door, wishing like hell that Lucy were coming with them. Or, even better, that he could figure out a way to spend another night on her sofa or in her bed.

But with Cora Lawford moving in with Lucy for the next couple of days, the likelihood of that was all but gone. He could only hope that during the time they'd have to be at arm's length, her passion for him wouldn't cool. Damn, but his bed had seemed lonelier than usual when he'd left her alone to take his daughter home.

Now that he'd tasted her passion, he wasn't about to give her up. There was too much about the woman he liked and admired, sex being only part of it. There were women at The River Lady who could take care of that problem if that were all he needed to make his life complete.

"Come on, Father, before someone gets our table!"

Mary was waiting for him a short distance ahead. He'd been so lost in thought that he'd drifted to a complete stop on the sidewalk. No wonder his daughter sounded so exasperated with him.

"Sorry, honey, I was thinking."

She waited until he'd caught up with her again, and took his hand. This time she wasn't taking any chances. She tugged him along as fast as her little legs would take them until they reached the hotel. He played the gentleman and opened the door for her. She accepted the gesture as no more than her due and sailed past him through the small lobby and right into the dining room.

The horror on her face when she realized that despite her best efforts, Mitch had gotten there first was a sight to see. Not only that, he was sitting at their favorite table. That didn't stop Cade's daughter. She marched right up to her normal chair and stared at Mitch until he realized that she expected him to pull out her seat for her.

"Sorry, Miss Mary, I don't know what happened to my manners." The tall lawman helped her into her seat and then pushed her closer to the table.

Cade took his own seat. "She was worried that you were going to hog all the shortcake."

Mitch laughed. "I wouldn't dare. Not when the prettiest girl in town likes it as much as I do." He winked at Mary, letting her know for certain she was the one he was talking about.

"Then I assume we can actually eat our meal and save the shortcake for afterwards?"

"I had Belle set three servings aside just for us, so we can eat our meal at our leisure."

The three of them placed their orders. Mary played with her doll while the two men made idle conversation. Cade knew Mitch had been keeping a close eye on the women of the Society, so he decided he should tell him about Cora.

"By the way, Cora Lawford will be staying with Lucy the next couple of nights. Her aunt left for Columbia on the stage, and Cora didn't want to stay alone."

"Thanks for letting me know. With all the stuff that's been going on, I like to know where those women are at all times." Mitch leaned back, balancing his chair on two legs. "I wish I knew who was stirring up trouble."

"You'll catch him eventually."

"I've got some ideas about that." Mitch looked pointedly at Mary and then back to Cade. "Maybe I'll stop by later when we can talk."

"I'll be home all evening. My brandy is better than what they serve at The River Lady." His mouth curved up in a slight smile. "Remind me to tell you about a conversation I had with Lucy Thomas and Cora Lawford this morning. I think you'll find it funny as hell."

"Father!"

"Sorry, Mary, I didn't mean to use that word in front of you." She'd taken to nagging him about his language, sounding much like her maternal grandmother. It didn't bother him, though, because he took it as a sign that Mary was no longer afraid of him.

Their hostess was bearing down on them with a tray heaped with food. Although his intentions were still to find a woman to cook for them, he'd yet to do much serious looking. The food at the hotel was better than most, but also he couldn't imagine any other woman in his kitchen than the petite brunette who lived next door.

That he also wanted Lucy in his bed only made the idea that much more appealing.

Meanwhile, the three of them tucked into their dinners, satisfied that there would be bowls of shortcake and strawberries to follow.


With Mary tucked into bed in her room upstairs, Cade was free to relax and wait for Mitch to come by. He'd already laid out a pair of glasses, two of his best cigars, and the promised bottle of brandy. While he waited, the need to watch the building next door had him lurking behind the curtain, watching for anything suspicious. The sun had set an hour before, and once again the darker side of life in Lee's Mill was starting to emerge.

Only a few minutes before, Oliver Turner had passed by with his much beleaguered wife at his side. If Turner wasn't already drunk, he was well on his way. Although he'd had a drink or two with the man, Cade never had cared much for mean drunks. He had nothing but pity for Mrs. Turner. From what Lucy had told him about the woman, Josie's life hadn't been easy to begin with, and her marriage hadn't improved it at all.

His reverie was brought to an abrupt halt by the sound of Mitch's big fist on the front door. Cade hurried to let him in before the racket woke up Mary.

"Sorry I'm late." Mitch stalked into the room. As soon as he spied the brandy, he headed straight for it.

Cade hung back and let his friend deal with his anger in his own way. Once Mitch had his drink and his smoke, Cade reached for his own glass.

"Something has you riled up. What happened?"

"Mayor Kelly." Mitch puffed his cigar until his face was lost in a cloud of smoke. "I sometimes wonder how in the hell he got elected in the first place."

Cade carefully framed his answer. "Well, I would guess that either he bribed everybody in town or else he held the election when no one was looking."

Mitch's answering laugh had very little in the way of humor in it. "I swear that little weasel doesn't give a damn about anybody or anything except holding meetings and throwing his weight around."

Cade motioned Mitch toward the sofa. "Skinny as he is, you wouldn't think that would work for him."

"Well, he does his damnedest to make my life miserable. Now he thinks I'm spending too much time worrying about the Society women. He figures they brought the trouble on themselves."

"The hell you say!" Cade tossed back half a glass of brandy, which burned its way down his throat.

"Even if I agree with him about that part of it, someone has to stop the threats before Lucy gets hurt!" Rather belatedly, he added, "Not to mention Miss Lawford and Miss Smythe."

Mitch arched an eyebrow in Cade's direction. "Well, I've been ordered to spend my time watching over the whole town, not just those three women. Hellfire, what does the man think I've been doing. I haven't had a full night's sleep in over a week, and my deputy looks half dead." He emptied his glass and reached for the bottle. "You were right, by the way."

"I usually am, but what about this time?"

"This brandy is better than that stuff they serve down the street."

Mitch sat in contented silence for the next few minutes, seeming to take great pleasure in the combined sins of alcohol and tobacco. Finally, he set his glass down and flicked the last of his cigar into the fireplace. He stared at the floor for several seconds before speaking.

"I've got a real bad feeling about this mess with the women. I know you don't approve of what Lucy and Melinda and the rest have been up to, but I don't see it myself. Take that Josie Turner." He shook his head. "She's never had even half a chance, what with a drunk for a father and another one for a husband. Those women, though, they've done what nobody else has ever done by helping Josie. She has a chance to make something of herself. Hell, half the time I don't think she gets enough to eat, not with Oliver drinking up every dime he makes."

He looked up to meet Cade's gaze. "For that alone, we owe them."

The pain in Mitch's eyes made Cade flinch. He had to wonder if the sheriff's protective instincts were a little stronger than they should be when it came to Josie Turner. But it was none of his business, especially considering his own feelings on the subject of men and other men's wives.

"Maybe we've all been a little harsh about the Society. I still don't hold with women in politics, even if some of what they've done is admirable." He frowned. "But my neck itches every time I'm over at Lucy's, like someone is out there staring. I thought I was imagining things, but then I found this sitting on my doorstep when we got home from dinner tonight."

Cade picked up an envelope off the mantel and tossed to Mitch, who unfolded the letter inside and quickly scanned the page. Then he started over at the top, this time reading it aloud.

> *Dear Editor:*
> *It would seem that the fine town of Lee's Mill has been deceived by two so-called ladies of the Luminary Society. Since only whores frequent The River Lady, it is therefore logical to assume that Melinda Smythe and Lucinda Thomas have now shown their true colors."*

Mitch paused and let out a low whistle.

> *"I am outraged to realize that unless we take immediate action, the children of our town will be taught by a woman of low virtue who has already corrupted our new pastor. It is bad enough that their parents continue to buy all their supplies from a slut. If no one else will stop this outrage, I will."*

"You going to print this?"
"Hell, no, but I don't see how we can ignore it

either." His worry over Lucy's safety had his gut churning.

"I'd better get back out there." Mitch handed the paper back to Cade. "Keep this someplace safe. I'll want to look at it again."

"Why don't you put it with the others at your office?" Cade asked as he put the letter back in its envelope.

"Because somebody has been going through my papers. At least one of the notes from the rocks is gone. I know it wasn't my deputy, because I asked, and I trust him. Until I figure out who it is, I'd just as soon not put anything else there that might go missing." Mitch picked up his hat.

Cade thought some more. "There can't be that many people who would be able to justify their presence in the jailhouse without arousing suspicion."

"Exactly. It's the first mistake this bastard has made." Mitch looked determined. "I even have my suspicions, but nothing to back them up."

"I don't suppose you want to tell me who you have in mind?" Cade asked as he unlocked the door to let the lawman out.

Mitch's teeth grinned whitely in the darkness outside. "No, but you're smarter than most. I bet you can figure it out on your own. Thanks for the brandy and cigar. I owe you."

As Mitch disappeared down the alley, Cade stared after him and pondered the various men who might be on the sheriff's list of suspects. No one immediately came to mind, but he wouldn't give up. Tomorrow he'd give the matter more serious thought. For now, he'd put out the lights and stand vigil for a while longer.

*   *   *

He chewed his nails and wondered if he'd gone too far this time. Every word in the letter had been heartfelt and sincere. For the good of the town, someone had to step up and point out that those women had gone too far. It sure wasn't going to be the sheriff; hell, he'd laughed about the whole thing.

And tomorrow he'd know for sure if Cade Mulroney was still on his side. After scouring today's paper from front to back, he was beginning to have his doubts. The real test would be if the man published his letter in the next issue.

If so, fine. If not, well, then there were going to be serious repercussions. The newspaper office was conveniently close to the store. What happened to one could easily happen to the other. In fact, he'd make damn sure of it.

Come to think of it, had anyone else taken note of how much time Mulroney was spending with Lucinda Thomas? Granted, he often left his daughter in the whore's care, but one had to wonder what else was going on. Had she succeeded in corrupting more than just the women in Lee's Mill?

She would have a high price to pay for her transgressions. They all would. For now, though, he would watch and wait to see which side of the fence Cade Mulroney would come down on.

"Melinda, I understand, but there isn't much I can do at this point."

Daniel knew his own limitations better than most men, and Melinda Smythe was pushing him hard. He hated refusing her anything, but this time he had no choice. If she was going to be a pastor's wife, she had to learn that he took his responsibilities very seriously. There were some things he would not—could not—do.

"But, Daniel, someone has to say something." Melinda stood across the room, her arms clasped around her chest.

"I know but . . ." His words trailed off. They'd been arguing for the past half an hour. It had all been said before.

Melinda shivered in the pale sunlight shining through the vestry window. "We're not wanting to take over the entire service, Daniel. Just long enough to tell folks what is going on."

"The pulpit is not the place to air public grievances. If I let you do it, then every time someone has a problem, they're going to demand the right to do the same. Can't you just see Mayor Kelly up there asking people to vote for him?"

"Not people, Daniel. Men."

Even with her back to him, he could see that his words hurt her. He crossed the room, wanting to offer what comfort he could, if she would accept it from him. He reached out to run his hands down her arms. When she didn't shrink from his touch, he tugged her back against his chest. At first, she remained stiff and unyielding, but gradually Melinda relaxed and leaned into his embrace.

As always, the scent of her hair, the warmth of her body, and her smile combined to make him ache with need. They'd yet to set the date for their wedding, but it had to be soon. A pastor, although subject to the same temptations as every other man, had to set the standard for his flock. He very much feared that his resolve would weaken if he and Melinda didn't make it to the altar soon.

He wondered what she'd think about riding to

the next town long enough to get the pastor there to speak the words over them. Melinda had made it clear that she wanted her friends to be part of their wedding celebration, but he figured they'd understand. Or at least forgive.

But before they discussed that idea, they needed to resolve the problem at hand.

"I will be glad to read a statement regarding the Society at the town council meeting if that would suffice."

Melinda looked up over her shoulder at him. "I know that, Daniel. I appreciate the offer, but once again it would be a man speaking on our behalf." Shaking her head, she sighed. "We are all capable of expressing ourselves. Just because we're women shouldn't mean that we can't speak our own words, our own viewpoints."

"I know very well what you're capable of, Melinda. Your intelligence is just one of the many things I love about you. But the truth is, right now if you want people to hear your message, it will have to go through me. Or maybe you should be talking to Cade Mulroney."

"Him? Whatever for?" Her head came up abruptly, bumping his chin. "Oh, Daniel, I'm sorry. Did I hurt you?"

"Nothing that a kiss wouldn't cure," he teased.

Very dutifully, Melinda turned to face him and slid her arms up around his neck. She kissed his chin and then his mouth. His chin might have felt better, but another part of him definitely started aching again. He wasn't about to tell her that, so he repeated his suggestion.

"I know in the past Cade hasn't been receptive to the whole concept of the Luminary Society."

"He hates the very idea of it."

"But I have reason to suspect that his attitudes may have softened. At the very least, he might be willing to publish a letter from the members of the Society."

"Last time we tried that, he twisted our words around to make us look like fools. Why should we trust him to do any differently now?"

His suspicions were based on his own observations, but he considered himself a good judge of people. He knew he could trust Melinda not to spread gossip if he were to share his thoughts with her.

"I think he has developed some feelings for Lucy Thomas. I'm not sure if they go beyond mere friendship, but I do believe he wouldn't want her hurt."

Melinda laid her head against his chest. "I've suspected the same thing. I would also go so far as to suggest that it isn't at all one-sided. She leaps to his defense every time someone complains about him or his newspaper." She looked up at Daniel. "I must admit that I find the idea worrisome. Her marriage was not a happy one. I fear that if another man were to treat her badly, she might never trust anyone again."

"I could have a talk with him, but I'm not sure it wouldn't do more harm than good. He doesn't talk much about his own past, but I've heard a few things that make me think his marriage wasn't all that good, either."

"It's scary, isn't it?"

She wasn't talking about Cade and Lucy anymore. He tipped her chin up to look into her eyes. "I promise to be the best husband I can be to you, Melinda Smythe. You deserve no less." He followed up his words with a kiss that said much the same thing.

When he finally broke it off, both of them were left breathless and shaky. A knock at the door announced the arrival of his next appointment. Melinda backed away, patting her hair to make sure that everything was still neat and tidy. He wished he had the time to make sure it wasn't.

"Would you like to have dinner with me tonight at the hotel? We can finish this discussion then."

"I'd like that, Daniel. Now, I'd better be going." She picked up her purse and opened the door to let herself out.

He hated to see her go. But knowing it was only for a matter of a few hours left him wishing the afternoon would speed by.

It was past dinnertime, and Cade was still hunched over his desk, trying to make up his mind about what to do next. He hadn't printed the letter from last night. There was no way he wanted that piece of filth associated with his newspaper, but his decision was likely to have dire consequences. It was a mighty short step from writing threats to carrying them out.

He almost wished the bastard would try something. The waiting and watching was taking its toll on them all. Before the last threats, Lucy had often left a dim light glowing in her room upstairs. He figured he wasn't supposed to know about that, but he had his own ghosts lurking in the dark. If a lamp helped keep them at bay, who was he to think less of her for it?

But the past few nights, the light had gleamed in her window like a beacon. She was badly frightened and had every right to be. Hell, he was having his own problems sleeping.

He'd made a list of names earlier. It had been

longer than it was now. For one reason or another, he'd crossed off all but three of his original suspects. If Mitch stopped by, he'd run the names past him, but that was all he could do. You could hardly accuse someone publicly just because you thought he drank too much or because he didn't do his job well.

He read down the list again. First, there was Oliver Turner, a drunk who mistreated his own wife. Thanks to the Society, Josie Turner had taken the first steps toward improving her lot in life. If Oliver resented her new independence, would he hesitate to threaten the ones responsible?

Cletus Bradford, the town banker. Cade had asked around but hadn't been able to find out much about the man's life prior to his coming to Lee's Mill. If he'd fought in the late war, no one knew which side he'd favored. He seemed honest enough, but appearances could be deceiving. Would he consider stirring up trouble for the sole purpose of making the mayor look bad? The thirst for power caused men to do strange things.

Finally, there was Mayor Kelly. He'd included him on the list solely because he was the only one Cade could think of whose presence in the sheriff's office wouldn't be questioned. The man wanted to be reelected, but there was nothing to be gained in that quarter by threatening the women.

Disgusted with the whole situation, Cade wadded up the piece of paper and tossed it in the trash. There were more productive things he could be doing besides playing name games. He had no evidence against any of the three. Mitch could hardly round up the three of them solely because one was a drunk, one was secretive, and the other inept.

He managed to concentrate on his editorial for

tomorrow's edition for all of two minutes before he muttered a curse and set down his pen. He didn't want to write. He didn't want to make lists. What he wanted to do was to slip next door and spend some time with Lucy Thomas.

Damn the woman, anyhow. He pinched the bridge of his nose in an effort to ease the headache that pulsed behind his eyes. If he had a lick of sense, he'd break off all contact with her immediately, while he had the chance. As if he could—the need for Lucy was like a siren singing temptation in his blood.

He pushed away from the desk and stretched his legs by retrieving the list in case Mitch might find it useful after all. When he bent down, he almost lost his balance. His left leg was stiff and hurt like a son of a bitch. It always plagued him worse when he was tired. He figured it had been a week or more since he'd gotten a full night's sleep. Even when he went to bed at a decent hour, the least little noise had him awake and listening for breaking glass.

If he didn't have Mary to worry about, he'd be tempted to spend a long evening at The River Lady. After a few hands of poker and enough liquor, he could stagger home in a pleasant fog and fall into bed. He might wake up with a headache in the morning, but at least he'd sleep.

"Boss, you got that editorial ready for me?" Will stood in the doorway, scratching his backside. He looked like hell, with bloodshot eyes and three days' growth of whiskers.

"Not quite. Give me ten minutes." He returned to his desk.

"I'll give you thirty. I could do with a walk to clear my head."

Cade figured what his typesetter really meant was five minutes to the saloon, twenty minutes to drink two beers, and then back again. "Fine."

Will moved much more lively going out than he had coming in. Cade called after him. "And, Will, keep it to two. After three, your spelling goes all to hell."

Because it was true, his typesetter laughed and waved his hand in acknowledgment. After the front door opened and closed, Cade reached for his pen. The small break had helped. With the renewed energy, the words started flowing again.

"Mrs. Overland, how can I help you?" The woman had been lurking at the back shelves with her husband until every other person in the store had finished their purchases and left.

The older woman looked around to make sure the three of them were alone and then plopped a handful of papers on the counter. "I brought these for you to look over."

Lucy had never seen Mrs. Overland blush before. "What are they? Letters you need mailed?"

"Ah, no."

Mr. Overland put a reassuring arm around his formidable wife. "What my lovely bride is trying to tell you is that she has written a paper on *Hamlet* to present at your next meeting. I've already told her that she'd done a fine job, but she would like to have your opinion on it before she reads it before the entire membership."

Lucy wasn't sure which was more amazing: that Mrs. Overland had taken upon herself to attempt a scholarly paper or that she was too shy to explain it to Lucy herself.

On the other hand, this was what the Society was all about—women learning to express themselves on matters other than the best recipe for biscuits and how to get stains out of children's clothes. If Mrs. Overland had taken the time to write the essay, Lucy would take the time to read it.

"I would be truly honored to read it, Mrs. Overland. I know it's scary to have someone else reading your words, but that's how we all learn. That you've even had the courage to put pen to paper is something to be right proud of."

"Thank you for saying so, Lucinda. I'm not sure I would have been so daring, but Mr. Overland encouraged me to try."

Lucy turned a bright smile on the woman's diminutive husband. "Mr. Overland, if only all the men in Lee's Mill thought the way you do."

For the first time, she saw beyond the henpecked husband to the intelligence that gleamed in his eyes. "Well, Mrs. Thomas, I've always known what my wife was capable of. I think it's wonderful that she has an appreciative audience for her efforts."

"We should let you get back to your work, Mrs. Thomas. Thank you again." With that, he offered his wife his arm, and the two of them sailed out of the store.

For several long seconds, Lucy stared after them. Although she'd never spent much time around Mr. Overland, she had always assumed that his marriage must not be a happy one. Instead, he genuinely seemed to adore his wife. Lucy wasn't sure if she was more surprised or envious. She picked up the papers and put them in a safe place behind the counter. Mrs. Overland's hard work deserved her full attention, so it would have to wait until later, when the store was closed. For now, she began recording the purchases of the last two customers before she forgot.

The bell over the door chimed. She set aside her ledger and prepared to greet her next customer. Her smile faltered only slightly when she recognized the mayor's profile as he studied the selection of shirts she'd displayed in the front window. In no hurry to deal with the man, she would allow him plenty of time to himself.

When she'd totaled the figures in the last column, she realized she'd forgotten that she was no longer alone in the store. Alarmed that she'd neglected a customer, she came out from behind the counter to apologize. At first she didn't see him. Knowing that he couldn't have left without the bell announcing his departure, she went from shelf to shelf, until at last she found him back in the corner.

"Mayor Kelly, I'm sorry—"

At the sound of her voice, the man jumped straight up in the air. He whirled around and glared at her. "Do you always go sneaking up on customers that way, Mrs. Thomas?"

She'd hardly been sneaking, but knowing anything she said in her own defense would fall on deaf hears, she merely continued with her apology. "I'm sorry, Mayor Kelly. I certainly don't make a habit of startling people that way. I assumed you heard me coming."

"Well, I didn't."

Something in the way he looked at her made Lucy wish that she had more than a couple of feet of floor space between them. There was no way she could retreat behind the counter without seeming more rude than she'd already been. She settled for trying to help him on his way.

"Was there something I could help you find, Mr. Kelly?"

"No. I was going to buy a shirt, but I find that your wares are too shoddy for my tastes."

His eyes raked over her, head to toe, making her feel unclean and not a little frightened. Was he even talking about her merchandise at all?

Rather than argue with the man, she did her best to placate him. "Well, I'm sorry you feel that way. I've sold quite a few of those shirts over the past couple of weeks. So far, no one else has complained about them, but if you want to tell me specifically what you're looking for, I will gladly place a special order."

"That won't be necessary, Mrs. Thomas. Considering everything, I will be taking my business to the store in White's Ferry."

Some threat. She'd be only too happy never to have the disagreeable man set foot in her store again. As much as she disliked him, she wouldn't stoop to exchanging insults with the man. The sooner he left, the better off she would be.

"When you do, please tell Mr. and Mrs. Davis hello for me, Mr. Kelly. They are nice folks. I'm sure you'll find their selection more to your liking. Good day."

She turned her back on him and walked away with as much dignity as she could muster. When the bell over the door confirmed his departure, she drew a shaky breath. No longer certain her legs would support her, she sat down on a nearby chair and tried to convince herself that the sudden weakness was because she hadn't eaten for several hours. When the worst of it had passed, she leaned back and tried to decide what to do next.

Both Cade and Mitch had told her not to hesitate to come to them when anything unusual happened. Did this qualify? No, she'd feel like a fool running to the sheriff to announce that the mayor had decided to take his business elsewhere. It wasn't all that unusual for folks from White's Ferry to make the trip to Lee's Mill to shop and the other way around. The two stores carried much of the same wares, but there was always some variation.

No, she decided. The whole incident wasn't worth mentioning. No doubt she was overreacting to the mayor's unpredictable temper. She'd lived far too long with her father and husband, both of whom lashed out with hateful words every time they were displeased with her. Maybe the effects of those years hadn't faded as much as she'd thought they had.

Rather than rush off to tattle on Mayor Kelly, she'd finish her paperwork. Perhaps later, if Cade stopped by, she might tell him about the mayor's strange behavior. She'd treat the matter lightly, even so far as to laugh at the man's odd behavior. At least that way, Cade would be aware of the situation. After all, he didn't have any more use for Mayor Kelly than she did.

Feeling better for having made a decision, she took off her apron and laid it aside. Perhaps she should slip upstairs for a light lunch in case that really was the reason for her weakness. After turning the sign to read *Closed*, she locked the door to keep anyone from coming for a while. That did more to calm her nerves than she cared to admit.

# Chapter Fifteen

Cade strolled in shortly before he knew Melinda and Cora were due to arrive. He'd brought Mary with him. As soon as they were inside, he sent her on upstairs. Lucy looked up from her notes, clearly surprised to see him. He'd stood outside the door for the longest time, trying to figure out what the hell he was doing here.

For a man who didn't approve of the Luminary Society and what it stood for, he felt it imperative that he attend tonight's meeting. Now all he had to do was convince Lucy that he should. The whole situation made him mad, with no handy target for his anger.

"Cade?"

Lucy's smile was a little tentative around the edges, but she'd been skittish around him since the other night. In fact, she'd made damn sure that the two of them were never alone. If Mary wasn't with them, Cora was. He didn't like the idea that somehow he'd frightened her. At the time, she'd seemed to enjoy their encounter as much as he had.

He'd made damn sure of it.

But right now, sex wasn't the first thing on his mind—a close second, maybe, but not first. He was more worried about the Society and its meeting. No one but he and Mitch knew about the threatening letter that been left for him. Although he felt strongly that it was the right decision, the man who wrote the words would no doubt disagree with that idea.

Who knew what fool thing the crazed idiot might try next? Cade's biggest worry was that a roomful of women might just prove to be too tempting a target to resist. Mitch agreed with him, as did Daniel Hayes. The three of them had talked it over and decided that they needed to take action.

Daniel was going to watch the front of the store from across the street. Mitch would keep an eye on things from Cade's house. And Cade had lost the coin toss. It was his job to attend the meeting or at least stand outside the door in case something did happen.

"Was there something you wanted?"

She sounded like a storekeeper talking to a new customer, rather than a woman speaking to her lover. He wanted to shake her until her teeth rattled. Or, better still, drag her back to the storeroom and remind her exactly what they'd shared on that sofa of hers.

For now, though, there were other, more pressing matters.

"How mad are you going to be when I invite myself to tonight's meeting?"

"Oh, no, you don't!"

She came charging out from behind the counter to face him down. It was cute.

"Yes, I do mean it. It's me or Mitch. Take your

pick." He grinned at her, knowing that would only inflame her temper more.

"I'll have you know, Cade Mulroney, this building is private property. If you continue to show up uninvited, I will have Mitch throw you in jail for trespassing."

"Fine. I'll leave, but like I said, it's me or Mitch. If you prefer his company, so be it." Then, to be outrageous, he leaned down and whispered, "But he's too tall for your sofa, don't you think?"

Lucy gasped and turned bright red. "Cade, just because we . . . you and I . . . I'm not . . ." she sputtered.

Deciding to stop her tirade by the most expedient method, Cade kissed her. She began to return the favor in a gratifyingly short time. When her arms slipped up around his neck, he knew that their one night of passion hadn't been a fluke.

Dimly aware that a roomful of people were due to come through the door any second, Cade gathered his scattered wits enough to break off the kiss, much against his better judgment. He kept Lucy tucked nicely in his arms, though. He wasn't about to let her take cover behind the counter again.

"I know you don't want me at the meeting, Lucy. Hell, it's not exactly my favorite way to spend an evening." He decided to go for broke. "I wasn't going to tell you this, but someone left me a letter at the *Clarion*."

"A letter? What kind of letter?"

"The threatening kind. Mitch and I both figure our rock-throwing friend wrote it. If so, he's sounding more scary all the time." Cade frowned as he thought about the letter and the venom it contained. "God knows why he hates the Society so much, but he does. We figure that if he's going to do something crazy, the night that you all meet seems like the logical time to do it."

She shivered and burrowed closer to him. "What did we ever do to make this man so angry?"

"I don't know, honey. If I did, we might be able to figure out who it is." He kissed the top of her head. "I'll be there to protect you, just in case. Mitch and Daniel will be watching the outside of the building."

The bell gave them a little warning that they were no longer alone. He felt her pulling herself together to face her friends. When she wanted to step free of his embrace, he let her go.

He caught her arm, long enough to whisper, "Mitch would rather no one else knew about the letter as yet."

"Why not? If we're all in danger, the others have a right to know."

"That's what I told Mitch. I also told him that I'd leave it up to you. In fact, if you decide to tell everyone, that could be my reason for attending the meeting. That way, you don't have to come up with some other excuse for my presence."

Then he grinned again. "Or you could just tell them your lover wants to watch you bang your gavel again."

"Cade, hush that kind of talk!"

"Yes, ma'am. I was only trying to help." He was still grinning as she marched away, leaving him to follow if he wanted.

She might not appreciate his teasing, but it brought the color back her cheeks and the spark to her eyes. He hated seeing what fear did to this normally strong woman—another mark against the man who had put it there. With luck, they'd find him before he did any real damage.

With that thought in mind, Cade waited until the last of the women had filed upstairs before locking the door. He lingered in the back of the store, gun in hand, for about ten minutes after the meeting had started. From his carefully chosen position, he watched for any latecomers as well as anyone who looked suspicious.

When all seemed quiet, he locked the front door and quietly slipped up the steps. He wondered if Lucy had announced his presence and the reason behind it. Avoiding the creaky board in the top step, he cautiously approached the door to the meeting room. Rather than barge in on the women of the Society, he pressed his ear against the door and listened.

He thought that the speaker was most likely Melinda Smythe, but he couldn't be sure. At best, he only heard the occasional word clearly, but it sounded as if she was trying to calm someone down. When she paused, perhaps to take a breath, several other voices spoke up, all at the same time.

Was it anger or fear that had the women all babbling at once? He had no intentions of allowing the women to turn the brunt of either one on Lucy and her friends. Without thinking much about his motives, he decided to give them a more suitable target for their ire.

He rattled the door handle a bit before actually opening the door, hoping the noise would distract the members of the Society. It worked. When he stepped into the room, every eye in the place was trained directly on him. From the looks he was given as he made his way to the front of the room, it was clear that the emotions in the room ran the full gamut from confusion to fury.

"Evening, ladies," Cade drawled, taking his hat off and bowing slightly. "I regret the need to interrupt your meeting, but the sheriff and I felt it was necessary."

To his surprise, Melinda and Cora both moved closer to where he stood, in an unspoken show of support. Lucy remained seated. He waited to see what her response would be.

So Cade had made good on his threat to invade their meeting again. She would be angrier about it, but she suspected that his timely arrival wasn't by accident. He'd opened the door at the exact moment the meeting had been about to break out into an all-out squabble. No doubt, he'd been listening at the door and decided that his intervention was necessary. Leave it to a man to think that women couldn't handle their own problems.

Resigned to his presence, Lucy slowly rose to her feet. "I think we should yield the floor for a very short time to Mr. Mulroney. After he has had his say, we will resume our own discussion."

"I want you to know that even as you have been conducting your meeting, Mitch Hughes, the Reverend Daniel Hayes, and I have been guarding your backs."

Mrs. Overland immediately broke in. "And exactly why do you feel that such an action is necessary, Mr. Mulroney? Considering your previous treatment of our group in that paper of yours, why we should be trust you?"

"Good question, Mrs. Overland. Make no mistake, my opinion of the activities of the Luminary Society remains largely unchanged. Politics and such are not for the likes of the fine women of Lee's Mill."

Melinda gave a small snort of disgust, clearly not buying his backhanded complement. "We don't have much time, Mr. Mulroney. Get to the point."

"As you wish, Miss Smythe. The letter I received at the *Clarion* contained very clear threats against the Society and its members. Until the sheriff can locate the man who wrote it as well as the other notes, we have no idea how serious those threats are. First and foremost, however, you must look to your own safety. We're assuming that the greatest threat will come when you are all together or on your way to and from the meetings. Sheriff Hughes suggests that none of you walk alone any more than absolutely necessary."

"Just what is the sheriff doing about this?" This question came from somewhere in the back of the room.

"I can assure you that he is doing everything possible."

When several women started talking at once, Lucy did the only thing she could do. She reached for the gavel and banged it several times as loudly as she could. A stunned hush fell over the room.

"Ladies, must I remind you of our rules? Only one person at time, please." She didn't spare Cade from her disapproving gaze. "Thank you, Mr. Mulroney, for your . . . ah . . . apparently sincere concern. Now, if you will please leave, we will return to the business of the Society."

Cade knew when he'd been outmaneuvered. He acknowledged her small victory with an arched eyebrow. "Thank you, ladies, for hearing me out."

But he didn't concede the field completely. "Mary fell asleep on your bed, Mrs. Thomas. I insist on staying nearby until the meeting is over and everyone is safely home. If you need me, I'll be on the sofa in the parlor." Then, with a smile and a wink, he was gone.

He was obviously paying her back for trying to dismiss him before he was ready to go, but did he

have to embarrass her in front of all her friends?
She fought the urge to flee the room when she realized that she was the only one who knew there
was an underlying meaning to his last comment.
There wasn't much she could do about the fact
that he'd made her blush, except to go on with the
meeting as if nothing were wrong.

As soon as the door was closed, she rapped the
gavel, more gently this time.

"I believe that Melinda had something she wanted
to say." Grateful to relinquish control of the discussion to her friend, Lucy did her best to compose herself. Of all the women in the room, only
Cora was giving her an odd look before turning
her attention to Melinda.

"I think it is very important that the Luminary
Society continue on as it has. We have already accomplished too much to give up now." Melinda
held up her hand and began ticking off each item.
"We have several members who have now learned
to read." A scattering of applause followed.

Melinda nodded emphatically. "That's right. Be
proud of yourselves!" She counted off another finger. "Our ability to conduct an orderly discussion
that allows for dissension without disrespect far
surpasses even the town council." The clapping
was louder this time.

"And finally, we are learning to express ourselves, both in writing and in a public forum. And
that, ladies, gives each of us power to affect the
quality of our lives. Men may not like it. Certainly,
they will try to ignore it. Let them try." She paused
for effect, then spoke out loud and clear, "But we
will be heard! If not now, then in the future!"

Instantly, every woman in the room was on her
feet and applauding. Lucy hurried to Melinda's
side and hugged her friend. Together, with Cora,

they stood arm in arm and smiled. If the Society could weather the threats of a madman, they could handle anything that came their way.

The meeting broke up a little later than usual, but only by a few minutes. No one had been in a hurry to leave the warm companionship and step back out into the darkness, where danger lurked. Mitch Hughes, bless his heart, was waiting outside with his deputy. The two men divided the women into groups according to where they lived in town, and proceeded to escort them home. Daniel stepped forward to see that both Melinda and Cora reached their destinations safely.

That left Cade waiting for Lucy upstairs in her parlor. On the sofa. She didn't know whether to hide out in the store until he gave up and took his sleepy daughter home or to run up the stairs as fast as she could. Temptation was a powerful force.

Deciding that hiding was a cowardly act, she picked up her lamp and walked up the stairs with as much dignity as she could muster. She half expected Cade to be waiting for her at the top with that same smug smile on his face, but there was no sign of him.

She found him right where he had said he'd be. Cade's long form was stretched out the length of the sofa, a soft snore filling the silence of her parlor. Some guard he turned out to be. The thought made her smile. Then it dawned on her that she'd never had the opportunity to really study the man. Perhaps she was intruding on his privacy by doing so, but after all, it was her sofa he was sleeping on.

The silver streaks in his hair didn't make him look older; they only added to the strength in his rugged features. She had to smile at the way he'd had to twist his long, lean body to fit the too-short sofa. Her eyes followed the length of his legs, wondering if his war wound pained him often. The thought that he'd come so close to death without her ever having met him bothered her more than she cared to admit.

Despite her resolve never to encumber her life with another man, somehow this one had come to mean something to her. Something powerful. Something that felt frighteningly close to love. She took a step back as the impact of that realization hit her full force.

Before she retreated any farther, Cade spoke. "Going somewhere?"

"I was going to go check on Mary."

"Liar. You were running out on me." He sat up and held out his hand, daring her to come closer.

She'd had the right of the situation. The man was sinfully attractive, making her ache all over with the need to touch him again. They'd lost control in each other's arms on that very sofa once before. Was she willing to risk it again?

Evidently, she was. Her hand settled trustingly into his as she let him tug her down beside him. He tucked her up close to his side and put his arm around her shoulders.

"How did the rest of the meeting go? Were the women upset?"

"Certainly, but we all agreed that no man, crazy or otherwise, was going to stop us. Not now, especially when we've come so far."

If she expected an argument, she didn't get one. "Does that surprise you?"

"Not particularly. Some of the women might waiver if left by themselves, but you are just too damn stubborn to give up. Melinda and Cora are almost as bad." He didn't sound particularly upset about the situation.

She realized that his wicked fingers were busy pulling out her hair pins as he spoke. She closed her eyes and enjoyed his touch. "I'm sure that my friends would be pleased to know you think so much of them."

When the last pin pulled free, Cade tangled his fingers in her hair, letting it ripple free down around her shoulders. He leaned in close and whispered, "It feels like silk. I dream of having you in my bed with your hair spread out over my pillow." He nibbled at her ear, sending shivers skittering through her as he whispered more of his plans for her.

She should be scandalized; she really should. Instead, she moaned softly as he picked her up and settled her in his lap. She kissed him first, but it was a close call which one of them deepened it as their tongues tangled and danced.

"Damn it, Lucy, I want to make love to you, but not here on the sofa. Come home with me."

The flames that were burning in her died. "I can't do that, Cade."

Anger replaced the passion in his eyes. "You want to, so don't try to deny it."

"Wanting to doesn't make it right."

She tried to stand up, but his arms pinned her against his chest as he kissed her again. There was nothing gentle, nothing coaxing in it this time. She did her best to meet his challenge.

When he realized that he wasn't going to convince her that way, he broke off the kiss and glared at her. "What would make it right for you, Lucy? Marriage? Is that what this is all about? Are you holding out for a proposal, Lucy? If you are, it won't do you a damn bit of good. There's no way in hell I'm ever going to make that mistake again. You've known that from the start."

This time, he let her go when she struggled to get free. She stood, glaring down at him. "And I've been honest with you, Cade Mulroney. I spent too many years of my life being ordered around by some pigheaded man. I won't put up with that again. Not from you, not from anybody."

When he stood up, she backed away until the full width of the room was between them. It wasn't enough. It hurt to stand there alone when all she really wanted was to be back in his arms.

"I'll be leaving." He didn't move an inch.

"Fine." She prayed he wouldn't go.

"Lucy . . ." He drew a ragged breath. "It doesn't have to be all or nothing. If neither of us wants marriage, then I don't see the problem." His eyes flickered to the sofa, as if to remind them both of what they'd already shared.

"The problem is that I'm not the one who deserves your anger, Cade. Your wife is dead, but you go right on punishing every woman you meet because of her."

"And what about you, Lucy? I don't think there's a man in this town that you trust any farther than you could spit."

"That's not true! I trust Sheriff Hughes and Daniel." And then honesty forced her to admit, "And I trust you."

"Then why won't you come home with me?"

She wanted to. She sure enough did, but there were some rules a woman couldn't afford to break. Feeling far older than her years, she told him the truth. "Because in this world, a woman's reputation is all that stands between her and absolute ruin. It's hard enough to be a woman in business for herself. If people in town found out that I was sharing your bed, they'd treat me like those who work across the street at The River Lady."

Cade's face hardened. "I have never treated you like anything less than a lady. I might have my blind spots when it comes to women, Lucy, but I do know the difference between a lady and a whore."

No, he didn't, not really. "The only difference is luck, pure and simple. Do you think any of them started out in life wanting to work in a place like that?"

His fists clenched in frustration. "Lucy, I want you. Isn't that enough?"

She almost collapsed with the pain from her heart shattering into a thousand pieces. "No, Cade, it isn't. It can't be."

If there was anything else he wanted to say, he kept it to himself other than to tell her, "I guess there's nothing left except for me to take Mary and go."

And when he left, he took joy with him.

Damn, his head hurt. He peeled his eyes open one at a time to find his daughter staring him straight in the face. She looked worried.

"Are you ever going to wake up?"

His mouth tasted like the bottom of a spittoon. "I'm trying to, honey."

"I'm hungry." She clutched her doll under her arm and waited impatiently for him to do something about it.

"Go on downstairs. I'll be along in a minute." He gave her what he hoped was a reassuring smile, but feared it was more of a grimace.

As soon as he heard Mary go down the stairs, he closed his eyes, glad for the relief from the glare of the morning sunlight. He couldn't hide in bed for long or she'd be right back up to nag at him, so he pushed himself upright to sit on the edge of the bed. He held his head in his hands as the room tilted and righted itself.

The empty brandy bottle on the floor told the whole story, or at least half of it. If he remembered rightly, there was another one just like it down-stairs. It had been years since he'd drunk himself senseless over a woman. It hadn't helped then, and it sure as hell wasn't helping now.

"Father, are you coming?"

"Yes, Mary. I'm up and moving."

The sound of his own voice rattled around in his head, all sharp points and ragged edges. Damn, he hurt. He splashed some tepid water on his face, wishing he could wash away the memory of Lucy Thomas along with the foul taste of last night's cig-ars and liquor.

Even the thought of the woman felt like a raw wound. Hell's fire, how had he been so stupid? She was right. Neither of them could afford to risk their reputations all for the sake of shared passion, no matter how much he wanted to have her. He couldn't even take the edge off his need with one of the women across the street at The River Lady— not after what Lucy had said about them. Damn her for reminding him that they were real people with problems and needs.

Coffee. He'd kill for a cup, but he'd have to wait until he got some made. Maybe there was some left in the pot from yesterday. It would be stronger than horse piss, but he'd drink it anyway. He kept the railing firmly in his grasp as he worked his way downstairs, doing his best not to jar his head un-necessarily.

Mary was waiting for him at the kitchen table.

She'd already set the table for two. Her part done, she chatted happily to her doll.

He added wood to the stove and picked up the coffeepot. There was maybe half a cup of inky-black liquid in the bottom, not enough to bother with. Resigning himself to the inevitable, he dumped out yesterday's residue and started a fresh pot. While he waited for the water to boil, he got out a skillet and made scrambled eggs for Mary.

He'd settle for coffee for himself. Breakfast would sound better when his stomach settled down.

"What time am I going over to Lucy's?" Mary asked between bites. "We're supposed to make a new dress for my doll today."

Oh, hell. He knew full well that Lucy would never hurt Mary, no matter how she felt about him. On the other hand, he wasn't sure he was up to facing her again so soon. He'd all but begged her to share his bed, and she'd turned him down flat. No matter how good her reasons were, a man had his pride. But for Mary's sake, he would walk into Lucy's store, head held high.

"I'm sure she's still expecting you, honey. Why don't you finish getting dressed while I clean up the kitchen?" *And drown myself in coffee and self-pity,* he added silently.

Mary skipped out of the room, happy to have her plans for the day all lined up. Cade wished his own life were as simple. He dried the last few dishes, poured himself another cup of coffee and trudged upstairs to his room to get dressed.

Half an hour later he took Mary by the hand and walked the short distance next door to the store. His footsteps echoed hollowly on the wooden sidewalk. Mary let go of him, eager to rush to her friend's side, leaving him to follow as he would.

He braced himself, unsure of his welcome. To his relief, it was Josie Turner behind the counter. He touched the brim of his hat. "Morning, Mrs. Turner."

"Mr. Mulroney."

Since she seemed unwilling to say more than the barest of greetings, he looked around the store. "Is Mrs. Thomas handy?"

"She's upstairs. She said to send Mary on up." Josie wiped the counter down with a damp rag. When he didn't immediately leave, she gave him a questioning look. "Was there something you needed?"

"No, I suppose not. Please remind Mrs. Thomas that I may be later than usual getting back. I have a meeting I have to cover over in White's Ferry this evening."

"I'll be sure and tell her, Mr. Mulroney."

The bell over the door rang out. Josie looked past him to see who had come in. For a brief second, her face lit up but then immediately settled back into its usual blank stare. Cade glanced back to see who had caused such a strange reaction.

Mitch Hughes headed straight for Cade. He acknowledged Josie's presence with a quick nod. "Morning, Mrs. Turner."

She gave him a shy smile. "Sheriff. Can I get you something?"

"No, thanks, ma'am. I'm here to see Cade."

Cade wondered if Mitch caught the look of disappointment that Josie gave him before she disappeared into the storeroom. Even if he hadn't, Cade wasn't about to say anything. He had enough problems of his own without messing in someone else's business.

"I'm on my way to the office. We can talk there if you want." He needed to get out of the store before he did something stupid, like charge up the stairs to tell Lucy she could hide all she wanted; it didn't change a damn thing.

Once they were outside, he asked, "Is this a social call, or did you have some business to discuss?"

"I'd rather wait until we're inside."

Although Mitch went to great lengths to appear casual and relaxed, from where Cade stood, the grim set to Mitch's mouth and the tension in his stance were all too obvious. Something had pushed the normally calm lawman to the edge.

Rather than waste time badgering him for details, Cade limped his way to the front door of the newspaper office. Mitch glanced down at Cade's leg but didn't say anything.

"Rough night," was all Cade was willing to give in the way of an explanation.

Figuring Mitch didn't want anyone eavesdropping, Cade called out, "Will, take a break." It wouldn't do to have the loquacious typesetter listening in. Sober, the man could keep a secret. Give him a couple of beers, and nothing was sacred.

Once the two of them were alone, Cade waved Mitch toward one of the chairs that faced his desk, and then sat down himself.

"What's going on?"

Mitch answered by tossing an envelope down on the scarred surface of Cade's desk. He recognized the handwriting immediately. Damn, he was in no shape to deal with another threat to Lucy right now. There was no way he wanted to tell Mitch that he and Lucy were no longer speaking to each other. Feeling cornered, he slowly picked up the envelope and stared at it.

"More of the same?" Maybe he wouldn't have to

read it if he could get Mitch to tell him what it said.

"I think you'd better read it." Mitch narrowed his eyes and frowned. "It mentions your daughter this time. Not by name, but it has to be her he's talking about."

Cade felt the floor drop out of his world as fear for his daughter's safety clutched his gut and twisted. With shaking hands, he ripped the letter from the envelope. In his haste, he tore the envelope in half, but he didn't give a damn.

> *I have warned you and you haven't listened. Not only do you allow the Luminary Abomination to continue to exist, but now you are allowing women of low character to influence and infect young children.*
>
> *Cade Mulroney, I thought to find an ally in you and your paper. Instead, you have betrayed both your gender and your ideals. Protect your daughter from the whores of Lee's Mill or you'll have to protect her from me.*

The words stopped, but the pain and dread they caused didn't. Cade looked up to meet Mitch's sympathetic gaze. "I'll kill the bastard."

Mitch, despite his pledge to uphold the law, nodded in agreement. "I'll help you."

A drink. Despite the early hour, he damn well needed a drink. He yanked open his desk drawer and reached for the bottle. After pouring them each a stiff one, he shoved Mitch's glass across the desk and downed his own in two quick, burning swallows.

"Where was this one delivered?"

"The man's got balls, I'll give him that. It was laying in the center of my desk this morning. After

I slept on the cot in the back of my office last night, I walked down to the hotel to pick up my breakfast. The letter was delivered during the few minutes I was gone."

"Did anyone know you were staying in town last night?"

"I didn't tell anyone, but it wasn't a big secret. He could have found out any number of ways—looking in a window, seeing my horse in the stable, following me on my rounds." Mitch looked purely disgusted.

"Got any ideas who it could be?"

"I've got a list in my head. Don't dare write anything down, especially considering the man we're looking for has managed to sneak in and out of my office undetected at least twice that we know of."

Cade had nothing to lose by showing his own list to the sheriff. He pulled it out of the drawer and tossed to his friend. "Does it look anything like that one?"

Mitch's eyebrows rose as he studied the three names. "Almost identical. I had to cross off Oliver Turner, though. He was locked in a cell this morning when the letter was delivered."

"Then why can't he tell you who brought it?" Cade knew the answer before he asked the question. If Turner had been in any shape to point a finger at someone, Mitch wouldn't be sitting here worrying.

"He passed out cold thirty seconds after I dragged his sorry hide in off the street last night. As far as I can tell, he hasn't stirred more than half an inch since. That reminds me—I need to tell his wife where to find him. This time I'm keeping him for a few days. I'm tired of him getting stinking drunk and then picking a fight with everyone who looks at him wrong."

Cade shook his head. "Can't think that she'd be surprised he's back in jail. Relieved is more like it. Hell, that cell is almost his second home."

"How a bastard like Oliver ever got hooked up with a sweet woman like Josie . . ." Mitch's jaws snapped shut, as if suddenly aware that he was revealing more than he'd meant to.

"What do we do next?" Cade needed to change the subject. Although he had some sympathy for Josie Turner's miserable lot in life, she was a married woman. As such, Mitch had no business thinking about her with that look in his eyes.

"Not much we can do but try to keep an eye on the mayor and the banker. Hell of a situation, isn't it? Those two are supposed to be our leading citizens, but they're the only ones I can point a finger at. Neither one has ever given any indication of hating women so much. Hell, Bradford is married to a damn nice woman. Could be we're way off the mark, and it's someone we haven't even thought of."

"Makes it hard to guard the women."

"Hard, hell. Damn near impossible. The son of a bitch keeps hinting and threatening without giving us anything substantial to go on. All we can do is wait and hope we can stop him before somebody gets hurt." Mitch picked up his hat and stood up to leave. "I'd better go talk to Mrs. Turner and then try to get some sleep. It will be another long night."

"Count on me to help any way I can." He hesitated before saying more, but if Mitch was going to do his job, he had to know all the variables. "I'm not so sure that Lucy Thomas will want me watching over her."

Mitch didn't ask any annoying questions, but he gave Cade a knowing look. "Women are tough to figure out. I'll stop by again later, after I've had enough sleep to clear out the cobwebs."

Cade picked the letter up off his desk. It felt as if he were holding hatred in the palm of his hand. "What do you want me to do with this?"

"Keep it with the other one. Like I said, my office isn't safe."

He started out and then stopped when Cade said, "One way or the other, we'll get the bastard."

"And let's hope, sooner than later."

When he was gone, Cade eyed the half-empty bottle on his desk. He forced himself to put it back in the drawer along with the letter. Mary deserved a sober, clear-thinking father. Besides, there was a paper to get out and a lunatic to catch.

# Chapter Sixteen

He'd warned and he'd threatened. None of it had made a difference, but then, he hadn't expected it to. Those women had turned the heads of the newspaperman, the sheriff, and even the preacher. Did the three of them think that they could stop him?

It had been a calculated risk delivering the last letter right to the sheriff's desk. If he'd been caught, or even if that stinking-drunk Turner had opened an eye, all would have been lost. The memory of his successful raid on the sheriff's office pleased him no end.

But the time for threats was over. Not tonight, but maybe the next. If not, the night after that. He was in no hurry at this point. The knowledge that lives lay in the palm of his hand pleased him, aroused him. If he were the type to consort with whores . . . but he wasn't. They were impure and filthy. The only difference between the ones who worked at The Lady and those in the Society was that the saloon girls were more honest about what they did.

He had no problem with them. It was the others,

the ones who pretended to be decent but didn't know their place—yet.

For now, he had a town to run and an election to win. Maybe it was time to go harangue the sheriff again to see what the incompetent fool was doing to catch him. He would demand results or fire him. Of course, if the sheriff did manage to do his job, then he himself would be in no position to fire anyone. But he was willing to accept the risks in order to do what needed to be done.

And it would get done—if not tonight, then tomorrow or the night after. The power to decide was his and his alone, just as it should be.

Cora shoved her needle into the fabric and managed to prick her finger. She held up the pillowcase and looked at it. "I got blood on it again. Well, now maybe Aunt Henrietta will quit trying to make me learn how to embroider." She shrugged indifferently as she bit through the thread with her teeth and then looked at her companions. "I still think one of us should attend the council meeting. I'll go if neither of you are willing to."

"You go right ahead and do that, Cora, and we won't see you outside of your aunt's house for a year and a half. Think of all the fine embroidery and other feminine arts you'll have time to perfect during that time."

Cora grumbled a bit under her breath but didn't argue the point, for the simple reason that Melinda was right.

Lucy's own curiosity was piqued by Melinda's behavior. Her friend's voice had an unusual hint of excitement in it despite her apparently calm demeanor. Even as she chided Cora, she kept her head bent over her needlework. Something was up; Lucy was sure of it. The only question was whether she should try to pry it out of her friend or wait until Melinda was ready to tell her.

A careful nudge wouldn't hurt. "So, have you and Daniel made any definite plans?" Melinda's response was all that Lucy could have hoped for.

Melinda, clearly flustered, blushed and looked both guilty and pleased at the same time. "No . . . yes . . ." she stammered. Then she demanded, "What has Daniel been telling you? We agreed to keep our elopement a secret!" When she realized what she'd just said, she covered her mouth with her hand as if that would keep anything else from slipping out.

"Elopement!" Cora squealed.

"And when is this supposed to take place? Are you trying to cheat us out of celebrating your wedding?" Lucy tried to look stern but couldn't quite keep up the pretense.

Melinda resigned herself to telling all. "You two have to promise not to say anything to anybody. We want to get married before school starts. We figured that even if we elope, we could have a party for all our friends afterwards." Her eyes pleaded with them to understand.

"Makes a lot of sense to me," Cora avowed staunchly. "You pick the day, and Lucy and I will put on a party that the town will talk about for years."

"Well, I don't know about doing something quite that elaborate, but we will sure do our best for you." Lucy reached over and patted her friend on the arm. "I know the two of you will be very happy."

Melinda's eyes teared up. "You know, I still mourn the loss of my family, but you two have made me feel like I've found two sisters. Finding a man like Daniel makes my life complete."

The three of them chatted for several more minutes about refreshments and additions to Melinda's meager trousseau. Finally, their conversation trailed off as they resumed work on their sewing.

After a bit, Cora brought them back to the original topic. "Why aren't we going to the town council meeting tonight? Don't you think that the mayor will think he managed to run you off if we don't show up?"

"And do we care what he thinks, Cora?" Melinda gave her a wicked smile. "Besides, if we were sitting there, it would take all the worry out of it for him. As it is, he will go crazy wondering if we're just running late."

Lucy and Melinda both laughed then; somewhat grudgingly, Cora joined in. "All right, but I still think we should have someone there to represent the women of Lee's Mill."

"Daniel is going to go tonight. He has a speech all prepared about the Society and what it means to us." Melinda looked at her friends, her eyes pleading for understanding. "I know how we all feel about a man having to speak our piece for us, but he wanted to do it. He's fed up with the threats and Cade's editorials being so one-sided."

Lucy bit back her first response, wanting to think it through. Finally, she gave a reluctant nod. "I think it is nice of Daniel to want to take up our cause. We shouldn't have to defend ourselves at all, but he will make a good case on behalf of the Society."

Cora checked the time. "Well, I have to be going. Aunt Henrietta is expecting several of her friends tonight, and I'm to be their maid."

"Now, Cora . . ." Lucy chided her.

"Well, what else would you call it? They all sit and pick everyone in town apart while I serve tea." She shoved her sewing into a sack, with little regard for the delicate fabric. "I can't wait until I can live alone."

Melinda met Lucy's gaze across the room. Both of them knew that the cost of living alone often was loneliness, but that was something Cora would have to learn on her own.

"Will you be all right walking home by yourself, or do you want me to come with you?"

"No, I'll be fine. Nothing is likely to happen in broad daylight, and I'm going straight home." When Lucy started to get up, Cora shook her head. "Don't get up. I'll let myself out."

"Try to enjoy yourself."

Cora's parting look said all too clearly how she felt about that prospect. There wasn't much anyone could do about Cora's situation except keep her company until she was old enough to take control of her money.

Only a few minutes later, the sound of heavy footsteps on the stairs startled both women out of their reverie. Before either of them had time to react, they heard Cade's deep voice responding to a question from his daughter. Melinda serenely went back to stitching, but Lucy's reaction was far more volatile. She and Cade had barely spoken to each other in days, saying only the minimum to discuss how long he'd be gone and when he'd need her to watch Mary again.

It wasn't much as conversations went. Lucy was ashamed to admit how much even those few words meant to her. She kept her own counsel, though. Cora had no comparable experience in her life, and Melinda was too blissfully in love to understand how Lucy felt. Her feelings for Cade Mulroney ran deep. But until he was willing to share more of himself than his bed, words were all she would accept from him.

Mary came skipping into the room. At least she was still happy with the arrangement. Cade followed behind her.

"Mrs. Thomas, Miss Smythe. Miss Lawford was kind enough to let me in." He nodded at each woman in turn. "The meeting may run a little later tonight. The debate over the new landing is heating up."

Lucy could be painfully polite, too. "No hurry, Mr. Mulroney. If Mary gets tired, she can always lie down on my bed." Although she'd rather have the father there than the daughter. Afraid that her wayward thoughts might show on her face, she turned her attention to Mary, leaving Cade to stay or go as he wished.

He went. The fading sound of his footsteps hurt Lucy far more than it should have, considering how the man felt about her. At least she had Melinda and Mary to keep her distracted. She'd done far too much brooding since she and Cade had argued. Trying to convince herself that she'd snap out of it sooner if she kept busy, she set up the chessboard and invited Mary to play. In between moves, she tried not to watch the clock, counting off the minutes until Cade would return.

Not for the first time, Cade wished The River Lady's bar remained open during the meeting. Cletus Bradford had finally backed Mayor Kelly into a corner on the landing, and the two were going to debate the issue after the rest of the council's business was concluded. To make matters worse, Daniel Hayes had gotten it into his head that the Luminary Society needed to be defended to one and all.

By Cade's watch, the good Reverend Hayes had

been going full steam for the past fifteen minutes and showed no sign of slowing down. Mitch, sitting next to Cade, shifted restlessly. Evidently, Cade wasn't the only one ready for the evening to end. Even the mayor had managed to slip out the back door. No use in hoping that he wouldn't be back in time for the debate.

"The good Lord tells his people not to hide their light under a basket. Who are we, then, to question the women of Lee's Mill joining together to enlighten themselves? Why the very name they have chosen, the Luminary Society, speaks to that very idea!"

Cade let his eyes wander right along with his mind. The pastor meant well, but he personally didn't want to listen to it. He had been doing some hard thinking about his own attitude about the Society and didn't like what he'd found. If he trusted Lucy with his most precious possession—his daughter—then surely he could trust her in other matters.

If she said the Society was good for the women of Lee's Mill, perhaps she was right. The whole idea made him uncomfortable, but that was his problem, not hers. Not once had Lucy Thomas done or said anything that made him think she was at all like Louisa.

For some time now, he'd been fighting some pretty strong feelings for Lucy. Maybe, just maybe, he didn't have to. Why, if he gave in to those feelings, he might ask Lucy to consider . . .

Daniel's voice intruded on Cade's thoughts as he brought his talk—in reality a sermon—to a close. "I thank you for your time."

Some lukewarm applause gave Cade the excuse he needed to shove that last thought to the back of his mind as the young pastor picked up his papers and walked away.

It was time for the debate. Cletus Bradford, looking self-important, took Daniel's place in front of the room. But when he and everyone else looked around for the mayor, he was nowhere in sight. The crowd stirred in their seats, but before anyone actually left, the back door of the saloon slammed open. Mayor Kelly hustled through the door, still buckling his belt.

"Sorry, gentlemen, that took a little longer than I thought." He finished tucking in his shirttail as he took up his position next to the banker.

A dissatisfied citizen yelled from the back of the room, "Just one more thing you don't handle well, Mayor."

The mayor flushed red as he looked around for the heckler. Realizing that everyone was laughing, he did his best to join in. Cade thought the man's response seemed rather forced even though his face was flushed with what appeared to be good humor and excitement.

Mitch leaned over and whispered, "He looks pretty worked up about the debate, especially considering how hard he tried to avoid it."

"Maybe he's managed to come up with better arguments than Bradford is expecting." Still wishing he could have a drink, Cade pulled out a cigar.

Mitch struck a match and held it up. "Let's hope so. If it's as dull as Daniel's speech, the snoring will drown out their speeches."

The mayor evidently claimed the right of going first. He spread out a distressingly thick pile of papers and put on his spectacles.

Cade resigned himself to taking notes. He pulled out his small notebook and a dull pencil and waited for the mayor to say something worth writing down. Five minutes later he was still waiting. Whatever possessed the fool to review the entire history of the town? What did that have to do with whether a new landing would improve commerce?

Cade's own questions were worth noting. If neither candidate answered them, then Cade would take great pleasure in pointing that out in tomorrow's paper.

The bat-wing doors of the saloon burst open. Daniel Hayes, his face streaked with smoke, looked panic-stricken as he searched the crowd for someone. He yelled something, but Cade couldn't make it out over the mayor's droning voice. When Daniel spotted Cade and Mitch, he waded through the clutter of tables and men until he reached them, still trying to out-yell the increasing noise in the room. This time, he was close enough for Cade to read his lips even if he couldn't quite hear the word.

"Fire!" Daniel yelled.

Mitch surged to his feet, his pistol in hand. He took careful aim at the floor and fired his gun. The sudden explosion brought an immediate hush to the room.

"Shut the hell up so the preacher can speak!" Mitch barked.

Daniel looked wild-eyed. "Fire!"

"Where, damn it?" The floor seemed to drop from beneath Cade's feet as he waited to hear what in his heart he already knew.

"The store. Please hurry." Daniel was already turning to leave. "Please hurry," he repeated.

Cade and Mitch led the charge out of the saloon. Cade let the lawman take care of organizing the others into fighting the fire. All he could think of was getting Mary and Lucy out of the store safely. Daniel was matching him step for step.

"I was supposed to meet Melinda at the store to walk her home," the pastor gasped out between steps. "When I got there, I noticed there was a trail of smoke coming out of the alley between your place and the store. The whole lower floor is full of smoke and flames."

He looked ashamed. "I broke open the door, but the smoke was too thick to see where to go. I thought I'd better run for help before trying again."

"You did the right thing. The smoke alone could have killed you before you had a chance to raise the alarm. The women stand a better chance of getting out with all of us helping."

Cade's assurances went a long way toward easing the pastor's guilt, but he'd told him nothing but the truth. As far gone as the fire was, it would take all of them and a miracle to get everyone out alive and unharmed.

They'd reached the front of the store. Daniel was right. It wouldn't be long before the entire building was engulfed in flames. His first instinct was to charge ahead. If he couldn't get to Mary and Lucy in time, then he'd just as soon die in the flames with them.

For their sakes, though, he forced himself to slow down and try to come up with a plan. The fire seemed to be coming mainly from the front. Maybe he could climb through the back window and make it to the staircase. Mitch came up beside him, carrying a couple of buckets.

"Soak me with water!" Cade stripped off his jacket, grateful that Mitch didn't question him but was already filling the buckets at the closest water trough.

He poured the water over Cade's head and then did the same to the pastor. Since Melinda was trapped upstairs as well, Cade wasn't about to argue about the man's right to come with him. Both men tied wet handkerchiefs across their noses to help keep out the smoke.

"We're going in the back and try to get upstairs. Be watching for us."

"If you can, take a rope with you. You may need to follow it to find your way back out if we don't get that fire and smoke under control fast enough."

"Good thinking. Let's go." He ran to the back end of the building and with his bare hands began to pry off the boards he'd put over the last broken window. When he had the last one off, he put his hands on the sill. "Give me a boost."

Daniel cupped his hands and gave Cade a quick thrust up and through the window. Once he was back on his feet, Cade reached out and pulled the young pastor in behind him. It took a few precious seconds to find a long coil of rope in Lucy's storeroom. He began to unwind it as he stooped close to the floor and tried to find his way through the choking cloud of smoke.

He literally tripped over the first step. "We're here!" he shouted over the roar of the fire to Daniel.

They held on to the railing as they dragged themselves upward, gasping for breath each step of the way. The staircase acted like a chimney, drawing the smoke upward in heavy black billows. When it became too difficult to breathe while standing, they crawled on their hands and knees, coughing and choking as they slowly made their way. More by memory than by sight, Cade worked his way to the parlor. To his relief, he found the two women and his daughter busy tying strips of cloth together. They had already broken out the window.

"One more sheet should be enough to reach the ground." Lucy began to tie the other end of the sheet around Mary's waist. "Now, honey, do just like we told you. Once your feet touch the ground, untie the sheet and run for help. I'll pull it back up and Melinda will climb down. Then me."

Mary looked terrified, but she nodded and held up her arms so Lucy could pick her up. Neither of the women had yet realized that they were no longer alone.

Cade reached them first. He wrapped his arms around Lucy and Mary, needing that immediate reassurance that they were both all right. "Smart idea."

He lowered his daughter out the window. Evidently, Mitch had been keeping watch for them, because he immediately moved into position to catch Mary as they lowered her down the side of the building. As soon as she was in reach, he quickly untied the sheet and handed her off to someone to carry her to safety. Melinda was the next to make the trip down to the alley.

When Cade pulled the makeshift harness back through the window, Lucy was nowhere in sight. He found her in the bedroom, throwing some of her belongings out of the window. No doubt she'd realized that the building was too far gone to save much of anything.

"Stop it, Lucy! Get over here and let me tie the sheet around you."

"Let Daniel go next. I need to get my mother's quilt."

"None of that stuff is worth your life! Damn it, woman, get over here!"

Cade had to haul her to the window. He tied the sheet securely. Before he let her climb out, he pulled her back into his arms and kissed her. "We need to talk," was all he had time to say before he lifted her up and eased her through the narrow window.

Slowly, inch by inch, he lowered her to the ground. The heat in the room was becoming unbearable as more dark smoke roiled up from the store below. If he and Daniel didn't get out soon, they very likely wouldn't. He helped Daniel out the window and had lowered him only part of the way when the parlor floor began to cave in. Cade stumbled back, trying not to lose control of the sheet until Daniel safely reached the ground.

A shout from below told him that it was his turn. With no one there to lower him, he fumbled through the smoke to tie the sheet to the sofa leg. When he eased out of the window, he tried to find solid purchase on the side of the building with his feet. His bad leg was already throbbing from the strain of helping the others. He could only be grateful that the store was only two stories high. Even if the sheet came untied, he didn't have far to fall.

When he felt it slip, he pushed off the building and fell the last few feet to the ground. Pain shot up through his leg as the impact knocked the wind out of him.

Mitch—or at least he thought it was Mitch— yanked him up off the ground and helped him stumble around to the front of the building, where the others were waiting. Lucy and Mary both came running to his side. Despite the horror of the blaze in front of them, the comfort of holding them both safe in his arms kept the fury of the fire at bay. Everyone was alive, and that was all that mattered.

Shoulder to shoulder, Cade stood with the sheriff as the town watched Lucy's home and store burn. It took everything people could do to keep the flames from spreading to other buildings. When nothing was left except the charred remains of Lucy's dreams, weary strangers and friends alike walked by, offering her their condolences.

She did her best to smile at everyone, but after a while it was more than even she could handle. Cade felt the tremors ripping through her before she gave any outward sign that she was about to fall apart.

He already carried Mary with one arm. There was no way he could catch Lucy if she actually collapsed.

"Mitch, can you take Mary?"

His daughter went readily enough to her friend the sheriff, so that Cade could turn his full attention to Lucy. He tugged on her arm, trying to get her to follow him. She stumbled forward a few steps before digging in her heels.

"Where are we going? I need to see about getting a room at the hotel."

Melinda was standing right behind them. "No, Lucy, you'll come home with me."

Stubborn, prideful woman that she was, Lucy refused the offer. "No, I won't be a burden to anyone. The hotel will be fine."

Knowing she'd stand there and argue all night if they let her, he decided to take charge. "She's coming home with me," he announced to one and all. He glared at the folks standing nearby, daring anyone to argue.

Some of the fight was back in Lucy's dark eyes. "I can't do that, Cade Mulroney, and you know it. I have my reputation to think of."

He'd almost lost her. Didn't she realize how damn scared he'd been? He wasn't about to let her out of his sight again until the bastard who started the fire was caught and behind bars. He had some thoughts on that subject, but now wasn't the time.

"I don't give a hoot in hell about your reputation, Lucy Thomas. You're coming to stay with Mary and me. I won't stand for any of your arguments."

The crowd now had something else to watch as the sparks of temper flew between Cade and Lucy.

She'd hate him for that in the morning, but right now getting her tucked away someplace safe where he could stand guard over her was more important than what the townspeople thought.

"Cade, for the last time. I'm an unmarried woman. I can't spend the night in a man's home with only his six-year-old daughter for a chaperon."

He was about pick her up bodily and carry her home when the perfect solution slipped through his mind. He poked and prodded the idea, looking for reasons it wouldn't work. When he couldn't give voice to even one objection, he announced it to the entire population of Lee's Mill.

"Fine. Then before we set foot across my threshold, we'll have Pastor Hayes marry us. Right here. Right now." He didn't have to look far to find the minister. He was glued to Melinda's side, much like Cade had been to Lucy's.

"Any reason you can't marry us, Pastor?"

Daniel was doing his best to look solemn, but a smile tugged rather persistently at the corner of his mouth. "Well, none except for the fact that I haven't heard Lucy answer your rather unusual proposal."

Cade didn't want to give her a chance to think, much less answer him. Considering her previous experience with marriage, there was every reason to think that her answer might well be no. Maybe if he asked her, this time more politely, she'd at least consider his offer.

"Well, Lucy, what's it to be? Are you going to marry me or not?"

The crowd grew silent as Lucy tried to make sense of everything that had happened in the past couple of hours. Her store had caught fire. She and her friends had almost died. Cade had come to rescue his daughter but also her. Now the fool was standing there ordering her to marry him.

Well, he could just wait a minute while she gathered herself up to consider his offer, even if it was more of an order. His light-colored eyes stood out in stark relief against his soot-stained skin. The set of his mouth was grim, but something in his expression sent her pulse tripping along at an alarming rate. No matter what the circumstances, he wasn't proposing just to protect her reputation. Cade was many things, but a martyr wasn't one of them.

The man, the real one behind the gruff manner, wanted her for his wife. Maybe it was wishful thinking on her part, but it felt right.

"All right, Cade Mulroney. I'll marry you, but don't think you'll always get away with ordering me around like this."

She had a few other things that she wanted to say, but just then Cade was too busy kissing her to listen.

Cade woke up alone, but then that's how he'd gone to bed. It was a hell of a way to start off a new marriage: sleeping on the sofa with his rifle on the floor beside him. Even though he'd bullied Lucy into coming home with him, his intention all along was to send her and Mary upstairs to sleep while he stood guard below. He wondered if Lucy had realized that yet.

In truth, as tired as he was last night, he wouldn't have been much of a husband to his new wife. His real worry was that if he left Lucy alone too long, she'd start having second thoughts about their rush to the altar.

Too damn bad. She was his, and that was the way it was going to stay. Feeling energized by that realization, he threw back the covers and sat up. His leg screamed in protest as soon as he put any weight on it, but he ignored the pain. There was work to be done today and an arsonist to bring to justice. It might be Mitch's job to arrest the bastard, but it had been Cade's women who'd been attacked.

A cold determination settled over him. He didn't make a habit of wearing his guns to breakfast, but this morning he'd make an exception. He headed to the small kitchen and set about fixing breakfast for himself and his family. It pleased him on some level to set the table for three instead of just two. The floor overhead creaked, warning him that he was about to find out how Lucy felt about it.

She eased warily into the kitchen, still showing the effects of the commotion from the day before. She'd lost everything in the fire, so the only thing she had to put on was the dress she'd been married in—torn, smoky, and blackened with soot. She managed to braid her hair neatly, but it was going to take a long soak in a tub to put her to rights.

Despite it all, Lucy had never looked lovelier to him. He wondered if she'd believe him if he told her so.

"Good morning, Mrs. Mulroney." His voice sounded gruff even to himself, but Lucy didn't seem to mind.

"Good morning yourself, Mr. Mulroney."

"Did you sleep well?" Damn, he felt like a callow youth calling on his first sweetheart, instead of a grown man speaking to his wife

She nodded. "But I still feel bad taking your bed."

"It's your bed, too." He wanted to make that perfectly clear. And with luck, starting tonight he'd be sharing it with her.

"Yes, well . . ." Her voice trailed off as if she'd lost her train of thought. She looked around the room, searching for something.

It hit him that she didn't know what to do with herself. This would be her home, but it didn't feel like it yet. She was used to keeping herself busy with the store. No doubt, she was still coming to terms with everything that she'd lost. And what she'd gained—a daughter and a husband.

"Would you mind seeing if Mary is awake? I should have breakfast on the table in about five minutes."

"Of course." She disappeared back up the stairs.

Maybe he was mistaken, but it seemed to him that there was more energy in her step. She was bound to need help finding her place in his house and in his life. Hell, even he hadn't quite come to terms with having another wife, especially after his past experience with the institution of marriage.

A rather sleepy Mary trailed into the kitchen right behind Lucy a few minutes later. She yawned and stretched a bit before running over to collect her morning kiss. Cade held on to her longer than usual, reassuring himself once again that she was safe and sound. When he released her, she gave him a puzzled look.

"Doesn't Lucy get a good-morning kiss and hug?"

Neither adult knew how to respond to her innocent question. Lucy was pouring the coffee. She froze, her dark eyes meeting his with a definite look of panic in them as she waited for him to answer his daughter.

Mary's suggestion seemed like a fine idea to him.

He set the skillet back on the edge of the stove and smiled.

"Why, you're exactly right, Mary. Lucy should get a morning kiss and hug." Before Lucy could bolt back up the stairs, he was across the small room, positioning himself between her and the doorway. Gently he crooked his finger under her chin and tipped her face up to the proper angle for kissing.

Slowly he lowered his mouth to hers, not wanting to frighten his obviously skittish wife. As their lips touched, he could feel the tension vibrating in her, but at least she didn't fight him. He took that as a good sign. Not wanting to push too far, he kept the kiss gentle and short.

"Good morning, Lucy," he whispered.

Her eyes opened slowly to meet his. Before he could decipher the look she gave him, someone pounded on the back door. Cade wanted to curse the interruption, but there was little doubt that it was Mitch Hughes. The two of them had plans to make and a criminal to catch. No one wanted to spend another night wondering who would be attacked next. Or if he'd come after Lucy again.

Mary scrambled to the door to let Mitch in while Cade and Lucy jumped to put some distance between themselves. There was no reason they shouldn't be kissing, but neither of them was accustomed to their new status as a married couple.

Mitch followed his diminutive friend into the kitchen. He took his hat off and nodded to Cade and then Lucy. "Sorry to disturb you, Mrs. Mulroney, but Cade here said he wanted to get an early start this morning."

At first Lucy looked at him blankly, as if trying to decide who he was talking to. Finally, she nodded. "That's all right, Sheriff. I have a few things to see to this morning myself. But please sit down and have breakfast with us."

"Thank you anyway, but I've already eaten. Some coffee would be appreciated, though." Mitch took a seat at the table while Lucy poured him a cup and set it down in front of him.

Cade finished serving up the simple fare of bacon and eggs before joining the others at the table. For several minutes, everyone seemed content to eat their meal and enjoy their coffee.

"Mary, why don't you go on up and straighten your room. I'll be up to help you with your hair in a little while."

"But I want Lucy to—"

"Mary Louisa!" Cade immediately gave her his look that said he would brook no arguments. Mary's mouth snapped shut as she begrudgingly left the room. Every few steps she sighed loudly, as if life had become too much of a burden to bear. Cade managed to keep a straight face until she was out of sight. Lucy and Mitch were already grinning.

"All right, you two. It's hard enough to deny her anything without folks laughing it up when I'm trying to be stern."

"Oh, yes. We all know what a hard man you are, Cade. Who else in town has ordered that many dolls from me, all for one little girl?" The mention of her store erased the smile from Lucy's face.

"You'll get your store back, Lucy, if I have to build it board by board myself."

Her eyes sparkled with unshed tears that she tried to wipe away without anyone's noticing. "I've got some money put by, but not enough to rebuild completely."

"Well, you'll be living here now, so the important thing is the store itself. Once Mitch and I finish our business, I'll be glad to sit down with you and start drawing up plans." He looked toward Mitch. "What's the name of the man who is building the school? Keller? I hear he's the best in these parts."

Once again a knock at the door brought their conversation to a halt. Cade looked through the curtain to see who else had come calling. "It's your friends, Lucy." He threw open the door and invited Melinda and Cora inside.

"Lucy is in the kitchen. She'll be glad for your company. Sheriff Hughes and I were just about to leave."

Cade wondered what the two women really thought of his unexpected marriage to their friend. Now wasn't the time to find out. He had other business at hand.

Mitch was already up and moving toward the door. "If you're ready, let's head to my office."

Cade stepped back into the kitchen long enough to tell Lucy where he'd be. He didn't like leaving her alone, but today there would be a reckoning. Then they'd all sleep safer in their beds.

Lucy watched Cade leave, not sure how she felt about it. He wasn't given to easy smiles, but this morning he seemed more grim than usual. She hadn't missed the fact that he'd been wearing his guns, or that he picked up the rifle on the way out the door. He'd been a soldier, she knew, but these days he usually fought his battles with words, not bullets.

There was something about the fire that he wasn't telling her. Did he think she didn't realize that it had been deliberately set? He and Mitch were out for blood. She wished them luck, even if the anger smoldering in Cade's eyes frightened her a little.

Melinda was holding a bundle of some sort. As soon as the door closed behind the men, she thrust it at Lucy. "I know we're not exactly the same size, but here are a couple of dresses for you. They'll do until we can get a couple of new ones made for you." She dropped her voice to a whisper. "I also brought you a new petticoat and some other things I thought you might need."

Lucy quickly unwrapped the bundle and spread the clothes out on the table. The dresses were fine—not new but in good condition. The other things, however, she recognized as items that Melinda had been sewing for her own trousseau.

"Melinda, I can't take these. You were saving these for your marriage." She tried to hand them back.

Her friend would have none of it. "No, I can always make more. Besides, as it turned out, you needed a trousseau before I did."

Cora threw her support behind Melinda. "You've done so much for us, Lucy. You have to let us give some back."

She had a bundle of her own to hand Lucy. Inside were several lengths of cloth ready to be cut and sewn into dresses, and another fabric that would make a lovely new nightgown. Lucy couldn't resist fondling the soft white cloth, already seeing the new gown in her mind. She'd always had a weakness for such things.

And she suspected that Cade would appreciate the gifts her friends had brought her as much as she did, not that she'd tell them that. How strange to be thinking of herself as part of a couple again. She wondered how long it would take her to get used to the idea.

"I do appreciate you bringing me all of this. I was afraid I was going to have to live in this dress," she said, gesturing at the soot and ashes that still clung to it, "until I can get Cade to take me to the store at White's Ferry."

"Tell you what, why don't you go on up and help Mary finish getting dressed and we'll put water on to boil for a bath for you."

Melinda laughed and shook her head. "Cora, how very tactful of you."

Lucy joined in. "Can't blame her for just telling the truth. I washed up as much as I could last night, but it'll take more than a pitcher of luke-warm water to make me feel clean again."

"Then go on up and check on Mary," Cora told her, making shooing motions with her hands. "We'll get the water ready. Afterwards, while you brush your hair dry, Melinda and I can start the new nightgown for you. If we work at it, it'll will be ready for tonight."

Then, to Lucy's amusement, Cora blushed. Evidently, her young friend, despite her forceful nature, was still a little shy about the idea of man and a woman sleeping together. No doubt, Cora's time would come, and she'd find out for herself what marriage was all about. Lucy could only hope that Cora made a better choice than Lucy had first time around. That thought made her wonder about her own rather sudden marriage. Not wanting to discuss her misgivings—or even her hopes—with her friends, she used Mary as an excuse to get away for a few minutes.

"I won't be gone long."

By the time she reached the first step, Cora and Melinda were already laying out the fabric for her honeymoon gown. It seemed like an oddly traditional thought for a couple whose courtship had been anything but traditional. And as she climbed the stairs, she decided maybe that was a good thing.

# Chapter Seventeen

Cade followed Mitch around the burned ruins of Lucy's store. He wasn't sure what they were looking for, unless the lawman thought the culprit had left some marker behind. After half an hour, Mitch stooped down and studied the ground.

"What did you find?" Cade asked, leaning over his shoulder to see what had caught Mitch's attention.

"I'd be willing to swear that this is the same footprint that I've seen before. There's no way to prove it belongs to the son of bitch who started the fire, but it sure seems likely to me. Not all that many men could have made a habit of skulking around out here without being noticed."

"Makes sense to me." Cade's hand caressed his pistol. A footprint wasn't much as evidence went, but it was more than he had expected to find. "Any idea who it belongs to?"

"No, damn it. Those two on our list couldn't have set the fire, unless they hired someone to do it. They were both at the council meeting last night when Daniel raised the alarm." He walked on, still studying the ground.

Cade followed close on his heels, trying to figure out why Mitch's comment seemed wrong. Then it hit him.

"Not Mayor Kelly, Mitch. Leastwise, he wasn't there the entire time. Bradford stood up front for several minutes while we waited for the mayor to get back from the privy. He left while Daniel was still speaking."

"Hell, I forgot. He even made a big deal of buckling his belt and straightening his clothes. I should have known he was up to something, because he never laughs at himself. Ever."

Cade checked his ammunition, ready to be judge, jury, executioner. "Any idea where I can find him?"

Mitch stepped in front of him, planted his feet, and shoved Cade back several steps. "I'll bring him in for a talk. Alive. In one piece."

The two men stared into each other's eyes, each taking the measure of the other's determination. Finally, Mitch spoke. "I swore years ago to never be party to a lynching. I know how you feel, but I've promised to uphold the law. And the law says he's entitled to a fair trial."

Cade tried to walk around Mitch, intent on taking care of the problem himself. Mitch, who outweighed him by a good thirty pounds of pure muscle, grabbed him by the shirtfront and yanked him back.

"Damn it, man, think about what you're doing. You shoot that worthless bastard in cold blood, where's that going to leave your womenfolk? Lucy's been your bride less than twenty-four hours. You think she wants her marriage to start off watching you get hauled off to jail for murder? And what about Mary? Hasn't your daughter lost enough?"

Cade didn't want to listen, didn't want to hear a

word of it, much less admit that Mitch was making sense. He quit pushing against the implacable sheriff. "Fine. I'll back your play."

"Now, that's help I will take." The two of them walked away from the stench of the burned building. Mitch wiped his sweaty face with his bandanna. "I figure the man has to be more than half crazy to pull a stunt like that. I mean, no sane person would burn the store with people still in it. If he's that far gone, there's no telling what he'll do when we corner him."

Personally, Cade hoped the crazy bastard would do something stupid, like go for his gun. He kept that thought to himself so Mitch wouldn't change his mind about letting him tag along.

They did their best to look casual as they made their way down the street to the small building that served as the center of government in Lee's Mill. There wasn't much to the mayor's office except a desk, a hatrack, and a cabinet of various legal papers. As far as Cade knew, the front door was the only way in.

Mitch eased up to the side of the front window and peaked in. "Hellfire and damnation, he's not here." Mitch looked up and down the street, trying to catch a glimpse of their quarry. No luck.

Cade had a bad feeling. "Let's look inside. Maybe we can figure out what he's up to next."

Once inside, it didn't take long to verify that Mayor Kelly was their man. The fool had left behind three empty oil cans. There was even a row of rocks sitting in the window, all of roughly the same shape and size as those he'd used to break windows. Most damning of all, though, was the wadded-up paper that Cade found in the bottom drawer of the desk.

He flattened it out on the desktop and read it. It was the note that had been stolen out of Mitch's office.

"He did it, all right."

Cade took another slow look around the office, not sure what he was hoping to find. He picked up one of the oil cans. Underneath it was a small slip of paper. It was probably nothing, but he held it up to the light of the window and read it anyway.

A ripple of terror shivered its way up his spine. It was a receipt for four cans of oil. There were only three sitting at his feet. He was running out the door before he even really had a chance to understand the significance. Mitch caught up with him before he'd gone ten feet.

"What's wrong?" he asked as they ran straight for Cade's house.

"Kelly bought four cans of oil. He only used three last night." Fear roiled through his stomach as his leg, already weakened by the fall last night, shrieked its protest at being further abused.

He refused to acknowledge either the complaint or the pain. With his wife and his daughter in danger again, he'd crawl if he had to. Both men reached the front of the newspaper office at the same time, guns in hand. Cade went through his office to the back window, which looked out over his house. Without a word being spoken, Mitch automatically went around the outside.

Caution won out over the need to see for himself that Lucy and Mary were safe. He hadn't forgotten that both Cora Lawford and Melinda Smythe were in his house as well.

He stared out the back window of the print shop for several long seconds, watching for any sign that something was wrong. It didn't take him long to spot trouble. The front window of his house had been broken out. A movement in the window caught his eye. The mayor was already inside, and unless he was mistaken, the man had his rifle aimed in Mitch's direction.

Craning his neck to the far left, he saw that he was right. Mitch was standing with his hands up, doing his best to talk the mayor out of the house. The two men were shouting at each other.

"Mr. Mayor, I know you have some business to see to back in the office. Why don't you come with me?"

"Why don't you go to hell, Sheriff? Actually, I've decided to replace you with someone who'll do the job right. I told you and told you to stop these women. You failed to do your duty. It's up to me to take care of the problem."

"Now, Mayor, you haven't hurt anybody yet. Let's not let this situation get out of hand."

"Go to hell, I said!"

"If you won't come out, then let me come in. We'll talk."

Mitch took a small step forward. The mayor immediately responded by shooting into the dirt right in front of Mitch's feet. The sheriff stood his ground.

"Let's be reasonable, Mayor. You know you won't get out of town. My deputy is already on his way. You can't shoot everyone in town."

Mitch kept his voice calm and all of the mayor's attention focused on himself, allowing Cade some time to figure out what to do. He eased back from the window and went back into his own office. The window there was smaller, but it offered him a clean shot at the mayor. Although he hadn't aimed a rifle at another man with the intent to kill since the early years of the war, he hadn't forgotten how. Or the sick feeling in his gut from knowing he was about to end another's life.

At least this time, there wasn't any doubt that the bastard deserved to die. Kelly wasn't just some poor fool who happened to wear a different color uniform. Crazy or not, he was doing his best to kill the two people who meant more to Cade than his own life.

And with luck, he'd live long enough to tell both of them how much he loved them.

He raised his rifle to his shoulder and took careful aim. A head shot would be the most effective, but he had to consider the women huddled inside his house. How long would it take Mary to get over seeing a man, even an evil one, killed in front of her?

He lowered the barrel of his rifle a mere trifle, but it was enough to change his target. Carefully squeezing the trigger, he absorbed the recoil and quickly took aim again in case one shot hadn't been enough. He could hear the mayor screaming in pain, but he was nowhere in sight. Luckily, Mitch was already disappearing into Cade's house.

Cursing the lack of a back door out of his office, Cade ran for the front door. Once outside, he limped along as fast as his leg would carry him. Lucy met him on the porch. She flew right into his arms with Mary right behind her.

Mitch would take care of whatever needed doing inside. For now, Cade had all that he could handle just verifying by touch and sight that his family was safe and sound.

"He seemed so normal, until you got a good look at his eyes." Lucy shuddered and sipped at the whiskey-laced tea that Cade had made for her and her friends.

"If I had known he was the one responsible for the fire, I would never have let him through the door." Guilt and fear had left dark circles under Cora's eyes.

Mitch tried his best to reassure her. "If we'd known even thirty minutes sooner, none of this would have had to happen. If I'd done my job . . ."

"Balderdash," Cade exclaimed. "You did your job just fine. No one was killed, and you've got the culprit locked up behind bars, where he'll stay for a long, long time. If I have anything to say about it, he'll be an old man before he gets out of prison."

Lucy had to ask the one question that remained unanswered. "Why did he do it? What did I ever do to make him hate me so?"

Cade moved around the table to put his hand on her shoulder. "It wasn't you as a person, Lucy, but more what you represented. Near as we can figure, the man had some twisted ideas about women. What they should be and how they should act. When the Luminary Society began to question how things were done around here, he saw it as a direct attack against him. The fact that Cletus Bradford was gaining in popularity for the job as mayor helped push him over the edge."

He gave her shoulder a slight squeeze. "Sometimes it's easier to blame an innocent party than face some unpleasant truths about oneself."

Lucy doubted that anyone else in the room realized that Cade was no longer talking about the mayor. Later, when they were alone, she'd tell him that his message had been received and understood. She had a few confessions of her own to make.

"Why don't you and Mitch go take care of whatever paperwork needs doing?" Lucy rose to her feet. "My friends and I have a project to finish. In fact, don't come back until dinnertime."

Melinda jumped into the conversation. "And while you're at it, why don't the two of you stop by the hotel and tell Belle that we'll all be there for dinner tonight. You'll need to find Daniel and invite him as well. We have a lot to celebrate, I think."

The two men accepted her orders without argument. Cade rather reluctantly left with his friend, leaving Lucy and her friends to see about finishing a certain nightgown.

The creak of a floorboard gave Lucy but a second's warning that she would soon no longer be alone. She pulled Cade's hairbrush through her hair one more time and then set it down. Tomorrow or the day after, she would really have to get to a store and replenish her personal possessions.

The doorknob slowly turned. She watched as the door slowly swung open and her husband stepped into the room. Their room. The bedroom. Her pulse raced as this man, who had given her both his name and his protection, came in and shut the rest of the world out.

"Is she asleep?"

He nodded, his silver eyes glittering in the soft glow of the lamplight. "I don't think we'll hear a word out of her before late morning. She was pretty exhausted after everything that's happened the past two days."

Lucy felt the need to rise to her feet. Cade always managed to make her feel small and feminine without even trying, but she wanted to meet him on equal ground tonight. She had words to say, something she needed him to know before